MR CAMPION'S
FOX

Previous Titles by Mike Ripley

The Fitzroy Maclean Angel series
JUST ANOTHER ANGEL
ANGEL TOUCH
ANGEL HUNT
ANGELS IN AMRS
ANGEL CITY
ANGEL CONFIDENTIAL
FAMILY OF ANGELS
THAT ANGEL LOOK
BOOTLEGGED ANGEL
LIGHTS, CAMERA, ANGEL
ANGEL UNDERGROUND
ANGEL ON THE INSIDE
ANGEL IN THE HOUSE
ANGEL'S SHARE
ANGELS UNAWARE

Other titles
DOUBLE TAKE
BOUDICA AND THE LOST ROMAN
THE LEGEND OF HEREWARD

Margery Allingham's Albert Campion
MR CAMPION'S FAREWELL *

Non-fiction
SURVIVING A STROKE

* available from Severn House

Margery Allingham's
Albert Campion returns in

MR CAMPION'S FOX

by

Mike Ripley

This first world edition published 2015
in Great Britain and the USA by
SEVERN HOUSE PUBLISHERS LTD of
19 Cedar Road, Sutton, Surrey, England, SM2 5DA.
Trade paperback edition first published 2015 in Great Britain
and the USA by SEVERN HOUSE PUBLISHERS LTD.

Ripley, Mike author.
  Margery Allingham's Mr Campion's fox. – (An Albert Campion mystery)
  1. Campion, Albert (Fictitious character)–Fiction.
  2. Murder–Investigation–Fiction. 3. Private
  investigators–England–Fiction. 4. Detective and mystery stories.
  I. Title II. Series III. Mr Campion's fox IV. Allingham,
  Margery, 1904-1966 associated with work.
  823.9'2-dc23

ISBN-13: 978-0-7278-8478-7 (cased)
ISBN-13: 978-1-84751-588-9 (trade paper)
ISBN-13: 978-1-78010-638-0 (e-book)

All Severn House titles are printed on acid-free paper.

Severn House Publishers support the Forest Stewardship Council™ [FSC™],
the leading international forest certification organisation. All our titles that
are printed on FSC certified paper carry the FSC logo.

MIX
Paper from
responsible sources
FSC
www.fsc.org   FSC® C013056

Typeset by Palimpsest Book Production Ltd.,
Falkirk, Stirlingshire, Scotland.
Printed and bound in Great Britain by
TJ International, Padstow, Cornwall.

This book is dedicated to the Margery Allingham Society, founded in 1988 to celebrate the life and work of one of the most distinguished writers of English detective fiction's 'Golden Age'.

The society meets regularly in London and East Anglia and publishes a journal, *The Bottle Street Gazette*, and a newsletter, *From the Glueworks*, both titles references to the London address of Margery Allingham's most famous creation, Mr Albert Campion.

www.margeryallingham.org.uk

Author's Note

In 2012, the Margery Allingham Society foolishly accepted my offer to try and complete a fragment of manuscript left by Pip Youngman Carter, Margery's widower, on his death in 1969. It would have been Pip's third 'Mr Campion' novel. Instead, as *Mr Campion's Farewell* in 2014, it became my first.

That book could not have been written without the expertise, enthusiasm and blessing of the Margery Allingham Society; nor could this one.

I am particularly indebted to Barry Pike (author of the indispensable *Campion's Career*), Julia Jones (Margery Allingham's biographer), cartographer extraordinaire Roger Johnson and the Albert Sloman Library at the University of Essex, which houses the Allingham Archives.

I have taken numerous liberties with the Suffolk coastline, though anyone familiar with that beautiful merger of sand, sea and sky will certainly recognize Orford, Orford Ness and perhaps a bit of Southwold in my fictitious Gapton. I feel in doing so I am following (most humbly) a fine Allingham tradition. Just as Mystery Mile wasn't quite Mersea Island in Essex, and in *Look to the Lady* the village of Sanctuary isn't quite Kersey in Suffolk, my Gapton and Gapton Thorpe are not quite real.

For the insatiable collector of trivia, British Passport number 1111924, which I have allocated to Francis Tate in this story, was in fact issued to Mrs Margery Louise Carter (née Allingham) in 1947.

Mike Ripley,
Essex.

Contents

Chapter 1: Pont Street Diplomatic   1
Chapter 2: Dean Street Confidential   20
Chapter 3: 'Orrible Murder   32
Chapter 4: Briefing at Darsham Halt   45
Chapter 5: Dark Room   53
Chapter 6: The Grimston Hybrid   61
Chapter 7: Cause of Death   75
Chapter 8: Sisters of the Sample Cellar   82
Chapter 9: Dead Lagoon   93
Chapter 10: Mud Cockles and Samphire   107
Chapter 11: Fox on the Beach   120
Chapter 12: Night Exercise   135
Chapter 13: Not Single Spies   147
Chapter 14: Air Cavalry   165
Chapter 15: Barter Economy   179
Chapter 16: Carry On Bodice Ripping   190
Chapter 17: Fermentation   202
Chapter 18: Low Treason   211
Chapter 19: Scouting for Peace   221
Chapter 20: Cobras in the Mist   232
Chapter 21: Smokescreen   239
Chapter 22: Run to Earth   250

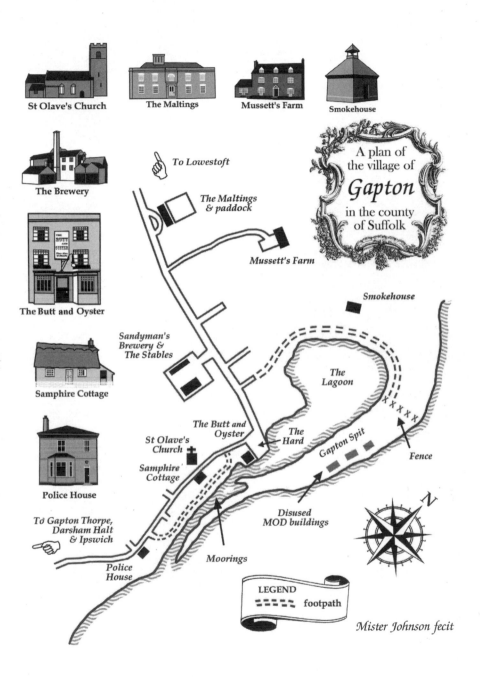

St Olave's Church

The Maltings

Mussett's Farm

Smokehouse

The Brewery

The Butt and Oyster

Samphire Cottage

Police House

To Gapton Thorpe,
Darsham Halt
& Ipswich

To Lowestoft

The Maltings
& paddock

Mussett's Farm

A plan of
the village of
Gapton
in the county
of Suffolk

Smokehouse

Sandyman's
Brewery &
The Stables

The
Lagoon

The Butt and
Oyster

St Olave's
Church

The
Hard

Gapton Spit

x x x x
Fence

Samphire
Cottage

Disused
MOD buildings

N

Police
House

Moorings

LEGEND
- - - - footpath

Mister Johnson fecit

ONE

Pont Street Diplomatic

'My wife's people have never quite forgiven you for the Battle of Maldon, Mr Ambassador.'

The diplomat smiled as diplomats are trained to do without effort, but no effort was needed here, for there was a definite twinkle in the speaker's voice.

'That would be . . . in the year 991, I believe,' he answered the twinkle.

''Fraid so. Awfully long memories my wife's family have; makes my life a positive trial at times.'

'And do they blame me personally, or my country?'

'I suppose they blame the Vikings,' the speaker said after a thoughtful pause.

'They are probably wise to do so,' said his host, 'but please forward my regret that while I am proud to represent His Majesty King Frederick IX and his government, I have no remit to explain or defend the actions of Sven Forkbeard.'

'What a pity; I had my petition already written out.'

A female and very feminine voice interrupted these somewhat bizarre diplomatic negotiations: 'Mr Ambassador, allow me to apologise for my husband. I have no idea what he was pestering you about, but pestering is his forte and as he has been out of my supervisory sight for all of five minutes, I think I can safely say he has moved in to full pestering mode. I do hope it wasn't about the canapés. He's quite obsessed with geometric patterns on plates of canapés, poor lamb. Never eats them, just likes the shapes. He's probably quite mad and it's surprising we still get invited to embassy receptions.'

The ambassador turned to the elegant, red-haired woman, who had quietly positioned herself at her husband's side with the smoothness of a closing Rolls-Royce door without the accompanying thunderous click. He proffered a hand in greeting, enhanced with a low, dignified bow.

'The exquisite Lady Amanda to the rescue, I presume.'

'Rescues gallantly and freely performed,' said the woman, performing a half-bob, quarter-curtsey with a smile and a tilt of her heart-shaped face. 'I assume you do need rescuing from my husband? Most people do after two or three minutes and I've had years of experience at it. I could even provide references and probably testimonials.'

The ambassador allowed himself a deep-throated chuckle.

'I have not yet been formally introduced to this gentleman, although of course I know who he is, and I am confident I am in no need of rescue.'

'Well, if you are absolutely *sure*,' said the woman, 'allow me to introduce Mr Albert Campion, who looks more harmless than he is but is, I suppose, a gentleman if you are willing to stretch a point.'

The tall, thin man with the pale-straw hair beamed from behind large, horn-rimmed glasses and offered an outstretched hand.

'Mr Ambassador. Please forgive my wife. She is younger than I and, as you can see from her dress sense, she has embraced the rebellion of youth.'

'I am Aage Westergaard,' said their host, 'and I welcome you to our little piece of Denmark here in England. I can say without hesitation that His Majesty King Frederick would approve of Lady Amanda's dress sense, which is surely the height of fashion for Swinging London.'

'I thank the ambassador,' said Amanda, 'and his king.'

'Of course, I cannot speak for that old Viking Sven Forkbeard, who probably had a rather . . . shall we say *restricted* . . . view of women.'

'As did my mother,' said Mr Campion, 'who would have been horrified at the thought of women wearing trousers at all, let alone at a diplomatic reception.'

The ambassador stared at Lady Amanda, his gaze sweeping from head-to-foot as if only now aware of her presence, noting her black velvet figure-hugging tuxedo suit, the white blouse with Peter Pan collar and cuffs and the square-toed heeled boots peeping out from beneath fashionably wide flares. With her mellowing red hair cut short, the ambassador decided it would be unwise to guess her age, but was wise enough to know he would be at least ten years wrong, though Lady Amanda required neither flattery nor defending.

'For goodness' sake, nipped waists, fitted bodices and long gloves went out of style years ago. In any case, if one has an Yves Saint Laurent, one should jolly well show it off.'

'Well said, Lady Amanda.' The ambassador bowed his head in genuine admiration. 'And may I suggest that you do so admirably.'

A waiter shimmered across the reception room bearing a tray of champagne flutes and presented himself smartly to attention at the ambassador's right hand.

'Please,' he indicated. 'The hospitality may be Danish, but the champagne is French and of particular quality; or so my staff inform me, for I have little taste in such things.'

'I find that hard to believe, *Greve* Westergaard,' said Mr Campion, concentrating on his champagne flute as if it held the secret of eternal life.

The ambassador sipped from his glass then waved it gently in front of him as he would wag a finger.

'Please, Mr Campion, let us not bandy titles about, for I suspect you have more to be embarrassed about than I. On these premises, "Mr Ambassador" will suffice, and outside these walls I answer perfectly well to Aage.'

Amanda fixed a steely eye on her husband and regretted that this had not been a sit-down affair so she could have kicked him under the table.

'Forgive me,' she asked politely, '*Greve*?'

'A Danish title, equivalent to your English count,' replied Ambassador Westergaard with a sigh. 'Like most titles, a hindrance more often than an advantage, especially in egalitarian Denmark, though often useful when booking a table in a restaurant in London or Paris. However, I am delighted to see that your husband has done his homework on me. I would have expected no less, just as I have done my homework on him, which is why you are both here tonight.'

'Drat! I thought I'd been booked as the cabaret,' said Campion with a straight face. 'I do a passable turn as a magician, am pretty nifty as a juggler and can play a mean boogie-woogie. Where do you keep the piano, by the way?'

Amanda pursed her lips, rolled her eyes upwards and shook her head slowly as if disapproving of the ornate chandelier hovering above them.

'Please, Lady Amanda, do not distress yourself. I was fore-warned that I might encounter the Campion sense of humour.'

'Don't worry, it's not catching,' said Campion quickly, 'but I'd love to know who has been flashing the warning signs.'

'Actually, it was a duke,' the ambassador said smoothly. 'Quite a senior one – a royal one, in fact. Your royal, that is, not mine; and everything he said about you was substantiated by another equally impressive gentleman.'

Campion, by now intrigued, questioned his host further: 'I can hazard a guess at the identity of the duke despite being both flattered and terrified by the fact that he has an opinion of me, but I am curious as to who the other gentleman is who has been providing character references for me. Impressive, you said?'

'Oh very,' the ambassador replied. 'A marvellous fellow and quite a character – almost larger than life. He claimed to have "all the dirt worth digging" on you.'

'Lugg!' chorused both Campions.

Less than two miles away in a north-easterly direction, across Green Park, over Piccadilly and into Soho, a long-haired young man wearing a leather 'biker' jacket was returning on foot from a very different sort of diplomatic meeting at a very different embassy.

The man, known as Frank Tate, with the easy skill of an experi-enced harbour pilot, navigated the shallow back alleys both north and south of Oxford Street, before crossing the main current of that thoroughfare with the collar of his jacket turned up as if to shield him from inquisitive street lights and the probing fingers of car and bus headlights. Entering the calmer – some would say stagnant – waters of Soho proper he closed his ears to the hum of pubs settling down to an evening's regular trade and his nose to the scent of the growing number of *trattoria* gearing up to serve platefuls of *spaghetti alle cozze* or *rigatoni all'amatriciana* at four-and-sixpence a go. Once in Dean Street, he stopped and looked around him as if taking bearings for the first time and, judging the coast clear, he strode full speed ahead into the dark, narrow inlet known to few apart from taxi drivers and the London Electricity Board as St Anne's Court.

At the third Dickensian doorway on his right he paused, alert to any minute changes which might have taken place during his absence. Sensing no obvious disturbances, he stepped into the door-less doorway and began to climb the wooden stairs, passing the stack of business cards drawing-pinned to the door jamb announcing: *Ground floor: Young Model; First Floor: French Model; Second Floor: Young French Model; Third floor: Francis Tate Photography; Top Floor: French Polishing.*

At the top of each landing he stopped to listen before continuing his climb. A series of indistinct grunts told him that the French Model was professionally engaged, while the muffled twang of guitar music suggested that the Young French Model was having an evening in listening to the radio. Neither situation disturbed or threatened him as both indicated that it was business as usual in the tenement.

Training and ingrained habit guided his feet to the exact spot of each stair tread which would not creak and give away his progress to anyone waiting above. No one was lying in ambush for him and never had been, but his meeting that evening had reminded him of the need for constant vigilance.

As he poised his key level with the door bearing a square plastic sign proclaiming *Francis Tate Photography*, his left hand automatically swept along the line where the top of the door met the door frame until his fingers brushed comfortingly on the undisturbed stamp-sized piece of card torn from a cigarette packet which he had placed there as he had closed the door earlier that evening. Reassured that his personal fortress had not been breached, he inserted his key and entered, catching the stub of card as it fluttered down in front of his face and slipping it into a pocket for future use.

There was nothing to distinguish the dusty bedsit from a thousand others within the same square mile: a single bed with a faded and frayed coverall, a small square card table and a single wooden chair and in one corner a sink flanked by a 'baby' electric oven and a double burner gas ring. On the draining board of the sink were a knife, a fork and an upturned plate and pint china

mug, utensils which, along with a scattering of photographic
magazines, were the only signs of regular human habitation. The
adjoining bathroom was, however, anything but undistinguished,
having been refitted at considerable expense as a very professional photographic darkroom. Such things were not unknown
in Soho, of course, but few bathrooms had a Yale lock on the
outside, and an inquisitive tax inspector might have wondered
how a photographer with Tate's declared income and sporadic
commissions could afford such state-of-the-art equipment and so
many cameras (though only a very diligent inspector or a detective would have found them all).

Only when Frank Tate had checked that the lock on his bathroom door had not been tampered with did he unzip his leather
jacket, taking a packet of cigarettes and a battered Zippo lighter
from the pocket. Sitting on the edge of his bed he lit a cigarette,
reached down to scoop up a plastic ashtray advertising a famous
vermouth from the floor, then sank down until supine, placing
the ashtray on his chest. Lying on that lumpy bed, which also
managed to be an irritating nine or ten centimetres short of
the length his long, skinny legs required, smoking and counting the
cracks in the ceiling plaster was Tate's way of combining relaxation
with stressful thinking. He called it his 'meditation time' and
was for him the equivalent of all those foolish and pampered
pop-stars trying to find inner peace with their own personal gurus
in India, but without the smells, bells and pretentions.

He had much to meditate on, for at his meeting that evening
with the man who was not a diplomat but was tenuously attached
to a foreign embassy situated a stone's throw from the BBC's
Broadcasting House, he had received new orders with which he
felt less than comfortable. His personal comfort did not, however,
come into it, for when the man-who-was-not-a-diplomat gave
orders, they had to be obeyed. Any dissent or deviation on Tate's
part could, it had been made abundantly clear, threaten his present
existence and while his current circumstances were far from
luxurious, he enjoyed pleasures and freedoms he had never known
as a youth and which he would forfeit should he be forced to
return to his previous life.

In order to get to his new objective, he would have to get
closer to the girl, which in itself was hardly an unpleasant duty,

though he regretted that he would be using her and eventually betraying her. Still, he had known that from the start. A pity, as he was genuinely fond of her and she was very attractive, but because of that she would have no trouble finding a more suitable suitor when the time came, inevitably, to leave her in the lurch.

Ironically it was thanks to the girl that his new objective had been identified at all. It had been one of his own reports detailing the girl's activities a month before which had sparked the interest – the close and sudden interest – of the man-who-was-not-a-diplomat and had resulted in his new orders. He had no idea what had prompted such a change in direction but he knew it was not his place to question orders old or new.

His random thoughts were interrupted by a soft knocking at his door and his body started as if electrocuted. He calmed himself instantly, remembering his training and taking assurance from the logic that his enemies, if they came for him, were unlikely to announce themselves so politely. Yet he still opened the door cautiously, standing well to the side in case his visitor(s) decided to shoulder-charge it once they heard the lock tumblers turn.

'Oh, hello,' he said in surprise, 'I wasn't expecting company.'

For a split-second the unkind thought occurred that he should have said 'I hadn't ordered company,' for his visitor was the Young French Model from the floor below, though she was in truth not particularly young and highly unlikely to hold French nationality. His second thought was more professional: how had she managed to climb the stairs without him hearing her footsteps, for this was a female never seen in public unless wearing shoes or leather boots with dangerously high and loud heels. His thought directed his eyes downwards to answer his question and discover that his visitor was wearing bright blue, furry, woollen slippers.

'Sorry to disturb, Mr Tate, just wanted a word on a professional matter.'

Dolores Pink – not her real name – smiled sweetly and looked up at Frank Tate from under thick, long and overactive eyelashes as he in turn stared down, mapping the contour of her body with his eyes, taking in the tautly stretched, lime-green cardigan, the black leather miniskirt not much wider than a blacksmith's belt, the black-stockinged legs and those incongruous fluffy slippers.

'Your profession, not mine, of course,' Miss Pink assured him. 'I've got sort of a business proposition for you.'

'Then you'd better come in,' said Tate holding the door wide for her, 'but there's nowhere much to sit except the bed . . .'

Miss Pink flashed him a smile, made a small fist of her left hand and gently punched Tate on the chest as she sashayed past him, leaving a spoor trail of cheap eau de toilette in her wake.

'Oh, I'm used to sitting on beds, Mr Tate. Well, perhaps not just *sitting* . . . Ooh! There I go. I promised meself I wouldn't do the old come-on with you and here I go teasing you before I've 'ardly got over the threshold. That's no way to start off a business proposition now, is it?'

Tate allowed Miss Pink to settle herself – with much wriggling of the derrière – until she was comfortably seated on the edge of the bed, her hands on her knees, her fluffy slippers making shunting movements as if they were two furry dodgem cars jockeying for position.

'Exactly what sort of business, Miss Pink?'

'Professional photography of course; that's your game, i'nnit? That's what it sez on yer door. Well, I wants to 'ire you. An' you can call me Dol, by the way.'

'OK . . . Dol . . . I'm a photographer all right, but I don't think I take the sort of pictures you're after.'

Miss Pink's expression soured and her lips pursed as if she had unwittingly bitten into a lemon wedge in polite company.

'Oh, I get it; you think I'm on the old badger game. Honey Traps – that's what the Russians call them, ain't it, it when they blackmail our businessmen into becoming their spies? Don't look so surprised, I read the papers, you know. And in any case,' Miss Pink continued in full flow, stamping her furry blue slippers silently on Tate's threadbare carpet, 'them's not the sort of pictures I was after.'

Tate held up the palms of his hands in surrender.

'I am sorry if I have offended you, Dol. All I was trying to explain was that my bread-and-butter is photographing buildings and places – landscapes or architectural pictures for brochures and advertising campaigns. I don't normally take pictures of people.'

'Not even intimate ones for private use?'

Miss Pink's voice had U-turned at speed, changing her from strident harpy to heavy-breathing Baby Doll.

'How intimate?'

'Well, little old me was thinking of branching out, you see.' The Baby Doll suddenly became just the baby, putting her knees together and coyly turning her slippers inward so the toes met. 'It's common knowledge that some of the newspapers – proper papers, mind, not the glam rags or the flesh mags – are thinking of making a regular *feechewer*, if that's how you say it, of pictures of young models. They'd be topless, but it would all be done in the best possible taste, nothing tatty, nothing sordid. I was thinking it might be useful to 'ave me own' – she took an unnecessary but very impressive deep breath before saying the word – 'portfolio. Something I could show to the agents or the scouts when they come calling. A nice set of tasteful shots which I'd keep very private, just to myself and of course I'd want the negatives. I'd pay for them as well, whatever the going rate is.'

'I'm sorry, Dol,' said Tate, his voice tinged with a genuine proportion of regret, 'but I couldn't do you justice. I don't photograph people and I don't do model shots. I haven't got a proper studio or the lights or . . . er . . . props.'

'Well, if that's your attitude!' The harpy was back, jumping to its feet. 'There's another matter I wanted to raise with you. Just you take a look at this.'

Against several laws of physics, Miss Pink hoisted her miniskirt even higher and turned the length of her right leg towards the startled photographer.

'Go on, 'ave a good butchers. That's your fault, that is.'

The speechless Frank Tate took in Miss Pink's short but very shapely right leg, from the unflattering blue slipper to above the knee where her black-stockinged thigh displayed an inch-wide tramline ladder.

'Ruined they are, ruined on that bloody great motorbike you keep in the 'allway on the ground floor where we 'ave to squeeze past it to get up the stairs. And these are good quality tights. It's not like they were stockings, you know, where you could just replace one if you got a ladder. You 'ave to replace the full set, both legs, and they ain't cheap.'

Dolores Pink, never one to underplay her hand, allowed her skirt hem to descend, as far as it could descend, very slowly until Frank Tate snapped out of his trance and said: 'Well, actually, I can help you there, as long as you don't go shooting your mouth off. Stand aside.'

Miss Pink stood aside and watched in amazement as Tate dropped to his knees and reached under the bed where she had been sitting, pulling out a battered tan suitcase. Clicking the catches he flipped the lid to reveal dozens of packets of fifteen-denier one-size nylon ladies' tights and, under Dol's widening gaze, selected two packets and handed them to her.

'There you go, one black pair, one sandy brown, for the trouble my bike caused. Don't let on where you got them from, though.'

Dolores Pink was no longer either harpy or seductress, but suddenly a happy and satisfied little girl. She treated Tate to a wide and genuine smile and a wink as she clutched the packets to her chest.

'Mum's the word, Mr Tate, your secret's safe with me.'

Over a hundred miles north-north-east of Soho in the North Sea off the Suffolk coast, the master of a small cargo ship, both of which had seen better days, sucked on an unlit blackened Brigham Voyageur pipe, producing a deep bubbling sound which seemed perfectly in tune with the rumble of the ship's engines.

The captain used the stem of his pipe to tap on the glass screen of the wheelhouse before he spoke to the bosun at his side.

'Make sure the look-out's awake,' he said in a language which was not English. 'He'll see two lights, one above the other, on the mast of a small motor boat. As soon as he sees them he's to signal us to stop engines. If we don't, we'll end up stuck in a mud bank. These waters are stiff with them.'

'He understands, Captain. He's a good lad.'

The ship's master re-clenched the pipe between his teeth.

'He knows he has to go below and stay there while we do our business, doesn't he?'

'He'll do as he's told,' said the bosun grimly. 'The purser will bring the stuff on deck and I'll help lower it over the side in the basket. What are we expecting in return this time?'

'The usual,' said the captain casually. 'Nothing to interest the likes of you and me, but stuff which should turn a few coins when we get home.'

'The man we're meeting, can he be trusted?'

'He's both thirsty and greedy so he can be trusted up to a point.'

'Aren't you worried that he'll have the police with him on one of these rendezvous?'

The captain removed his pipe and the bosun saw him smile in the dim light of the wheelhouse.

'Now that, my friend, is the least of our worries.'

Mr Campion and Amanda had been spirited away from the whirlpool of the main reception and into the calmer waters of an empty drawing room where they stood gazing out of a wide sash window, watching the lights of large, chauffeured cars creep quietly in and out of Belgravia.

'Can you remember,' Amanda said dreamily, 'when people said it was "Pont Street" to do this or "Pont Street" to do that, meaning it was fashionable and absolutely the done thing? It was a craze just after the war. "My dear, that hat is positively Pont Street" – things like that. I've no idea what was special about Pont Street.'

'My grandmother had a thing about Pont Street,' Mr Campion mused.

'I thought your family had "things" about everything,' murmured his wife fondly, brushing the back of her fingers over his cheek.

Mr Campion inclined his head, trapping Amanda's hand gently against his shoulder.

'The old girl had a hatred of public displays of just about everything, especially public protests, but back in 1884 or thereabouts, she was out on the streets leading a protest march, parasol flailing at any policeman's helmet to come in range. She even got an official caution from a local Inspector, though of course that was kept out of the papers.'

'I never thought you had suffragettes in the family, darling.'

'Oh, it was nothing to do with politics; it was to do with St Andrew.'

Amanda gazed at her husband with an expression that was one part sympathy but nine parts love.

'Oh, very well then, I suppose I have to ask: why St Andrew?'

'The Church of Scotland had built a new church in London, here on Pont Street and they wanted to call it St Andrew's – patron saint of Scotland and all that – but Grandmama was a patron of a society to help fallen women based on another St Andrew's, over in Stepney, and demanded that the Church of Scotland change the name. Made quite a nuisance of herself, apparently, and so they did, and called the new church St Columba's. It's still there, down by Lennox Gardens.'

'Not that grey, concrete thing which looks like a battleship made out of paving slabs?'

'That's not the original, of course. St Columba's was pretty well blitzed on the tenth of May 1941. The one that's there now has been built on the same site though. Grandmama would have taken exception to it and probably resorted to civil disobedience again. I think she had it in for the Church of Scotland, but quite why is a bit of a mystery.'

'Don't tell me, my darling hero, that there actually was once a mystery you managed to resist getting to the bottom of?'

'*Mea culpa*, my dear, *mea* totally *culpa*. In my youth I would tackle gangsters and gunmen till the cows came home and swash buckles with the dirtiest of dirty dogs, but I drew the line at quizzing Grandmama. A very formidable lady. You never met her, did you?'

'You know I didn't, although of course I've seen pictures of her, everybody has. But don't we have something of a mystery on our hands at this very moment? Why have we been secluded here, away from the party? Come to that, why were we invited to the party at all, and at such short notice? Are we here just to make up the numbers? We're not going to war with Denmark, are we? And if we are it's not of your doing, is it? Please tell me it isn't, Albert.'

'I have no idea why we're here. Clearly we were deliberately invited, but as to why, I am completely in the dark, as I often am. In fact you should think of putting that on my headstone: "Albert Campion, Permanently in the Dark". How's that for an epitaph?'

Amanda's fingers squeezed the lobe of his left ear until he squealed softly.

'Don't be morbid, darling. What would you really like to see on your headstone?'

'Somebody else's name,' said Mr Campion, placing an arm around his wife's shoulders as she collapsed against him in a fit of giggles.

It was in this affectionate pose that the Danish Ambassador discovered them as he entered the room followed by a frock-coated waiter bearing a tray of champagne cocktails.

'Lady Amanda, Mr Campion, my apologies for putting you in isolation but these parties are a terrible bore because everyone has to be so polite and I am confident I have saved you from dreadful lectures about wine surpluses, fishing quotas, the arms race, the space race, employment prospects, unemployment prospects and the price of cocoa beans in West Africa. I needed, you see, to ask a personal favour.'

The waiter dispensed their drinks and made his exit so quietly Campion wondered if he had been there at all. The fizzing flute in his hand told him he had not been dreaming.

'Mr Ambassador,' said Amanda, 'forgive me if I am being presumptuous, but before you ask anything of my husband I must tell you – for he will not – that he is supposed to be retired. He may, at a pinch, be available to open a garden fête, present the prizes at a school Speech Day or draw a raffle, but those are roughly the limits of his abilities these days.'

'Were it not a delicate family matter, dear lady, I would not think of imposing on your husband,' the ambassador replied sincerely, 'but I was recommended most strongly to seek his advice.'

'By a duke,' Amanda whispered in a resigned way.

'By *the* duke,' said Mr Campion, 'which I suppose means I come "By Appointment" and the least I can do is offer advice if I can.'

'You're forgetting that you also come recommended by Lugg, my dear,' said Amanda, unable to resist a wry grin.

'True. I suppose that must count against me. Do tell us, Mr Ambassador, how you managed to obtain these character references for yours truly?'

The ambassador shepherded his guests towards three leather armchairs surrounding a small circular table of white pine on which they placed their drinks.

'I attended a luncheon at Brewers' Hall recently,' he began. 'They do very good lunches.'

'So I've heard,' observed Campion, things already becoming clearer.

'I was not present in any official capacity but as the guest of an old friend from the war years. The duke was there to give a short speech to encourage your brewers to export more and, when he saw me, to have a little dig at a well-known Danish brewery which he visited some years ago only to be distinctly unimpressed by the beer he sampled there. He spoke very highly of you, by the way.'

'I am extremely flattered – almost humbled – but whose idea was it to ask the duke for a reference for me?'

'Why, Lugg's of course. That is his name, isn't it? I found his Christian name very odd . . . Magersteen or Magerfountain . . . is it?'

'Magersfontein; it was a battle in South Africa during the Boer War and it is an odd name, but then Lugg is an odd fellow.'

'He makes a very impressive Beadle of Brewers' Hall, has the place running like a military operation and the staff there seem to adore him.'

Mr Campion turned to his wife and beamed. 'I told you he'd fit in.'

'I thought at first, when he greeted me, that the Brewers' Company had employed a circus bear as a doorman. Have you seen him in his full Beadle regalia? The long fur gown, the gold chain of office and the ebony staff all make him a most formidable figure.'

'I've seen him in his pyjamas and that's frightening enough,' chirped Campion.

'Yes, he said the two of you shared a rather colourful history and when he overheard me discussing my little problem he suggested you might be able to help me.'

'So he was listening in at keyholes again, eh? That sounds like Lugg all right.'

'Something he learned during your colourful history, no doubt,' breathed Lady Amanda.

'There were no keyholes involved,' the ambassador assured them. 'Mr Lugg was doing his duty as Beadle, patrolling the back of the top table, "keeping an eye on the silverware" as he put it, when he accidentally overheard the conversation I was having with my friend, and host, Bernard Sandyman. He asked permission if he might interject an opinion or two' – Campion smiled broadly as he imagined Lugg torturing the phrase – 'and, well, joined in the conversation.'

'Did he pull up a chair and help himself to the port?' asked Amanda without malice.

'Not at that point, though he did later persuade the duke to try a bottle of the "well-crusted" that he had found in the cellars.'

'Oh, my stars,' muttered Mr Campion, shaking his head. 'What have I done?'

'I'm sorry, I don't understand . . .'

'I got Lugg that job as a sort of pension, to keep him off the streets. I do apologise, Mr Ambassador, pray continue.'

Count Westergaard did exactly that. 'So I was telling Bernard Sandyman – and Mr Lugg – that I was worried about my daughter Vibeke. She's eighteen and very headstrong, very independent.'

'And so she should be!' chimed Amanda. 'If an eighteen-year-old girl can't be independent these days, there's something wrong with the world, and if an eighteen-year-old girl isn't headstrong, there's something wrong with *her*.'

'You are a feminine liberationist, Lady Amanda? Good for you; jolly good for you. My daughter too has radical views and has been known to paint "This degrades women" over the lingerie advertisements on the Underground, but I have no quarrel with her views. We have, I think, more enlightened views on the role of women in Denmark than you British have.'

'I'm glad to hear that,' said Amanda, 'and I apologise for interrupting. You were saying you were worried about Vibeke because . . .?'

'Because like all fathers – and I should tell you that Vibeke's mother died ten years ago, so I am a lone parent – I am concerned about her choice in men. I know it is the normal reaction of a protective father, and I have tried to protect but not be over-protective. It has not been easy, especially since being posted to London, where there are many temptations for a young girl. I do not mind the fashions and the music; all that is very exciting, vibrant even, and Vibeke will have nothing to do with drugs, of that I am sure. She does not even smoke cigarettes. But she has formed a strong attraction to a most unsuitable young man.'

The ambassador held up a hand to ward off criticism which was not forthcoming.

'Oh, I know all fathers of daughters say that. No boyfriend is ever good enough for their precious daughter, especially when she is an only child. But I know there is something not right about this boy.'

'You have had him "checked out", as our American cousins would say?' asked Campion.

'I have, on the pretext that he was applying for Danish citizenship.'

'Can you do that? Legally, I mean?' Amanda scolded.

'Legally, yes; ethically I am on less sure ground,' admitted Westergaard. 'Your Home Office and the Metropolitan Police could find nothing against him, at least on paper, and I was in no position to press them further. I am at an impasse. I cannot use the security officers here at the embassy on such a purely personal mission and I am not willing to risk the reputation of my government or my country by employing a private investigator who could sell the story to one of your Sunday newspapers.'

'Yes, they do have a tendency to do that, I'm afraid,' Campion sympathized. 'Perhaps we don't pay them enough or they had unhappy childhoods or something. I'm sure if I put my thinking cap on I could recommend one who wasn't *totally* dishonest; merely seedy, unsound in wind and limb and probably slightly odorous.'

'Mr Campion, *you* have been recommended to me; recommended most highly.'

Campion sighed and flicking out a blindingly white handkerchief from the breast pocket of his jacket with the languid aplomb of a stage magician who could do tricks in his sleep, removed his spectacles and began to polish the lenses. His wife, with resignation, recognized the action as the first sign that her husband was taking an interest in the ambassador's concern.

'I am naturally flattered that the duke provided me with a character reference and both flattered and slightly amazed that Beadle Lugg did so too, but I fail to see what I can do that the

Home Office and police force cannot. I am, after all, only a private citizen.'

'A *retired* private citizen,' said Amanda firmly.

'Mr Lugg said you would say that.' The ambassador grinned.

Campion replaced his spectacles and replied, 'Oh, he did, did he, the old recidivist?'

'He told me not to believe a word you said about retirement and that you'd jump at the chance of "slummin' it in Soho for a few days" – as I think he put it. If I wanted to make sure of your help all I had to do' – and here the ambassador sat bolt upright in his chair, thrust out his stomach and dropped his chin on to his chest in a Churchillian pose – 'let me see if I remember correctly. Oh, yes: "Tell 'is nibs there's been an 'orrible murder and he'll be on the scent quicker than a Jack Russell down a rat hole." I think those were his exact words.'

Mr Campion turned to his wife and smiled sweetly.

'That does sound like Lugg. I mean not just the words, but don't you think the ambassador's got him off to a "t"?' His smile was not reciprocated and he returned quickly to Ambassador Westergaard. 'There hasn't actually been a murder, horrible or otherwise, has there?'

'Of course not; I merely want you to keep an eye on this young man for a few days. He lives and works in Soho, and I need an intelligent assessment of what sort of a life he leads.'

'I am afraid,' Amanda interjected quite forcefully, 'my husband's knowledge of the rat-runs of Soho is not what it used to be – or at least I sincerely hope it isn't – and he has reached an age where physical exertions should be limited to stamp collecting or alphabetizing the novels in his library. He certainly shouldn't be tearing around Soho spying on a couple of young lovebirds. What if they decided to go to a disco? Albert would stand out like a vicar at an orgy!'

'Actually, in Soho—'

'Albert, please don't be coarse!'

'I was merely going to agree with you, my love,' Campion soothed. 'I was going to say that actually, in Soho, a much younger man would do a much better job.'

Amanda eyed him suspiciously.

'You didn't have anyone particular in mind, did you?'

'No, my dear, did you?'

The ambassador saw the need for more diplomacy, which was, after all, his forte.

'Personally I was delighted at Mr Campion's nomination for he has the required experience, local knowledge and, most importantly, the discretion which comes only with age. It would not be a case of following two young lovebirds as Lady Amanda delicately puts it, but only the boyfriend and only during the working week. He consorts with Vibeke at the weekends, up in Suffolk.'

'What does she do there?'

'I persuaded her to take a job for a year before she goes to university, preferably in America or Germany.'

'To be far away from the worrying boyfriend, I suppose?' observed Amanda.

'That is my hope, I admit. At the moment he only sees her at the weekend when he zooms up to Gapton on his motorbike. He is something of a . . . what do you call them, not Mods, but—'

'Bike boys? Greasers? Hell's Angels? Rockers?' suggested Mr Campion, not altogether helpfully.

'Rockers, that's it,' decided the ambassador.

'I thought their day had waned and we were now in the age of hippies and the psychedelic,' Campion mused, 'though perhaps it's just what they call "a fashion statement" these days. Did you say Gapton, as in Gapton-once-on-sea as we used to call it, home of Sandyman's Seaside Brewery? Of course, it must be; you've told us you were at Brewers' Hall as a guest of Bernard Sandyman. So daughter Vibeke is working in a brewery? That must be a temptation for any red-blooded English lad.'

'That's part of my concern, Mr Campion; you see, I don't think Frank Tate is English. Of course, you may think I'm not one to judge, but sometimes it takes a foreigner to know a foreigner. And Vibeke isn't working in the brewery, but for my old friend Bernard's son Torquil, who is the firm's sales director. He is married with three young children and they needed an au pair.'

'Good heavens,' Campion exclaimed. 'Torquil Sandyman was at school with our son, Rupert. I've even been press-ganged into watching them play cricket on the same team and stumping up for the cream teas afterwards when they lost. Now Rupert—'

'Albert Campion,' said his wife in a voice which suggested she was strongly resisting the urge to stamp a dainty foot, 'I know what you're thinking; and stop it immediately!'

TWO
Dean Street Confidential

One of the fondest – and one of the few clear – memories of his time at drama school had been, for Rupert Campion, the tutorials of Mr Martin Halliday, who had specialized in 'mime, interpretation and improvisation'. As these particular classes required no learning of lines (always a chore for a young man with an overactive brain), few if any props (he was self-consciously prone to clumsiness), and a bare minimum of dressing-up (apart from an exercise exploring naturism, where 'bare' was the apt description), Mr Halliday's seminars were among Rupert's favourite parts of his training as a thespian, although he had soon realized that while he longed for the roar of the crowd, the smell of the greasepaint, and that of dusty and faded provincial repertory theatres, nauseated him slightly.

Rupert had decided after a year that the Actor's Life was perhaps not for him, although the role of Director had begun to appeal, but still he felt he owed the patron saint of actors a huge vote of thanks as his apprentice years in the profession had blessed him with the opportunity to meet, woo and marry Miss Perdita Browning, for whom acting was not so much a vocational choice as a military objective.

Not that Rupert had too much faith in the patron saint of acting, St Genesius, for as far as he knew the fourth century jobbing actor Genesius had experienced an epiphany and converted to Christianity while performing in a play about the dangers of converting to Christianity. Sadly misjudging his audience – the pagan Roman Emperor Diocletian – Genesius had his religious conversion on stage and refused to renounce his subversive new faith when the curtain came down. Consequently the imperial curtain came down on Genesius and he was beheaded. It was, Rupert thought, one of the most extreme critical notices in history and had they been around at the time, Equity would surely have had something to say about it.

The theatre was, Rupert now realized, never going to provide him with fame or honours or even a regular wage, but it had provided him with Perdita and he felt himself almost churlish to ask for more. Martin Halliday's drama school classes were, however, finally proving both useful and practical.

For one regular session Mr Halliday would turn his students out on to a busy West London thoroughfare and tell them they could be anything they liked but had to remain on the street in plain sight and not hide behind hedges or in shops. Giving them half an hour to disperse and prepare themselves, Mr Halliday would then travel the length of the designated street on his irritatingly noisy Italian scooter without stopping or slowing, but spotting as many of them as he could. Halliday played the game scrupulously and fairly spotting with ease ninety per cent of the class each time, but never managing to 'tag' Rupert. The 'chameleon class' or the 'hide in plain sight' game became Rupert's favourite exercise as he delighted in slipping effortlessly into the persona of casual pedestrian, a lost stranger asking directions from a policeman, a council worker smoking idly while leaning over the barriers around yet another hole in the road, or on one occasion holding an impossible number of shopping bags for a lady with an impossible number of children in tow at a bus stop in the rain. He found the trick was to keep on the move where possible, but never seem to hurry; to interact with the other 'civilians' on the street; and that it was far better to look openly innocent and lost than be cautious and, consequently, furtive. It was only after successfully avoiding Mr Halliday for the third time that he realized he owed his innate skill at the game to years of observing his father quietly and unobtrusively going about his, or someone else's, business.

To blend in to Soho, Rupert had dressed in jeans and an American denim jacket salvaged from his student days, which seemed to be the uniform attire of the young men rushing between Wardour and Dean Streets. He carried two large but empty film reel canisters, borrowed from his old drama school, because all the rushing young men were delivering or collecting something and nobody questioned somebody carrying cans of film in Soho, except perhaps the Vice Squad.

The one thing that had worried him was his bright flame-red hair, inherited from his mother and he had seriously, albeit briefly, considered the possibility of hair dye to make himself less conspicuous. As virtually no male of his age wore a hat these days, unless they were pop musicians who patronized the militaria boutiques of the King's Road or Carnaby Street, he judged that he would be more noticeable with one than without. His mind was put at ease as soon as he entered Soho Square and immediately spotted two ginger-headed youths dressed as casually as he was and also carrying film canisters, one heading north and the other south. He himself took the western exit from the Square on to Carlisle Street where his olfactory senses told him without looking that he was passing The Toucan, Soho's famed 'Irish pub' where the pavement seemed sticky and the woodwork stained with an even more famous black Irish stout.

All over London, offices would be spluttering into life and thousands of golf ball electric typewriters beginning their machine-gun rattle, but at this hour of the morning, as Rupert crossed Dean Street, he had to conclude that Soho was a bird which didn't mind terribly if the early worm got away. He had, however, slipped into the ideal persona, for those who were about at the clearly ungodly hour before nine a.m. were all scurrying rather than walking and the vast majority carried packages which simply had to be delivered to someone important, somewhere.

Using a hop-skip-and-jump technique remembered from damp afternoons on a school athletics track, Rupert negotiated Dean Street without being run over by two cyclists and a speeding Vespa coming one way and a furious Fiat 500 the other. He then strode purposefully into St Anne's Court, as if cutting through to that hub of the British film industry, Wardour Street.

In fact, he was following a mental map given to him the night before and looking for the doorway which lay beyond the bookshop and then the tobacconist-newsagent on his right, but before he reached the licensed betting office opposite a large curtained window and vertical neon sign announcing 'Striptease'. The doorway was not difficult to miss, for it was a doorway without an outside door and a series of postcards thumb-tacked to the frame advertising a variety of services, only one of which he was interested in.

The briefing Rupert had received had assured him that Francis Tate Photography was a part-time occupation and its principal and only shareholder worked in a Soho film laboratory for a modest wage, Mondays to Fridays. As there was no way of surreptitiously discovering whether Frank Tate had left for work, short of disturbing a model of dubious Gallic origin, Rupert strode on by the gaping doorway until he reached the dog-leg in the Court where it turned towards Wardour Street. There he waited with his back against a wall, observing the door-less doorway, attempting to look as if he was loitering without intent even though in Soho, loitering – at least until the pubs opened – was a mass-participation sport taken very seriously by local residents.

He did not have to loiter long. At exactly ten minutes to nine Frank Tate – or the man fitting the description Rupert had been given – emerged from the door-less doorway, looked quickly to his right and left, hefted a military-style rucksack over one shoulder and took four long strides before disappearing into the newsagent/tobacconist shop.

Rupert did not move and for a moment thought this was Tate being clever and acting unpredictably in order to flush any pursuers or watchers. But then Tate emerged, a newspaper tucked under one arm and his hands busy opening a new pack of Guards, popping one between his lips and flicking a cigarette lighter as he walked. When he reached the end of the Court, he turned right and Rupert followed the cloud of his exhaled smoke around the corner into Dean Street.

Frank Tate, oblivious to his tracker, crossed the street and continued to walk and smoke while Rupert remained a firm fifty paces behind him on the opposite pavement until somewhere between Leoni's Quo Vadis and The York Minster, he simply disappeared from the street.

Rupert experienced a moment of panic before he spotted the gap between two brick buildings only wide enough for pedestrian traffic and realized that Tate had side-stepped into one of the many anonymous yards that nestled in Soho's shadows. They had once probably been used for stabling horses but now tended to be temporary storage facilities for the refuse bins used by the restaurants and cafés. Rupert's nose told him this particular yard was currently being used for that purpose, but a sign on the wall – a proper, printed sign, not a handwritten postcard – informed him that the entrance to Pan Europe Film Labs was to be found there also.

Hovering across the road, Rupert watched three more employees (he guessed) arriving for work do a similar disappearing act from Dean Street into the yard and then a courier, such as he was pretending to be, called with a pile of stationary boxes and Rupert saw the door of Pan Europe open to receive the delivery. He waited for fifteen minutes but observed no further movement and so hurried on to Shaftesbury Avenue to find a telephone box, mercifully complete with a directory.

Having found a number for Pan Europe Film Laboratories, he rang it and in a fair fist of an East London accent (he had failed 'Accents' at drama school and had been listed as 'Received Pronunciation Roles Only'), he claimed he had a delivery to make to them but couldn't get there for a while, and did they close for lunch? An authentic East London voice told him not to 'bovver callin' between one an' two when we're in the pub'.

As Rupert had no reason to doubt this information, he found a café which offered him a sticky Formica table, milky coffee and a view of Dean Street through nicotine-smeared windows. There he settled into his watcher's role, already bored and regretting he had agreed to play the part.

Four days later, Rupert was given time off for good behaviour and joined his father for an early dinner at Beotys on St Martin's Lane. It was a restaurant staffed by a platoon of shuffling Greek and Cypriot waiters, who perked up and seemed to shed many of their collective years at the sight of Mr Campion.

'I'm known here,' said the elder Campion. 'Allow me to recommend the slow-cooked lamb with a bottle of Othello – a little rough, but the staff will approve – and then something sticky with honey and nuts.'

'Order away, Pa, I'm in your hands.' Rupert surrendered gracefully. 'All I ask is that you tell me why I'm wasting my time down in Soho every day sitting in a dingy coffee bar bored out of my mind.'

Campion smiled fondly at his son. 'I hope you took an improving book with you as I doubt you'd find one on Dean Street. But tell me what you've discovered, just the main points, leaving out the local colour.'

'That won't take long,' said Rupert. 'The man identified to me as Frank Tate – I think that's how a policeman would give evidence – leaves the premises he shares with several . . . shall we say professional ladies . . . at almost the same time every morning, buys his newspaper and cigarettes at the nearest shop and is in work, just around the corner, by nine o'clock. I presume he does a useful morning's work in the film laboratory because at one o'clock he emerges and takes lunch with work colleagues at either a nearby sandwich bar or in The Crown and Two Chairmen. He goes back to work and between five and five thirty he leaves and returns to his flat. I'm guessing that's his regular routine.'

'Does he not have a social life?'

'I have only had three evenings to observe him and I wish to lodge a formal protest on behalf of my beautiful wife, since this little task you volunteered me for is certainly ruining her social life.'

'Ah, yes, poor Perdita,' said Mr Campion genuinely, 'I must crave her forgiveness for getting you involved in this.'

'And Mother also.'

'Of course, though it was she who put the idea into my old and befuddled brain.'

'How on earth did she do that?'

'When you were but a lad, a mere scamp in short trousers and dirty knees,' Campion beamed angelically at his son, 'she used to call you Young Sexton Blake. I suddenly remembered that and everything seemed to click into place.'

'I doubt Sexton Blake ever had such a dull case,' said Rupert attacking his plate of lamb shank with a fork, though hardly any force (and certainly not a knife) was necessary. 'This man Tate does go out in the evenings, or at least he has the last two, though not for long. At first I thought he was a budding alcoholic because he visited four different pubs or drinking clubs each evening, but he never stayed more than two minutes in each and was back at his flat by eight-thirty. At which point I decided I had earned my corn for the day and I popped home for a well-earned sleep.'

Mr Campion sampled his dinner and observed greedily that his lamb could be carved with a spoon then he resumed his interview.

'Did Tate meet anyone on this rapid pub crawl of his?'

'I have no idea as I didn't follow him into any of the establishments. A couple of them were real third-rate dives I wouldn't have fancied going into in daylight let alone after dark. But he didn't stop in any of them long enough to qualify as a social visit.'

'So it was business then?'

'Possibly, though I'm baffled as to what sort of business. He had his army rucksack with him, the one he takes to work every day, but I've no idea what he carries in it.'

'His sandwiches?' Mr Campion blinked behind his spectacles as if pondering the problem seriously. 'I've known many a senior civil servant carry very expensive hand-tooled leather briefcases with nothing more than their potted meat sandwiches in them.'

'Frankly, I neither know nor care. I'm fed up with Mr Frank Tate. Why am I following him anyway?'

'Observing, my boy, you've been observing. That's all we were asked to do, it's all we can do. In a sense the fact that we have nothing suspicious to report is good news.'

'Do you want me to hang around his lair over the weekend?'

'No need for that, he won't be there.' Rupert gaped at his father, his fork in mid-air. 'He'll be on his motorbike burning up the old Roman road into East Anglia by now. That's why I suggested dinner.'

'You knew this?'

'I was told he goes up to Gapton in Suffolk every weekend to see a young lady, so you get the weekend off.'

'Well, I'm grateful for that,' said Rupert, 'and I'm sure Perdita will be. That also explains Tate's behaviour today at lunchtime.'

'Behaviour? What sort of behaviour – good, bad, strange, illegal?'

'Slightly odd, to say the least. Instead of going for a drink with his workmates, he nipped out earlier than usual and beetled

off down to Oxford Street where he jumped on a bus going up
to Marble Arch.'

'Did you follow him?'

'Like a foxhound on the scent, though much quieter. I managed
to pile on the same bus and jump off just after he did, dead
opposite Marks and Spencer, which turned out to be where he
was going.'

'He didn't see you?'

'Never looked round; in fact, he kept his head down and
charged straight into the lingerie section.'

'Lingerie?' Mr Campion allowed his eyebrows to raise a
semi-quaver.

'I thought it a bit strange, but now you've explained about the
girlfriend, it makes some sort of sense. He must be taking her a
present, though tights aren't exactly the most extravagant gift;
practical perhaps, but not very romantic.'

'Tights as in female hosiery or as in a Jester's multicoloured?'

'Ladies Cantrece nylon stretch tights in American Tan – that's
the colour all the sales assistants wear.'

'You seem to have made a study of the subject.'

'Perdita told me that. She wears them; actually she goes
through a pair a week if she's rehearsing a play and she always
carries a spare pair. Mind you, Frank Tate's girlfriend must be
even more careless. Either that, or he's heard there's going to be
a shortage and he's stocking up. Sorry, no pun intended.'

'None taken,' said Campion automatically.

'I mean,' Rupert mused, cleaning his plate, 'what sort of girl
wants fifty pairs of tights as a present?'

'Don't go near the water, Dido.'

The high-pitched female voice skimmed across the calm,
moonlit lagoon, seemingly ignored by canine ears.

'Oh, don't fuss over the dog, Hyacinth,' echoed a second voice.
'She won't go in for a swim this time of year, it's too cold.'

'It's not the water I'm worried about; it's if she goes galumphing
off into the mud. When she does that she stinks to high heaven
and has to be given a bath, and you know what a handful she
can be then.'

'Then keep her on the lead.'

'But that's so unfair, Marigold. She's a sensitive animal and she's shut up in the house all day and you know she doesn't get on with the horses, so her walks are her only relaxation time.'

'Stupid bitch.'

'Marigold!'

'The dog, Hyacinth, the dog. I don't know why you ever took her in.'

'She was a waif, if not a stray. No one has any use for a greyhound when its racing days are over and poor Dido was abandoned in a pub car park, or so Sergeant Davies said. Tied to a fence post with baling twine, poor thing.'

'Was it one of our pubs?' asked her sister with a thinly curtailed sneer.

'No, as a matter of fact it wasn't. It was a free house on the Lowestoft Road.'

'Then you are absolved of all responsibility as far as I can see. Now shine that torch on the path, would you? I don't care about Dido but I really don't want to end up thigh-deep in mud.'

A pool of pale orange light illuminated a patch of gravel path into which a pair of wellington boots stepped forcibly.

'That's better. Let's get on, it's getting chilly.'

The two ladies – ladies of a certain age and formidable disposition – continued their evening stroll arm in arm. They wore identical Royal Navy duffle coats, woollen balaclavas and rubber boots, displaying a sense of sartorial style which would have appeared ludicrous and faintly pathetic in daylight and in public but which was ideally suited for an Autumnal late evening trudge out along the desolate finger of sand, mud and marram grass known as Gapton Spit, a prime example of longshore drift much beloved by geography teachers, but long despised by generations of Gapton inhabitants who had seen a once thriving trading and fishing port strangled by the unstoppable movement of the coastline.

'Dido! Dido! Heel!' Hyacinth tried again.

'She won't come,' Marigold said ruefully. 'That dog was built for speed, not for brains.'

'Don't be such a meany,' her sister replied sharply. 'I can't help worrying about her, poor little thing.'

'If she'd gone in the mud or the water, we'd have heard her splashing. It's a high tide tonight and the water's like a mill pond.'

'What if she's got into a fight with the fox that lives over by the smokehouse? She's done that before.'

'You worry too much, Hyacinth, and always about the silliest of things.'

'I can't help it; I feel responsible for her. Sergeant Davies entrusted the poor little thing to my care.'

'Sergeant Davies wanted the bitch off his hands so he didn't have to buy dog food out of his own pocket and he's too lazy to even try to find her real owners.'

'Dido was abandoned! Someone had to take her in,' wailed Hyacinth.

'And Davies knew you would, you being the softest touch in the town.'

'There are worse things to be in life. Oh, here we are, journey's end.'

'Do you have to say that every night?'

Hyacinth had said no more than the literal truth, for the path the sisters had been following had ended suddenly in a high mesh wire fence which artificially truncated the length of Gapton Spit, stretching from the edge of the lagoon on the town side to the pebble beach at which the North Sea licked hungrily.

Out of habit rather than ritual, Hyacinth flicked her torch upwards until the beam illuminated the sign she knew was there, hanging above head height, and as she did every night, she silently mouthed the words printed on it: MINISTRY OF DEFENCE PROPERTY: KEEP OUT.

'Come on, let's head back and have cocoa,' said Marigold. 'Let the damned dog find us.'

The sisters were less than halfway back along the path, the few lights of Gapton now before them across the lagoon, when Dido – neither lost nor damned – ambushed them silently out of the long, sharp grass and thrust her muzzle under the hem of Hyacinth's duffle coat.

'There you are, darling,' gushed her mistress. 'What have you been up to, wandering off like that?'

'It's probably a good thing she can't answer you,' said Marigold drily. 'Dogs are rarely up to anything good; not like horses, which are useful animals who earn their keep.'

'You're being mean again, Marigold; it's really not nice.'

'And you're being soft, but then you always were.'

This traditional squabble between the two sisters was cut short by a deep throated roar which seemed to bounce off the still black water of the lagoon from the southern edge of Gapton. The roar grew quickly louder and a single headlight became visible, flickering between the buildings until it came level with the sisters' eyeline. The motorbike's engine dropped a note as it turned left in the town square, then growled back to full throttle as the machine accelerated, its red rear light disappearing at speed up the Lowestoft Road.

As the throbbing bass notes faded, Marigold drew up her slender frame within her duffle coat and said, in a voice which brooked no argument:

'Now there's a dog up to no good.'

To celebrate him 'having the weekend off', Mr Campion insisted on calling a taxi to convey Rupert home to his long suffering wife.

'Please let me have a note of all the places Tate visited, would you? Those pubs and shady dives you mentioned. When you've a minute, of course, no rush,' he said as he held the cab door open so that Rupert could climb in. 'You get off, I'll walk from here.'

'Do I return for duty on Monday morning?' Rupert asked, looking up at his father from the back seat of the cab.

'If you wouldn't mind, old chap. Another week of nothing-much-to-report should do us very nicely.'

'Well, I still don't see the point of it all.'

'We must hope there isn't a point to it,' said Mr Campion thoughtfully. 'You are sure you weren't spotted?'

'Pretty confident. No, I'm absolutely sure he didn't see me shadowing him.'

'Good, well done.'

Mr Campion smiled benignly and raised a hand in salute as the cab pulled away. He too was sure that Tate had not spotted his Rupert shadow, just as he was also sure that Rupert had not seen Campion himself shadowing his son, as Amanda had commanded that he do to keep her maternal instincts in check.

Yet so absorbed had he been in watching his son play the role of surveillance operative, the fact that he himself was being watched had gone quite unnoticed.

THREE
'Orrible Murder

I t is generally accepted, especially by people who have never been there, that the most famous inhabitant of the small coastal town of Gapton goes by the name of Sandyman, although not one of the three generations of the family Sandyman presently resident there. The most famous Sandyman of them all is not a person but a small group of buildings and equipment – that collection of pots and pans which offered the potential of riches "beyond the dreams of avarice" as Dr Johnson once told Mrs Thrale – which comprised Sandyman's Seaside Brewery, an institution whose fame since 1890 had spread far beyond the confines of Gapton throughout Suffolk and even into those undiscovered countries of South Norfolk and North Essex.

In fact, the town's most famous human inhabitant, based on the criteria of visual sightings rather than the fond but insecure memories of ale drinkers, was a woman in her mid-forties called Dorothy Monk. Few people, however, realized this; not even her fellow residents and near-neighbours in Gapton. A close observer of this lady as she went about her quiet domestic routines would have perhaps noted an air of sadness around her, a withdrawn introspection that was clearly not aloofness. She was briefly polite to all who attempted to talk to her but gave the impression that her business was her own and she had no interest in anyone else's. Sightings of her in Gapton were rare, though not rare enough to merit concern. She was known as a customer in the Post Office and by the town's sole butcher, two of its fishmongers and its general grocer, yet none could say anything about her except that her credit was good and she paid her bills in cash and on time. It was common knowledge that she had a key to the redundant church, St Olave's, and it was said she used the empty church for private prayer and contemplation in exchange for some light cleaning duties. An observant woman of a similar age might have noted – in fact, almost certainly had – that Dorothy Monk seemed to have foresworn the use of cosmetics and adopted a policy of dressing in a deliberately dowdy way reflecting the fashion precepts of the austere 1950s rather than those of the 'swinging' or at least brighter 1960s and exemplified by the fact that she never appeared out of doors without a headscarf shrouding her sharp but undoubtedly pretty face and a long coat, even in summer, disguising her still-shapely figure. Gapton's men, as all men are easily fooled, hardly gave Dorothy Monk a second look if they saw her on the street and the few that did might have agreed with Gapton's women that she was either a widow or, more interestingly, a divorcee. The tradesmen she dealt with deferentially and automatically referred to her as 'Mrs Monk' without any idea of her real status, and both Gapton sexes would have been surprised to discover that Dorothy Monk was not her real name. Though they did not realize it, all would have instantly recognized the name she had been known by in a previous life, that of Jean Learner-Scott, though that was not her real name either.

It was rare that Dorothy Monk had visitors to Samphire Cottage, her small thatched home which lay on the edge of Gapton proper on the road to the expanding secondary settlement of Gapton Thorpe, at any time, but unheard of at seven o'clock on a grey Sunday morning, just as dawn was spluttering to get up a head of steam. Anyone observing the scene as a mud-spattered Land Rover ground noisily to a halt by the cottage's white garden gate might have seen a bedroom curtain twitch and a curious feminine eye assuring itself of the arriving visitor's identity before he had taken two anxious paces down the garden path.

Mrs Monk's visitor was a very recognizable face – and name – in Gapton, for it was a Sandyman; specifically, Torquil, son of Bernard and grandson of Ewart Sandyman, the brewing dynasty on which the town now depended for much of its employment as well as its refreshment. And he was clearly in a hurry, covering the distance to the cottage's front door in a few long, rapid strides and wielding the small brass knocker shaped like a fox's head with far more violence and volume than was seemly so early on a Sunday.

The visitor seemed to realize he had violated some unwritten law as soon as the door creaked open and he immediately apologized to the woman standing before him, backlit by a living-room standard lamp.

'Mrs Monk, I am so sorry to disturb you at such an ungodly hour.'

The reply he received was casual rather than judgemental, and delivered in clear, calm tones with just a wisp of a continental accent.

'Should not all the hours of a Sunday be godly, Mr Sandyman?'

'Er . . . yes . . . of course,' Sandyman stumbled, 'but you see we're in a bit of a state back at the house.'

Torquil Sandyman was not a man easily intimidated. His education and background had instilled in him supreme self-confidence and a dynastic sense of responsibility for all Gapton residents, yet had he been less flustered and his business less urgent, even he might have failed to retain eye contact with the sharp blue eyes which fixed him from that angular and impassive face, which though plain and unadorned was still icily attractive. He had forgotten how tall Dorothy Monk was until it registered that those unblinking blue eyes were on a level with his, and how naturally imposing a figure she cut framed in the doorway of Samphire Cottage, even when wearing a long, pink silk dressing gown, through the sleeves and neck of which protruded far more practical winceyette nightwear.

'Again, I am so sorry to bother you so early,' Torquil resumed.

'Please do not concern yourself; I am a very light sleeper. How may I assist you?'

'It's about Vibeke, our au pair girl up at The Maltings. I believe she comes to visit you.'

'She does – occasionally,' Mrs Monk replied carefully – perhaps too carefully, though Torquil in his red-faced fluster did not notice.

'I don't suppose you've seen her recently, have you?'

'Not since last week,' the woman said, then after a pause, 'but I heard her last night.'

'Heard her? How? Where? When?'

Torquil realized he needed to take a deep breath and did so. Mrs Monk watched him exhale, as if waiting for a cue in a script.

'To be accurate, I heard her boyfriend's motorbike – it's quite distinctive. I don't think there's another one like it in Gapton and I've seen her riding on it before. She loves going motorbiking with Francis, she's told me so many times.'

'Does Vibeke talk much about Francis, when she visits?'

'Oh, yes, she's deeply in love, I think, but then she is so young.'

'So she seems happy with him?'

Mrs Monk nodded seriously. 'As happy as an eighteen-year-old can be when she thinks she has found true love, which is to say ecstatic.'

'But has she told you anything *about* him?'

'Nothing that I suspect is not common knowledge. She has been seeing him for many months. He works in London and comes up to Gapton to see her at weekends, staying, I believe, in one of your public houses. He comes by motorbike and they go for rides into the countryside or to Yarmouth and the beach in summer, or to Ipswich and the cinema in the evening. I assumed that was where they were going when I heard the bike engine yesterday evening. It would have been around six o'clock.'

'Did you see which way they were going?'

'I have told you, I did not see them at all. I merely heard a motorbike and assumed it was Vibeke and her young man. As there clearly seems to be a problem, might I ask what it is? I am very fond of Vibeke, you know.'

'Yes, she said you get on well.'

'Considering the difference in our ages?'

Torquil Sandyman blushed and cleared his throat.

'I merely meant that she speaks fondly of you and looks forward to her visits. That is why I thought she might have told you her plans, or even that she might have stayed with you last night. You see, Mrs Monk, she left our house just before six to meet that boyfriend of hers – and his motorbike – and never came home.'

Many believe it to be an old wives' tale, or a story spread by newspaper editors short of hard copy, but the majority of the dead bodies found in rural England are discovered not by detectives

of any hue, but by ordinary law-abiding citizens out walking
their dogs. On that Sunday morning, just as full daylight was
yawning the mist off the gentle swell of the lagoon encased by
Gapton Spit, it was an abandoned and then adopted greyhound
called Dido who fulfilled that traditional role.

It was said that the screams of Dido's mistress, Miss Hyacinth,
could be heard all over Gapton, and those old enough to remember
claimed that she did a better job of waking the population than
the now-silent bells of St Olave's church ever had.

Two weeks had passed since Mr Campion had released his son,
Rupert, from 'surveillance duty' in darkest Soho, but only after
he had turned in his homework in the form of a single sheet of
typewritten paper listing without comment some twenty pubs,
clubs and drinking dens which Frank Tate had visited on his
evening patrols, though never staying for more than a minute or
two in any of them. Campion senior had sent Campion junior's
list to Count Westergaard with a handwritten summary concluding
that other than his unusual evening perambulations and occasional
odd shopping expeditions, nothing specifically criminal or anti-
social could be levelled against the character of the boyfriend of
the ambassador's daughter.

And that, he thought, was that, and gave the matter no further
thought apart from an exchange with his wife when Amanda had
said, 'Well, that was a complete waste of Rupert's time,' and
Campion had spiritedly replied: 'Nonsense, he's still young
and has plenty of time to waste. It was a useful training exercise
for him.' For the sake of domestic harmony Lady Amanda had
gently bitten her lower lip and refrained from asking exactly what
her husband had in mind when it came to their son's 'training'.

It was on a dull, overcast Monday afternoon in London, the
sort of afternoon when the streetlights came on early, that Mr
Campion was reminded of the name Frank Tate. He was walking
towards his Bottle Street flat – an inefficient drain on his finances
given the amount of time he spent in London these days, but a
welcome bolt-hole full of memories nonetheless. In fact, given
the price of hotel rooms it was, he felt certain, a justifiable
extravagance.

Mr Campion was in town to attend what promised to be a

rather dull recital of chamber music in the Wigmore Hall in aid of a charity of which he was a patron. He was there out of duty rather than pleasure and had considered – fleetingly – whether he could in all conscience sneak off to Ronnie Scott's club where the American trumpeter Miles Davis was currently causing quite a stir, but as he crossed the street, overnight suitcase in hand, he had a premonition that his evening was destined to be anything but musical. He claimed no special psychic power but knew from experience that a police car parked outside the street door to his flat usually involved a change in the best-laid plans.

'Mr Campion, is it?' asked the uniformed sergeant climbing out of the passenger seat of the Metropolitan Police Rover.

'I'm afraid it may well be, Sergeant, depending on what he's wanted for,' Campion replied cheerfully.

'He's not wanted for anything in the conventional sense, sir. But he is wanted by someone in authority. If, that is, he could spare the time.' The policeman gave the speech as if he had rehearsed it and Campion smiled to himself, for the only thing he could think of was how young the officer was. *When the police sergeants start looking younger*, he mused, *one knows one is getting old.*

'An appointment with someone in authority; how could I resist? Do you have a time in mind?'

'Immediately would do very nicely, sir.'

The sergeant nodded to his driver who brought a radio microphone up to his mouth, then opened the rear door of the Rover and indicated that Campion should climb in.

'I'll come quietly, Sergeant, but only on condition you sound your siren all the way there. Where are we going, by the way?'

'Aldermanbury Square, sir, in the City.'

'Ah,' breathed Campion, bending his long legs to fit them into the car, 'Love Lane police station, I suppose.'

'Not exactly, sir.'

It was true. In his ceremonial Beadle's robes with his hands behind his back, Lugg did look like a bear. In fact, only a few inches of razor-creased pinstriped trousers and a pair of highly polished black shoes protruding from under the hem spoiled the ursine illusion. The bald pink head and wobbling jowls were definitely human but gave the impression of a human head glued on to the body of an aggressive teddy bear.

In his heavy finery, Lugg stood on the steps of Brewers' Hall flexing at the knees. He made no effort to open the rear door of the police car for his old friend but waited until the constable driving leapt out to perform the task. A friendship older than most marriages and a devoted, if argumentative, loyalty were all very well in their place, but Campion knew that Lugg had an inbuilt reluctance to touch police property on the reasonable assumption that such an action might be used in evidence against him.

'Good afternoon, Mr Beadle,' said Campion jovially. 'I must say you cut a fine figure in your formal robes. It seems that Beadling agrees with you, though I would have thought they could have supplied you with a suitably impressive tipstaff to keep recalcitrant brewers in check or to lay about unruly orphans, as they did in Dickens.'

'As it 'appens,' Lugg said majestically, 'they do provide a handy length of ebony tipped with a good clout o' silver to weight the end. Trouble is I'm only allowed to use it to bash on the floor when I'm announcing Grace. Anyways, I'm glad you're 'ere.'

'It was no trouble at all. I found a taxi waiting for me at Bottle Street before I'd got through the front door. How did you know I'd be there and just when – and I have to ask – did the Metropolitan Police start working for you as a mini-cab company?'

'Ho, they don't work for me,' snorted Lugg, rocking back on his heels as if reeling from the very idea. 'They works for 'im h'inside, 'im who you'll meet in a minute if you'd be gracious enough to cross our threshold. As he'll be on duty, so to speak, I'll have to put the kettle on, but that doesn't stop you and me having a drop o'somefink stronger. There's a ripe barley wine just tapped and the first of the winter ales 'ave arrived, or there's a nice Hock left over from luncheon and mebbe a snoot-full of claret, but we don't 'ave spirits in the 'ouse. Not good for the image; us bein' brewers an' not distillers.'

'I think I get the distinction,' said Campion, 'but tea sounds just what's called for. My magical mystery tour seems to require a clear head. One minute I was reaching for the keys to my flat, then the next I'm here at this hallowed hall courtesy of a police escort. To coin a phrase popular among the recidivist classes, how did they know where to pick me up?'

'I told 'em,' Lugg said proudly, stooping to pick up Campion's case with a hand the size of a ham. 'They came to me 'cos they knew we 'ad previous—'

'An unfortunate turn of phrase, old fruit, but do carry on.'

'I rang your place and talked with the guv'nor – Lady Amanda, that is – and she tells me you're on your way to town and your train gets in just after four. Knowin' yer 'abits better than you do yerself, I reckons you'll head for Bottle Street for a wash and to get changed into your penguin suit for the evening's fun and festivities or whatever it is you 'ad planned. I didn't think you'd mind being hijacked for an hour or so.'

'Well, old dear, you've got me here, so lead on. Who exactly is it am I here to meet?'

Lugg's grin turned the lower half of his face into a slice of watermelon.

'You'll hardly credit it, but it's another Elsie who wants to see you.'

As he followed Lugg up the oak staircase to the first-floor rooms of the Brewers' Hall, Campion had the fleeting impression that the broad, swaying figure before him could blot out the sun.

'So how are you finding life among the Livery Companies of Old London, me old china?'

'Musn't grumble, though probably will,' said Lugg over his shoulder. 'This ain't a bad place to work even though it's a modern building, the h'original 'aving been flattened by the Luftwaffe. The clerk is a bit tight-fisted when it comes to making up the pay packets and I reckon he's the only man in England to go into mourning when the halfpenny stopped bein' legal tender. But the perks are good. We gets our meat direct from Smithfield, so if you ever wants a nice beef fillet, you know where to come.'

'I'll file that away for future reference,' said Campion, 'as we see so little fresh meat in the countryside.'

'Have to hunt yer own, so I hear,' said Lugg, pausing at the top of the stairs in a circular lobby. 'I'll leave yer case here, the gentlemen that wants to see you are in the Court Room.'

'Gentle-*men*? Plural?'

'If that's what the educated classes calls more than one,' Lugg scowled, 'then yus, they're in the plural. There's Mr Bernard Sandyman, one of our brewer members and the aforementioned Elsie.'

'You're enjoying this, aren't you?' Campion smiled.

'Brightens the day, old cock, brightens the day,' Lugg smirked, turning a handle and pushing open a door.

The two men waiting in the Court Room stood formally, if not quite at attention, on either side of an impressive fireplace of Verona marble. Campion's quick eyes took them both in before settling on the exquisite blue-white Carrara panel insert showing, fittingly, infant Bacchanals which a distant memory told him were the work of Sir Charles Wheeler.

The rigid expressions on the faces of the two men could have served as models for Janus bookends; the older man's stern, severe and possibly angry, the younger man's fixed in a welcoming smile which could have been applied with lacquer. It was the younger, more sharply suited man who spoke first, stepping forward with a hand outstretched, his smile unflickering.

'Mr Campion, so good of you to see us. Allow me to introduce Bernard Sandyman. I don't believe you've met.'

'Not in person, no; but I know his products well.' Campion shook hands and fixed his host with the lenses of his glasses. 'And you, I suppose, must be Elsie?'

The smile never wavered.

'An affectation, but also a coincidence,' said the smile. 'I believe you knew my predecessor, L.C. Corkran.'

'Very well. He always said that rumours of his retirement from the security service were greatly exaggerated.'

'Well, I'm afraid they are true; time's winged chariot and all that. I'm his replacement in the Department and, wouldn't you know it, I have the same initials: L.C., so I got the "Elsie" nickname as well. I don't mind, it's quite an honour given the old boy's track record. My name's not Corkran, though – that would be rather incestuous – it's Deighton, actually.'

'Like the writer of those clever spy stories?' Campion asked innocently.

'Who?'

'Never mind.' Campion turned to the man closer to his own age and took his proffered hand. 'Delighted to meet you, Mr Sandyman; speaking as a grateful customer.'

'Campion,' the brewer acknowledged stiffly. 'Sorry to drag you into this. I met your uncle once, the Bishop of Devizes, about thirty years ago. Fancied himself as a bit of a wine buff, though he was more of a wine-bore if you ask me. No offence intended.'

'None taken, you clearly knew him well. As I'm here, you might as well make use of me, though I have no idea *why* I am here.'

'Allow me,' offered the grinning Elsie. 'I believe you two gentlemen have a mutual acquaintance: Count Westergaard, the Danish Ambassador.'

'More than an acquaintance,' barked Mr Sandyman, 'I've known the count since the war. An honourable man and a brave chap; must be going through hell this morning.'

'What has happened?' Campion asked gravely, slightly disturbed by the fact that Elsie's smile had not waned a single watt.

''Orrible murder!' hissed Lugg from behind his right ear.

'A smidge overdramatic perhaps,' smoothed Elsie, 'but forensically quite accurate, I'm afraid.'

'Good Lord, not the ambassador's daughter?'

'We don't know – that's the problem. Vibeke Westergaard was last seen in the company of Frank Tate on Saturday night in Gapton and we have no idea where she is now. Frank Tate, on the other hand, was found dead yesterday morning, the back of his head smashed in quite thoroughly.'

'Told yer,' Lugg whispered.

'You're sure it's Tate?'

'The body hasn't been formally identified yet – we're not sure who could do that – but local sources are sure it's him. His motorbike was found nearby when the tide went out round something called Gapton Spit.'

'Somebody had pushed it into the lagoon,' Sandyman

interrupted. 'I don't know if you know our little town, Campion, but it used to be a thriving port until longshore drift cut us off and now we have a dead lagoon instead of a harbour. Good for birdwatchers but damn little else apart from these Government wallahs from Defence' – the brewer jerked his head towards Elsie – 'and their top secret fiddle-faddling.'

If L.C. Deighton was disturbed by Sandyman's outburst, his smile did not show it.

'It's no secret that the Ministry of Defence owns most of Gapton Spit but I'd hardly call the work being done there fiddle-faddle.'

'But it is why you are here.' Campion did not make it a question.

'There's a question of whether Tate's body was found on ministry land. We await a ruling from the police on that,' said Elsie, all sweetness and light. 'But I'm here because of the diplomatic implications.'

'The ambassador's daughter.'

'Exactly. She's missing; disappeared completely.'

'My son and his family are distraught,' said Sandyman, 'because the girl lived with them as their au pair. Torquil feels responsible somehow but I've told him that's nonsense. He's been out since dawn with the search parties and the children are very upset. They were very close to Vibeke and she's the count's only child, so naturally he's taking it very badly and I came up to London to offer any support I could. He'd do the same for me.'

'I'm so sorry for all of you,' said Campion, locking eyes with Elsie, 'but I have to ask: is Vibeke Westergaard a suspect in Tate's murder?'

'Good God, man, I didn't expect that from someone like you!' Sandyman spluttered. 'Of course not.'

The man from the security service continued to smile, but his voice was without humour.

'Officially, she cannot be ruled out as it seems she was the last person to see Tate alive, but it is highly unlikely from what we know about her that she will be a suspect. We have, of course, to find her before we can be sure, but where you can help us is with the victim, Tate.'

Campion raised an eyebrow. 'I'm not sure how, I never met the poor man.'

'But you followed him, put a watch on him, for the ambassador,' Bernard Sandyman stated, his chest puffed out. 'I was there – here in Brewers' Hall – when your name was suggested to Aage Westergaard. Suggested by that fellow Lugg right there and supported by the Duke of—'

Mr Campion held up a calming hand. 'Yes, I am aware of my references, and yes, I did agree to have an eye kept on Frank Tate for a few days, but only in London. I have no idea what he got up to in Suffolk. The ambassador knows all I know and it was my son who did the actual surveillance.'

'Ah,' breathed Lugg behind him, 'that's a relief. At least Rupert's still light on his feet.'

Campion turned his head sharply to scowl severely over his shoulder, then turned back to the young man known as Elsie. 'I'm sure Rupert will tell you everything he knows, and if we can borrow that police taxi outside I'll take you to him right now. I believe he and Torquil are old school chums and I guarantee he'll be happy to help.'

Mr Sandyman nodded in appreciation. 'That's good of you, Campion. This is a devil of a mess and could get messier.'

'Quite,' said Campion. 'I just need a moment in private with your Beadle, if I may.

Campion walked and Lugg waddled out of the Court Room back to the circular lobby, where Campion's overnight case stood unmolested. Campion dropped to one knee on the thick carpet and opened the case, removing an envelope from on top of a pile of white shirts and underclothes.

'You might as well have this,' he said, passing Lugg the envelope. 'It's my ticket to the Wigmore Hall concert tonight. You probably won't like the music and you certainly won't appreciate it, but that just serves you right for getting me into this. And for Pete's sake, don't go down Wigmore Street dressed like that in the dark – they'll think you've robbed the fur department in Selfridges. The ticket's paid for but you'll be expected to put your hand in your pocket when the plate comes round at the end. Just smile, dig deep and remember it's for a good cause.'

'Never turned me back on a drop of free culture,' observed Lugg, 'and I'll take this as a thank-you-very-much.'

Campion stood up and brushed the knees of his trousers with his hands.

'Thank you for what?'

'For making you a present of an 'orrible murder. I told the duke you couldn't resist one. Mind you, being respectably employed these days, I'll have to ask for time off if we're going to Suffolk.'

'We,' said Campion firmly, 'are not going anywhere. I am too old to go hunting murderers by the seaside and you're just too old, full stop.'

'So you'll give the boy Rupert his head, then?' Lugg beamed, his chin jutting out.

'I'll see how he feels about it.'

'Tell him to watch out for young Elsie back there.' Lugg jerked a thumb towards the Court Room. 'You noticed how he never stops smiling? You can't trust a man who smiles all the time. It's like he's had his teeth painted and he's waiting for 'em to dry.'

FOUR
Briefing at Darsham Halt

'I don't want to sound callous, Rupert, but I don't think I can play the ministering angel to a family I don't know from Adam when I should be crawling round the West End on my knees begging for an audition. Of course, if those damned reviewers hadn't taken against *Lucky Strike*, it wouldn't have closed after ten days and I wouldn't be resting. I'm not as used to resting as you are, darling.'

Perdita Browning, as she was known to Equity, paused for breath then clutched at her perfect mouth with a well-manicured right hand, as if trying to retract her words.

'Oh, God, that was so *theatrical*, wasn't it? Real diva stuff – bitchiness of the highest order. I thought we had a pact that if either of us went that way the other was free to shoot them.'

Rupert Campion patted his wife's hand, smiled beatifically and sighed. 'You are reprieved this time, darling, but I reserve the right to keep my powder dry for future outbursts, of which there will no doubt be many. And don't blame yourself – or the critics – for *Lucky Strike* closing; it was a pretty awful show. I mean, who wants to go to a musical about striking car workers from Essex? Anyway, a few days in Gapton with the Sandymans will take your mind off things.'

'It's hardly a holiday, though, is it?' protested Perdita. 'Won't we be intruding on private grief? I mean, there's been a murder and a girl is missing, though I haven't seen or heard anything on the news about it.'

'I think they're keeping it quiet.'

'Who? The police?'

'They and the Ministry of Defence and probably the Foreign Office – it's complicated, as the girl is the daughter of a diplomat.'

'Which is no doubt why your father is involved and none of that adds up to a relaxing few days by the seaside. The North Sea seaside – in November.'

Rupert put on his best boyish grin. 'I didn't say it would be relaxing, I said it would take your mind off things. Torquil and I were at school together and his wife, Victoria, is a charmer. If we can help them out, I'd really like to.'

'Won't we get in the way?'

'He told me on the phone last night that they could use all the moral support they could get and if we find ourselves under-foot and more of a hindrance than a help, then we go back to London. Anyway, the die is cast, as somebody famous once said in Latin.'

'Julius Caesar,' said his wife primly, 'as he crossed the Rubicon, but he would have said it in Greek, not Latin.'

'I bow to your superior knowledge in all things, darling. All I meant was that we've arrived.'

'Arrived where?'

'Darsham Halt.'

Perdita pressed her nose up against the carriage window. 'But we're in the middle of nowhere!'

When they descended from the train – the only passengers to do so – on to what seemed to be a makeshift platform Rupert was tempted to agree with his wife. As the train shuffled off down a long straight track to nowhere, but probably Lowestoft, the young Campions took stock of their surroundings. There was an official railway sign board announcing that this was indeed Darsham, a disused goods shed, level crossing gates where a road totally devoid of traffic crossed the lines and a large, square, badly rendered building which might have been a pub. The only moving entity was the wind coming from the north-east, which carried a tang of sea salt and a portent of winter.

'I don't think it's the middle of nowhere, but it might be the end of the world,' Rupert tried gamely. 'Don't worry, Torquil said he'd send somebody to collect us.'

'I expect it'll be a ghostly Victorian hangman in a horse and trap come to carry us off across the misty marshes, like something out of a Dickens or Wilkie Collins novel on a bad day,' Perdita grumbled, pulling up the collar of her coat.

'I very much doubt it will be anything quite so melodramatic. They'll most likely send a . . .'

Rupert cut short his thought and exchanged rapid glances with his wife, for she too had heard the distinct sound of approaching hoof beats.

'Good grief! I don't believe it,' Perdita gasped. 'For goodness' sake, pinch me really, really hard and tell me I'm dreaming.'

'I'm not dreaming but I still can't quite believe it.'

Perdita's hand grabbed her husband arm and squeezed. 'They've sent a hearse!'

'That's not a hearse,' Rupert said, wincing under Perdita's grip. 'It's a carnival float – no, it's not. It's a brewer's dray, of course it is; what else would they send?'

'A car, perhaps,' Perdita said under her breath, 'with seats and a roof?'

Both of them had to blink several times before they fully believed their eyes, but it was indeed a brewer's dray which rattled and clunked over the level crossing towards them. It was powered by a pair of magnificent Suffolk Punch horses, their leather and brass harnesses creaking and jangling in time with their regular effortless tread. They looked like noble beasts who could have carried a knight in full armour, or perhaps even two, without complaint. They were being steered by two seated draymen, one holding the reins, the other a long, thin whip, though neither piece of equipment seemed necessary. The draymen, both small – tiny compared to the huge horses – were in formal traditional attire: tweed jackets and waistcoats, brown bowler hats and thick sacking aprons around their legs. They sat on a sprung bench seat under an arched metal sign advertising Sandyman's Seaside Ales.

The horses clopped up to the waiting couple and came to a halt close enough for Rupert to feel their warm breath on his face. From the driving seat of the dray came a distinctly feminine voice.

'Are you Campions?'

Rupert and Perdita looked up into the faces of the horses as though one of them had spoken, and both nodded silently and in awe to the gentle giants in front of them.

'Oh, good,' said the voice. 'Say hello to Horatius and Belisarius, and then climb aboard and we'll take you into Gapton. I'm Hyacinth, by the way, and the one in the driving seat is Marigold.

We'll be there in no time. Everyone round here gives way to the Sandyman Shires – if they know what's good for them.'

Perdita might have baulked at riding in a vehicle without a roof, but she did have a seat, albeit one which had started life as a metal park bench and was now bolted firmly to the planks of the dray just behind the driver's seat. She and Rupert sat there swaying precariously, clutching their overnight bags, as Horatius and Belisarius powered them smoothly on their way while the bowler-hatted Hyacinth, with minor interruptions from Marigold, who was concentrating on driving, provided the running commentary over the soundtrack of the rhythmic clip-clopping of metalled hooves.

'We'll be passing through Gapton Thorpe, which was originally a secondary settlement to Gapton – a sort of medieval overspill town – but it continues to expand while we in Gapton shrink. We will go through Gapton and you will see all the sights: St Olave's church, redundant for many years sadly, the popular public house The Butt and Oyster down on the Hard and of course the famous Gapton Spit enclosing the Gapton Lagoon, as we call it. Which is where' – she took a breath for dramatic purposes – 'I discovered the body!'

'Calm down, Hyacinth!' barked her companion from the driving seat. 'You'll get yourself overexcited and have another of your turns.'

Hyacinth was unmoved by such concern and continued in jovial mood, glossing over her gruesome announcement. 'Then we will pass the brewery gates and the stables where these lovely boys live and we'll deliver you to Torquil at The Maltings. Of course, it's not a real maltings, it's just a house called that, though I believe there was quite a trade in malt when Gapton still func-tioned as a port. You are aware, I take it, that Gapton is one of the most quoted examples of a Grimston Hybrid, which shows—'

Perdita, who was far more familiar with scene-stealing actresses than her husband, could stand it no longer. 'I'm sorry, but who exactly are you?'

Their tour guide turned to face the passengers, who were clutching their iron bench seat with white knuckles. 'We are the sisters Mister,' she said pleasantly.

'I beg your pardon?'

'That's our name,' snapped their driver without turning. 'I'm Marigold Mister and this mop-head is my sister, Hyacinth Mister. It's a perfectly good name, but a bit strange if you're a man because you'd be Master Mister to begin with and then Mister Mister later on.'

Perdita let her jaw drop and gaped in silence at Rupert, who promptly recovered his manners and said, 'It was awfully kind of Torquil to send you to collect us.'

'Needs must,' said the bowler-hatted driver. 'Torquil's out with one of the search parties and every vehicle in the place has been pressed into service by the police, scouring the area. We volunteered as the boys needed a bit of exercise and they're not on delivery duty today.'

'I suppose they're out searching for Vibeke Westergaard,' said Rupert, gently placing a hand under Perdita's chin to encourage her to close her mouth.

'Such a sweet girl; so helpful to Victoria and so good with the children,' said Hyacinth, resuming her role as Mistress of Ceremonies. 'We're godmothers to the two boys, you know. We have one each, so to speak. I suppose you'll be wanting to interview me about finding the body of Vibeke's young man?'

'Have you not talked to the police?' Rupert said uncertainly.

'Oh, yes, but you know what the police are like, they never *listen*, do they? It's not like talking to a famous detective like you, Mr Campion, is it?' She turned the brim of her bowler towards Perdita. 'And I'm sure you'll be a great help too, Lady Amanda.'

Rupert looked at his wife and this time both their mouths fell open into competing circles.

'Anyway, this is Gapton Thorpe,' their guide continued, dangerously pointing out things with her ridiculously long whip. 'Not much to see except some quite ghastly new houses and even uglier *bungalows*.' She said the word as if reaching for mouthwash. 'A few shops and our little public library and there, on your right, just out to sea is the very tip of Gapton Spit, that freak of nature which has brought ruin to old Gapton.'

Bemused, the young Campions did as instructed and gazed out between the houses, over the cold grey seascape until their eyes focussed on a bar of sand around which licked gentle white-topped waves. On a bad day, thought Rupert, it could have been mistaken for a submerging submarine or a dead porpoise. But when the dray turned a sweeping bend in the road and the ugly houses of Gapton Thorpe came to an end, they had an unobstructed view of the shifting coastline and the extent of Gapton Spit which formed a strange ethereal boundary between two mirrors of water, the calm steel blue of the trapped lagoon and the white-flecked, battleship grey ocean beyond it. The only sign of life on either watery horizon was provided by a squadron of gulls on a desultory low-level patrol over the lagoon.

'We are now entering Gapton proper, where you will observe that motor vehicles, cyclists and even pedestrians all give way for the Sandyman horses,' resumed Hyacinth.

'Quite right too!' her sister shouted in agreement. 'It should be a by-law.'

Perdita risked a look over her shoulder and noted from the queue of traffic building up behind them that a by-law was probably unnecessary.

'Coming up on our left is St Olave's Church, named, I believe, after a Viking king of Norway and famously described by somebody or other as "the flintiest church in a county of flint churches", which sounds a very smart thing to say even if I don't quite understand it. And on our right' – on which command, three heads swung in unison – 'Samphire Cottage, the home of Gapton's very own mystery woman, Dorothy Monk.'

'Why is she a mystery?' asked Perdita, despite hushing motions from Rupert.

It was Marigold, with a snap on the thick leather reins which the horses ignored imperiously, who answered. 'Because the woman keeps herself to herself and doesn't join in the local gossip. Hyacinth here thinks that's unnatural in a woman and possibly subversive. If the woman doesn't want to join the basket-weaving-and-bingo set then good luck to her is what I say.'

'Vibeke Westergaard got on very well with her,' Hyacinth retorted, 'and used to visit her at the cottage – the only person ever allowed across the threshold.' Then she leaned over her seat so that her face was only a foot away from Rupert's. 'You'll be wanting to question her too, won't you, Mr Campion?'

'Well, I'm not sure if—' Rupert stammered.

Hyacinth sat upright again. 'Of course you will,' she said to herself, and then another tourist attraction came into view and she was back on the job. 'On our right, one of our flagship pubs, The Butt and Oyster down by what used to be the old harbour, famed for its seafood platters. When the tide's out, it has a car park; when the tide's in, it has a handy launching dock for small sailboats. Pity the poor motorist who gets his tide times wrong.'

'Serve them right,' growled Marigold, clearly an advocate of horse power in the more literal sense, as the dray turned left as if on automatic pilot and on to what was clearly the main, if not the only, street of Gapton.

The scent of warm malt as comforting as breakfast cereal and warm milk on a winter's morning, told them they were approaching the brewery, the beating heart of the town.

'This is the High Street and you will have noticed how the boys' ears pricked up because they know they're home,' gushed Hyacinth, 'but you'll have to wait a little for your second breakfast, my lads.'

To Rupert's relief, the giant horses did not seem to mind when Marigold snapped their reins and Hyacinth leaned forward and tapped one of them (Belisarius?) ever so gently on the flank with her long whip. Their sedate pace did not falter as they passed the open gates to Sandyman's brewery yard. From the buildings abutting the yard came the rattle of metal and the clink of glass and the hum of machinery, though the only signs of a workforce were two men in brown overalls who were attaching sacks of hops taller than themselves to a chain to be hauled up into the air by a second-storey hoist.

'When you come to question me,' Hyacinth broke Rupert's reverie, 'just go into the brewery yard and ask for the stables. That's The Stables with a capital T and a capital S, of course, which is the name of our house. The horses live in the real stables next door.'

'I think Mr Campion is clever enough to work that out,' said Marigold drily.

'A common mistake,' Perdita chimed in impishly. 'This Mr Campion likes things spelled out for him slowly and clearly.'

'I think most men do, Lady Amanda,' Hyacinth said innocently, 'a bit like dogs, so I'm told.'

Perdita suppressed a fit of the giggles and winced playfully as Rupert's elbow nudged her in the ribs.

'Almost there. That's the Sandyman place up there on the right. We can pull into the drive and drop you at the front door. All part of the service!'

To emphasize her point, Hyacinth turned to the passengers and briefly lifted her bowler hat in salute, revealing a pile of pinned-up white hair and a tear-drop face crisscrossed with age lines.

For the first time Rupert – some great detective he! – realized that Hyacinth was of a venerable age, perhaps eighty, although undoubtedly spry for it. He wondered if her sister was of a similar vintage and strained his neck to try and catch a glimpse of Marigold's hands for he had been told, by Mrs Christie no less, that a woman's age was always betrayed by the backs of her hands. His researches proved inconclusive however.

'You've been most kind,' he said to the back of both their heads. 'Do you mind if I ask what your connection with the brewery is? You told us you lived there and you called The Butt and Oyster "one of our flagship pubs" and you obviously have access to brewery transport, but I'm not clear how you are connected to Sandyman's.'

'Why, my dear boy,' said Hyacinth sweetly, 'we own it.'

FIVE
Dark Room

While his son and daughter-in-law were being given a whimsical open-top tour of the Suffolk coast, Mr Campion was ascending a dingy staircase in Soho and taking in, from the various postcards on display, the range of Anglo-French services on offer. He was following the creaking footsteps of Mr L.C. Deighton, who, Campion had on reliable authority, was 'something not too junior in security'.

'Do you have a warrant for this visit?' Campion asked casually, his words echoing in the dusty stairwell.

'Not as such,' said 'Elsie' without breaking stride, 'but I could rustle up a post-dated one if the need arose. It's unlikely that Mr Tate will demand to see one, though.'

They were on the second landing when the staccato beat of high heels in a hurry brought a heavily scented female form on a collision course. The two men leaned into the wall as the figure slowed to squeeze past them. Mr Campion caught a glimpse of shiny thigh-high boots, a very short black skirt and a very small red jacket straining against a single brass button. Mr Deighton, he felt, took a much more studied view.

'Looking for anything in particular?' the woman asked without pausing in her descent towards the street.

'Francis Tate, the photographer,' said Campion.

'Best of luck; I haven't seen him since last week. If you want to wait for him, Dolores one floor down will look after you. Don't be put off by the sign on her door, she don't speak a word of French.'

Mr Campion raised his hat to the retreating figure swaying like a metronome and with a broad grin said, 'We are grateful for your advice, miss.'

For his politeness he received a raised hand and a swirl of bejewelled fingers, but the woman did not give them a second look.

'We really shouldn't draw attention to ourselves,' Deighton admonished him as they continued upwards.

Mr Campion, who had made a career out of going unnoticed, took the reproach cheerfully.

'Oh, I doubt she would remember little old me from the hundreds who have trod these stairs and anyway, isn't our proposed bit of breaking and entering likely to draw attention?'

'Not if we are discreet, and it won't bother Mr Tate, will it?' said Deighton, pausing before the door advertising *Francis Tate Photography* and reaching into his jacket pocket for a large bulb of keys on a thick metal ring.

Keeping his back firmly towards Campion, he fumbled through various keys and quickly found one which produced a satisfying click, then pushed open the door with his fingertips as carefully as if he was expecting an explosive booby trap.

Campion followed him into the flat and his nose reacted faster than his eyes became accustomed to the gloom, immediately detecting the layers of old cigarette smoke and the sour scent of poorly washed (or rather washed, but un-rinsed) clothing which is often the mark of a solitary male life, especially a male who has spent time in prison. There was also a third smell in the musty air, a faintly chemical one which Campion could not immediately identify.

'Please snoop around to your heart's content, Campion,' Deighton instructed him, the older man noting that he still held his impressive bunch of keys – keys of all shapes and sizes – and was concentrating on what Campion guessed was the bathroom door, a door guarded by a Yale lock.

'Am I looking for anything in particular?' he asked, adopting his most vacuous expression.

'I think the rule is that you'll know it when you see it.'

'Not a rule that has served me well down the years,' said Campion ruefully, but nevertheless set to with a will and an expertise that suggested some experience in the art.

Deighton began his personal lottery, matching the keys on his ring to the lock on the bathroom door, which was, thought Campion, an odd place for an external lock; just as it was odd that Deighton had not remarked on or expressed surprise at the fact. He was trying his fourth key, swearing softly under his breath, when Mr Campion discovered and pulled out two cheap suitcases from under the bed. Both were unlocked and he allowed himself a restrained whoop of victory.

'I think I've discovered Mr Tate's treasure trove, though it's not what you might call pirate gold, more like contraband.'

'Drugs or dirty magazines?' Deighton asked casually, still fumbling to fit a key to a lock. 'Both are as good as currency around here.'

'Well, I suppose it could be currency of a sort, if the wartime Black Market was still functioning, but I believe that disappeared when we all realized that we'd never had it so good.'

Finally he attracted Deighton's attention, though he felt the younger man was humouring him as he examined the contents of the open cases with that fixed smile of his as statuesque as ever.

'So what have you found? Cigarettes? Well maybe he was a heavy smoker, and what're those? Stockings?'

One suitcase did indeed contain enough cigarettes, in cartons of two hundred, to keep the dedicated addict happy for some time. The contents of the other were more surprising.

'They're ladies' tights,' said Campion, 'bought from Marks and Spencer and, from what I hear, Mr Tate was a regular customer.'

Deighton prodded each suitcase in turn with the tip of a highly polished brogue. 'So he chain-smoked and had a thing about women's hosiery, but I can't see how that gets us any further forward.'

'That would depend on where we are going,' said Campion.

'I think where we should be going is beyond that bathroom door,' said Deighton selecting another key. 'His personal habits are just red herrings and signify nothing.'

'I'm not too sure about that.'

'Oh, come on, Campion. This is Soho and you'll find booze, fags and ladies' underwear in every bloke's flat.'

'I'm sure you're right, but our Mr Tate seemed to go in for things on an industrial scale . . .' he paused as if the thought had only just come to him, '. . . but is it not curious that a man with a substantial stock of cigarettes in unopened cartons under his bed should stop off every morning to buy a packet at the shop on the corner on his way to work?'

Deighton stared at him and Campion thought that, for a milli-second, the permanent smile wavered.

'What I'm curious about is what he has behind that door in his darkroom and one of these blasted keys just has to work.'

In fact, it was the fourth blasted key which worked and Campion had manfully resisted the temptation to offer Deighton the small metal nail file he kept in his wallet, the curled end of which had been carefully shaped for use on just such a lock. It was only polite, he felt, to allow the younger man his moment of triumph but as the door clicked open and he reached around for the light switch, Campion offered a warning.

'Do be careful, old boy.'

'Careful of what?' smiled Deighton as an eerie red light came on in the bathroom.

'I was thinking of booby traps, that's all. I knew a chap during the war, an awesomely brave little Belgian, who kept a very illegal radio transmitter under his bath and took the precaution of taping razor blades around the light switch so that he'd know if anyone had been snooping around.'

'That sounds a bit drastic. Was the chap paranoid?'

'No, the Gestapo really were out to get him. He was being careful, just like our Mr Tate was when he marked the door to his flat. What was it, a piece of paper? You did jolly well to keep me from seeing it.'

'A square of card in the top of the door jamb,' admitted Deighton.

'A single hair works just as well if you lick it and paste it across the crack where the door meets the frame,' said Campion conversationally.

For the first time L.C. Deighton's smile disappeared completely. 'Just what are you trying to say, Campion?'

Mr Campion took off his horn-rimmed spectacles, pulled a silk handkerchief from his jacket's breast pocket with a small flourish, and began to polish out an imaginary grease spot. 'I think I am implying,' he said slowly and deliberately, 'that you know more about Francis Tate than you have admitted, and that the late Mr Tate was almost certainly in a profession similar to yours, though not, of course, on the same side.'

'Look, Campion, I know you were thick as thieves with my predecessor, but that was then and this is now.' The smile returned. 'There's a lot less trust around than there was in your day, the stakes are higher and we have to play things closer to our chests.'

'I can understand all that,' Campion said reasonably, 'though I am not sure why I am involved at all.'

'You are here because the Danish Ambassador brought you into this business and, quite frankly, he wants you to remain involved. In fact, he insists upon it, and it's his quid pro quo for going along with the news blackout on the disappearance of his daughter.'

Mr Campion replaced his glasses. 'That must be hard for him, very hard,' he said softly. 'I will of course do anything I can to help without asking awkward questions such as how you knew Tate had converted his bathroom into a darkroom long before you got the door open.'

'I guess that was careless of me,' said Elsie, and for once his smile appeared genuine. 'Shall we take a peep at his happy snaps?'

'After you, *mon Capitaine*,' said Campion with a mock salute and a gaiety which masked the concern he felt that L.C. Deighton knew already what they would find.

Yet in a bathroom converted to a photographic darkroom, what else should one expect to find but strips of 35 mm negatives dangling like lazy snakes from a makeshift washing line hung over the bath. The hanging film rolls were interspersed with ten-by-eight inch prints pegged out to dry as if they were tiny sheets and it was laundry day in the doll's house. In the bottom of the bath lay shallow trays which had once contained fixer and developer, and with a blithe disregard for safety, a tangled wire hung like a jungle creeper from the light socket, taking electricity first to a red bulb on a spur and then to a light-box balanced precariously on a three-legged stool. There were wet towels sulking in soggy lumps dotted over the linoleum floor.

'Not exactly the tidiest of chaps,' Deighton observed as he and Campion peered along the washing line of negatives and black-and-white prints.

'A pretty good photographer, though,' said Campion, detaching a print from its peg. 'That must be Vibeke Westergaard.'

The picture was a head and shoulders shot, full face, of a shiny-complexioned girl with light, probably blonde, hair cascading in curls to her shoulders. It was one of many of the same smiling face staring happily down on them.

'It is; and it's a better photo than the one the ambassador gave us. I'll get copies made and have them circulated. It could help with the police search.'

Mr Campion held up a strip of negatives and examined them closely. 'Do you think the girl is alive? It's been three days now.'

Deighton chose another length of film to study, neither man willing to confront the multiple images of the ambassador's missing daughter dangling before them. 'We must continue to believe so. I have certainly no reason to think Tate may have harmed her.'

'But she,' Campion said softly, 'might have harmed him?'

'We can't rule that out. Let's find her first before we start that hare running.'

'I agree entirely. Is the search concentrating on the Gapton area?'

'So far, yes. There's been no sign of her in London and we presume if she was here she'd try to contact her father. At least in Gapton we can keep things contained and so far the newspapers and the TV boys are playing along with us.'

Mr Campion raised a finger to point along the line of hanging prints. 'All these pictures were taken out of doors on a beach of some sort. The background is sea or sandbanks by the look of them. I presume that's Gapton Spit?'

'Yes,' said Deighton firmly as he began to unclip the prints. 'I'm going to have to take these with me. Could you see if you can find a bag or a large envelope or something for me?'

'Happy to be of use, old boy,' Campion chirped, leaving the 'finally' unsaid.

He drifted back into the living area of the apartment and

conducted a desultory search until, under a pile of photographic magazines by the bed, he found an empty box which had once contained photographic paper, that would fit Deighton's requirements. Before he presented it, however, his eyes swept the room to see if there was anything he had missed.

'That will do perfectly,' said L.C. as he began to pack Tate's prints in the box. 'I'll get these back to the department for proper scrutiny. We have people there who know what they're looking for.'

Mr Campion wondered whether he was being dismissed or insulted, or both. 'What about Mr Tate's private supply of cigarettes and tights?'

Deighton looked faintly surprised and rather vacant, an expression Mr Campion matched with ease. 'Oh, yes, those . . . er . . . I think we should leave those to the local police, don't you? They'll be along in due course.'

'As you wish; it's your show. Does that mean we're finished here?'

Deighton's smile slipped a fraction at the sudden steel in Campion's voice.

'Unless you've found something important here I've missed . . .?'

'It's what I haven't found – and what you don't seem to be interested in looking for – which might be important, or perhaps just a fraction suspicious.'

'What's on your mind, Campion?'

'Tate is – was – a photographer, fairly obviously. You've scooped up all the photographs and negatives in his darkroom, but not once have you mentioned the fact that there does not appear to be a camera on the premises. Neither have you made any attempt to look for his documentation: his passport or driving licence, a gas bill or a library card even, which would prove he was who we think he was.'

'And you find that suspicious?'

'Slightly; I think you already know where Tate's camera is and probably where his documents are and that you're not worried about proving his identity.'

Deighton tilted his head on one side as if considering a deep philosophical proposition. 'Are you suggesting that Francis Tate, photographer and film technician of this rather seedy parish of Soho, was not exactly what he seemed to be?'

Now it was Campion's turn to smile. 'Of course he wasn't, otherwise you wouldn't be wasting your time here.'

'Or yours.'

'Oh, don't worry about my time, old chap. I'm retired; I've got oodles of it.'

SIX
The Grimston Hybrid

R upert replaced the telephone receiver on its cradle and hurried down the hallway of The Maltings back to the dining room where a small crowd, holding plates and cutlery, surrounded an oval oak table which might have been made from the timbers of a man-of-war, and were hungrily eyeing the display it bore of two large carved Suffolk hams and a bowl of steaming boiled potatoes.

'I do apologise,' he said to the poised faces. 'That was my father checking that we had arrived safely.'

'Think nothing of it. Let's tuck in, shall we?'

Torquil Sandyman resumed his duties as host, filling glasses from a large jug of ale and urging those gathered to help themselves, while his wife Victoria, looking more haggard than a woman of her age should, staggered in from the kitchen bearing a large wooden tray crammed with an assortment of bowls and jars each with a spoon or fork in them standing to attention.

'I've brought pickles and mustards,' Mrs Sandyman announced, her knees bending under the weight of the tray. 'There's sweet pickle, piccalilli, pickled onions, red cabbage, gherkins and just about anything else you can think of.'

Perdita stepped forward, hands outstretched, offering to share her hostess's burden. 'Please let me take that. I'm Perdita, by the way. Perdita Browning . . . I mean, Campion. Browning's my stage name.'

'Thank you,' said Victoria once she was relieved of her burden, 'and welcome to Gapton. I'm sorry if you've been shanghaied into coming here, I'm afraid everything is a bit chaotic just at the moment.'

'That's perfectly understandable given the circumstances. I only hope we won't be under your feet. If there is anything I can do to help, you only have to ask.'

Mrs Sandyman reached behind her perfect waist and undid the bow of the white baker's apron she wore, removing it to reveal a tight-fitting black roll neck jumper, black ski pants and black leather boots. A single string of pearls around her throat, her wedding ring and a thin silver watch were her only adornments, yet Victoria Sandyman, Perdita judged, could never and would never be mistaken for anything less than a strikingly beautiful woman, even without make-up, her hair dishevelled by steam from standing over a hot stove and clear beads of perspiration on her forehead.

'Are you any good with children?' she asked, flicking a wayward strand of hair out of her eyes.

'I'm not sure,' said Perdita, caught slightly off guard. 'I don't know that many.'

Victoria Sandyman tilted her head and examined Perdita as if she was coming into focus for the first time.

'You're an actress, aren't you?' Perdita nodded. 'Have you ever played the part of a nanny, or an au pair?'

'No, never.'

'Do you think you could? Just for a week, say? The twins are really very well-behaved and won't give you any trouble.'

'Twins?' croaked Perdita, her mouth dry.

'Jasper and George, they're absolute sweeties, though I admit I'll be glad when they start school. Perfect angels, they are; just remember not to let Jasper anywhere near open water and George can get a bit naughty if he gets hold of matches. Beatrice won't be any problem as long as you keep her strapped into her pushchair.'

'Beatrice?'

The baby of the family; the twins are four, both of them – well they would be, wouldn't they? – but Beatrice is fourteen months and has just discovered walking. No matter how much she screams, keep her tied down once you're out of the house, or she'll be off like a shot. Oh, and don't ever leave an outside door open and make sure the cat-flap on the kitchen door is locked.'

'Look, Mrs Sandyman—'

'Victoria, please. One treats one's au pair as a member of the family, not as a servant.'

'Victoria, I'm sorry but I really don't think I could do that. I have absolutely no experience of dealing with small children. I have enough trouble keeping big ones like Rupert in check.'

'Oh, but you offered to do *anything* . . .' sulked Victoria, showing she was as good an actress as Perdita, '. . . and Torquil told me that Rupert had more or less volunteered you when they spoke on the phone. It was a glimmer of hope for me; I was relying on getting some help before I go absolutely mad. It's been a nightmare since Vibeke disappeared. The children liked her so much they'll be heartbroken if they have to suffer another rejection.'

'Well, I suppose that as we're on the premises, so to speak . . .' Perdita started, wilting under Mrs Sandyman's wide cow-like eyes.

'Excellent! That's all settled, then.' Victoria Sandyman suddenly had no further need of sympathy. 'I'll give you the kids' rotas – bedtimes, bath times, that sort of thing – when I show you your room, just as soon as we've got this lot fed and watered. Do find somewhere to put that tray down, my dear – it looks quite heavy.'

Throughout this exchange, Rupert had carefully avoided catching his wife's eye and had happily surrendered himself to Torquil Sandyman, who was introducing him to the motley crew of men crowded into the dining room, drinking deeply of the free ale and carving rather thick slices of Suffolk ham. It quickly became apparent that he was being introduced to a search party, and a considerate search party at that, as all the men were in their stockinged feet, having left, Rupert deduced, their muddy boots outside.

Torquil reeled off a list of names like a schoolmaster taking the morning register – 'Sam Jones, John Jones his brother, Cyrus Beeton, Joseph Dugard . . .' – and Rupert acknowledged them in a daze, remembering little about their serious faces and knowing he would be hard pressed to put the correct name to the correct face. '. . . Josh Cooper, Rufus Ebberley, Sam Eades and Geoffrey Bradley . . . in fact, we've got most of the brewery staff here. They all volunteered to join one of the search parties, and this is their leader, Superintendent Appleyard.'

The name rang a faint bell in the back of Rupert's overcrowded mind, but the face of the large man now in front of him, stonily featureless apart from prominent coal-black eyebrows, meant nothing to him.

'*Detective* Superintendent,' corrected granite visage, 'Suffolk CID. You must be the son.'

'I suppose I must be; well, we all are really – sons, I mean. Sons of somebody.'

Rupert realized he was in danger of sounding quite mad but his experience of policemen of such rank was limited to the second acts of humdrum plays in repertory concerning murder in a country house where, more often than not, the butler did do it. He concentrated and told himself that although he was now a guest in a country house and there had been a murder, or at least a very suspicious death, *Detective* Superintendent Appleyard was a real policeman and this was not a play where by Act III the cast obviously couldn't care less who had done it and, usually, neither could the paying audience. An old adage of his father's suddenly sprang to mind: *Never forget that senior policemen, even when they've had a snoot-full of gin and they've got their boots off, warming their gigantic feet by your kitchen fire, they are never – never – off duty.*

'Son of that Albert Campion, I meant,' said the policeman, as though reading from a charge sheet.

'I'm afraid so. Do you know my father? I know he has a chum on the Suffolk force called Bill Bailey – like the song.'

'I crossed paths with your father,' growled Appleyard, 'a couple of years ago down the coast at a place called Brett. It wasn't exactly a mutually beneficial experience. And Bill Bailey is stationed at Bury St Edmunds over in West Suffolk. I'm here from Ipswich, because the East is my bailiwick and I'm sure my boys can handle things without outside help from amateurs. This is a murder case, not a parlour game.'

'Rupert and his wife are here as guests of my family in my house, Mr Appleyard,' Torquil intervened, leaving Rupert in little doubt that it was the Sandyman family to whom people looked for law, order and employment in Gapton. 'They are here to help us cope without Vibeke; if they can help us find her, so much the better.'

If the detective superintendent had been reminded of his place, if not put in it, he gave no outward sign.

'Did you know this Miss Westergaard then, Mr Campion?'

'No, but I have' – Rupert chose his words carefully – 'a passing acquaintance with Frank Tate, or rather the late Mr Tate.'

The policeman's eyebrows rose like two black slugs. 'Did you now? Did you know him well enough to formally identify his body? I warn you, it's not a pretty sight if you have a delicate stomach.'

'I never actually met the chap or spoke to him,' Rupert said, suddenly nervous, 'but I saw a man who was pointed out to me as Francis Tate several times in London about two weeks ago.'

'And just how did that come about?' asked Appleyard, the eyebrows now slanted into a threatening chevron.

Never off duty pulsed through Rupert's brain.

'I had been asked to . . . keep an eye on him . . . follow him, see what his routine was.'

'Following him, were you, sir? Are you some sort of *private detective*?'

'Certainly not!' retorted Rupert, but restrained himself from adding that he was an actor. 'I was following him as a favour to Miss Westergaard's father.'

The eyebrows twitched violently. 'So you're a friend of the ambassador then?'

'No, I can't claim that. My father asked me to watch Frank Tate.'

The black slugs on Appleyard's forehead came to a self-satisfied rest. 'Ah, there we have it – the hand of Albert Campion. Meddling seems to be a family trait.'

'Now look here, Superintendent,' Torquil galloped to the aid of his old school chum, 'this is my house, I pay the wages of the men in your search parties, you are eating my food and drinking my beer, and Rupert is my guest and I will not have him bullied. I would remind you that *my* father is a very close friend of Ambassador Westergaard and both of them seem very happy to have a bit of meddling, as you so pithily put it, from the Campions. Goodness knows, they cannot contribute any less to this awful business than your chap Davies, who is hardly a shining advertisement for you boys in blue, is he?'

Rupert had no idea who 'your chap Davies' was but he recognized a dart striking home when he saw one; even the most peripheral contact with the theatre taught you that.

'If you have any concerns about the local constabulary, Mr Sandyman, there are proper channels as your father, as a senior magistrate, knows well. I am sure he is also aware that interfering with a police investigation can lead to a charge of perverting the course of justice.'

It was time, thought Rupert, to throw himself on the fuming policeman's mercy. 'Please, Detective Superintendent, my wife and I have come to Gapton purely to help Torquil and his family. I have neither the ability nor the intention to get involved in your investigation, but if I can help in any small way, I will. If you want me in a search party, I am yours to command.'

He delivered his little speech with his arms at his side and a straight back, looking Appleyard square in the face although avoiding those eyebrows, and he was quite proud of his perform-ance. A touch of Rattigan-style dialogue usually went down well with figures of authority, and it seemed to have worked as the policeman gave a grunt of quiet acceptance.

'There is one way you could make yourself useful, Mr Campion,' Appleyard said pleasantly and with a smile for good measure.

Never off duty . . .

'Whatever I can—'

'Good. I'll have a car brought round as soon as we've finished this excellent lunch.'

'A car?'

'To run us down to the Ipswich and East Suffolk Hospital, so that you can formally identify the remains of Francis Tate for me,' said Appleyard with more than a hint of smugness. 'You said you would do anything to help.'

'But I told you, I never even spoke to Tate, I just observed a man I was told was Tate, I didn't know him.'

'Unfortunately, sir' – Rupert noted the selective police use of the personal title – 'the only person in Gapton who really knew him is missing. Some people saw him around the town and were told his name was Frank Tate, but nobody really knew if that's who he was. At least you can corroborate that our body was the same Frank Tate you saw in London. That would be a great help. Sir.'

As Detective Superintendent Appleyard disappeared to borrow the house telephone and Torquil consulted his brewery workers as to which area they would search that afternoon – the general consensus being that it should be 'off the Lowestoft Road beyond Mussets' – a rather dazed Rupert chewed listlessly on a slice of ham until his wife accosted him, speaking in a violent whisper.

'You've dropped me right in it! I appear to be the replacement au pair girl, thank you very much.' Rupert winced but it did not slow his wife's quiet tirade. 'I haven't even unpacked or had a wash or anything, and I'm expected to take all three Sandyman children out for some fresh air this afternoon. Children! You never said there would be children. Three of them and two of them are twins. How am I supposed to know which is the evil one?'

'Do calm down, darling, you're gibbering. What do you mean "evil one"?'

'There's always an evil twin – stock character in Rep and Panto.'

'Well, you'll just have to grin and bear it,' Rupert hissed. 'I'm being dragged off to a mortuary to look at a dead body.'

Perdita's face softened immediately and she clutched her husband's arm, making the plate he was holding shudder so that the potatoes on it danced towards the edge. 'What on earth for?'

'I think mainly to punish my father for some ancient sleight.' Rupert sighed. 'While I'm gone, keep your beautifully proportioned ears open and see what you can find out.'

'About what?'

Rupert shrugged his shoulders.

'Anything.'

Victoria Sandyman was perfectly happy to hand over her three children to a complete stranger 'to get some fresh air' as long as they were wrapped up warmly and on condition they were returned to The Maltings before it got dark, which would be around five o'clock. Perdita Campion was less enthusiastic about the arrangement, but had been brought up in the belief that house guests should submit quietly and without objection to any small domestic task their host asked them to perform. Whether keeping Victoria's children out of her expensively coiffured hair for a couple of hours counted as a domestic task was perhaps open to question, but Perdita held her tongue. Torquil Sandyman, however, felt a slight pricking sensation in the region of his conscience and offered to accompany Perdita, partly to show her the splendours of Gapton and partly to 'ride shotgun' over his unruly offspring.

As her own husband had been whisked away in a police car, seated uncomfortably next to a very smug detective superintendent, Perdita had no qualms about borrowing Victoria's for the afternoon. Indeed, she was grateful for his presence when she saw the raw physical effort required to get baby Beatrice strapped into her push chair. In contrast, the twin boys George and Jasper quietly put on wellington boots and matching duffle coats and patiently waited for their baby sister to calm down. Perdita examined them closely but could not determine, as yet, which was the evil one.

'I thought I'd give you the sixpenny tour,' Torquil said as he buttoned his coat, 'to get you orientated. I was going to offer to do it for Rupert, but that pompous prig Appleyard wouldn't be denied. I hope Rupert's got a strong stomach.'

'I'm afraid not. He's had trouble with Kensington Gore in the past.'

'With what?'

'Fake blood, as used on the stage and in films. Actors call it Kensington Gore.'

'Oh dear. I'm afraid Frank Tate wasn't . . .' Torquil checked to see if his sons were listening, which of course they were, so he mouthed the words, '. . . a pretty sight.'

He held the front door open so that Perdita could negotiate Beatrice and her pushchair out on to the drive and told the twins to walk ahead, out of earshot.

'Almost did a bit of an up-chuck myself when I saw the body, the back of his head all smashed in like that, and Sergeant Davies actually *swooned*. I never knew people actually did that except in women's fiction. He was rocking on his heels fit to keel over and I think he would have fainted dead away if Marigold hadn't told him to pull himself together and not be such a softy.'

Perdita was not sure why Torquil was briefing her on the murder, but as Holmes was absent it fell to Watson to pay attention. 'You actually found the body?'

'No, Hyacinth did, or rather her dog Dido did.' He allowed himself a chuckle. 'I'm sure there's a song in there somewhere: *Did Hyacinth? No, but Dido did.* Sorry, I'm rabbiting, aren't I. Anyway, I'll show you where it happened – don't worry, from a safe distance.'

They had reached the end of the semi-circular drive, and Torquil ordered the twins to turn left and stay on the pavement. 'There's not much danger from traffic,' he explained because he evidently felt he had to. 'Everyone drives very slowly through Gapton because of our horse-drawn drays. They're quite a tourist attraction.'

'Rupert and I experienced them this morning,' said Perdita, pausing and stooping to pick up the damp fabric toy animal, which might have been a rabbit, flung aside by Beatrice to highlight her boredom.

'Of course you did. It's actually quite a convenient way of picking people up from Darsham Halt, if we can match the train times with deliveries to our pubs on the way. Of course, the brewery business has been a bit up in the air since Sunday. Most of our men are out looking for' – he lowered his voice – 'Vibeke, our au pair, so we're just ticking over at the moment.'

'I thought that the murd . . .' Perdita also remembered the Not In Front of the Children rule. 'I'm surprised recent events haven't resulted in an invasion of gawpers, snoopers and ghouls.'

'Things have been kept out of the papers, thank goodness,' Torquil said airily. 'Though The Butt and Oyster is doing excellent business as the locals argue about who . . . about what happened. It's a topic which seems far more interesting than anything on television.'

'*How* are things being kept out of the papers?'

'I'm not sure. The police, I suppose. No, Jasper, we stay on this side of the road.'

One of the twins moaned loudly in disappointment but Perdita could not tell whether it was Good or Evil expressing an opinion. Both boys had halted on the kerb as if preparing to cross the road to what Perdita's nose had already warned her were the premises of Sandyman's brewery.

'We'll pop in and see the horses on the way back,' Torquil told them. 'I want to show Perdita the Hard and the lagoon and we can count how many boats there are today.'

This went some way to mollifying the boys for whom boat-spotting seemed to be a good use of a dank afternoon and the party pressed on, passing the empty brewery yard on the other side of the street.

'Hyacinth and Marigold live in there, in a little cottage near the stables. They absolutely refuse to live anywhere where they can't see the horses morning noon and night.'

Perdita, concentrating on keeping Beatrice's pushchair on an even keel, felt she should play up her Watson role. 'We gathered they were heavily involved with the horses. In fact, it was quite a surprise when they turned up at Darsham Halt. We had been expecting a taxi but it was quite an experience. They were utterly charming but what I don't really understand is what they *do*.'

'Actually,' said Torquil with a sheepish grin, 'they own the brewery.'

'Yes, they said that.'

'But you didn't believe them, did you? Not many people do, but it is true. The brewery, when it was incorporated as a company back in 1890 or thereabouts, was an amalgamation of two busi-nesses and the result was the Mister and Sandyman Brewing Company. Pretty soon, somebody realized that 'Mister Sandyman' was open to having the mickey taken out of it and when the local temperance movement started a 'Don't leave your children with Mr Sandyman' campaign, the board called an emergency general meeting and the Mister family agreed to drop out of the limelight. So the business became Sandyman's Brewery, but the Misters hung on to fifty-five per cent of the shares. They still do, in the shape of the sisters Mister, Marigold and Hyacinth.'

'But they surely don't have to live in the stables!' protested Perdita, her arms and shoulders aching from her efforts to steer the pushchair over a particularly rocky patch of pavement.

'Of course they don't. They're rich enough to live in Switzer-land, probably could buy one of the cheaper Cantons, but they love Gapton and the dray horses are the children they never had.'

'One of them, Hyacinth, I think, told us this was a Gapton

Hybrid or something but I was too busy hanging on to the dray for dear life to ask her what she meant.'

'She would have said Grimston Hybrid,' Torquil corrected her. 'Gapton is a Grimston Hybrid – quite an oft-quoted one, I believe. It means the name of the town indicates it was a Saxon settlement taken over by the Vikings. The *ton* bit is Saxon for 'town' but it is thought the *Gap* is derived from the Viking name *Gabbi*, so originally it would have been Gabbi's Town, whoever Gabbi was. He probably settled here after he'd done the required amount of raping and pillaging.'

'So it has nothing to do with there being a gap in the cliffs or the shoreline? That would have been my guess.'

Torquil chuckled politely. 'That would be really ironic as the whole problem with Gapton is that it doesn't have a gap to the sea any more. It once did, and was a flourishing port mentioned in the Domesday Book, but now we've been cut off. That's what I'm going to show you.'

'The famous Gapton Spit?'

'The very same; it must be cited in every geography text book in every school in the country. Kids doing O-levels must hate the sound of the name Gapton.'

Perdita was conscious of the fact that ahead of her the road dissolved into what she had earlier (on Hyacinth's guided tour) learned was called the 'Hard' but she now realized it acted as a watery town square. Where road and concrete ended there was smooth dark water reflecting the wilting afternoon light and, beyond, the humpbacked sand bar that was the Spit.

'Is that where Hyacinth found the you-know-what?' Perdita asked delicately, though she was sure that the twins walking ahead of them were so involved in an argument about sailing boats that they were unlikely to be listening to boring old adults.

'Actually, it was along that path just there,' said Torquil, nodding to his left. 'Of course, it's out of bounds to everyone just now, but you can see the scene of the crime from the Hard. In fact, the best view is probably from the Lounge Bar of The Butt and Oyster, which I have to admit has been jolly good for business.'

Perdita looked to her left and noticed a gap between two weather-beaten cottages and a fingerpost on the arm of which had been burned rather shakily the words Public Footpath. It was just wide enough to take a small car, perhaps the second-hand Mini Cooper which she had her eye on, but to make sure no joyrider tried to drive along the path, a very solid bollard in the shape of a capstan had been concreted in a central position. It would have been possible for a bike or a pushchair to negotiate the bollard but all, including pedestrians, were dissuaded by the triangular metal sign propped up against it which announced Police: No Admittance.

'The path goes out across Mussett's Farm, curves around the edge of the lagoon then runs the length of the Spit, or at least as far as you can go these days. That's the way Hyacinth goes to walk that mangy excuse of a dog of hers, but you can see where she found the you-know-what from down here on the Hard.'

As they approached the square which tilted ominously down towards the water's edge, one of the twins turned a shining face to address the adults bringing up the rear of their small column.

'Can we go to Grundy's, Daddy?'

'I suppose so,' said Torquil in mock resignation. 'Did you bring any money?'

'I've got fourpence but Jasper's got nearly a shilling,' answered the twin who must be George, with a sigh.

'You know the rules: you pool your resources and share the sweets.'

The Solomon-like judgement of his father was clearly what George had hoped for and he smiled broadly and punched his brother playfully on the shoulder. His brother responded with a desultory 'Ow! That hurt!' but did not falter in his determined stride to the small weatherboard shop ahead, which Perdita presumed was Grundy's.

The shop, which performed the function of ship's chandler, newsagent, off-licence and post office among other duties, was perched on the highest corner of the Hard, clear of the water line, opposite the much more imposing The Butt and Oyster with its two bay windows looking into the square and out over the lagoon. The eastern wall of the pub met with the water's edge and a high tide mark had discoloured the Suffolk pink lime-wash rendering to within two feet of a side sash window.

While the twins disappeared into Grundy's shop clutching their pennies, Torquil said they would be perfectly safe under Mrs Grundy's eagle eye and indicated he and Perdita should take a few steps on to the Hard and look at the water.

'Does the tide come up that high?' asked Perdita, pointing at the stain line on the pub wall.

'Quite often,' said Torquil, 'especially when there's a full moon. The landlord keeps a cask of our best bitter on stillage at that end of the bar so he can serve through that window.'

Perdita looked at him quizzically.

'In the summer,' he explained, 'we get a lot of boats in the lagoon – there's only a few this time of year – and those who are sleeping on board row up to the window in their dinghies and knock three times for service. If the tide's right, that is.'

Perdita checked the brake was on the pushchair, for the Hard sloped downwards and the last thing she wanted to spoil her first shift as an au pair was to have to watch Beatrice hurtling towards the water. Only when she was convinced the wheels were locked did she join Torquil down at the water's edge and take in the view.

Torquil raised an arm and pointed across the lagoon to the prickly undulations of the Spit.

'If that's twelve o'clock, then the body was at about quarter to eleven, over there, half in mud, half in the water. Of course, there's nothing to see now. The path I showed you runs down the side of the mud and that's where Hyacinth takes the dog for its morning walk, which she does alone. Marigold only goes with her in the evenings. If Marigold had found it, I suspect she might have pushed it back into the water and trusted the tide to get rid of it.'

Perdita averted her gaze from that gruesome spot of mud, sand and waving marram grass and took in the length of the lagoon, automatically counting (before the twins did) the number of motionless small skiffs and yachts moored in it. Only an occasional puff of wind raised a white fleck on the dark water, and the wind also brought the soft thud of the more aggressive North Sea pounding against the far side of the Spit.

'I can see it being quite beautiful here,' she said.

'Vibeke used to say that; said it reminded her of the Jutland coast she visited as a child.' Torquil cleared his throat. 'It would be terrible if Gapton becomes known for a second Danish mishap.'

'I'm sorry?'

'The whole Grimston Hybrid thing – Gapton's in all the text books for being the most southerly example, most of them are up in Lincolnshire and Yorkshire – but if *Gabbi* was the Danish Viking who made us famous, Vibeke could be the one to make us infamous.'

'You mean if we don't find her?'

'No, actually I meant if we *did* find her.'

SEVEN
Cause of Death

Perdita had never seen Rupert so desperately in need of a drink before. Indeed, Rupert had never felt so great a need before. Examinations, his driving test, his audition for drama school, the morning (though not the night) of his wedding day and almost every First Night performance – none of these, singly or combined, had shredded his nerves so much as his afternoon in Ipswich, but he managed a weak smile at the thought that many a stand-up comedian on the variety circuit of yore may well have used a similar line in their patter.

He had been delivered back to The Maltings by a police car with a uniformed constable driving; a driver who clearly thought it a demotion to be transporting white-faced and shaking civilians rather than authoritative, and authoritarian, detective superintendents. Arriving at the indeterminate hour of 5.45 p.m., he found to his relief that he was too late for Sandyman's children's favourite meal, high tea, and to his dismay that he was too early for the serving of alcohol.

Torquil explained, with embarrassed boyish charm, that The Maltings, like all the brewery's properties, followed the licensing laws of the land, at least when it came to opening hours; closing times being perhaps a little more flexible in private, if not public, houses. It was a rule which had been established by the Misses Mister and was closely patrolled by the eagle eyes of those majority shareholders, such eyes being the sharpest in the world of business.

Resigned to the fact that the world seemed to have turned against him, Rupert mumbled his need for a wash and brush-up before dinner and was directed to the stairs and the bedroom he and Perdita had been allocated. His heavy footsteps telegraphed his arrival and his wife appeared on the landing to greet him.

She was holding a large white towel and using it to dab inef-
fectually at her damp neck and soaked blouse.

'Hello, darling, I hope you don't want to use the bathroom. The
twins have just had their bath and the place looks as if the mael-
strom has taken up residence. I've been in charge of the children
all afternoon . . .'

She raised her voice in order to be overheard, said, 'It was
such fun,' and immediately began shaking her head at her husband
as she mouthed the words, 'No, it was not!' and her facial expression made sure that the exclamation mark was emphatically, if
silently, conveyed. But then she saw into Rupert's hollow eyes
and melted towards him.

'My God, darling, are you all right? You look like Hamlet's
father with a hangover. Are you rehearsing the part or have you
actually seen a ghost?'

'As a matter of fact, I think I might have,' said Rupert, taking
Perdita and bunched-up wet towel in his arms. Her hair smelled
of cheap bubble bath and indeed contained a few small unex-
ploded soap bubbles. 'Can we go to our room and be alone?'

'Of course we can.' Perdita smiled. 'I thought you'd never
ask.'

If she was disappointed that all her husband wanted to do was
sit on the bed and be held tightly in her embrace as he told his
story, she did not show it and listened in silence apart from the
occasional dutiful and sympathetic coo.

From the moment they had left The Maltings, Detective
Superintendent Appleyard had treated Rupert as at best a suspect,
at worst as the murderer of Francis Tate. At one point, just north
of Ipswich, Rupert had felt that sharing the back seat of a police
car with the aggressive Appleyard was akin to being in the dock
at the Old Bailey eyeball-to-eyeball with the most eloquent and
well-briefed barrister ever to take silk and with blood dripping
from his hands.

'I half-expected him to slap a pair of handcuffs on me when
he marched me into the hospital,' sighed Rupert.

'He sounds a perfectly horrid policeman,' soothed Perdita.
'Why has he got such a down on you?'

'It's not me he's got a chip on his shoulder about, it's Dad.
They had a run-in somehow, somewhere, and Appleyard's nose

was put out of joint. Not that he let slip any details, just constant snide references to "dilettante adventurers" and "outsiders". He seems to have a thing about "outsiders" – probably because he is one. He let it slip that he's from Norwich and the North Folk of Norfolk are not generally trusted by the South Folk of Suffolk. Apparently it goes back to the time of the Angles and the Saxons.'

'It seems a lot of things do around here,' said Perdita thoughtfully. 'But forget about the pompous policeman, what happened at the hospital?'

'That I do wish I could forget. They took me down to the basement, to the morgue, where they made me look at Frank Tate's body.'

'My poor love!' Perdita's hand made a fist and the fist shot to her mouth, though she realized immediately it was a gesture straight out of *Melodrama for Beginners*. 'You didn't have to watch an autopsy, did you?'

'No, thank God, though Appleyard would have loved that. As it was, he gave me the full treatment: the ghoul's ringside seat view.'

Perdita snaked her arm around her husband's shoulders and when she realized he was trembling, and pulled him closer. 'Was it really horrible?'

'Yes, it was.'

'But you could tell it was Frank Tate?'

'Well, I recognized the face as that of the man I'd been told was Frank Tate, but it wasn't his face that was the problem.' Rupert took a deep, quivering breath before continuing. 'That perfect swine Appleyard made them turn the head so I could see the back of it . . . only . . . there wasn't much left to see, because somebody had bashed it in. One of the doctors or pathologists, or whatever they're called, said it had been done with a blunt instrument – just like in one of those corny two-act murder mysteries we do in Rep, only this wasn't done with a length of lead piping or a brick in a sock. From the size of the wound, they reckon someone came up behind Tate and hit him with some sort of medieval mace or a flail – you know, one of those heavy metal balls on the end of a stick-and-chain. The sort of thing the Knights of the Round Table or El Cid waved about. Just the

ticket for belting somebody in a suit of armour, or so Appleyard
said.'

Perdita remained silent for a moment, then said quietly, 'Could
you see Vibeke Westergaard wielding one of those flail things?'

Rupert stared at her in surprise. 'I can't imagine anyone bashing
a bloke's head in like that, let alone a chap's girlfriend. What
made you say that?'

'Because I think the prevailing theory in Gapton is that Vibeke
was the one whodunit.'

In another house in Gapton, a much smaller more modern one
inhabited by a single occupant, a telephone rang and was answered
nervously.

'Gapton 289.'

The caller was anything but nervous. 'My name is Dieter. You
know who I am?'

'Frank said someone would call if . . . if anything happened
to him.'

'It appears something has happened to him – something bad.'

'As bad as it can get, but I can't talk about that.'

'I do not expect or want you to. Frank is no longer with us
and his death is of less interest to me than his possessions. Do
you have them?'

'If you mean what I think you mean, I might have.'

'I think you know exactly what I mean and I think you will
do exactly what I say, otherwise the consequences for you would
be rather tragic. Your position in Gapton would, at least, be
untenable. Prison cannot be ruled out. Now listen to me very
carefully and do what I tell you to . . .'

'Ain't you too old to be a Private Dick, Pops?'

'Oh, absolutely,' Mr Campion agreed politely. 'But one is
never too old to be a concerned uncle.'

'You talk real funny.'

'So do you, Mr Daniloff, but then, as you might say, you're
not from around here, are you?'

Once he had got over his surprise at finding that a dark, pungent
basement drinking club in Old Compton Street would advertise
itself as The Green Dahlia, Mr Campion had determined that

nothing else would startle him that evening. It was a promise to himself which he could not keep for long, for his descent into the Stygian gloom of the club down steep steps bare of carpet but sticky with an ancient varnish of spilled beer had brought him almost immediately into a face-to-face confrontation with the ape-like Daniloff.

Mr Campion considered whether 'ape-like' was too pejorative a term, but, no, there was definitely something Simian about the man. He was not muscular or frightening enough to be a gorilla, nor did he exude the world-weary wisdom of the orangutan, but his general rangy stance, long arms dangling at his side and legs bowed definitely gave the impression of an anti-social chimpanzee. It was an impression cemented by the fact that he wore no jacket and his short-sleeved white shirt, unbuttoned to the waist, revealed a thick carpet of curly black hair sprouting vigorously over chest and stomach, from belt buckle to chin. His biceps and forearms bulged as if artificially inflated and his right arm was decorated with a large purple tattoo.

It was difficult not to stare or think of Jacob's confession that his brother Esau was 'a hairy man', but the chimpanzee had placed himself directly in Campion's path, blocking any further exploration of the club. Rather than displaying aggression, however, the chimp had his face on one side as if struggling to comprehend Campion's last remark.

'How come you know my name and where I come from, Pops?'

'Answers for answers, Mr Daniloff,' said Campion with more confidence than he felt, for the man in front of him, although almost a foot shorter, was at least two feet wider, fifty per cent heavier and twenty years younger. 'I assumed that from the alacrity with which you greeted my arrival you were the licensee of this establishment and I was told the licensee was a Raymond Daniloff. I'm sure there's a sign somewhere which says that in legal gobbledygook. As for you not being from "around here" – by which I mean not just Soho, or London, or even this Sceptred Isle in all its glory – well, that was easy. You display a tattoo – I presume proudly – of the eagle, globe and anchor badge of the United States Marine Corps, which I suspect is a reminder of service past rather than simply decorative. Your accent, of course, gives you away as American straight away, as does your use of the terms "Private Dick" and "Pops" – expressions I find rather crude and claim no association with either professionally or paternalistically.'

The chimpanzee's lower jaw sagged and a waft of exhaled breath carried a breeze of sweet, spirituous liquor. 'I said you talked funny.' This time there was menace in the voice and the hairy paws had become fists. 'Just what the hell do you want in my club? And let's have it in English this time.'

Mr Campion's eyes blinked rapidly behind his spectacles as they peered over the head of the creature blocking his way and tried to accustom themselves to the dank shadows of the club's interior. Soft piano jazz floated out of a tape recorder or gramophone and there was an orange glow from a backlit bar displaying an array of bottles, but only the glowing red tips of half-a-dozen cigarettes indicated that The Green Dahlia had any customers.

'I'm looking for a girl,' said Mr Campion, and was not at all surprised at the bare-toothed lascivious grin this produced on the chimpanzee's face.

'Whoa, Pardner; this ain't that sort of a joint; well, not this early in the evening.'

From the darkness came two or three deep chortles of laughter and Daniloff turned his head and bowed to acknowledge his audience.

'A specific girl,' Campion said, unperturbed, and from his jacket pocket he produced one of the head-and-shoulders shots of Vibeke Westergaard which he had successfully palmed from under the nose of Mr L.C. Deighton earlier that day. He held it out towards the American, who furrowed a hefty brow at it.

'Never seen her before in my life and believe me, I would remember a pretty piece of skirt like that. What's your interest in her, Pops?'

'I told you, Mr Daniloff, I am here in the role of concerned uncle, not in any official capacity,' Campion said amicably, replacing the photograph in his pocket. 'My niece, as I will call her, may have been brought here by one of your regular customers – Francis, or Frank, Tate.'

'Never heard of the guy – and we're a members' club. We have members not customers.'

'I am sure,' said Campion drily, 'your membership lists are the envy of the Garrick and the Athenaeum. You do have a list of members, I take it?'

'I sure do, but you don't get to see it, Pops; it's confidential.'

'And you can't tell me if Frank Tate is on it?'

The chimpanzee spread his arms in supplication. 'Now that would be breaking confidentiality, wouldn't it?'

'Heaven forfend, I wouldn't have you do that, but I was under the impression he was a regular visitor to this establishment, always round about this time in the evening, though he never stayed long – no more than a few minutes. Still not ringing any bells?'

The chimpanzee did not respond to Mr Campion's rather frivolous tone and began to look more like a gorilla. 'Not a ding, not a dong,' said the American coldly, 'and you never told me your name, Pops.'

'That would be breaking confidentiality,' said Mr Campion, performing a smart about-turn and climbing the stairs at a deliberately steadied pace.

It was only when he reached the damp, dimly lit street that he allowed himself to exhale. He had taken no more than ten paces and was only ten more from the safety of the lights and crowds of Shaftesbury Avenue when two dark shapes travelling with speed and purpose came out of the darkest shadows and tumbled him violently towards the unforgiving pavement and even deeper darkness.

EIGHT
Sisters of the Sample Cellar

I t was a dank, chilly morning in Gapton, with fine sprays of
sea fret gusting gently through the streets as a constant
reminder that the ocean was close and getting closer every
day.

Rupert, his hands thrust deep into the pockets of a borrowed
duffle coat, was following his nose, quite literally, to his destina-
tion. It was a scented trail of sweet malty goodness which would
have led a blind man into Sandyman's brewery yard without
incident, and the background noise of metal casks rumbling across
concrete and the constant chink of bottles jolting along conveyor
belts would have signalled his arrival.

Across the yard and around a wall Rupert's olfactory skills
detected another clue – the warm smell of horses. Sure enough,
there were the brewery stables and at least two of the brewery's
shire horses loomed inquisitively over the bottom half of stable
doors to prove it. Rupert had no idea if the horses were Horatius
and Belisarius, who had powered his taxi from Darsham Halt,
but he thought it wise to smile and nod deferentially in their
direction as he passed by on his way to the 'other' stables – a
chocolate-box thatched cottage painted 'Suffolk Pink' approached
through a maze of trellises and a garden devoted entirely to
savagely pruned-back dormant roses.

'You found us, Mr Campion!' Marigold Mister greeted him,
opening the front door before Rupert got there. Then, over her
shoulder, she shouted back into the interior: 'Hyacinth! Mr
Campion's here to grill you!'

From deep in the comfortable depths of the cottage, a sisterly
voice responded. 'I'm almost decent. Is Lady Amanda with him?'

'No, dear, she's not,' Marigold shouted in answer and then,
as Rupert crossed the threshold, she said quietly, 'Humour her,
would you?'

Rupert smiled and nodded, silently agreeing to join the conspiracy. 'What a lovely place you have here,' he said politely. 'I bet in the summer you have roses-round-the-door to complete the idyll.'

'We have bloody roses everywhere!' scoffed Marigold. 'Something like fifty-seven varieties, though I've lost count. It's the only thing we seem to be able to grow, though at this time of year the garden looks like a bunch of sticks poked into a Somme battlefield. Fortunately, roses love the spent hops we get from the brewery and we have plenty of those, which is just as well as all the horse manure from the stables is spoken for by local farmers – bit of a tradition, with which we dare not interfere. Anyway, have a seat, get comfortable. You didn't come here to discuss fertilizers and as soon as Hyacinth has finished putting her face on, she'll want to get down to being interrogated. She's been looking forward to it since Sunday.'

'Haven't the police talked to her?'

'Only our dozy local bobby, Sergeant Davies, but that doesn't really count. The oaf was so shocked by the sight of the body he couldn't move. Rigid, he was, rigid with inertia if that's possible. We simply had to take charge, throwing an old blanket over the corpse and making Davies fetch his little boat to get the motorbike.'

'Motorbike?'

'It was in the water, in the lagoon, just like the body was. Somebody had run it in there, but we didn't see it at first. It was only when the tide started to go down that the handlebars poked up out of the water. That poor boy Frank used to zip about everywhere on it, usually with young Vibeke sitting behind him hanging on for grim death. The thing made an awful racket around the town and the horses didn't like it, but at least you could hear him coming.'

'And what happened to the motorbike?'

'I told you, we made the Dreadful Davies fetch his boat. It's a little cabin cruiser thing with a putt-putt engine and pretty ancient, though it's a mystery how he can afford it on what can't be more than a village bobby's salary. Anyway, Dreadful picked up a couple of chaps from one of the houseboats down by The Butt and Oyster and they got a rope round the machine and with a lot of swearing managed to haul the thing aboard. If you ask me, our local guardian of law and order was far more interested in claiming the bike for salvage than he was in the body washed up on the Spit.'

'Now, Marigold, don't be beastly about dear old Enoch,' admonished Hyacinth as she swept into the room, wearing what Rupert guessed was her church-going outfit: a grey woollen suit over a white blouse with a high lace neck, white gloves and very sensible lace-up brown brogues. 'Aren't you ready yet? We mustn't be late on parade.'

'It won't take me a moment to change . . . unlike some people,' her sister retorted, 'and I'll be as beastly as I like about "dear old Enoch" because I think he's a disgrace. You only have a soft spot for him because he found that soppy dog for you.'

Marigold flounced out of the room as smoothly as her sister had floated in, without waiting for the retort she knew would be forthcoming.

'Don't call Dido soppy, she's proved herself to be at least part-bloodhound!'

As if responding to her name, a rangy, oddly proportioned hound of (in Rupert's opinion) distinctly mixed parentage padded into the room and burrowed its muzzle under the hem of Hyacinth's long skirt.

'Now you know you can't come with us, Dido.' Hyacinth bent over and spoke directly into the dog's large brown and pleading eyes. 'I'll take you for walkies just as soon as the parade is dismissed.'

Disorientated by the way the sisters Mister changed topic as rapidly as they appeared to change their clothes, Rupert took a deep breath and attempted to get his thoughts in order. 'Who is "dear old Enoch"?' he asked tentatively.

'Our policeman,' said Hyacinth, taken slightly aback at her guest's ignorance. 'Marigold calls him Dreadful Davies but his proper name is Enoch David Davies. I think it may be Welsh, but one can never be sure these days.'

'And you said something about being late on parade . . .?'

'If my dear sister doesn't get a move on, we will be,' said Hyacinth loudly, reaching down with a gloved hand to stroke Dido's head. 'We thought you'd like to join us on Morning Parade. You might even be useful with that hair colour of yours.'

'I'm sorry . . .?' Rupert started but was distracted by rapid
and noisy footsteps followed by the unmistakably Prussian sound
of heels being clicked.

Marigold was back in the room, dressed in a crisp white shirt
with a red cravat bunched at her throat, hacking jacket, jodhpurs
and shiny riding boots, heels firmly together. 'Right then,' she
ordered, 'if we're all present and correct, quick march!'

'Er . . . march where?' Rupert asked meekly.

'Why, to the sample cellars over in the brewery, of course!
Can't you see I've got my drinking boots on?'

Mr Campion had slept remarkably well, all things considered;
the things having to be considered including the shock of being
tumbled to the ground by unknown assailants and momentarily
losing consciousness, the disorientation and nausea engendered
by being lifted like a baby from the hard, cold street and bundled
into the back of a vehicle (a taxi?), the rather humiliating experience of being carried like a baby from the vehicle and up the
stairs to his Bottle Street flat, and the utterly disconcerting
discovery of finding Lugg wearing a long white apron busying
himself in the kitchen, warming milk laced liberally with Watson's
Trawler rum.

Before sleep claimed him, there had been a rather confusing,
but polite, conversation with a large stranger, a telephone call
and then a less polite fruitless argument with Lugg, from which
Mr Campion remembered clearly only one segment.

'How did you get in?' he had asked once emboldened by milky
rum. 'I've invested in new locks since you camped here.'

'Yer didn't invest enough,' Lugg had answered with a vulpine
grin. 'Took me no more than three minutes and you won't find
a scratch on 'em.'

And now it was morning – a dank, gloomy, November London
morning – the noise of traffic humming outside and inside the
scent of frying bacon wafting seductively from the kitchen, where
Lugg, still fully aproned, was once more in command.

'Have you been here all night?' Campion enquired, tightening
the tasselled cord of his dressing gown.

''Course not,' growled Lugg, forsaking his frying pan for a
white china pint pot full to the brim with a steaming liquid the

colour of run-off from an iron works. 'You ain't got to the stage where you need a night nurse, 'ave you?'

'If I should, I will bear in mind the image of you as my personal Florence Nightingale. That pinnie really does suit you, you know.'

Lugg slurped tea noisily, only his piggy eyes and shining bald pate visible above the lip of his pint pot. When he had fortified himself he lowered the mug and smacked his lips with relish. 'There's a brew in the pot, just made. Help yerself. If yer waiting for silver service, you'll 'ave a long wait. I don't work for you no more.'

'It's a moot point whether you ever *worked* for me at all, old fruit,' said Campion cheerfully.

Lugg made a face. To him it was a perfect imitation of a middle-aged, Bible-carrying spinster having accidentally heard a ribald double entendre by a particularly blue comedian. To an outsider observing from a safe distance, his expression indicated something between severe indigestion and demonic possession.

'Got a clear memory of events last night, 'ave we?' he asked slyly.

'Almost perfect recall,' Campion replied. 'There may be one or two *minor* points of detail which require clarification, following the attack upon my person by overwhelming odds—'

'Gaaar . . .' Lugg snorted. 'Yer fell over!'

'I was set upon, out of the shadows, by a positive horde of marauding Mongols, though they may have been Tartars – it was dark – and beaten to the ground, despite valiant resistance.'

'An' as I 'eard, yer fell over and 'it yer 'ead on the pavement, which if yer will go slouchin' round Soho at night – a man of your age – is no more than you should expect.'

'All right, Matron, fill in the blanks for me. How did I get here? Did you carry me up the stairs? Somebody did.'

'Not I, Your Honour,' said Lugg, as if his character had been impugned. 'It's more than twenty years since I carried a body up them stairs and then I 'ad help. No, you've got Mr Milton to thank for the piggyback. Actually, he carried you like a baby, said you was light as a fevver.'

'And just who is this Mr Milton? Have we been formally introduced?'

'Well, I don't know whether yer know him, but he knows all about you. He's yer minder, courtesy of our friend Elsie, and he's been keeping an eye on yer. Just as well, I reckon, a man of your age wandering around Soho . . .'

'If you say "man of your age" one more time,' Campion threatened, 'I'll start comparing birth certificates and you know I'll win.'

Lugg straightened his dignity along with his shoulders and made a futile attempt to suck in his stomach. 'You might 'ave me there, but I wasn't the one who 'ad to be picked up out of the gutter and brought home to safety.'

'This Mr Milton did that?'

'So he said. He rang me at Brewers' Hall, where we had a dinner on; though naturally I missed out on any tips thanks to having to leave early and meet him here to see you tucked up in bed. I didn't pick the locks, by the way – I lifted the keys out of your pocket. You didn't notice.'

'Don't be smug, just finish the story.'

'Not much to tell. This Milton chap – and he ain't half a big lad, a real heavyweight who 'as to come through doors sideways, but light on his feet; you should be glad he's on yer side – well, he was keeping an eye on yer as yer perambulated around darkest Soho and he was there when a pair of the local low-lives jumps out at yer.'

'A pair?' Mr Campion trilled, feigning outrage. 'They were at least brigade strength.'

'Mr Milton says there were two of them and in fact he knows them both by sight. It was knowing their type that made him pile in straight away and he persuaded them to move along as soon as he saw you fall over and crack yer 'ead. The hooligans didn't need much persuading, not given the size of Mr Milton. I'd say he could be very persuasive in such a situation. You was lucky; he saved you from a good kicking.'

'I am sincerely grateful,' said Mr Campion.

'You should be. It was a good thing the new Elsie put a guardian angel on your shoulder.'

'So it would seem. Did my guardian angel mention whether the gang of professional assassins – and I still maintain there were at least thirty of them – were in any way connected to the rather bizarrely named drinking club called The Green Dahlia, which I had just visited? Purely for professional reasons, you understand.'

'Pah!' Lugg exhaled rudely. 'There was two of them and they were local tearaways who never laid a glove on you because you fell over before they could! Our Mr Milton said they'd been hired that very evening by the management of a place called The Maltese Cross in cahoots with the management of a dive called Tortuga's, the managements of them two h'establishments being fraternally related. I believe you'd visited them both earlier in the evening.'

'So I had,' admitted Campion, 'again, purely in the line of duty.'

Lugg shook his massive head slowly and tut-tutted through pursed lips. It was Lugg's 'Here Comes the Sermon' face and it always reminded Campion of a giant puffer fish.

'Yer shouldn't be trawling round back-street dives in Soho at your age,' the Reverend Lugg admonished. 'It's not fitting. If yer fancies a drink in Bohemian company there's plenty of pubs with well-lit Snugs and Four Ale bars to choose from. Them's much safer for a gentleman of your age, particularly one prone to falling over when somebody says "Boo!". You'll get yourself a reputation hanging round the places you were hanging around last night. Goodness knows what Lady A thought of it.'

Mr Campion's brain snapped to attention. 'Amanda? Good grief, you haven't told her about my little mishap, have you?'

'Not me, soul of discretion I am. It was that security man, Deighton – Elsie. He called round to see how you were but you were tucked up in the Land of Nod by then. It was 'is idea to give the boss lady a ring and tell 'er you'd had a little accident, but yer'd be fine after a good kip.'

'Oh dear,' said Campion, 'that was indiscreet of him – or rather clever. I'd better phone home and throw myself on my good lady's mercy.'

'Well, best of luck with that,' said Lugg phlegmatically. 'And I'd take 'eed of Elsie's message, if I were you.'

'What message?'

'Didn't I mention the message?' asked Lugg at his most

annoyingly innocent. 'He said you were to stay out of Soho and concentrate on finding the girl. Just the girl.'

In a way, Rupert could understand Marigold's jokey reference to her 'drinking boots' better than Hyacinth's decision to dress up in her Sunday best, for as he discovered they were only doing what they did every day, and although it may have been an unusual occupation for a pair of diminutive ladies well into their eighth decade, it was just that: their occupation. The sisters Mister were going to work. The most baffling thing about it all was why they insisted that Rupert accompany them.

Not that he protested too much once he discovered the precise nature of their profession. Whether by experience, natural talent or privilege of shareholding, Hyacinth and Marigold, along with a small, wiry Scotsman in a white coat, were the official beer tasters for Sandyman's brewery and it was, it seemed, a vocation from which one did not retire.

'As we say, it's a dirty job but somebody has to do it,' announced Marigold as she held a half-pint glass almost two feet below one of several small metal barrels on wooden stillage chocks and turned a brass tap.

'She says that every time we have a visitor,' sighed Hyacinth wearily, 'along with that rather vulgar crack about her drinking boots. It grates somewhat after thirty years.'

'Stop talking, start tasting,' ordered her sister, handing Rupert the glass of clear, sparkling ale. 'Drink with your mouth open, dear boy. I know it sounds stupid but take in air with the beer, that way you get all the flavours.'

Realizing that resistance was futile, Rupert did as instructed while keeping one eye on the white-haired, white-coated Scotsman, who had been introduced as Mr Ross, the Head Brewer, and following his lead. As he could not see a spittoon or similar receptacle he assumed that beer tasting, unlike wine tasting, involved swallowing, and he did. He found the experience refreshingly pleasant, if short-lived, for as Hyacinth relieved him of his empty glass, Marigold pressed another full one upon him.

'Now try that one and tell me which is which,' she ordered.

'Which is which what?' said Rupert foolishly.

'I dinna think the laddie understands,' Mr Ross growled at the sisters. 'Ye haven'a told him why you've selected him, have ye?'

'I've been selected for something?'

Rupert looked down at the glass in his hand as if it was a foaming magic potion giving off purple fumes.

Mr Ross sipped gently from his own glass then said, with a twinkle in his eye: 'Och, the sisters Mister here have always had a thing about redheads. I bet they had your card marked as soon as they saw you.'

'Redheads?'

'Aye, Gingers, Carrot Tops, Redheads, like I was meself when I was your age, before these Harpies kidnapped me and brought me down south.'

'I'm sorry, but I'm totally confused,' said Rupert honestly, 'and not by the ale, excellent though it is.'

'We know it's *good*,' Marigold scolded, 'but which is which?'

'Again: which is which what?'

Marigold, struggling to control her exasperation, took a deep breath. 'Which one is thirteen days old and which is fourteen days old? You should be able to tell. It's important because our ale should be matured to perfection.'

'And I should be able to tell because I have red hair?'

'Of course, haven't you heard a word we've said? Ginger-haired people have certain pigments – or lack them, I'm never sure. Anyway, what it means is that they can taste certain things normal people cannot.'

'No offence intended,' Hyacinth added quickly.

'None taken, I'm sure.' Mr Ross winked boldly at Rupert. 'After all, we Gingers have to stick together, but Miss Marigold has a point: we can pick up tastes and flavours that mere mortals never savour. Can you tell which was the younger brew?'

Rupert considered he had a fifty per cent chance of being right and then considered that if he made a mistake, a repetition of his task would not be too onerous and it was perfectly possible it might take him several attempts to reach the right answer . . . But no, that was thinking like an undergraduate; he had to keep at least some of his wits intact.

'I think – yes, I definitely think – the first one was fresher, slightly thinner and with a faint tang of citrus, while the second certainly had more body and more rounded flavours,' he said carefully, silently thanking his good fortune in once having played the part of an insufferable wine snob in a pretty insufferable drawing-room farce. 'So the first, I would say, was slightly immature and therefore the younger one.'

'An almost perfect answer!' chirped Hyacinth.

'I knew he had the gift,' Marigold pronounced with satisfaction. 'Now, Mr Ross, give Mr Campion a glass of this year's barley wine as a reward. Oh, don't look so worried, Mr Campion, we won't be quizzing you further. I'm afraid even your very intelligent palate would be dulled by the time we got to the third or fourth ale, so we restrict our special guests to two.'

Mr Ross had busied himself at another brass tap at a cask further down the line. He produced a half-pint of flat, dark brown liquid and handed it reverentially to the sample room's star guest. 'Now you be careful, young Mr Campion. It's not something we normally drink during daylight hours round here.'

'Yes, do be careful with that stuff,' Marigold advised, 'I've seen grown men get very childish after a pint or two. Now if you'll excuse us, Mr Ross and I have some quality control to do.'

She waved an empty glass to indicate the line of small casks on stillage. Rupert estimated there were at least ten of them and after tasting his barley wine was quite proud that he could count so accurately.

'You have to taste all those?' he asked, trying to curb the admiration in his voice. 'Every day?'

'Every day,' said Marigold. 'We may not brew every day during the winter months but our beers are fermented and vatted for different periods and we have to assess their progress towards maturity.'

'Towards *perfection*,' added Mr Ross, 'though there's usually more of us to spread the load. I've trained up quite a few of the work force as tasters, though of course they're not up to the standard of the sisters Mister. We once had the postman as a regular – he was a Scot and a Ginger too – but he got to like it a bit too much and when the second post never got delivered for three days on the trot, the Post Office complained and transferred him to Great Yarmouth, which was a bit severe as punishments go if you ask me. What with every able-bodied man out searching for that missing girl from Mr Torquil's house, it's left to me and Miss Marigold to do the hard work.'

'I really think I ought to be helping out with the search parties,' said Rupert, his eyes rapidly scanning the sample cellar for a place to secrete his glass of barley wine.

'Nonsense,' said Marigold firmly. 'They're searching the woods down the Lowestoft Road today and you don't know the area so you'd be next to useless. Not that they're going to find her, if you ask me. Anyway, you're here to grill dear Hyacinth and she's really been looking forward to it, so you get on and leave Mr Ross and me to our work. Hyacinth will take you to the scene of the crime.'

Hyacinth stepped forward as a very willing volunteer. 'Allow me to help with your enquiries, Mr Campion, but first we must get Dido, for she'll be your key witness in the case.'

NINE
Dead Lagoon

Wearing a decidedly self-satisfied expression, Hyacinth Mister walked – no, *promenaded* – down Gapton's High Street with Dido linked to her left arm by a leather lead and choker and Rupert Campion equally tightly controlled by her right arm looped through his left. If anything, thought Rupert, the dog was allowed more slack; but happily for him, and sadly for Hyacinth, there were few Gapton residents around to appreciate the sight.

With the awful inevitability of the *Titanic* heading for the iceberg, Hyacinth and Dido swung to port and steered Rupert around the corner of a cottage and on to a footpath straddled by a triangular metal warning sign advising the unwary that admittance was forbidden by the police. Unlike the unfortunate captain of the *Titanic*, Hyacinth smoothly manoeuvred the willing Dido and the hesitant Rupert around the obstacle.

'Shouldn't we—?'

'Oh, that doesn't apply to us, Mr Campion. We have permission.'

'We do?'

'I have requested that Sergeant Davies join us at the scene of the crime.'

Rupert felt the spinsterly grip on his arm tighten, moving from the cloying to the painful as the woman breathed the words 'scene of the crime', but he allowed himself to be led along the pathway which, once it had cleared the back gardens of the cottages, offered a view of undulating sand dunes bristling with marram grass and gorse, a few stunted and wind-sculpted trees to one side and on the other the flat, grey bowl of water that formed the rump of the lagoon imprisoned by Gapton Spit.

As they walked briskly around the curving path – Hyacinth's brogues easily keeping pace with Dido's busy paws – Rupert

took in the vista from an angle he had not seen before. He realized immediately that he was in a magical and disorientating
place where the sky, sand and water blended as if painted on
transparent overlays, and the only sounds were the grumble of
the North Sea, out of sight but not out of mind, over the Spit
and a trio of gulls squawking angrily at the elements as they
wheeled and glided overhead. Then he tuned in to a third alfresco
sound: thumping noises, the sound of somebody hitting wood,
irregular but repetitive, somewhere to his left over the grass and
sand rather than over the water.

But it was the water which, as it always does, drew his eyes.

It was disconcerting to be on dry land and see Gapton from
this aspect; from the front as it were, albeit at an angle, as it was
a view usually reserved for those afloat. Even though it was a
damp and gloomy morning with the sun hiding behind a blanket
of low cloud, Rupert could identify the impressive frontage of
The Butt and Oyster and the grey concrete Hard it stood by,
sliding into the water of the lagoon like the dropped ramp of a
landing craft. Beyond the pub, a line of low weather-boarded
houses, which Rupert had seen only from the rear as he and
Perdita had been taxied by brewers' dray from Darsham Halt,
stretched southwards. No planning restriction or local ordinances
had inhibited the residents of Gapton; at least not those who
owned property with a sea view as they had expressed their
individuality through a paint palette. No two houses seemed to
have the same coloured front door and if they did, the owners
had made sure that none of the window frames or gutters matched.

There were flashes of more autumnal colour from the boats
bobbing gently at anchor in the sheltered channel provided by the
Spit beyond, mostly browns, but interspersed with fluttering folds
of rust-red sails and blue and red pennants. To Rupert's left stretched
Gapton Spit, the long sausage of sand and sparse vegetation which
had strangled the port but protected the boats at anchor. It was
impossible for him to judge the thickness of that coastal bar but
in places it rose to the height of a house above sea level and indeed,
as Rupert screwed up his eyes to try and focus, there did appear
to be the roofs of small houses peeping above the dunes.

'Are those buildings out on the Spit?' he asked his companion.

'Remnants and remains,' said Hyacinth quietly so that Rupert had to strain to catch her words, 'from the war. Marigold and I did our bit there, you know. Nothing dramatic or dangerous, just helping out the backroom boys and girls. Of course, being connected to the local brewery made us very popular and we made sure there was a well-stocked NAAFI.'

'What went on there?'

'Huff-Duff.'

'Excuse me?'

Hyacinth smiled a superior smile. 'You are too young, of course . . . Huff-Duff is what we did. The Spit was a Y Station during the war, just one of dozens all around the Suffolk and Norfolk coastline. It was a listening station; listening for the enemy, intercepting radio messages and direction-finding work. Technically we used HF/DF – High Frequency Direction Finders – which we called Huff-Duff.' Hyacinth began to giggle. 'All our reports went to Room Forty at the Admiralty, which I think was Hush-Hush as well as Huff-Duff.'

'It's hard to think of the war impinging on such a remote spot,' Rupert said thoughtfully.

'Oh, the war made quite an impression on all of us who lived through it. You'd be just a baby, I suppose' – Rupert nodded – 'so you can't be expected to know, but we were on the front line here for a time. Remember, on the other side of the Spit the next thing you came to was Occupied Europe, which was full of very nasty people trying to do us harm. The Y Stations were there to give advance warning to our Navy and Air Force.'

'And it all stopped when the war ended?'

'For Marigold and me, yes, but the Spit remained Ministry of Defence property – still does. There were boffins around in white coats for a few years dismantling secret equipment and such like, but eventually they stopped coming and left the place to the birds, which is why we get a fair number of birdwatchers visiting. Until last year, that is, when the army turned up.'

'The army have a base here?'

'Oh, no, they don't stay, just visit. Several times, in fact, and quite dramatically, by helicopter. Two or three helicopters at once – big ones – landing right in the middle of the dunes. It provides quite a spectacle for the local yokels, though the birdwatching fraternity always complain, especially in the mating season.'

'What are they doing?'

'Well, the official story they gave Bernard – Torquil's father being our most prominent citizen so to speak – is that they are removing potentially hazardous material left over from the war. The gossips in the public bars, however, maintain that it was a bit of private enterprise and they were stripping out copper wire and brass fittings for scrap, though I don't personally hold with the theory that the defence cuts have turned our soldiers into rag-and-bone men – not yet, anyway.'

Hyacinth bent down to let Dido off her leash and the dog, with a surprised yelp, bounded into the dunes and grass, away from the lagoon. As she straightened, her arm locked back into place through Rupert's, who realized he was not to be allowed the same courtesy of freedom.

'Don't go looking for that fox, Dido,' she shouted at a disappearing tail. The tail took little notice. 'You know it will only end in tears.'

'I thought Dido would have made a beeline for the water,' observed Rupert. 'Most dogs do.'

'Dido doesn't like swimming; she much prefers chasing the fox who lives here.'

'You have a fox here on the Spit?'

'Quite a brazen little vixen, actually not quite so little these days, she's been patrolling the Spit for a couple of years now living off birds' eggs and careless ducks. We see her most days and Dido always goes chasing with hope in her heart, but she never gets close to an actual confrontation. The fox is far too clever for her. If Dido is the vixen's only natural predator, then the vixen has little to worry about.'

'Isn't that a farm over there, though?' Rupert pointed in the direction Dido had taken. 'I thought farmers were rather intolerant of foxes.'

'Normally yes, but the Mussetts aren't exactly normal farmers; in fact, they're not normal at all.' Hyacinth hooked Rupert's arm again and, with irresistible force, steered him along the path. 'And I'm not just saying that because they're Methodists or Rechabites or what have you.'

'So they don't drink, then, the Mussetts?' said Rupert, proud that he had followed Miss Mister's disparagements.

'Not a drop. A terrible advertisement for a brewery town, but at least they don't organize Temperance meetings or go out of their way to frighten the dray-horses, or anything like that. In the main they keep themselves to themselves but they're a very odd family.'

Rupert was not convinced that the word 'odd' had the same meaning in Gapton as it did in the wider world, but he was curious to see how Hyacinth applied it. 'Odd in what way?'

'Well, they have such ridiculous names for one thing,' said one of the sisters Mister without irony. 'The old clan leader was Bram Mussett, that's Abraham, but he's been dead ten years now. Old Bram was buried at sea, which is a little odd for a landlubber farmer, don't you think? Mind you, he was a pretty bad farmer, though one shouldn't speak ill of the dead unless you're an archaeologist or a historian, in which case you're paid to do so.

'He did very well out of the war, did old Bram. He claimed all the land from the farm down to the lagoon here, even though it's mostly sand and scrub and good for very little. Look, there's the farm through those trees.'

Rupert's eyes followed Hyacinth's pointing hand and, now the leaves had fallen from the thin, wind-bent trees, made out a stone outline perhaps five hundred yards away and several dark uneven shapes which might have been outbuildings or barns. 'Where's the access to it?' he asked. 'You'd need a tank to get across these dunes.'

'Oh, the entrance is round the other side. There's a farm track which comes out on the High Street just short of The Maltings. Torquil may not have mentioned it, but the Mussetts are the Sandymans' next-door neighbours in a sense, though the last thing they do is mix socially. In fact, the Mussetts don't mix much with anyone. As I said, old Bram did well out of the war by claiming a lot of sand and pebbles that probably weren't his, but the War Office didn't check too closely and nobody else claimed it, so Bram got a pile of compensation when they set up the Y Station. In a way, no one begrudged him it as the farm wasn't much of a living, and when his brother Eppy came back from Burma after four years as a POW, everyone felt a bit sorry for them. Poor lad wasn't right in the head. Still isn't.'

'Eppy?'

'Short for Ephraim. I told you they had odd names. Bram's son, who farms the place now, was christened Pelagius of all things, though everyone calls him Tinker. I think that's because he was always thick as thieves with the gypsies who toured the county at harvest time and he even married one, a real raven-haired beauty called Mercy Lee. It seems to have been a good match as she's still there and they've had six children so far. Goodness knows what their names are. One hardly dares to ask.'

'Did Vibeke Westergaard know the Mussetts? They being neighbours, as it were,' Rupert asked carefully.

'I shouldn't think poor Vibeke even noticed the Mussetts were there and she certainly wouldn't have let the twins play with their unruly horde of urchins. Victoria would not have allowed it. That's Eppy now.'

'What is?'

'That noise, that thudding noise we've been hearing. That'll be Eppy splitting logs for his smokehouse. He smokes fish and eels mostly, but oysters if he can get them and he has a customer for them. His smokehouse is over there, low down in the dunes, and unless he's got a fire smoking you'd hardly know it was there, though if the wind was in the other direction you'd certainly smell it. It drives Dido mad. I'm convinced our local vixen has a den near Eppy's smokehouse, perhaps even under it. Dido follows her scent that way but then gets confused by the smell of kippers. They're very good kippers, by the way, and we serve his smoked eel in some of our pubs.'

'So you do business with the Mussetts?'

'Not with Eppy; he can be rather . . . er . . . difficult. We deal with Pelagius or Mercy Lee when we have to. Ah! I spy a policeman.'

A figure was indeed approaching them along the path from Gapton; a stout figure with a rolling gait wearing a long belted raincoat and gumboots. Only his peaked blue-black hat suggested officialdom.

'Good morning, Enoch, so glad you could join us.'

The approaching man removed a hand from a raincoat pocket, touched the peak of his cap and returned the greeting. 'A very good morning to you, Miss Hyacinth, though by rights you shouldn't be out on the Spit, what with this still being a crime

scene. Superintendent Appleyard would definitely not approve.'
The policeman spoke with a gruff formality but Rupert sensed
he was paying no more than lip service to the sensibilities of his
superior. 'And you must be the Mr Campion I've heard so much
about.'

No hand was offered to shake, which presumably meant the
sergeant regarded himself as, if not on duty, then not off duty,
so Rupert smiled his most charming smile in greeting. 'Guilty
as charged, I'm afraid, and it's a dead cert that Mr Appleyard
does not approve of me.'

'Superintendent Appleyard is regarded as an incomer around
these parts,' said Hyacinth primly, 'and so we look to Sergeant
Davies for our law and order here in Gapton.'

'I understand you were first on the scene, Sergeant,' Rupert
encouraged the new arrival.

'After Miss Hyacinth, that would be.'

'And Dido – don't forget Dido.'

'How could I, Miss Hyacinth?' Davies said with a twang of
Suffolk deference. 'What with me being her godfather, so to
speak.'

To Rupert, Hyacinth positively *simpered* at the memory of
Dido's acquisition and he realized that if the Gapton police force
had only one fan, it had a loyal one.

'So you want to see where Dido found the body, do you, Mr
Campion?' Davies turned a round, ruddy, weather-beaten face
with a fleshy nose two shades too red to be healthy towards
Rupert.

'If it's not too much trouble, I'd be fascinated.'

'Can I ask why you would want to do such a thing?'

'Curiosity,' said Rupert carefully, 'though not of the idle
variety, at least I hope not. I had to make an identification of the
body Dido found for Mr Appleyard. You see, I had some . . .
dealings . . . with Francis Tate in London.'

'Dealings, eh?' Davies's brow creased and his chin seemed to
shrink into the collar of his raincoat. 'Did you know Frank well?'

'I didn't *know* him at all, except by sight. Never actually spoke
to the chap. I was just asked to keep an eye on him.'

Now Davies contorted his thick lips into an exaggerated pout
as would an end-of-the-pier comedian expressing outrage at an

audience. 'Keeping an eye on him, were you? What was he suspected of?'

'Nothing that I know of,' Rupert answered honestly. 'I was doing it on behalf of Miss Westergaard's father, the ambassador.'

'Quite understandable,' said Hyacinth in support. 'Any responsible father would want to be as sure as he could be about his daughter's boyfriend, especially in a foreign country. You knew Francis, Enoch. I've seen the two of you propping up the bar in The Butt and Oyster on many an occasion. You've got to admit that in that motorbike get-up he could be mistaken for a tearaway, though I'm sure Vibeke would not have associated with him if he had been one, the poor lad.'

'So you and Tate were boozing buddies?' Rupert experienced an illicit thrill when he realized that, in a bizarre way, here was a policeman helping him with his enquiries.

'Oh, oi'd hardly claim that.' Sergeant Davies's smile was less than sincere and his Suffolk accent became more prominent, which Rupert recognized as defence mechanisms. 'Young Frankie stayed at The Butt and Oyster when he was in Gapton. As the village bobby – so to speak – oi saw it as moi dooty to check out any strangers that hung about regular.'

'How long had Tate been coming to Gapton?'

''Bout a year, oi'd say. Started visiting to photograph the birds what live on the Spit. Then he met another sort of bird and he was down here so often he could have got a place in the darts' team.'

'Please do not refer to Miss Westergaard as a "bird", Enoch. It's vulgar,' Hyacinth scolded.

Sergeant Davies's smile disappeared in a flash. 'There's some will call her much worse than that if she don't turn up soon.'

'You think she's involved in Tate's death?' Rupert pressed, feeling slightly guilty at Hyacinth's theatrically loud intake of shocked breath.

'Well, the longer she's missing the more suspicious it looks. That's how my superiors see it,' Davies said smugly, straightening his shoulders and jutting out his chin.

'Then why are you not out searching for her?' snapped Hyacinth, clutching at Rupert's arm almost as if she was about to poke the policeman with it.

'Technically, I'm not on duty until two o'clock this afternoon, Miss Mister. I'm only here now because you requested this little tête-à-tête. There are plenty of men searching the woods down the Lowestoft Road as we speak, not that it will do much good. If you want my opinion, which you probably don't, I reckon Vibeke Westergaard has somehow got herself back to Lunnun and is sitting snug and warm somewhere. Anyhow, I probably shouldn't be talking about such things; not even to you Miss Hyacinth. So, shall we press on?'

Hyacinth Mister responded with what could only be called a 'harrumph' and allowed Sergeant Davies to take the lead on the path as it curved around the northern bulge of the lagoon.

The path here ran through proper sand dunes rather than sandy scrub and in places the dunes rose above head height giving the impression, Rupert thought, that they were walking up a desert valley or wadi, albeit a cold and damp desert where the air carried a heavy tang of salt. Lest he forget himself totally, the booming of the waves beating inexorably against the seaward side of the Spit to his left was there to remind him.

'The Suffolk coast is a magical place,' said Hyacinth, reading his mind. 'It's what drew us here in the first place.'

'That and having a brewery to run,' Sergeant Davies observed tartly over his shoulder.

'Nonsense – we could have put managers in to look after our interests or sold our holding to the Sandymans had we been so inclined, but Marigold and I fell in love with the coast at an early age, when we saw the genius of Steer.'

'I take it that would be Philip Wilson Steer?' said Rupert.

'I knew *you* would get the reference,' said Hyacinth pointedly, glaring at the back of Sergeant Davies's head. 'One of the finest English Impressionists – or should that be "Post-Impressionists"? I'm never sure. It was his *The Beach at Walberswick* and *Girls Running on Walberswick Pier* which made us fall in love with the coast here. Marigold and I *were* those girls running. It's a wonderful picture. Have you seen it?'

'Not in the flesh, so to speak, but I was introduced to Steer on a visit to the Uffizi in Florence, where his work is held in high regard.' Rupert thought it added to his credibility to omit the fact that it had been on a school trip. 'So I mugged up on him and discovered that my father is a big fan of his. In fact, he has a Steer squirrelled away somewhere, or at least he says it's a Steer. It's from his later period, a small oil-on-canvas of sailing barges at Maldon in Essex, painted sometime between the wars, though I'm not sure it forms part of the official Steer catalogue.'

'If I can interrupt the art class,' announced Davies loudly, 'we're here, though there's nothing to see now.'

The path had curved again and the dunes were lower, offering a view of the lagoon, flat and cold, and across it the houses of Gapton. Directly in front of them the path ended in a ten-foot high wire fence which ran down into the lagoon on their right where it was anchored by vicious-looking rusted iron stakes crossed in the way which reminded Rupert of beach obstacles in film of the D-Day landings. To their left, the fence undulated away across the dunes, presumably to the sea, effectively amputating ninety per cent of the length of Gapton Spit. The sign which hung from it, courtesy of the Ministry of Defence, reinforced the suggestion that anyone who could read should Keep Out.

'He was down there, face down, floating in the water.' Hyacinth pointed with a hand which shook visibly. 'His jacket had snagged on those metal stanchion things, otherwise he might have floated down the lagoon and out to sea.'

'Tide hadn't turned when you found him,' Davies offered.

'When Dido found him,' Hyacinth corrected automatically.

'We pulled the body out and laid it just about where you're standing, Mr Campion. He was quite a weight was young Frankie, being all waterlogged.'

'But the two of you managed to get him ashore without falling in?'

Rupert realized his question may have sounded fatuous but he could not imagine Hyacinth hauling a sodden body over the mud and sand and Davies hardly seemed the type to take off his boots and dive in to the rescue.

'Oh, no,' said Hyacinth coyly, 'I was too busy trying not to swoon clean away, and then of course I had an overexcited Dido to get back on the leash. Fortunately those nice birdwatchers from the houseboat spotted our predicament and rowed over in their little dinghy to help. I suppose that's the thing about bird-watchers – they're always watching out for things.'

'Birdwatchers? This time of year?'

'Oh, we get 'em year-round here, watching the lagoon. It seems there's always something going on with their feathered friends. Mustn't grumble about it – they're good for business, 'specially at The Butt and Oyster.'

'And they were so helpful with poor Francis. They got terribly wet and muddy but they didn't complain and they even stood guard over the body while Enoch went to telephone for a doctor to come over from Beccles. The Gapton doctor, that nice Dr Milne, is away on holiday, you see. He always goes away for two weeks to somewhere hot in the autumn before the arrival of all those winter chills and sniffles he has to deal with.'

From what he had tasted in the brewery sample cellar, Rupert was of the opinion that Sandyman's barley wine could immunize the local population against all known germs and was surprised that an enterprising doctor had not yet offered it on prescription.

'You left the body with the two birdwatchers? That's not normal police procedure, is it, Sergeant?'

'Needs must, Mr Campion, when you're not in the metropolis. How many phone boxes do you see round here? We have to make do out here in the sticks.'

'And it isn't as if they were total strangers we dragged off the street,' Hyacinth sided with the policeman. 'Mr Carruthers and Mr Smith have been here for nearly a month. Their house-boat is on one of The Butt and Oyster's moorings and they often take their meals there. Charming men, and no trouble at all. In fact, they helped with the motorbike as well, didn't they, Enoch?'

'True enough.' Sergeant Davies nodded sagely but offered no further details until Rupert prompted him.

'I understand you didn't spot Tate's bike at first.'

'Not possible, it being underwater. It was only when the tide started to go out that we saw the handlebars poking out, so I ran back round to my place and got *Betsan* fired up – that's my little cutter, is the *Betsan* – and brought her over the lagoon while there was still water to float her, not that she draws much, mind.

The chaps from the houseboat helped get some rope around the bike and pull it out of the mud. We lashed it to the side of *Betsan* and took it over to the Hard by The Butt. Couldn't have done it on my own and the least I could do was stand them both a pint when the pub opened at twelve.'

'Tate's bike,' Rupert mused vaguely, 'was it ridden into the lagoon or pushed in?'

'Couldn't rightly say, Mr Campion, and not sure I should if I knew. Best you ask Mr Appleyard about such things. Now I've got to be off, unless I can do anything else for you.'

'You could help me find Dido,' said Hyacinth. 'She always comes to you.'

'She's not off after that blasted fox again, is she?'

'You know what she's like, Enoch, a hopeless optimist, convinced she'll catch it one day, though goodness knows what she'd do if she did. Let's stroll back, she'll come to us.'

They set off back on the curving, sand-blown path. Rupert was disconcerted by how quickly the wire fence, the view of Gapton and indeed the lagoon were lost from sight as the dunes – lifeless and naked except for scrawny bunches of marram grass – hemmed them in again.

'Will you be in Gapton long, Mr Campion?' Davies asked.

'I'm not sure. A few days, perhaps a week.'

'You putting up at The Butt? It's very comfortable, I hear.'

'My wife and I are staying with the Sandymans; Torquil's an old school chum of mine and my wife's sort of helping out with their children now that Vibeke isn't there . . . Didn't you mention that Frank Tate stayed at The Butt and Oyster when he was in Gapton?'

'Well, oi don't know that oi did, but it happens to be roight.'

Rupert noticed the return of Davies's convenient Suffolk accent.

'Tate had a regular room there when he come up courting that young Danish girl. I think they gave him a special rate.'

'Did you search his room after you found him?'

Davies glared at Rupert from under the peak of his cap. 'No real need to, was there? What do you think we should have been searching for, Mr Campion?'

'A crash helmet, perhaps? I've seen the body,' Rupert said grimly, 'and there's no way he would have had his head smashed in like that if he'd been wearing one – oh, I'm sorry, Miss Hyacinth!'

Hyacinth uncoupled herself from Rupert's arm and flapped a hand in front of her face as if fanning herself. 'There's no need to spare my feelings, my dear; after all, I saw it too, but I'd rather not think about it, so I'll go and find Dido.'

They were rounding the bulge of the lagoon now and the dunes had flattened out. Hyacinth strode purposefully off the path and up one of the smaller ones in the general direction of Mussett's Farm, whistling the five-note whistle which dog owners always adopt and dogs usually ignore.

When he judged she was out of earshot, Rupert continued: 'Frank Tate was a biker and would probably have worn a helmet for a long run like London to Gapton, even though the law doesn't insist on it. He wasn't wearing one when somebody bopped him, so what was he doing and where was he? Find the helmet and we might find out.'

Davies stopped walking and studied Rupert through narrowed eyes. 'I was told that your father fancied himself as a bit of a detective,' he said with just a hint of menace, 'but I didn't realize it was something that passed down from father to son. Some things are best left to the professionals, don't you think, sir? We might not be flash and brash but we tend to get there in the end.'

Before Rupert could compose a riposte, the attention of both men was drawn to an anguished cry from Hyacinth Mister, who was shuffling through shifting sand atop a dune with much arm-flapping as she tried to keep her balance. Her anguish was not, however, because of her own ungainly predicament.

'You leave that dog alone!' she shouted. 'If you harm her, I'll have the law on you and I've got the law right here with me!'

'Now what?' muttered Sergeant Davies, but realizing that duty called, he hurried to Hyacinth's side and Rupert accompanied him, reaching Hyacinth in time to offer a supportive arm before she lost her footing completely.

From the top of the dune they saw and heard Dido, some twenty yards away, her front paws splayed, confronting and barking at a short stocky figure dressed in dungarees, gumboots and some form of khaki army tunic. The man, balding and in his mid-fifties, had a face which was tanned a deep brown. From further away he could have been mistaken for Indian or Pakistani, but Rupert could see there was something unnatural about his colouring.

There was nothing Asian about his voice, although Rupert had great difficulty penetrating the Suffolk accent.

'Git yor 'ound out o' moi bizness. Oi shan't tell ye again!'

When the man – though Rupert could think of him only as a brown elf – spoke, it was a shout, not of anger, but rather that of a man trying to be heard over a crowd or a television with the volume turned too high. And when he spoke, or shouted, the man/elf cupped the palms of both hands to the already prominent brown ears which formed handles to his shiny brown face.

'Don't you dare call Dido a hound, Eppy Mussett, and don't you presume to tell me anything. I'm a person of some standing in this town!' Hyacinth retorted while struggling to control her slipping, sliding feet as the sand shifted beneath her. All in all, thought Rupert, it was an object lesson in maintaining balance as well as the social order.

'Well, yew keep 'er away from moi smokehouse, otherwise there'll be trouble, and that's straight,' the small brown man shouted back and, to emphasize his point, he parted his khaki blouson and pulled from a wide leather belt a three-pound lump hammer which he whirled, frighteningly, about his head. 'Trouble, oi say!'

Sergeant Davies raised an official hand in a part-warning, part-threat gesture, calling for, if nothing else, order. It either did the trick or was totally superfluous to requirements, for the small brown man had already turned his back on his antagonists, both animal and human, wedged his hammer back inside his belt and was stalking away across the sand and scrub.

'That was really quite disturbing,' said Rupert, Miss Hyacinth still balanced on his arm.

'You're telling me,' observed Sergeant Davies, genuinely surprised. 'I ain't never heard old Eppy so talkative before.'

TEN
Mud Cockles and Samphire

Rupert did not really want a drink. In fact, he would have preferred food or a brisk walk in the fresh air to mitigate the rigours of his morning session in the sample room, but he quickly realized that he was not to have much say in the matter. Sandwiched between the formidable Miss Mister, her dog and her favourite local policeman, he found himself guided along the path, round the edge of the lagoon and on to the High Street only to be turned left and eased (he was mentally rehearsing 'frog-marched' for when he had to face Perdita) towards the Hard and The Butt and Oyster, which looked out over the lagoon like a Napoleonic sea fort.

To be fair, the interior of The Butt and Oyster was nothing like the interior of a Napoleonic sea fort, or at least not one that Rupert imagined. It was decorated in the traditional style of all British pubs claiming an affinity with the sea, either by location and genuine heritage or, perhaps more commonly, by the whim of a brewery executive and a tame sign painter. Beams and exposed timbers were of a uniform shiny dark-brown hue, whether from age or tobacco smoke it was impossible to be certain, although nicotine stains on the walls and low ceilings favoured the theory that two hundred years of salty patrons puffing on clay and then briar pipes reinforced by one hundred years of cigarette smokers were probably responsible. The decoration also had a sea-faring theme comprising lobster pots (fortunately vacated by recent residents) and cobwebs of fishing nets edged with ancient cork floats dangling from every crossbeam. The upright beams were liberally dotted, as most pubs seemed to be these days, with horse brasses and enough of them to keep a parish church brass-cleaning rota busy for a week. They had been chosen, however, for their maritime connection and designs were strictly limited to anchors, lighthouses, fish, and yet more anchors.

In case any unwary stray visitor was left in any doubt, the areas of plaster wall between timbers (which themselves had probably been 'shivvered' and reclaimed from a pirate ship) were hung with framed prints on a nautical theme, usually one which showed the grimmer side of life on the ocean waves. There were prints of Scapa Flow, warships entering Dover harbour and *HMS Terror* from paintings by Sir John Lavery during World War I, interspersed with prints from the *Illustrated London News* of the 1870s showing the hardy life aboard the smacks of the Great Yarmouth fishing fleet.

By contrast, the main and only bar of The Butt and Oyster was refreshingly plain and uncluttered; a solid structure of varnished wood against which a man – sailor or landlubber – could lean with confidence. Large rectangular ashtrays advertising the Sandyman name were strategically placed a yard apart but otherwise the bar counter was bare save for, in one corner, an illuminated lime green square plastic box housing a dispensing tap for a liquid unknown to Rupert but which proclaimed garishly to the world that it was 'Husky Lager'. Sandyman's own beers were dispensed, more discreetly, straight from tapped casks on an extensive stillage arrangement even more impressive than that in the sample cellar, some six feet behind the counter. None of the metal casks were identified other than by paper labels pasted across the ends bearing cryptic, handwritten, single-word descriptions such as: Bitter, Mild, Old, Stock, Best, Winter, IPA and Barley.

'I know what you're thinking,' said Hyacinth, pointing to the luminous green box. 'That plastic monstrosity is totally out of keeping – and you'd be right, but we have to have it. In the trade we call it a "reciprocal": we supply our barley wine to another brewery and in return they supply us with *laager*' – she wrinkled her nose as she stretched the word – 'which is supposed to be the coming thing. Torquil says we must keep up with the times but we don't sell much of it, hardly any; and the locals refer to it, politely, as 'Husky Piddle' when there are ladies about.'

Rupert had a strong suspicion he knew what the regular patrons might call it if ladies were absent.

'Now order a pint of whatever you fancy, on the house, of course,' said the perfect hostess. 'Are you on duty yet, Enoch?'

'Not for another half-hour, Miss Hyacinth,' answered the sergeant with a ramrod back and a huge grin. Rupert noticed that his raincoat was now buttoned up to the throat and his official cap had disappeared as if by magic.

'In that case, you'd better have one too and you can keep Mr Campion company while I take Dido over to see Mrs Grundy, who always has a dog biscuit for her; won't be long.'

And with a snap on Dido's lead, she turned and made her exit, leaving Rupert bemused but in the capable hands – when it came to free beer – of Sergeant Davies, who ordered two pints of best bitter with an authority unlikely to be questioned.

'I think,' said Rupert, 'that I could live in Gapton for a year and still only follow a quarter of what the sisters Mister are talking about.'

Sergeant Davies raised his glass, took a long and noisy slurp before replying. 'A year? You could spend a lifetime and not fathom those two. Still, she's a lot more easy-going than Miss Marigold; she's got corsets of steel, that one. But don't be fooled by the animal-loving-little-old-lady act. She says she's taking the dog to see Mrs Grundy at the shop across the Hard like it was a social call, but really it's to see how the shop's stock is holding up. She owns it, you see. The Misters own most of Gapton, picked up a lot of properties during the war when a load of the locals moved out. They thought the listening station on the Spit – what Miss Hyacinth calls her Huff-Duff work – would not so much detect the Luftwaffe bombers as attract them. Never did though. All those Gapton properties remained undamaged and very cheap at the price, compared to what they'd fetch now. What the Sandymans and the sisters Mister don't own between 'em don't leave much of Gapton apart from my police house, a redundant church and a handful of cottages on the Darsham road.'

'And Mussett's Farm, I believe,' observed Rupert between sips of beer which he found very tasty, even though a still small voice of calm at the back of his head was telling him to be careful.

'True enough. The Mussetts wouldn't take orders from anybody nor pay rent to anybody. That's their way.'

The sergeant nodded solemnly into his pint glass, as if imparting great wisdom.

'I got that impression from the Mussett we met out in the dunes,' Rupert agreed.

'Oh, don't mind old Eppy. He can't help himself; he had a really bad war out East. Left him sixpence short of a bob, if you know what I mean. It's best to give him a wide berth, not that he allows many to get alongside. The Gapton doctor, Dr Milne, is the only one who can really get through to him.'

'Is he dangerous?'

'I doubt it, though he can get riled up.'

'Did he know Frank Tate or Vibeke Westergaard?'

'I can't see Eppy Mussett knowing either of them socially,' Davies said without humour. 'He's not the sociable type and certainly wouldn't have taken to strangers, not for a few years anyway.'

'So who did know Frank Tate in Gapton? Apart from Vibeke, that is?'

'I really couldn't say. It wasn't like he lived here full-time.'

'But he must have talked to somebody,' Rupert persisted. 'He had a room here in the pub, you said. Perhaps the landlord would know if he met up with anyone in particular.'

Davies drained his glass, lowered it slowly on to the bar and began to unbutton his raincoat from the neck downwards, revealing his police uniform beneath and, clasped between his knees, his peaked cap. Slapping it once against his legs, Davies replaced the cap on his head and quivered the peak until it sat square and he was clearly back on duty.

'Like I said before, Mr Campion, it's probably best if you leave police enquiries to the police. If it's local gossip you want, Miss Hyacinth is more than qualified to supply that.'

After Sergeant Davies had marched out without another word, Rupert declined the offer of a refill from an anxious barman and concentrated on swirling the dregs in the bottom of his glass as though inspecting the entrails of a sacrificial horoscope. He received no divine inspiration but when Miss Hyacinth and Dido re-entered the bar, he realized he had no need of supernatural assistance.

'Now have you done anything about ordering some lunch, Mr Campion?'

'No, I haven't, I'm afraid,' said Rupert, suspecting he was in for a scolding.

'Would you allow me to be your guide to the local specialities?' Miss Hyacinth asked formally but with a twinkle in her eyes.

'I place myself entirely in your hands,' Rupert replied with a polite bow. It was a phrase and a gesture he had learned from his father at an early age.

'Well, the real *specialité de la maison* is mud cockles and samphire, but of course the samphire is not in season now. Now don't look so aghast, Mr Campion – mud cockles from the local river estuaries are plump and juicy and I think superior to the sea cockles you get on Yarmouth front, which have to be doused in vinegar to make them palatable. Samphire always was the poor man's asparagus and it grows in abundance in the salt marshes around here in July and August. Down the coast, in Essex' – her voice lowered as she named the neighbouring county – 'they make a big song and dance about Colchester oysters, but I think our Suffolk mud cockles are superior in flavour. Odd, really, for a pub called The Butt and Oyster, but we don't serve oysters. But as our most famous dish is not on the menu today, let me treat you to our second-most popular.'

She rapped a set of dainty knuckles on the bar counter, attracting the immediate attention of the ruddy-faced middle-aged man who had been tending the array of casks on stillage with great solicitude.

'Two pints of Specials please, Stanley.'

'Oh, I don't think I could manage any more beer,' protested Rupert.

Miss Hyacinth gave him a withering look of pity. 'The "Special" here is a pint of prawns served with a pot of Marie Rose sauce and doorsteps of brown bread and butter. Of course, we'll have beer with it, but only a half of Mild. I *know* a nice Chablis or a fresh Muscadet would be the proper accompaniment but in my position I simply cannot be seen to be doing anything other than supporting our native ale. Now let's grab the table in the window so we can watch the world go by, though in truth the world passed Gapton by many years ago.'

They settled themselves into oak captain's chairs around an

iron-framed table in the bay window, looking over the lagoon towards the false horizon of Gapton Spit.

'In the summer, there's usually a queue to get this table,' said Hyacinth proudly. Dido remained unimpressed and flopped down between their feet, yawned once and went to sleep.

'I can see the appeal,' Rupert agreed. 'It's sort of tranquil and yet slightly threatening at the same time. Perhaps that's just because I know what you found over the other side. Why did no one spot Tate's body from here in the pub?'

'It was very early on Sunday morning, long before opening time and after a busy Saturday night Stanley and Barbara – they're our licensees – deserve a bit of a lie-in.'

'Tate had a room here, didn't he?'

'Just bed and breakfast when he was in Gapton, it wasn't a permanent thing.' Miss Hyacinth's eyes widened. 'Oh I say, am I being interrogated? I do hope so.'

'Just a few questions, if you don't mind, so that I can get things straight in my rather slow brain,' Rupert said, trying not to disappoint his hostess. 'Didn't anyone notice he hadn't come back that night?'

'There was no reason why anyone would. He often kept late hours, or so I'm told. He would have had a key to the kitchen door where there's a back staircase to the upstairs rooms. Stanley and Barbara could have locked up the bar and the cellar and gone up to their quarters, leaving him to his own devices. On the morning in question' – she almost hugged herself as she uttered the phrase – 'they would have thought he was merely late down for breakfast, which is nothing unusual for a young man who has been out courting his girlfriend the night before.'

'Would it be possible for me to see Tate's room?'

'I'm not sure of the protocol on such things,' Miss Hyacinth started primly, then her nose wrinkled and her mouth turned up in a cheeky smile, 'but it would be quite exciting to go searching for clues . . . I'm not sure if it is quite proper, though.'

'I have no idea if there will be any clues there,' Rupert said hastily. 'In fact, I really have no idea what we would be looking for.'

It was a masterstroke by Rupert to say 'we' rather than 'I' and, thus included, Miss Hyacinth quivered with excitement.

'Let's ask Stanley the landlord – of course, he's not actually the landlord, I suppose I am, but he is the licensee and we should get him on side.'

At that moment, a white-aproned Stanley was negotiating his way from behind the bar, his tongue protruding from between fleshy lips in concentration as he gripped a large wicker tray at chest height. With a lightness of footwork which belied his size, he avoided treading on the inert Dido and managed to lower the tray safely on to the table.

'As you ordered, Miss Hyacinth,' he said proudly as he unloaded a plate of thickly cut and thickly buttered brown bread, two bowls of steaming hot water with a saucer of cut lemon wedges, an empty white china pudding basin, a pile of paper serviettes and two veteran ten-sided fluted pint glass beer mugs overflowing with plump, pink prawns.

'Thank you, Stanley.' Miss Hyacinth mimed an imaginary pen signing an invisible bill to indicate that no cash would be changing hands. 'We were wondering if it would be possible to have a look in the room poor Francis Tate rented. You see we are both frightfully worried about Vibeke and we thought that Francis could have left a clue as to where she might have gone.'

Stanley wiped his hands down his apron as he considered this. 'Well, I don't see why you can't. I mean, it's your pub after all.'

'Yes, I suppose it is,' giggled Hyacinth demurely. 'Of course, we wouldn't want to do anything to get you into trouble with the police . . .'

'Can't see how you could,' said Stanley phlegmatically. 'They've been and gone and as far as they're concerned I can let the room if I have a visitor.'

'The police have searched the room?' Rupert asked. 'Do you know if they found anything?'

'Well, there wasn't much there to begin with, I reckon. Young Tate was only booked in for two nights – the Friday and the Saturday – and Sergeant Davies took most of his things away on Sunday morning, while you and those two birdwatchers from the houseboat were with the body out on the Spit.'

'But I thought Sergeant Davies was with you when you found Tate . . .?'

'Technically, it was Dido who found the body,' explained Miss

Hyacinth patiently, 'and then I screamed. Rather loudly, I'm afraid, and sound does carry across the water when the lagoon is calm. Sergeant Davies was working on his boat, which is moored not far away down towards the inlet to the sea, and he heard me and came running round by the path – well, I say running, but he's hardly what you might call athletic. He pulled poor Francis out of the water and by then those two young men from the houseboat – Mr Carruthers and Mr Smith – were rowing across in their dinghy to help. Once they were there to keep me and Dido company, Enoch charged off to telephone for a doctor.'

'He phoned from here,' said Stanley. 'Used the public phone by the door. I know 'cos I had to open up the till to give him some change. He made two or three calls, I reckon; said it was quicker than for him to run back to the police house.'

'Odd,' murmured Hyacinth.

'Why so?' said Rupert softly.

'Because he had to go his police house anyway, to get *Betsan* – his little chug-chug boat – so he could pull Francis's motorbike out of the water.'

'Which he did, as soon as he'd left here,' said Stanley, 'but when he'd finished on the phone, he asked for a key to the poor lad's room and went up there.'

'Did you go with him?' Rupert asked, riding the coattails of Hyacinth's authority.

'No, I'm afraid I was standing right here gawping across the water at what was going on,' admitted Stanley. 'When Mr Davies came downstairs, he had the lad's haversack with him. He said he was taking charge of it and there was nothing of Tate's left in the room, though his boss, Mr Appleyard, might want to have a look round before I let anybody in there. That's what I told the two birdwatchers when they asked.'

'When who asked what?'

Stanley baulked at the abruptness of Rupert's question, but a regal nod from Miss Hyacinth reassured him.

'Them two chaps from the RSPB or whatever it's called; the two who rowed over to help you like stand-up citizens.'

'Carruthers and Smith,' supplied Hyacinth.

'Yes, them. They came in late on Sunday lunchtime just before closing time, so it would be two o'clock, and we stretched a point to make sure they got served with some food and some ale, 'cos of what they'd been through that morning. Hope you don't mind, Miss Hyacinth, but Barbara and I just thought it was the right thing to do in the circumstances.'

'It was, Stanley, just don't make a habit of it.'

'Of course not, Miss Hyacinth, we don't want a reputation for doing "afters" here at The Butt, but them two birdwatchers seem decent lads and good customers, hardly the type to take advantage.'

'But they wanted to see Tate's room?' Rupert pressed.

'Said they'd loaned him a book on photography and wondered if they could have it back, but I had to tell them Sergeant Davies had taken charge of his things. Not that I'd ever seen Tate with a book – though he liked his photography and always had a camera about him – and Barbara, who cleans the rooms, never saw one either.'

'Where did you say the phone was?' Rupert asked.

Even though she had been slaving over a hot stove for more than an hour, preparing enough chicken and pearl barley soup to feed twenty hungry men, Mrs Victoria Sandyman looked a pin-up of domestic sexiness, a fact which Perdita acknowledged with only a slight twinge of resentment rather than jealousy for she was not by nature a person to waste time being jealous. Her resentment of Victoria and the confident way in which she wore – modelled might be a better description – a scoop-necked, knee-length black jersey dress (Saint Laurent perhaps?), adorned centrally with a single emerald brooch, sheer black stockings and impressive high heels which click-clacked across the kitchen tiles, was deepened by the fact that she herself felt desperately in need of a bath and clean clothes.

While Victoria had been creating lunch for a soon-to-return search party of volunteers – just managing to squeeze in enough time to do her hair, nails and make-up to Hollywood standard – Perdita had found herself assigned to playing ('constructively') with twins Jasper and George, who still remained indistinguishable, changing the nappy of baby Beatrice (twice) and 'running the Hoover' around the children's bedrooms. All this only, Victoria had insisted, if she really didn't mind helping out in a crisis, just as Vibeke would have. Good manners and the lack of a quickly thought-up excuse meant that Perdita had not only agreed to her domestic chores, but had bitten her tongue and resisted pointing out that Vibeke *was* the crisis. As a consequence, her fingers were sticky with strawberry jam (where had that come from?), there were chocolate stains down the front of her check shirt top and crushed red crayon embedded into both knees of her jeans, her nose felt blocked with dust and she was convinced there were cobwebs in her hair.

The only positive she could take from a morning of servitude and drudgery – or so she would call it as soon as she got Rupert in her sights – was that it had given her the perfect opportunity to snoop around the room occupied by Vibeke Westergaard, even though Superintendent Appleyard's detectives had swept it clean already, albeit stopping short of hoovering. Either the police had removed all useful clues or there were never any there to find, or at least not there to be found by Perdita.

She found Vibeke's clothes, the ones she had left behind, which were typical of any eighteen-year-old girl's wardrobe: jeans, flared trousers, miniskirts, blouses with puffed sleeves, tie-dyed T-shirts and flamboyantly patterned tights which could only be worn on young legs without giving the appearance of a medical condition.

There were film posters on the walls from *The Graduate* and *Thoroughly Modern Millie* and on a bedside table, a portable gramophone and a small pile of 45 r.p.m. discs, which Perdita shuffled through as she would a pack of cards, noting the artists. Amen Corner, The Hollies, Love Affair, Manfred Mann and something called Status Quo, all of which she put down as typical pop ephemera representative of the musical taste of an eighteen-year-old: mop-haired musicians who would be forgotten within six months. And that very thought made her stop in her tracks.

'For heaven's sake, I'm not much older than she was!' she said out loud, and almost immediately felt a wave of guilt over her automatic use of the past tense.

'Than she is; than Vibeke *is*!' she spat the words, angry with herself. 'Wherever she is.'

But the room yielded no clues, at least to Perdita, as to where Vibeke Westergaard might be, and it seemed that the search party which had returned to The Maltings for lunch in sombre and subdued mood had discovered none in the woods to the north along the Lowestoft Road.

Victoria Sandyman, who had sliced and buttered bread in platoon strength without a hair falling out of place or chipping her nail polish, asked Perdita if she would 'be an angel' and take beans-on-toast to the twins in their play room so the men of the search party could have the kitchen to themselves. The last thing she wanted the boys to overhear was their speculation on Vibeke's whereabouts, or even worse, of the discovery of Vibeke's whereabouts.

As soon as Perdita's good manners had compelled her to agree to these further domestic duties, Victoria informed her, with more enthusiasm than was perhaps necessary, where she could find sliced bread and a tin opener, and that there was no need to worry about Beatrice, for a bottle of 'formula' was already warming in a pan of hot water on the stove.

At least Beatrice seemed happy with her lunchtime feed and didn't complain, unlike the twins – which one was Jasper? – who regarded baked beans as ammunition and their knives as ballistae.

Order was restored only by Perdita promising to let the twins choose what they wished to do that afternoon, by which time, she reckoned, Rupert would have returned from whatever fun he had been having and she could tell him in no uncertain terms that her morning had not been *fun* at all. In fact, she considered, wiping yet more tomato sauce from her jeans, she might use physical violence against her husband to enforce her point.

And then Jasper – or was it George? – said: 'Can we go and see Dotty this afternoon? She always gives us tea and cake.'

'And just who is Dotty?' Perdita asked politely, picking up yet another piece of discarded toast from the play room carpet.

'Vibeke's friend. She takes us there all the time,' said George, or possibly Jasper. 'She said Dotty was the only stranger we were allowed to talk to, but once she started giving us tea and cake she wasn't a stranger, was she?'

'That's very interesting,' urged Perdita, 'but would you know Dotty's proper name and where she lives?'

An answer came loud and clear as though well-rehearsed. 'Mrs Dorothy Monk, Samphire Cottage, Darsham Road, Gapton.'

'Well done. You're a very clever boy, Jasper.'
'I'm George,' said George.
'Of course you are,' smiled Perdita.

Rupert's telephone call to his father, a mutual exchange of situation reports, took longer than he had intended and, by the time he returned to the bay window table, Hyacinth was squeezing lemon juice on to her fingers and then splashing them delicately in one of the bowls of water. In front of her were an empty pint mug and a small mountain of shellfish detritus.

'I just couldn't wait,' she said without a trace of embarrassment, 'I find prawns simply irresistible.'

'They do look good,' Rupert agreed, 'and my apologies for deserting you, but I simply had to check something with my father.'

He began to behead and then undress a prawn as Hyacinth leaned closer over the table while wiping her hands on a serviette.

'Was it something to with the . . . case?'

'Case? Oh, I see. Well, yes, it was connected to the unfortunate Mr Tate.'

'Have you spotted a clue? I suppose it was right in front of me all the time, but I missed it. Marigold says I'm terribly stupid that way. In every way, actually.'

Rupert's fingers tore into more victims. 'No clues yet, I'm afraid, just a few thoughts and a chance to compare notes with Father, who really is much better at this game that I am. In fact, I sometimes think he's always one step ahead of me.'

'Don't put yourself down, dear boy, I'm sure you're doing a wonderful job.'

'I'm not sure I am. I'm not sure I even know what I'm supposed to be doing and when I told Father what I'd found out he didn't seem surprised by anything. He even bet me he knew the name of the houseboat those two helpful birdwatchers, Carruthers and Smith, live on, though I swear he'd never heard of their existence until ten minutes ago when I told him about them.'

Rupert took solace in a chunk of brown bread then went back to tearing at his lunch with gusto. 'I mean, I just don't see how he could know. Do you know?'

'Do I know what, dear?'

'The name of the houseboat Carruthers and Smith are staying on.'

'Of course I do – they've rented one of our moorings. It's the *Dulcibella*.'

'Damn!' said Rupert, taking out his frustration, rather messily, on an innocent crustacean. 'I owe Dad a fiver.'

ELEVEN
Fox on the Beach

Victoria Sandyman, still busy dispensing victuals and encouragement in equal proportions to the search party while playing the role of Lady of the Manor to perfection, was delighted with Perdita's offer to take the children out for some fresh air. Only a wisp of a scowl flitted across her face when she estimated the amount of washing up she would have to tackle single-handed, but Perdita was already heading upstairs to change into more child-friendly clothes.

She vaguely remembered Hyacinth Mister announcing Samphire Cottage as a point of interest on the guided tour she had provided on the brewers' dray ride in from Darsham Halt. What was it Hyacinth had called it – the home of Gapton's mystery woman? There was no doubt in Perdita's mind that she could find it for she had already worked out that Gapton comprised basically three streets which joined together in one long snaking thoroughfare. As she guided Beatrice's pushchair out of The Maltings, she knew that to her right was the Lowestoft Road; to her left the High Street which led past the brewery to the Hard and the Darsham Road they had come in on in such style. In any case, she had the twins to direct her and with the promise of a slight detour into Mrs Grundry's sweet shop she had secured their loyalty.

Once suitably bribed with a bag of sherbet-filled 'flying saucers' and a Milky Bar each, Jasper and George proved to be conscientious and helpful guides, pointing out with great pride, in case Perdita managed to miss its sharp and flinty features, St Olave's church, clearly a local attraction even though the church was now 'redumbdant' as Jasper put it, which meant 'closed for business' as George explained with the seriousness of a four-year-old going on forty.

It was only when George, or perhaps Jasper, was holding open

a white gate bearing War Office-style stencilled lettering announcing Samphire Cottage, that Perdita realized she had not rehearsed
her opening line. As the door of the cottage and its impressive
brass fox-head knocker loomed larger, she toyed with 'Hello,
Mrs Monk, you don't know me but . . .' and 'I hope you don't
think me nosey but . . .' then dismissed them both.

As Jasper and George scuffled to be the first to place a sticky
hand on the fox-head, Perdita decided to leave the stage to the
children. She parked Beatrice right in front of the doorstep and
crouched down beside the pushchair as if comforting the child,
so that the eyeline of whoever opened the door would be automatically drawn downwards to the toddler's cherubic face. She
ordered the twins to knock once each and then stand politely (a
command she had heard their mother use whenever she required
order). Surely the sight of three cherubim would break the thickest
of ice.

Once the cottage door swung open, Perdita decided that her
crouched position had put her at a distinctive disadvantage for
the figure which now loomed over her was slim, glacial and very
tall. The little tableau thus presented to a casual observer, had
there been one, must have looked like a Rackham illustration for
a fairy tale involving an ice queen and four supplicant dwarves,
albeit an ice queen wearing a Bri-Nylon housecoat which successfully blurred any feminine outline.

'Good afternoon, children,' the queen addressed her subjects
regally, 'how nice to see you.'

Perdita straightened her legs, resisted the urge to curtsey, and
rose to her full height which brought her fringe level with the
ice queen's chin. 'I do hope this isn't an imposition, though it
probably is, but the boys did so want to come and . . . er . . .
visit.' Transfixed by a pair of unblinking blue eyes, Perdita felt
her mouth drying. 'If it is at all inconvenient, I'll whisk them
away, take them out of your hair.'

Hair? Why had she mentioned hair and subconsciously drawn
attention to the fact that the queen of Samphire Cottage was
wearing a pearl grey scarf turban-style and knotted at the crown,
as women had done in films of the Home Front during the war
when they had to make do and mend, which concealed all but a
few wisps of damp (dyed?) black hair.

'Please allow them to visit. I am overstocked with cake and chocolate and would welcome hungry mouths. My name is Dorothy Monk. You are . . .?'

'Perdita Browning, well, Campion, actually; we haven't been married long, but my husband's a friend of the Sandyman family.' Perdita offered a hand which was accepted in a surprisingly limp grip.

'Bring the children in and I'll make tea. Jasper and George take their tea like proper grown-ups and I put milk in a plastic cup so Beatrice can join in.'

Mrs Monk released Perdita's hand and her own hovered around Beatrice in the pushchair. Perdita thought she was about to chuck the toddler under the chin or pat a rosy cheek, but the hand faltered and then, as if nervous of actual contact, withdrew and only fluttered in blessing as the woman stepped back into the cottage and waved them all inside.

Jasper and George were clearly familiar with the geography of Samphire Cottage and made a beeline for a living room rather overstocked, to Perdita's eye, with chintzy furniture which promised comfort but always failed to deliver. The twins, to Perdita's relief, did not climb over chairs or wipe sticky fingers on any surface but waited patiently for Mrs Monk's orders – orders which they obeyed quickly and without a murmur of dissent.

'Come on, boys, help your sister out of her pushchair and keep her amused while the grown-ups get the tea things ready.' Mrs Monk raised her pencil-line eyebrows and gently jerked her head as a signal to Perdita, adding: 'In the kitchen.'

Perdita, an actress who had never missed a cue, obediently followed the tall woman through an archway which was brushed by Mrs Monk's turbaned head and into a small, functional galley kitchen where her hostess immediately busied herself opening cupboards and drawers then filling a kettle from the sink tap. As water cascaded noisily on to metal, she leaned over Perdita and asked softly: 'Is there news of Vibeke?'

Perdita glanced over her shoulder to make sure the children were out of earshot and replied in a similarly conspiratorial whisper, 'She hasn't turned up yet. The men are still out searching for her.'

Mrs Monk closed her eyes slowly as if blotting out an

unpleasant thought and concentrated on assembling cups, sugar
and milk on a wooden tray and slicing a Battenberg cake with
the precision of an office guillotine.

As she busied herself, Mrs Monk asked the regulation questions demanded of good-mannered small talk and listened to the
answers with just the right amount of polite attentiveness. Had
Mrs Campion – it was 'Campion' wasn't it? – known the
Sandymans long? Barely twenty-four hours; but her husband and
Torquil Sandyman were old school friends and they were visiting
to offer moral support (and free child-minding, Perdita added
silently) in the current circumstances. Had Mrs Campion been
to Gapton before? No, she had not, but the Sandyman children
had been helping her explore, and she had received a potted
lecture on the place thanks to being met from the train by the
sisters Mister.

Mrs Monk furrowed her brow at that, as if she had never heard
the expression before, until realization dawned. 'You must mean
Hyacinth,' she said firmly. And when Perdita nodded, she
continued, choosing her words carefully: 'Miss Hyacinth is one
of the great characters of Gapton.'

'She said you were the most mysterious,' Perdita said with a
smile.

'I value my privacy,' said Mrs Monk, concentrating on the
dexterity always required when a teapot, a tea strainer and cups
are involved, 'and that, to an old Englishwoman of Hyacinth's
class and breeding, makes me mysterious. Because I mind my
own business rather than other people's and also because I do
not own a dog or a cat or a horse – though I have no room for
a horse and I don't think that one can technically *own* a cat – I
do not enter Hyacinth's sphere of influence. As far as she is
concerned, I am beyond the pale.'

Perdita thought that a rather enigmatic statement and one of
which Mrs Monk clearly did not expect to be contradicted. Not
that there was any opportunity to do so for it was time for children and cake to collide.

Not for the first time in their short acquaintance did Perdita
notice that the twins were far better behaved when in front of
adults other than their parents and when anywhere except at home
at The Maltings. Like Mrs Monk, she had perched on the edge

of a badly stuffed armchair so that she was in position to launch herself, or at least a rescuing hand, to intercept spillages or broken crockery as the Sandyman brood knelt on a synthetic fleece rug and enjoyed their repast picnic-style.

'The children are well-behaved with you,' observed Mrs Monk.

'I was just thinking the same of you,' acknowledged Perdita with a smile. 'Do you have any of your own?'

Mrs Monk met Perdita's eyes but not her smile. 'The circumstances were never appropriate for me,' the older woman said vaguely. 'What about yourself?'

'My husband and I have talked about a family, but we have no immediate plans until we see how my career develops.'

'So you are a career woman? That is good. I hope it is a fulfilling one.'

'Well, it's certainly not a stable one,' Perdita laughed. 'You see, I'm an actress.'

Perdita had become accustomed to a range of reactions when she admitted, under oath, to new acquaintances that she was an actress, ranging from joyous exclamations of pleasure and good-humoured envy, to sneering disgust and sympathetic pity. But never could she remember getting absolutely no reaction at all, for Mrs Monk remained rigidly straight-faced, staring at the cup and saucer she held balanced on her clenched knees. It was a long half-minute before she spoke.

'The children seem to have finished. Let's take them into the garden where they can see the water and the boats. They like the boats.'

It was only as Mrs Monk rose from her chair that Perdita realized that the faint tinkling sound she was hearing came from the cup rattling in the saucer which the tall woman held in her violently shaking hands.

The small garden at the rear of Samphire Cottage led directly down a slight slope to the muddy bank of the lagoon and, to Perdita's relief, was protected by a low flint wall big enough to contain young children. Little Beatrice, she knew, had to be restrained in open spaces and the safest way to do that was to pick her up and carry her on her left hip, where the toddler seemed comfortable enough as she burbled and gurgled sweet nothings on marzipan-scented breath into Perdita's face. She was sure, however, that Victoria Sandyman had advised her about one of the twins and the proximity of water, but both boys seemed content to lean on the flint wall, pointing and commenting on the boats moored along the lagoon from The Butt and Oyster to their left and almost as far as they eye could see on such a grey afternoon away to the right to where the lagoon narrowed and met the sea.

Unlike the twins, Perdita showed no interest in the lines of stationary vessels, as her eyeline was firmly fixed on the hypnotically impressive sandbank that was Gapton Spit, the geographical quirk which, technically, prevented Samphire Cottage from having a sea view.

'It must be beautiful here, in the summer,' Perdita said wistfully.

'It is beautiful all year round to me,' replied Mrs Monk, who checked to be sure the twins were preoccupied before continuing. 'Vibeke always said it reminded her of home.'

'In Denmark?'

'Yes, she said it was just like the Jutland coast where her family had a holiday home.'

'You were close to Vibeke?'

'I knew her and we got on well together, but "close"? I can't say I have ever been "close" to anyone in my life.'

Perdita felt a twinge of sympathy for the woman who, profiled against a dull, overcast sky, leaning on the sharp flint wall, was looking particularly gaunt and exuding loneliness. Had she not been so oddly dressed, she could have been the model for an especially severe ship's figurehead.

'Did you know her boyfriend, Frank Tate?'

'I met Francis two – perhaps three – times, when he came to Gapton to see Vibeke.'

'What did you think of him?'

'Nothing. What should it matter what I thought of him? Vibeke liked him very much and he was besotted with her; that was clear to see. He was always taking photographs of the poor girl. I felt quite sorry for her but she seemed to like the attention and that was all that mattered.'

Perdita checked on the position of the twins, who were still busy arguing about boats, before she said: 'Do you think it possible that Vibeke had an argument with Frank Tate and she . . .?'

'Well, something caused her to disappear. Perhaps they had a row and she has run home to her father.' Mrs Monk shrugged her angular shoulders dismissively.

'On foot? After bashing her boyfriend's brains out?'

'I would think that highly unlikely but not impossible, for people do strange things when they are in love.'

'And Vibeke was definitely in love?'

Again the shoulders moved more expressively than the face. 'Who can be sure, except her? I am a terrible judge of human emotions and the last person to ask.'

'What a dreadful thing to say!' exclaimed Perdita. 'I'm sure you are being far too harsh on yourself.'

Mrs Monk did not reply and turned away to stare out over the lagoon with her chin jutted out and face upturned, soaking in the damp salty air as a sunbather would strain for a better tan.

'I like the wildness of this place,' the tall woman said at last.

'I like the fact that there are no crowds. Some days the only living thing I see is my fox who lives over there on the beach.'

'Your fox?' Perdita asked, resigned to the fact that the subject had, most firmly, been changed.

'A vixen appropriately enough, though of course she is not really mine. She trots the length of the Spit almost every day; hunting, I suppose. Perhaps she has cubs to feed. The birdwatchers hate her and say she disturbs the wildlife, but it's the helicopters which frighten the birds the most.'

'Helicopters?' Perdita asked automatically, her eyes drawn to the Spit across the lagoon as if either foxes or helicopters, or perhaps both, would appear at Dorothy Monk's bidding.

'When the army comes they come by helicopter. It's quite a sight and the whole population turns out to watch,' said Mrs Monk staring unblinking out towards the dunes.

'What on earth is the army doing out on the Spit?'

'No one knows, but it is their land so they can do what they want.'

'Do they have a base there?'

'Not since the war, when there was a radio station or something there, but they held on to the land and for the last nine months or so there have been helicopters landing and taking off. Always on the seaward side, over the dunes, just out of sight so no one in Gapton can see what they do,' Mrs Monk said dreamily.

'It must drive the locals mad with curiosity,' observed Perdita, still scanning the sandy false horizon.

'The "locals", as you call them, are remarkably *un*curious about most things, but I have not lived here long enough to be classed as one of them. *I* am curious, just as I was curious when I saw the lights out there on the Spit at night.'

'Lights? I'm sorry, I don't follow. I thought the Spit was uninhabited.'

'It is, that's why I was curious, but I definitely saw lights out there – moving lights – late at night on two occasions.'

'Did you see them on Saturday night, when Vibeke . . .?'

'Oh, no, I'm talking about a month ago or perhaps more.'

'And did you report them?'

Mrs Monk's expression changed for the first time, as if a dark cloud had settled on her brow. 'Why should I draw attention to myself? If I saw them, others must have, but as I said, Gapton is a most uncurious place. In any case, who would I report it to? The police or the newspapers? I distrust one and despise the other.'

Perdita studied the profile of the tall woman, whose gaze was fixed immovably on the grassy sand dunes across the flat lagoon and oddly, for an actress who had never once in her career to date required a prompt, could not think of a single thing to say.

They were halfway back to The Maltings, entering the High Street from the Hard with Beatrice fast asleep in the pushchair, when Jasper – or possibly George – added to her confusion.

'Don't you speak the secret language, then?' asked the twin with the seriousness which comes naturally to a four-year-old-going-on-forty schoolboy.

'What secret language is that, my darling?'

'The language Vibeke and Mrs Monk spoke when we visited and they didn't want us to hear what they were saying,' said the twin earnestly, like a prosecuting counsel presenting evidence.

'They were probably just being grown-ups,' sighed Perdita wearily.

'No, they were talking for real, it wasn't made up like Mummy and Daddy do sometimes. Dotty said they all talked like that where she came from,' said one of the twins.

'It's called Danish – what they were speaking – and Vibeke said she spoke it all the time with her Daddy,' said the other.

'It sounded funny,' added his brother.

'Now that's really interesting, George.'

'I'm Jasper,' said the boy.

'And so you should be,' said Perdita graciously.

Victoria Sandyman's smiling face was positively aglow as she welcomed Perdita back to The Maltings. At first, Perdita put it down to the fact that she returned all three children and all seemingly intact, but it soon became clear that Mrs Sandyman had *news*.

'I had Lady Amanda on the phone not five minutes ago!' she gushed before the twins had taken off their overcoats.

'Amanda? My mother-in-law?'

'Yes, *Lady* Amanda.'

'Was she checking up on Rupert?'

'She seemed to be checking up on you, or at least asking how you were. I said you'd ring her back as soon as you got in. You will tell her that we'd love her to visit us here in Gapton . . . when things have quietened down that is. I could organize a little party one weekend. There are lots of interesting people who would like to meet her, you know.'

Perdita, who was well aware of the charisma of the Fitton name in Suffolk, had no doubts there were. 'Actually, your children have just introduced me to a very interesting Gapton resident: Dorothy Monk.'

Mrs Sandyman looked surprised, then concerned. 'Did she talk about Vibeke in front of the boys?' she asked quietly.

'Only briefly, and very discreetly,' Perdita reassured her. 'Were they close?'

'She was Vibeke's only friend here in Gapton and despite the difference in their ages they seemed to enjoy each other's company. I suppose it was the language thing.'

'They spoke Danish together, I believe,' said Perdita casually.

'Well, they would; the two of them being Danish.'

'I didn't realize Mrs Monk was also Danish.'

Victoria took pity on her young, and clearly ignorant, house guest. 'Well, it stands to reason, doesn't it? I mean it's not as if anyone who *isn't* Danish would speak Danish, is it? It's not like French or German, which come in handy when abroad, or even Italian which is often useful at the opera.'

'How peculiar that Vibeke managed to find another Dane living in Gapton,' Perdita said innocently.

'Hyacinth thought it amusing. She called them her "tame Vikings", but it's hardly peculiar. It was through Vibeke's father that Dortë Munk – that's her Danish name I believe – came here in the first place ten years ago.'

'Vibeke's father? The ambassador?'

'Well, of course he wasn't Ambassador then, but he and Torquil's father knew each other during the war, I think, and always kept in touch. The story is that he asked Pa-in-Law Bernard if he knew of any vacant property up here on the coast which might suit a respectable middle-aged lady with a taste for privacy. Hyacinth and Marigold had acquired quite a few properties during the war, including Samphire Cottage and the last tenant had just died. The sisters didn't want to sell, but they were happy to rent and Mrs Monk has been there ever since.'

'Did Vibeke know her before she came to au pair for you?'

'I don't know. Vibeke would have been no more than eight when Mrs Monk came to Gapton but her father might have mentioned her. Count Westergaard is an absolutely charming man by all accounts. Have you met him?'

'No, but my pa-in-law has – and so has my ma-in-law, who I'm supposed to telephone, am I not?'

'Use the phone in the hall, dear,' urged Mrs Sandyman, who then joined the children in their play room which would still be in listening range. Fortunately for Perdita, and unfortunately for Victoria, the Sandyman boys had been well-schooled in manners and George – or perhaps Jasper – thoughtfully closed the door to allow her some privacy.

She dialled the number of the Campion family home and the lady of the house answered almost immediately, upon which

Perdita found herself being asked to give an assurance on oath that she was not being misused by her wayward husband as an unpaid policewoman, a stalking horse or a bloodhound.

Perdita allowed herself a throaty laugh into the receiver. 'You have a rather strange view of your son, Amanda!'

'You forget, my dear,' soothed Lady Amanda down the line, 'I've been married to his father for almost thirty years and I know what a bad influence he can be. Seriously, though, is there any news?'

'Not so far,' Perdita said cautiously, 'and I'm afraid this is a situation where no news is not good news. The search parties are still out scouring the countryside but there is an opinion here that if she turns up it will be in London.'

'The implication being that she's on the run because . . .'

'Exactly, though I find it hard to believe. By all accounts she was madly in love with this Tate chap.'

'All accounts, eh? Have you been snooping, Perdita? Are my husband's bad habits spreading to you as well as our son and heir-to-not-very-much?'

'I am gathering intelligence by a sort of osmosis. It comes with the job.'

'The job?' Down a telephone line, Perdita thought, Amanda could definitely make a fist of playing Lady Bracknell.

'Well, I've sort of been dragooned into taking on Vibeke's duties as an unpaid child-minder while we're staying here.'

'You poor thing. Albert will be appalled. When he was your age he was absolutely terrified of children. How many chicks are there in the Sandyman coop?'

'Three, but the baby's no trouble and the twin boys' – Perdita registered a sharp intake of breath in her ear – 'are polite and well-behaved. It was the children who got me an introduction to Gapton's most mysterious resident, a Mrs Monk who turns out to be Danish as well as Vibeke's friend, and she settled in Gapton – years ago – thanks to some favours being called in by Vibeke's father.'

'Interesting, but does it have anything to do with the girl's disappearance?'

'I can't see how it can,' admitted Perdita, 'but Mrs Monk – or Dortë Munk, as I'm told is her real name – is certainly odd. I doubt she has many visitors, doesn't own a television and almost turned into a pillar of salt when I mentioned I was an actress. She dresses as if dowdy was the latest style, doesn't wear make-up and lives alone in a seedy little cottage which is clean enough but absolutely devoid of any personal touches. I suspect the wallpaper is the same as it was in 1959, there are no paintings on the wall, no ornaments on the shelves, just a few books, and not a single photograph anywhere.'

'You appear to have made a study of the woman,' Amanda said drily.

'Do you know,' Perdita confessed, 'I had no idea I was noticing all those things when I was with her. I thought I had been concentrating on her, as she's quite a striking woman, almost enigmatic somehow – could be a real beauty with a bit of effort, I would think. But she's strange; really strange. And another thing: there wasn't a single mirror in her house. I didn't go into the bathroom or the bedrooms, mind you, so that might not be terribly important after all. Am I rambling?'

'Completely, my dear, but it is rather endearing, although I don't like the way you seem to be taking to this snooping lark. I know it's a family trait, but you don't have to go along with it. How is Young Sexton Blake getting on, anyway?'

'I haven't seen Rupert since breakfast. He was soaking up the local colour this morning and I think the plan was for him to join one of the search parties this afternoon.'

'Leaving you to babysit.'

'Oh, I don't mind really. But that reminds me: Victoria Sandyman made me promise to tell you that you are welcome any time here in Gapton. I've got a feeling she's already pencilled you in on her social calendar.'

There was a moment of silence on the line.

'I'll report everything you've said to Albert, who sees himself as some sort of Mission Control, pulling strings from his Bottle Street hidey-hole,' said Lady Amanda, 'and we'll see if we can't take Mrs Sandyman up on her offer of hospitality. An autumnal sea breeze might do Albert good.'

'I thought you didn't approve of his "adventuring"?'

'At his age he ought to know better, though he clearly doesn't.

I suppose I'll have to come with him to make sure he doesn't get up to any mischief.'

Mission Control, as his wife called it, did not appear to be the hub of activity, though a casual observer – a passing street sweeper or a suspicious traffic warden, for example – might have been slightly curious at the number of visitors to a certain door in Bottle Street throughout that afternoon. Not all the callers were men, though all were of a certain age and all, at least from a distance, were respectably turned out. A very close observer might have noticed that some of the men wore sports jackets desperately in need of dry-cleaning over shirts spotted with ciga-rette burn holes and ties flecked with tomato ketchup or worse, and that several of the ladies who called were perhaps a little unsteady on their high heels. Had it not been the entrance to a private residence and had there not been a former police station virtually on the doorstep, the procession of visitors might have been mistaken for patrons of a licensed betting office intent on following that day's race card.

Not that any of the motley crew who pressed the Bottle Street doorbell actually made it across the threshold. They were met by either a tall, thin, bespectacled, silver-haired gentleman or a balding, wide slab of a man, were listened to and then dismissed. All of them departed clutching pound or ten-shilling notes, and a select few also received a brace of the new fifty-pence pieces which they regarded with suspicion and contempt in equal measure.

'I make it that three out of eight of your Dean Street Irregulars earned their corn,' said Mr Campion, pacing the living room, 'which is not a bad rate of return, I suppose, given the time we had for recruitment and training.'

'What d'you mean "we"?' spluttered Lugg. 'It was me who signed that lot up.'

'Dare I ask how you found them? Put a personal ad in *Horse and Hound*, did you?'

'Cheek!' huffed Lugg. 'I couldn't let yer go back into Soho, could I? I mean, there might be a high kerb or a crack in the pavement and yer could fall to your death. So I braved life and limb and hung around The York Minster – or what we h'afficiondos

call "The French"– at opening time and nobbled some of the reg'lars on their way in. Told 'em there was a bob or two in it if they asked about yer photographer friend among the clientele of those shady clubs you mentioned. The Green Dahlia, The Maltese Cross and Tortuga Bay or whatever it was.'

'And amazingly, three of them came up with something useful, or at least interesting.'

'You reckon?' Lugg's moon face widened in surprise. 'I didn't fink we got much for our money.'

'What do you mean "our" money?' Campion scowled over his spectacles.

Lugg raised his hands in surrender. 'Point taken. If you're poorer but wiser then that's a result, but I can't see it meself.'

Campion sighed loudly. 'That's because, old fruit, when you hear of somebody behaving suspiciously or illegally it just doesn't register as unusual. Our three most useful informants all reported that Frank Tate was a known frequenter of said shady premises, but not as a customer. He seems to have been that rare bird, a man who takes drink *into* a drinking club and then leaves withou having a drink.'

'Yus, I'd call that suspicious behaviour,' Lugg agreed sagel

'One of your Soho spies actually called him "The Vodka Man He was delivering bottles of Polish vodka to regular custome – clubs which were quite happy to pay cash for them. A cour of bottles here, a couple there, easily explained away if he w caught in possession.'

Lugg nodded his giant head. 'Earned himself a nice bi pocket money, I suspec'.'

'I would think so. No excise duty, no income tax – and it in with some of the things in his flat.' Campion stopped pa and performed a slight bow with a flourish of his arm. 'It l like young Frank Tate was a bit of a smuggler.'

'Wot? As in "brandy for the parson and 'baccy for the cle

Mr Campion feigned surprise. 'I had forgotten you ha perfect voice for declaiming good old Kipling. You kno course, how his poem continues?'

'You're going to tell me, ain't you?'

'Naturally. It goes: "Brandy for the Parson, 'baccy f Clerk. Laces for a lady; letters for a spy."'

'And does that get us anywhere?'

'I don't know,' Campion said slowly. 'It might just be a muddying of waters which are already pretty murky. We need to do some serious thinking, and by "we" I mean, of course, me. You should return to more menial duties, I think.'

The telephone rang, preventing a quivering Lugg from the riposte clearly frothing up inside his domed brain.

'Such as answering the phone,' said Campion sweetly. 'And if it should be my wife worrying about me, be a good egg and tell her I am absolutely fine and fit as a fiddle and I've just popped out to Evensong or something.'

Lugg bit his tongue and settled for a withering stare before scooping up the receiver and jamming it into the side of his face in one swift, violent movement. 'Good h'afternoon,' he said in sepulchral tones into the instrument, but his voice melted almost instantly. 'Why, hello, Lady Amanda, it's always lovely to hear your voice.'

Then, shooting a vengeful and totally malicious glare at Mr Campion, he said, 'Why of course, he's right here dying to talk to you. The bleeding's almost stopped and the bruises will fade eventually . . . I'll hand you over . . .'

TWELVE
Night Exercise

As darkness began to fall over the North Sea, a small freighter bearing the registration of a Baltic port but flying no national flag altered course towards the East Anglian coast.

'If we maintain this speed,' said the bosun, consulting a chart, 'we'll be at the rendezvous in just under three hours.'

'Good,' answered the captain in the same language. 'When we get near to landfall I'll take the wheel. I want you personally to replace the forward look-out and be sure our passenger makes the transfer without falling in and drowning.'

'Our passenger is going ashore?'

'So he says, but that's none of our business,' said the captain, the stem of a dead pipe rigid between his clenched teeth.

'Will we be doing any of our *usual* business?'

'There's the usual case of *wódka* for our friend but we should not expect any goods from him this time.'

'Pity. My wife was very appreciative after the last trip.'

'And your girlfriend too, I'll bet. Don't make them any promises about future supplies either. I've a feeling this could be our last trip here.'

'Because of our passenger?'

The captain nodded his head in silent agreement, his unlit pipe keeping time like a conductor's baton.'

'Is our British friend expecting our passenger?' the bosun persisted.

'I don't know; that's his problem.'

'Just who is this Dieter character?'

'It's best we don't know, lad, because then he'd be our problem,' said the captain grimly.

Rupert had spent the late afternoon in a pair of borrowed wellington boots searching the fields, copses and ditches of land

ten miles north of Gapton with Torquil Sandyman and a group
of volunteers drawn from the brewery's workforce. As the light
dimmed, whistles were blown and the searchers mustered on the
Lowestoft Road where a tractor with a low flat trailer was waiting
to collect them.

The tractor deposited them at the brewery yard where three
police cars were parked with their headlights on. In the arena of
light they provided was a trestle table in danger of buckling under
the weight of glasses and jugs of beer being served by the sisters
Mister putting all their wartime NAAFI experience into the roles
of ministering angels. There was not enough light to identify the
liquid they were dispensing, but smell and taste confirmed it was
a Sandyman product and Rupert overheard one thirsty searcher
identify it, with satisfaction, as 'a fine glass of mother-in-law'
which he knew was an affectionate term for a mixture of two
ales: Old and Bitter.

This was neither the time nor place, however, to exchange
tasting notes or pleasantries. The overriding mood of the gathering
matched that of the evening, being dark and gloomy, and it was
not lightened when Superintendent Appleyard strode into the
circle of light and took command.

'Ladies,' he began, acknowledging Hyacinth and Marigold,
'and gentlemen, I'd like to thank you all for your efforts and
in particular Mr Sandyman and his father for allowing you
time off work. With your help, we have searched rough ground
and farmland to a radius of ten miles of Gapton. Police in
Lowestoft to the north, Ipswich to the south and west as far
as Diss have all been on high alert and we have had the full
cooperation of the Coast Guard, the railways and the bus and
coach companies.

'There can be little doubt that Miss Westergaard is no longer
in the area and in view of the fact that she is still wanted for
questioning in a murder enquiry, I have no option but to recommend that the hunt be escalated into a national one, with the help
of television, radio and the press.'

Rupert felt a cold tingle on the back of his neck when he
realized that in Appleyard's words, a 'search' had become a
'hunt'.

'It is my opinion,' Appleyard continued unprompted, 'that

Miss Westergaard will be found, either in London or attempting to leave the country, so a watch will be placed on airports and the Channel crossings.'

There was a low, murmured hum as the men in the yard digested this, mostly with resigned nods of acceptance. Rupert, standing close by Torquil Sandyman, noticed that his host was shaking his head quietly in disagreement.

'You don't go along with that?' he whispered.

'She'll have trouble leaving the country without her passport,' Torquil said out of the corner of his mouth. 'It was in the safe in my study at The Maltings until I handed it over to the police along with her handbag and purse.'

Briefly Rupert wondered if there was such a thing as diplomatic immunity for the family of a diplomat, but was distracted by the fact that Appleyard was speaking again.

'In view of the fact that thorough searches of the Gapton area have proved negative, I am calling a halt to this portion of the investigation and so there will be no further calls for volunteers. I thank you for your cooperation and efforts and please enjoy a drink courtesy of Mr Sandyman, though I have to say that if you are driving home, please limit your intake. There are laws about drinking and driving, you know,' he concluded with a prominent wagging of a finger.

If Appleyard had been expecting his captive audience to laugh or applaud, he was disappointed, for the men in the yard responded with only a few quiet groans.

'Typical policeman,' Torquil confided to Rupert, 'never off duty.'

'That's what my father always says, and he knows far more coppers than I do, though I get the impression that Mr Appleyard there was *born* on duty.'

'You might be right,' Torquil answered him with a soft chuckle. 'I suppose we get the policemen we deserve. Come on, let's go back to the house and have some dinner. There's nothing more we can do here unless you want to help the draymen load the drays for tomorrow's deliveries, or volunteer to help Hyacinth wash the glasses.'

Together they strode out of the brewery gate and turned left along the High Street towards The Maltings.

'Are they really giving up looking for Vibeke?' Rupert asked his host as they walked.

'It looks that way. Once Appleyard says something in public he never goes back on it; he's very stubborn.'

'I can think of other words to describe him.'

'I thought it a bit insensitive, making you identify Tate's body. That must have been grim.'

'It was.' Rupert winced at the memory. 'And it was totally unnecessary. The police had Tate's wallet with his driving licence, and his passport funnily enough, they'd been drying out in a tray. He must have had them in his jacket when he went in the lagoon. Appleyard didn't really need me to identify the body; he was just getting back at my father through me for some sleight he thinks he suffered.'

'He's certainly the sort of man to hold a grudge, but that's being rather petty, isn't it?'

'Yes, it damn well was petty. What was the point? The people who found the body said it was Frank Tate, the local Bobby said it was Frank Tate, the landlord of the pub where he stayed said it was Frank Tate and to top it all he was carrying Frank Tate's driving licence and Frank Tate's passport, with his picture in it. I actually sneaked a look at it: British Passport Number 1111924.'

'I say, that's jolly impressive.'

'What is?'

'Your Memory Man act remembering that number; comes from having to learn lines, I suppose.'

'I suppose it must, I hadn't remembered that I'd remembered it, if you see what I mean.'

Rupert stopped in his tracks and put out an arm to rein in his old school friend. 'Hang on,' he said, his tongue between his teeth in concentration, 'I've just remembered something I should have remembered.'

'It's probably the Sandyman ale, old boy. It catches up on you if you're not used to it.'

'No, it's not that,' Rupert insisted. 'I've just remembered that Tate's wallet was found on his body – and back there, in the brewery, you remembered that you had handed in Vibeke's purse and handbag.'

'So?'

'So if she's run away to London or points beyond, she's done so without any money. Frank Tate might have been murdered, but he wasn't robbed.'

'Steady on, old chap. Where are you going with all this?'

'Well,' Rupert drew a deep breath and attempted to marshal his confusion, 'if we couldn't find Vibeke by scouring the country-side and she had neither transport nor money with her, what happened to her?'

Torquil lowered his voice, almost in reverence. 'She could have chucked herself into the sea after . . . well, you know . . .'

'Or . . .' said Rupert, taking a firm grip on his friend's arm, '. . . she might still be here in Gapton.'

Any speculation over dinner on search parties, policemen or the plight of Vibeke Westergaard was strictly forbidden by Victoria Sandyman, who declared herself utterly exhausted by having had to bathe and put the children to bed by herself and then assemble a dinner of cold cuts and baked potatoes. As she listed her trials and tribulations, she pointedly avoided looking at Perdita who, totally unconcerned, was sedulously slathering butter into a bisected King Edward.

It was not until the Campions insisted that they do the washing up – an offer gratefully received by Torquil, who had 'paperwork' to do in his study, and Victoria, who had a television programme she really had to watch – that they had the opportunity, in the privacy of the Sandymans' kitchen, to compare progress reports.

'I spoke to my father at lunchtime,' Rupert began, piling dishes into the ample butler's sink, 'on the phone from the pub. There's been no sign of Vibeke in London and I should think he's had his ear to the ground, but he did give me a few ideas.'

'That sounds dangerous,' said his wife, preparing to dry as Rupert washed.

'Well, more food for thought really, but I'll have to ring him again and tell him the local search has been called off. I'm not sure we can be of much more help here, not that we've been much so far.'

'You speak for yourself,' Perdita said casually. '*I've* been *very* helpful as a stand-in au pair. In fact, your mother was rather worried I was being used as a bit of a skivvy.'

'Mother?'

'Yes, we had a chat this afternoon. She was very interested in my description of Gapton's mystery woman – oh, and she did mention you in passing.'

'What mystery woman?'

'Dorothy Monk, Vibeke's one and only friend in Gapton, and she's Danish too. Strange woman. Lives on her own in a cottage which looks out on to the Spit, where she sees foxes and lights in the night.'

Rupert, up to his elbows in lemon-scented washing up bubbles, looked at his wife and raised an eyebrow in what he called, as part of his theatrical repertoire, his 'caddish quizzical pose'. 'Tell me about her.'

Torquil Sandyman said it was hardly a nice night for a stroll around the lagoon to show Perdita 'the lights of Gapton' but if Rupert insisted on going he could provide duffle coats and torches and, if the rain threatened by the weather forecast did come in off the sea, they could always run for shelter in The Butt and Oyster. Victoria Sandyman, having checked that all the plates, dishes and cutlery that needed washing had in fact been washed and that the kitchen was in a presentable state, had no objection and offered to leave the front door unlocked as she deserved an early night and her full eight hours 'beauty sleep'.

Out in the cool night air which smelled of approaching rain, their torch beams making ghostly shapes of the sandy lumps and spiky grass as they scuffed along the path which bordered Mussett's Farm, Perdita was not sure their excursion had been a good idea.

'Remind me, husband mine. Just what are we doing here?'

'We're going snooping on Gapton Spit,' her husband said confidently.

'At night?'

'I don't want anyone to see us snooping.'

'And just why are we snooping? Or should I be asking what are we snooping for?'

'Foxes . . . lights in the night . . . Vibeke Westergaard? Who knows? All I know is that a lot of people keep a keen eye on the Spit, so there must be something to see out here.'

'That's deliciously vague, darling – or do I mean irritatingly vague?'

'I'm sorry, my love, but I can't explain it any better. The Spit has started to bug me. There are those two birdwatchers from the houseboat watching it. Your new best friend, Mrs Monk, watches the fox there and sees mysterious lights. Stanley at the pub has a ringside view of it. The sisters Mister walk their dog out here every day. That strange old man Mussett from the farm spotted us this morning before we'd been out here two minutes. Yet with all those eyes trained on the Spit, nobody sees – or hears for that matter – Frank Tate and Vibeke ride out here on a motorbike on Saturday night, or what happened between them.'

'Or happened *to* them,' Perdita observed. 'But it was dark.'

'Just like now,' Rupert said as if he had just had a flash of inspiration, which in fact he had. 'Humour me, darling; I've just thought of an experiment we could do.'

'Experiment?' said Perdita suspiciously.

'If only to prove a negative . . . Look, you nip back round the path and go down to the Hard by The Butt and Oyster. When you've got a clear view over the lagoon, signal me with your torch. You could use Morse code.'

'I could, if I knew any.'

'You could do P for Perdita, that's dot, dash, dash, dot.'

'How on earth do you know that?'

'Boy Scouts, I'm afraid.'

'You kept that quiet. Can't I just do a circular twirling motion, like when you have sparklers on Bonfire Night?'

'That would be fine as a signal.'

'So what will you be doing? Pretending to be a motorbike? Promise me you won't make *vroom-vroom* noises.'

'I won't go that far,' Rupert said, hoping that blushing could not be seen by torchlight, 'but I will run around a bit and use my torch as a headlight. All you have to do is keep me in sight, or more importantly, notice if I drop out of your sight line. It might tell us something about what happened last Saturday night.'

'I'm not convinced it will and I warn you, if I get cold and bored, I'm heading straight for the Lounge Bar. I do not have any female reservations about women going into public houses alone.'

Rupert bent his face to kiss his wife on the end of her pretty, if icily cold, nose. 'Take care on the path, darling, and don't fall in the lagoon.'

'Don't you either.' Perdita blew him a return kiss.

'Don't worry,' Rupert laughed, 'I won't.'

'Frank Tate did.'

Perdita trudged around the curve of the lagoon, one hand flicking the beam of her torch at the path in front of her, the other clutching the hood of her borrowed duffle coat to her throat. She felt faintly ridiculous and she just knew Rupert would appear ridiculous running about pretending to be a motorcycle, but then they had both done ridiculous things in the service of the god of theatre Dionysus. Still, Dionysus was also the deity responsible for wine and revelry, so Perdita reassured herself that if she got too bored, she would be entirely justified in going to the pub.

Rupert, determined to execute his role to the best of his imagination once he had given his wife a head start, also followed the path back towards Gapton, keeping the lights of The Butt and Oyster in sight, but concentrating on the patch of darkness alongside it, which he estimated was the Hard. When he was eventually rewarded by a small light being waved in a large 'O', he went into his act.

Clutching his torch to his chest, which he estimated to be headlight height, he ran back along the path, veering from side to side and often off the path and into the dunes to create the impression of a machine in motion. At least that was the impression he was aiming for. He was sure Perdita would review his performance under a sub-heading of 'An idiot running at night' or similar.

He stumbled from the path more than once and had to kick his boots free of the sand. On those occasions the beam of the torch he was clutching stabbed in multiple directions which Rupert felt only added to the accuracy of his impersonation of a powerful motorbike bouncing over rough terrain.

Breathing heavily, he realized he was approaching the area where the dunes grew high on either side of the path. That morning, walking the dog with Hyacinth Mister, it had reminded him of a desert landscape: a wadi, with the man-made path representing a dried-up river bed. Now in the dark, illuminated only by erratic flicks of torchlight, the piles of soft sand became a hard, cold, very alien moonscape and bizarrely, Rupert was oddly comforted when he saw the forbidding wire barricade ahead of him and its less than welcoming Ministry of Defence sign telling him to Keep Out.

He could see the lights of The Butt and Oyster again, across the dark mirror of the lagoon and working on the assumption that Perdita would have a clear line of sight he turned his torch off, counted to five, then turned it on again and holding it at arm's length made a wide circular motion. To his great relief – though he was not quite sure why he was so relieved – he saw the same light circle being returned from across the water and at almost exactly the same moment, he heard the engine.

There must have been a change in the direction of the onshore wind, Rupert reasoned. His ears had become so accustomed to the muffled rolling hum of the sea beyond the dunes that another, intrusive, note surprised him. The sound was the regular diesel throb of a marine engine, which did not surprise him as he stood on a sandy peninsular with one docile body of salt water on one side and the entire North Sea on the other. As he could see out over the empty lagoon, he deduced that whatever the engine was powering, it was powering it on the seaward side of the Spit and it was definitely getting nearer.

Intrigued, Rupert trotted along the line of the high wire fence and up the rise of the dunes, a vague childhood memory of the thrill of scampering along a deserted beach mingling with the effort of running uphill through damp sand in rubber boots. At the summit of the highest dune he paused and with the salty tang of the sea in his face, he screwed up his eyes and tried to locate the source of the rhythmic throbbing noise but could see nothing except the dark, glassy surface of the sea flecked with white waves. If it was a boat, it had passed the point where the Ministry of Defence fence extended off the Spit and into the sea, presumably held in place by metal stanchions similar to those at the lagoon end which had snagged the floating body of Frank Tate, and must be heading roughly southwards parallel to the Spit.

Except that it wasn't heading anywhere, Rupert realized, because the sound of its engine had suddenly stopped. Whatever the craft was, it had either sunk like a stone or it had berthed somewhere along the Spit – a strip of sand and grass where, to the best of Rupert's knowledge, there was no natural harbour or landing place.

In frustration, Rupert clawed at the wire mesh of the fence and cursed the dark dunes on the other side which rose even higher, blocking his view. Not that he could realistically have seen much at night, but a boat would surely be running with lights and it suddenly felt very important for him to see them.

He stumbled back down the dune, his left hand brushing against the fence to keep his balance, until his feet hit the path and his torch showed him he was directly under the sign telling him to Keep Out. Taking the warning for an invitation, he thrust his torch into a pocket and hooked his fingers into the cold metal of the wire mesh. Heaving himself up, his wellington-ed toes scrabbling for purchase, he used the sign kindly provided by the Ministry of Defence first as a grab-hold and then, straining upward, as a foothold. Although the wire fence swayed under his weight, the sign remained solid and allowed Rupert to stand on it on one leg providing enough of a platform for him to lie over the top strand of wire, which to his relief was neither barbed nor electrified.

Using his midriff as a fulcrum, in the 'lazy vault' way he had seen many a middle-aged farmer by-pass a five-bar gate without the effort of opening it, he swung his legs up and over the top wire and then released his grip. Only as he let go did he think that it would have been wise to use his torch to check his landing ground for obstacles. Fortune, however, favours the foolish as well as the brave, and Rupert landed on a cushion of soft sand, for which he allowed himself a moment of self-congratulation before realizing that his precious Ministry of Defence foothold was now on the inconvenient side of the wire, and that a return vault over the fence might require a rather long and sturdy pole. He would, however, jump that fence when he came to it.

He began to climb the steep dune which sheltered him from the sea, moving diagonally and clutching at clumps of sharp, spiky marram grass to pull himself higher. Panting with exertion, he reached the summit of his personal sand mountain only to find that another peak, even higher, blocked his view down the

Spit. With a sigh of resignation he set off at a stumbling run, leaning back to stop himself pitching face-first down one slope and then he was straining upwards, the muscles in his calves reminding him most urgently that they were not happy with this type of exertion.

At the top of the second dune he flung himself down, his arms embracing a clump of especially sharp grass, and flexed his legs and feet in an attempt to dislodge the sand which had accumulated inside his boots.

From this vantage point, Rupert now had a view of the seaward edge of the Spit, or as much of it as he could make out in the dark, but nowhere could he see the lights of the passing vessel whose engines he had heard quite distinctly. Turning his face away from the sea, he concentrated on the Spit itself and considered whether the next dune in line might offer a better vantage point.

It was some minutes before Rupert realized that what he was looking at was not actually a natural sand dune but a regular geometric shape, definitely man-made, against which sand had drifted. What had Hyacinth said about buildings on the Spit? 'Remnants and remains' she'd called them, presumably the remains of the wartime Huff-Duff station. But if they were the remains of wartime military buildings, he knew that could involve sharp-edged concrete, protruding steel rods and rusty barbed wire at the very least; a minefield or a slit trench to ensnare the unwary at worst. If he strained his eyes in the dark he could imagine other regular shapes – a pill box or a tank trap, perhaps? It was not a terrain to explore blind.

Rupert pulled out his torch and clicked it on, then struggled upright and began to slide, stumbling down the slope towards the sea.

'There's somebody out there with a light.'

'You said the place was uninhabited.'

'It is, it's been deserted since the war,' said the man wearing oilskins. 'That's why I stash my supplies there.'

He hefted the wooden box he was holding and the bottles in it clinked together almost musically.

'I am not in the slightest interested in your petty criminality,' said his companion, a man of medium height but stocky frame encased in a seaman's thick wool pea coat, whose accent suggested that it originated on the other side of the North Sea. 'Get us out of here.'

'Look, whoever's out there has no business to be there,' said the man in oilskins. 'If he saw me he'd probably run a mile.'

'Being seen is the problem,' said the other man, planting his feet firm and wide against the swelling movement of the boat and slowly tugging an ugly but undoubtedly efficient automatic pistol from the pocket of his pea coat. 'Now start the engine and get us away from here.'

'Steady on, Dieter,' said the man in the oilskins, the box he was holding now shaking and rattling of its own accord. 'We're not carrying anything worth killing for.'

'Oh, yes, we are. Me.'

THIRTEEN
Not Single Spies

Perdita had obeyed orders. She had made her stupid signal and had noted her husband's Boy Scout response. Then she had seen, across the dark lagoon, the erratic beam of Rupert's torch thrust and parry along the path which led out to the Spit. At times the beam disappeared completely, then reappeared pointing into the night sky or sometimes directly downwards. When she saw Rupert's circular signal, she allowed herself a sigh of relief, then plunged her hands deep into her coat pockets and settled down to wait, leaning against the weather-boarding of Grundy's shop. She only hoped the exercise made more sense to Rupert – bless him – than it did to her.

After five minutes of twitching and stamping her feet to keep warm while growing increasingly envious of the happy customers she could see through the windows of The Butt and Oyster, Perdita spotted, briefly, the faint, flickering beam of Rupert's torch out on the Spit. And that was the point. It was out on the Spit, not tracing the path back around the edge of the lagoon to where a dutiful wife was waiting outside a public house like a jilted girlfriend.

What did the stupid boy – curse him – think he was doing?

Rupert halted his ungainly downhill rush down one dune by the simple expedient of running headlong into another. His fumbling hands confirmed his suspicions that this dune was at least in part made of concrete rather than sand and that he was standing behind the one remaining wall of a small building.

Cautiously, with his shoulder pressed against this solid support, he inched his way along, his torch beam seeking an edge and locating the corner, turning it to find himself facing the dark swollen sea, so close that he could feel fine salty spray on his face. The beam of his torch showed him a pebble beach lapped by small, white waves less than twenty feet away and, further out, a dark shape bobbing on the dark water.

It took Rupert's brain several seconds to realize he was looking at a small cabin cruiser, seemingly deserted, moored prow on to the beach. He trained his torch on to the vessel's bow and discerned that a long plank had been run off the bow and into the water, resting at an angle of forty-five degrees, providing a simple if precarious gangway for anyone leaving or boarding the boat assuming they did not mind getting their feet wet for the last two or three steps on to the Spit.

His torch was not powerful enough to give him any more details of the silent craft but starved of facts, his brain fed on fancy. There was a boat, there was a beach. What if someone had walked that gangplank and was now on the Spit, behind him?

Rupert turned on his heels and swung his torch in an erratic arc, illuminating sand, grass and the partial skeletons of more ruined buildings. It was purely by chance that he saw, out of the corner of his eye, a small spark in the dark – a cigarette lighter being clicked into life? – from the direction of the boat.

It was a full second, perhaps two, before his brain registered the muffled *crack* and another two, perhaps three, before he realized he was being shot at.

Across the Spit and across the lagoon, hunkered down inside the folds of her coat, Perdita bit into her bottom lip to stop herself cursing her husband out loud. For several minutes, though it seemed like hours, she had seen no shards of light from the Spit and had even made another circular signal with her torch, though answer came there none.

She considered shouting into the dark but doubted the sound would carry over the water and across the Spit, and in any case she had spotted a rowing boat pulling out on to the lagoon for the Gapton bank below The Butt and Oyster. She could not identify the dinghy's two passengers but had no intention of making a fool of herself in front of them. Any despairing wail from her in her current location would surely make her appear like the pathetic child left outside the pub with a packet of crisps and a bottle of pop while Mum and Dad were inside in the warmth, having a good time. She regretted her *braggadocio*, when she had told Rupert that she had no qualms about entering a public house alone, for she was a victim of her class and a self-consciously decent upbringing and it simply was not true. Added to which, she was a stranger in Gapton and, as an attractive if not modest young woman, she would attract even more attention. Plus – and this was possibly the clinching factor – she had left her purse back at The Maltings and though she had once, in Rep, convincingly asked if there was 'a sailor willing to buy a girl a drink' she had no intention of using the line in real life.

Stamping her feet to fire up her circulation, she decided that her wayward Boy Scout of a husband had been allowed out to play far too long and deserved to be chastised and put to bed without any supper. She set off with grim determination to find him, scold him and drag him home by his ear right now, however much he was enjoying himself.

Later – much later – Rupert would congratulate himself on his quick thinking and catlike reflexes, and would tell anyone who asked, and often those who did not, that he realized immediately that his assailant was actually shooting at the light he was waving. This was why he had thrown his torch one way as a diversion while diving for cover in the opposite direction, thus avoiding a hail of bullets.

In fact, there had been only one shot and he had honestly no idea where it had gone, and he had not so much flung his torch as dropped it like a hot iron and then sought strategic cover by tripping over his own wellington-booted feet and landing face first in the sand.

As he spat sand from his mouth and cautiously wiped sand from his eyelids and eyebrows, his ears – one of the few senses he had left in working order – registered the bass notes of a diesel engine being fired up. Rolling over so that he lay supine in the sand, he raised his head slightly and by parting his feet to splay them out in the 'ten-to-two' position, he was able to look down the length of his body. It was not the most dignified of positions but, he comforted himself, it was one which offered little in the way of easy targets.

Through the 'V' formed by his boot, which made him think

uncomfortably of a gun sight, he could see the boat as well as hear it. With a revving of its engine, the stubby silhouette pulled back from the beach, leaving its gangplank to splash down into the surf. It then turned in reverse through ninety degrees and chugged off southwards, running parallel to the Spit. Within half a minute the night had swallowed it completely, but Rupert waited until the noise volume of the engine had dropped several notches before he risked getting to his feet.

At no time had he seen anyone on the boat and there was nothing, with the possible exception of an abandoned gangplank somewhere among the waves, to prove it had ever been there. Similarly, there was nothing except a spent bullet somewhere among the millions of pebbles and tons of sand to prove he had been shot at; if indeed he had. Rupert was feeling distinctly light-headed and quite happy to believe he was dreaming all this.

He picked up his torch and a perfunctory sweep illuminated, as he had suspected, the remnants of rudimentary brick and reinforced concrete buildings half-buried, as the entrances to Egyptian tombs always were in films, in the sand. Only one structure was identifiable, a hexagonal wartime pill box with dark gun slits and an even darker entrance hole which seemed impenetrable to Rupert's torch beam. Not that he had any intention of playing Howard Carter and venturing any deeper into this ghostly realm.

What Rupert needed was firm ground under his feet and the light and warmth of human contact. Satisfied that the mysterious boat and its murderous but invisible crew were out of range if not out of mind, he put his back to the sea and strode inland – as far as the Spit could be considered as land – working on the theory that from the dunes which formed the central spine of the Spit, he would be able to see the lights of Gapton and from there take his bearings.

His geography and his navigation were both accurate and, as he breasted the summit of the dunes which formed the spine of the Spit, he could see the lights of Gapton and, slightly to his right, the un-curtained bay windows of what had to be The Butt and Oyster. Perdita was probably in there in the warmth, sipping a whisky mac (or a 'Whisky Macdonald' as his father always insisted), although she might, stubbornly, be still waiting for him on the Hard in an increasingly filthy temper.

The least he could do, thought Rupert, was make the circular signal to show her he was still in one piece. He clambered on to the very peak of the dune and extended his arm and torch, but he had made only one complete revolution before two shadowy figures rose up from the other side of the dune and began to lay about him with extreme violence.

Stunned and frightened, his feet slipping in the loose sand beneath him, Rupert sank to his knees under the onslaught of fists and something harder and colder that was being pushed into his cheek. He had lost his torch again and the two men pummelling him were determined to keep his head and face pressed down. Bizarrely, memories of being underneath a collapsing scrum during a particularly spiteful rugby match with a rival school came to mind, but there he had tasted mud and grass and now his mouth was filled with sand.

He felt a knee pressing on his shoulder and fingers clawing at his hair, pulling his head up and back, allowing him a close look at one of his attackers. At first he thought he was staring into the face of one of the great apes, though not one of the human species, but then his befuddled brain, clogged as it was with messages of pain from his chest, his scalp, his kidneys and a dozen other places, registered that he was looking at a man wearing a balaclava.

And then the balaclava spoke. 'Welcome to England,' it said, just before a dark cloth bag was pulled over Rupert's head and the night sky disappeared.

Rupert felt himself rolled on to his back, his upper body restrained but his feet allowed to scrabble uselessly for purchase in the slipping sand beneath him. He spat at the fabric of the hood, which was being held in place over his face by a hand at his throat, and felt the first icy tendrils of real fear as the cloth became damp and then wet around his nose and mouth.

Who was it who had once told him that if you can smell the sweet, cleaning-fluid scent of chloroform, then you are inhaling a dangerous dosage?

Lugg, that was who – it had been Lugg in a mood to share some of the arcane knowledge he had acquired during his colourful career and, blast the old rogue, he had been absolutely right.

Head down and giving her husband a good piece of her mind under her breath, Perdita strode up the High Street until she could turn back on to the path to the Spit for the second time that evening. She gripped her torch uncomfortably tightly as the path curved into the larger dunes, muffling sound and casting ghostly shadows in the corner of her eye. More than once she hefted the torch, taking comfort in its weight and solidity as a weapon. If her darling husband was playing hide-and-seek with her and planning to jump out of the dark and scare her, then she was quite prepared to bop him right between the eyes.

On the part of the path which formed a canyon between the largest dunes, she had the sudden chilling conviction that she was not alone on the Spit and mentally comforted herself that of course she wasn't – Rupert was here somewhere. Where else could he have gone?

She was sure there were eyes on her, yet also convinced that that would be exactly what a young woman more used to the theatrical jungle of cities and provincial towns would imagine if alone, at night, out in the real wild. Yet she could not shake the feeling and realized that she had put her tongue behind her teeth and was whistling softly, a ritual she always performed in the moments before she stepped out on to a stage. The tune she had unconsciously chosen was the long chorus to a recent Beatles' hit, which for all its dirge-like qualities always boosted her spirits, though not always those of fellow actors waiting in the wings.

The height of the dunes isolated her completely. She could see neither the Gapton lagoon to her right nor the sea which she knew to be over to her left. Perhaps most unnerving of all was the muffler-effect the sand dunes had, which reduced the night to an unnatural silence.

Perdita was quite relieved when the beam of her torch picked out the hanging grid of the Ministry of Defence's wire fence. Here at least was something she recognized, and as the dunes were lower she was offered the reassuring sight of the lights of The Butt and Oyster in the distance across the glassy expanse of water.

For a moment she thought she heard a noise from the lagoon
– a deep thump, followed by a splash – and she started to swing
her torch to her right towards the water.

It was then that she saw the pair of ghostly eyes watching her.
Eyes that were shining unnaturally brightly and which were
luminous, spectral and green.

'For God's sake, be careful with him, you clumsy sod!' hissed the
man who went by the name of Carruthers.

'He's heavier than he looks,' replied the man called Smith
through a black balaclava which had slipped over his mouth so
that it muffled his voice.

'He'll be a damn sight heavier if he falls in the water.'

'It's me who has the wet boots, not him. I don't see why we
had to drug him. He's just a dead weight now.'

'You think he would have come quietly? If this is who we
think it is, he's one of their top operators and therefore extremely
dangerous.'

'You have your pistol.'

'Better a dead weight than just dead. Now push us off this
mud and see if you can get aboard without falling in again. I'll
row. Oh, and do try and keep your feet off our guest, there's a
good chap.'

It was a fox.

It was probably the famous fox of Gapton Spit, and it was
staring through the wire fence at Perdita from a distance of less
than ten feet.

Whether it was a dog or a vixen, she had no idea. Whether it
was big for a fox, Perdita could not judge. Was it dangerous?
She doubted it, but she had no intention of offering to stroke it
and the fox seemed quite happy with that arrangement.

Did the fox have supernatural powers? For a moment, Perdita
was convinced it did, as the animal had somehow materialized
on her side of the wire mesh. By holding her torch steady
and concentrating the beam at the base of the fence, Perdita
discovered a small depression in the sand and the key to the fox's
magic trick. The Ministry of Defence had clearly not buried
its fence deep enough to prevent this cunning predator from

tunnelling into and out of what by default had become both a wildfowl preserve and a convenient larder.

The fox seemed untroubled by the light from Perdita's torch and it appeared to see through the beam, examining and assessing the intrusive human who had disturbed its nightly patrol. Although Perdita could not in truth discern any such expression, she imagined the fox had given her the sort of look a cat would during a reprimand for sharpening its claws on a valued piece of furniture; the sort of look which said, with impunity, 'what business is this of yours?' And then, in a dark blur, the beast was off into the dunes, leaving Perdita only a fleeting glimpse of a bushy tail and a trail of scuffed paw prints in the sand.

Perdita remembered to breathe again, but on the whole found herself heartened rather than frightened by her nocturnal encounter. It would be something to tell Rupert if she ever found him, or consented to speak to him again. If he was not prepared to be where he was supposed to be, Perdita saw no point in waiting around forlornly like some model for a Victorian 'Home from the Sea' watercolour.

Oddly, given that the fox had disappeared from sight, Perdita was sure she could *smell* it. Perhaps the light evening breeze had shifted direction, but she was definitely not imagining it.

Wasn't one of the foxy genders supposed to be especially rank? Was it the dog or the vixen? It would almost certainly be the male, she decided, though she had no idea where she had acquired that particular nugget of natural history. Yes, it was a distinctly musky scent, very masculine. The closest Perdita's olfactory memory could get to it was of old, hardbacked books which had been read and re-read by an enthusiastic pipe-smoker with an aversion to ventilation.

'You shouldn't be here,' said the smell.

Perdita screamed.

'Is he secure?'

'I've tied his hands and feet so tight he'd have to do Alexander's trick with the Gordian knot to get free, but I don't see why we couldn't use handcuffs. Much less effort.'

'And what if someone had come on board and found pairs of handcuffs lying around a houseboat used by two birdwatchers?

We stay in character and we use only what does not arouse suspicion.'

'Thank God we didn't get many visitors then, or they might have spotted the pistols, the bottles of chloroform and radio equipment which wouldn't look out of place on a nuclear submarine but might seem a touch surplus to requirements for a canal longboat which doesn't move more than six inches from its moorings unless there's a neap tide.'

'You really can be an old woman when you want to,' said the man who called himself Carruthers. 'Now stop your moaning. I'll get the cylinder and we'll give him a whiff of oxygen. You get the hood off him.'

'Can I take mine off?' The man who went by the name of Smith tugged at his balaclava.

'No, we'll leave them on. It will disorientate him; maybe even scare him into telling us what his mission was.'

'Really? I thought he was supposed to be one of their top men, tough as nails, impervious to pain, all that rot. Anyway, weren't we supposed to report in to London as soon as we made contact?'

'It's a question,' Carruthers stated pompously, 'of making the most complete report we can. That way we impress our lords and masters.'

'I'm not so sure about that. Mr Deighton's orders were quite clear to me: this was a watching brief only.'

'So we've shown a bit of initiative and the big prize has just fallen into our lap. We should make the most of it – of him. So let's get him talking.'

They had laid the trussed-up Rupert out on a narrow bunk and as Smith removed the hood from his head, Carruthers held a plastic mouthpiece connected by a short pipe to a small, red gas canister to his mouth.

'A couple of squirts of O_2 will bring him round good as new.'

He was in the process of turning the screw valve on the cylinder when a loud thumping noise sounded above his head – the noise of something large landing on the deck of the houseboat – resulting in two pairs of eyes staring at each other from balaclava-framed faces.

'What the hell was that?'

'Have we hit something?'

'We're not moving, you idiot! We've been boarded!'

Both balaclava-ed heads turned towards the narrow double doors at the end of the long, low cabin and slowly both men straightened up. On the bunk, Rupert groaned softly behind the oxygen mask but his abductors ignored him, concentrating instead on the approaching sounds of footsteps on the deck above their heads.

The man whose name was not really Carruthers lifted his dark blue fisherman's sweater and pulled a snub-nosed revolver from the waistband of his trousers.

'What the hell are you doing?' hissed the man who was not called Smith in an angry whisper. 'Are you trying to make this look even more incriminating than it does already?'

'Oh, grow up, you stupid man,' his companion hissed back. 'Who do you suppose that is on deck? The milkman? The vicar dropping in for tea and toast? If it's some local tart you've invited back to see your etchings, you've picked a really bad night for it.'

And then the bad night got worse as the double doors to the cabin were wrenched open with such force that the hinges squealed in protest and the doorway was filled by a khaki-clad figure so large it seemed impossible that he could squeeze into the cabin without bursting the hull's wooden planking.

He was wearing a military uniform – complete with hobnail boots, gaiters and peaked cap – which identified him as a sergeant in the military police, and it would be a brave man who questioned that identity.

'Good evening, gentlemen,' said the massive uniform.

'Stay where you are. Don't come any nearer,' said the man not just holding the pistol but pointing it, rather shakily, at the intruder.

'You must be Carruthers,' said the giant military policeman reasonably, 'and if that gun is loaded, then put it away carefully or be prepared to have it removed surgically. I'm never at my best when people point guns at me. Oh, and you might as well take off that stupid ski mask. It's far too late to worry about being compromised.'

'Compromised? What the hell are you—'

The huge figure seemed to cover the distance between the cabin entrance and the gun with supernatural speed and without a sound. Suddenly the gun was pressed up against a khaki blouson and seemed in danger of melting into it, becoming part of the uniform.

'I won't tell you again about the gun, Mr Carruthers. Either you lower it or I make you eat it.'

The pistol barrel slid limply down the khaki frame it was supposed to be threatening until it was pointed loosely at the deck.

'That's a good gentleman,' said the MP, whose large square face twitched a smile as he seemed to notice the supine Rupert for the first time. 'I do hope you haven't damaged your guest. That wouldn't look good on my report. Chloroform, was it? Hmm . . . a bit basic but effective if you know what you're doing, which I doubt very much.'

The second man, who had remained silent until now, stripped off his balaclava almost as if it was burning his skin.

'Now look here, *Sergeant*,' he sneered, 'you have no idea who he is and you'd better show us some credentials before we say another word.'

The bear-like soldier planted his boots wide apart and placed his bunched fists on his hips so that his elbows seemed as if they touched the sides of the hull. It was as if the small wall lights in the cabin had dimmed of their own accord, perhaps in fear.

'I happen to know exactly who your guest is, but do you? His name is Campion, does that ring any bells? It should ring bloody great Big Ben-sized bells. This is the son, Rupert, and a couple of weeks ago I spent a few days trudging round Soho making sure he didn't clock me. He didn't, because I'm very good at not getting noticed, which you might think surprising for a man of my size. Then again, you might not think that because not getting noticed is something you two twerps are not very good at. My name's Milton, by the way. You can call me *Mister* Milton. This uniform's borrowed and I'm not really a sergeant, just as you're not Carruthers and Smith.'

The big man threw back his shoulders and chuckled loudly, his red-banded peaked cap – the Redcap's red cap – threatening to wobble free of his head.

'Why did you have to come up with such daft names? I mean, that was kids' stuff. Two English public schoolboy types on a boat called the *Dulcibella* . . . I guess you just couldn't resist the reference to *The Riddle of the Sands*, could you? So one of you had to be "Carruthers" but the other couldn't be "Davies" like in the book, because one of the people you're supposed to be keeping an eye on here is Davies, the local copper. So you made it Carruthers and Smith.' Mr Milton snorted in disgust. 'Why didn't you just call yourselves Butch Cassidy and the Sundance Kid? You were bound to be rumbled by somebody with a few brain cells, and believe me the senior Mr Campion has many more than a few.'

A blushing Carruthers pointed towards the inert, bound figure on the bunk, seemingly unaware that he was still holding a pistol.

'But he's not Campion Senior, is he? He's not the Campion who lectured us during induction training.'

'I told you,' said Mr Milton, exhaling wearily, 'but you just don't listen, do you? This is Campion's son who only arrived here yesterday, but had you two clocked by lunchtime today. He rang his old man and the old man rang Mr Deighton and asked why a couple of schoolboys were playing *Riddle of the Sands* down in Gapton. I think the words "this year's Cambridge entrants" were used, but not in a nice way, if you follow. Mr Deighton pulled me in and told me to get down here and throw a bucket of cold water over you two before you made any more of an exhibition of yourselves. You were supposed to be inconspicuous, or didn't you understand that bit of the brief?'

'You don't exactly blend in to the local fauna in that uniform,' said Smith bravely.

'That's where you're wrong, sonny. I trained it up to Colchester and got kitted out at the garrison there – well, the Glasshouse, to be precise. That's where I borrowed this uniform and the military police Land Rover that's parked down the road a bit. Everyone round here knows that Gapton Spit is military property and there's been a murder here, so a member of the military who is also a policeman isn't going to raise many eyebrows, I reckon. And if anybody was to ask, my story would be verified by the army. I doubt yours would be by the Royal Society for Bird Spotting or whatever it's called.'

'You're bluffing,' said Carruthers, puffing out his chest. 'I don't believe our cover's been blown at all.'

The man in uniform inflated his own chest far more impressively. 'Oh, you've been noticed all right,' said Mr Milton, and then his eyes flicked to the pistol dangling from Carruthers' hand, 'and do put that gun away somewhere safe. Don't make me take it off you; that would just disrupt my train of thought. As I was saying, you'd been noticed. Mr Deighton was a bit upset to hear, second-hand, that you'd been spotted by the Campions. He'll be mortified when I tell him I saw you row out in your little dinghy, ambush poor Mr Rupert here, put a bag on his head and truss him up like a chicken.'

'You couldn't have!'

'Not without a little technical help, I admit, but my army chums supplied me with a night-vision scope, a useful bit of kit that. It's called Starlight and of course it's American and they use them out in Vietnam. It gave me a ringside view of you two clowns rowing out to that sand bank to play Cowboys and Indians. Trouble is you kidnapped the wrong Injun. You nobbled Tonto when you should have been ambushing Crazy Horse.'

'You mean he's on our side?' asked Smith, pointing at Rupert as if his body had just materialized on the bunk.

'You're not as stupid as you look, sonny.' Mr Milton turned to scowl at Carruthers. 'But *you* must be, because you haven't got that gun out of my sight yet.'

Carruthers needed no further warnings. From a side cupboard in the galley area of the cabin he produced a square biscuit tin, dropped his pistol inside with a metallic clunk and pressed the lid back.

'That's better,' said Milton soothingly. 'Now I don't have to worry about accidental discharges and you don't have to worry about where the nearest hospital is.'

'There's no need to be rude, old boy,' Carruthers said sulkily.

'Oh, I'm not even warmed up yet, my lad. Now get young Mr Campion untied and give him a whiff of that oxygen. Gently now, let him come round gently. I'm told he's staying somewhere called The Maltings. Know it?'

'Into Gapton and follow the High Street, it's the only road,' Smith said, eager to be of help. 'The brewery is on the left and

The Maltings is about a quarter of a mile further on, on the right. Big house, set back, with a horseshoe drive.'

'I'll find it. Now, has Mr Campion got all his possessions about him?'

Milton's question was answered with blank looks.

'Documents, wallet, money, concealed suicide pill, that sort of thing.' He paused, considered the inane expressions facing him then shook his head. 'You didn't even search him, did you? Bloody amateurs.'

'What are you going to do?'

'I'm going to take him to his bed or at least as far as his front door and then zip back to Colchester to await orders.'

'What about us?' Carruthers pulled the last loose length of rope from under Rupert's body.

'I suggest you two keep your heads down and get back to birdwatching until you hear different – now budge over.'

Milton gently shouldered Carruthers out of his way so that he could lean over Rupert and slip one arm under his back and one under his knees. He straightened up, lifting his burden like an elongated baby, with ease.

'This is the second Campion I've carried this week,' he said, more to himself than the two onlookers, 'and this one's got a bit of meat on him. His old man was as light as a feather.'

'You shouldn't be here. You've no right.'

If Perdita had been startled by the voice, she was physically jolted when the torch beam showed her its owner. Her first thought was that it wasn't human but then she began to breathe again and realized that it was and the curiosity before her had not in fact escaped from a travelling circus. Her second thought, a more rational one, was that she had mentally used the words 'it' and 'curiosity' in a way she ought to be ashamed of, for the figure which had startled her was clearly human – a wizened old man, smaller than she, who spoke with a Suffolk accent – and surely no danger to her. On third thought, that dark brown wizened face did look angry and more twisted with fury than age, and that face was getting nearer and nearer to hers.

Instinctively she took a step backwards and then another and then two more hurried ones as if engaged in a dancing lesson without music. The figure closed in, aping her steps as if leading the bizarre foxtrot. He was so close now that Perdita could have leaned forward and kissed him on the forehead, though that thought did not so much cross her mind as bounce off it like a stone skimmed on water for her senses were overwhelmed by the sheer stench coming off the man. His clothes, his hair, even his skin seemed to reek of smoke, of fish, even of meat. It was an unholy perfume, brewed in a cauldron somewhere hellish.

As the menacing voice said, 'You shouldn't be here' again, Perdita felt herself gagging with fear. Involuntarily she jumped backwards away from her dance partner, only vaguely conscious that she had by now been backed up against the wire mesh fence.

Realization came with pain.

Her left foot landed on firm sand but her right leg seemed to give way into nothing as her booted foot sank into the hole the Gapton fox used as its personal entrance tunnel on to the Spit. She sank awkwardly and felt the ankle twist but another, sharper, shock distracted her. She fell with her back against the fence, and as she slid down it, a broken but very sharp length of regulation strength Ministry of Defence wire penetrated her coat and stabbed her in the right shoulder.

Perdita howled. Perdita sobbed. She could not move her foot and her shoulder was on fire. She was alone, at night, in an uninhabited dunescape, skewered to a wire fence; except she wasn't alone.

'Oi said you shouldn't be here!'

Perdita screamed now, an unthinking, animal scream of frustration and pain as she was now convinced that her attacker – and she was by now convinced beyond a scintilla of doubt that the figure meant her harm – had her at his complete mercy.

And mercy came, but not in ways she could have imagined.

Her first piercing howl had stopped her would-be assailant in his tracks. At her second full-lunged scream (which, she thought later with pride, would have sent shivers down the spines of an audience at the back of the Gods), her demon had smacked the palms of his hands against his ears and emitted a low keening noise of his own, though Perdita, maintaining her own high-volume emissions, failed to notice as she was distracted by yet another frantic animal noise.

This sound was an earthly one – that at least penetrated Perdita's confused thought process – a dog barking, and for no rational reason she assumed that help had arrived.

She had somehow kept a grip on her torch with her right hand and despite the burning pain in her shoulder she raised its beam so that she saw the face of her tormentor, framed by the hands clasped to his ears, twisted in agony.

Perdita did not move; she could not. She was transfixed by a metal spear to the fence and her right foot dangled uselessly in a fox hole in the sand. She could not even summon the breath to scream again, but then she realized that other people were screaming and that the satanic figure illuminated by her shaking torch beam was clasping a long and writhing creature to his chest.

'Down, Dido, down!'

The wriggling composite split into two entities as her assailant repelled his own assailant by hurling the squirming dog to the ground, and then he himself disappeared out of her poorly guided spotlight.

'Sit, Dido! Stay!'

Suddenly there was more light, which was just as well, as Perdita's efforts as a follow-spot operator would have earned her a reprimand from the most amateur director in amateur dramatics.

'My heavens!' gasped Hyacinth Mister.

'Good God!' agreed her sister Marigold, then added: 'What the devil have you done to yourself, Mrs Campion?'

Perdita composed several witty, if not biting, responses and then decided, purely for dramatic effect, to faint instead.

The sisters Mister had coped with emergencies many times before and their roll of honour could have included the recapture of a bolting dray horse, the repair of a burst boiler in the brewhouse, maintaining morale on the Home Front in a pair of World Wars, the storm surge and floods of 1953, the unmasking of a tenant licensee prone to pilfering and the arrest and conviction of numerous poachers, litter-louts and dangerous motorists. They took the rescue of Perdita in their stride, though Hyacinth would always insist on sharing the credit with Dido.

Perdita's faint lasted only a few seconds and she was dreamily

aware of two pairs of elderly hands helping her off the wire and
out of the fox hole. She heard Hyacinth bemoan the fact that she
no longer carried smelling salts with her at all times (as her
mother had advised) and Marigold scoff at the suggestion and
say it was a jolly good thing that she always carried something
far more efficacious. Perdita felt a cold and metallic taste on her
lips and then her mouth filled with a fiery liquid which warmed
her stomach and made her forget the pain in her shoulder the
way only a well-aged cognac could.

Once Perdita was back on her feet, albeit unsteadily, Marigold
took a secretive swig from her silver hip flask before snapping
the top back in place while Hyacinth re-attached Dido to her
lead. The sisters then took up guard positions port and starboard
in support and began to guide Perdita back to the path, using
their own torches to light the way.

'Where is . . . that . . . man?' Perdita managed to ask.

'Don't worry about Eppy Mussett, my dear,' said Marigold,
heaving Perdita's right arm across her shoulders and taking her
weight. 'He's quite barmy and a bit scary if you're not used to
him, but the dog saw him off.'

'That's my brave Dido,' Hyacinth agreed. 'But I don't like the
way Eppy's been behaving lately. We should call the police and
tell Sergeant Davies.'

'What? Davies of Dock Green?' scoffed her sister. 'He's about
as much use as a chocolate teapot.'

'I just want to get home – to the Sandymans – have a hot bath
and go to bed,' said Perdita, adding to herself that she would
quite like to know where her husband was as well.

'We'll get you to The Maltings, dear, just lean on us,' said
Hyacinth, 'but if you change your mind after a nice bath, just
ring the police house. It's Gapton 289. Can you remember that?'

'I'll remember,' said Perdita, hobbling along in step with her
two supporters and thinking: *I'll remember because I might have
to ring the police and report myself for murdering the husband
who left me stranded!*

'Is there any more brandy?' she asked.

The three women, arm in arm, staggered up Gapton High Street
with only the dog on her lead to spoil the outline of a small

string of cut-out paper dolls. The trio encountered no other pedestrians and only one vehicle, a Land Rover which passed them at speed going in the same direction. They were so intent on keeping their balance, not to mention their dignity, that they hardly noticed, except to screw up their eyes against the oncoming headlights, that the same Land Rover passed them travelling in the opposite direction only a few minutes later.

As they limped into the horseshoe drive leading to The Maltings, Hyacinth said comfortingly, 'Almost home, dear.'

Exterior porch lights had been left on, making the front door and porch an obvious target for the three linked women staggering as one to aim for. It seemed, though, that they were not the only moths drawn to that particular flame that night.

'There's somebody lying across the doorway,' Marigold observed casually, 'and I think they're drunk.'

'I think *they're* my husband!' squealed Perdita, lunging forward, dragging her human stabilizers with her. 'Rupert!'

The figure in the porch struggled to his feet, swayed and stumbled forward just as Perdita broke free of the two sisters, almost tripped over Dido and hopped on her good leg towards her husband. They were still six feet apart when they both spoke, saying in perfect unison: 'You won't believe the evening I've had.'

FOURTEEN
Air Cavalry

'It was my old mess-mate, Lugg,' said Mr Campion, 'who gave me the priceless advice that one should never go on holiday anywhere the local population looked up in wonderment when an aeroplane went over.'

Bernard Sandyman arched an eyebrow. His moustache bristled under its own steam.

'I hope you're not casting aspersions on the good folk of Gapton, Campion. That sort of attitude doesn't sit well with us country bumpkins, though I dare say quite a few local heads were turned upwards at your rather flamboyant arrival. Was the helicopter absolutely necessary?'

Both men turned their heads to look back across the paddock, over which they had just walked, to where the dull blue-green machine in question rested, its rotor blades almost stationary now, its turbines sobbing rather than roaring, looking for all the world like a large metallic insect getting its breath back.

'They're splendid things, aren't they? I really must get one of my own,' enthused Mr Campion.

'Don't be ridiculous, Albert,' chided his wife. She swung a BOAC flight bag over her shoulder and linked arms with her husband. 'You can't even rub your tummy and pat your head at the same time. You'd never have the coordination to fly a helicopter.'

'Oh, I'd insist on a chauffeur.'

'Pilot. They're called pilots.'

'Does your pilot require bed and board?' asked Bernard Sandyman, remembering his duties as host.

'Timothy?' said Amanda, turning to give the helicopter a regal wave. 'No, he'll be heading back towards St Albans once he's worked out his route. I only borrowed him for the morning.'

'Must be nice to be able to whistle up a whirlybird like that,

Campion,' Sandyman said with genuine envy. 'Even if it does frighten the locals.'

'But not the locals that matter,' said Mr Campion. 'Timothy had specific orders not to fly his little mosquito over the brewery stables and startle the horses.'

'I told you, it's not a mosquito, it's a Wasp, a Westland Wasp,' Amanda corrected him, 'and technically it's not Timothy's, it belongs to the Royal Navy, but when it's not carrying homing torpedoes, my company services and repairs it and that includes regular test flights.'

'Ah yes, I remember now, you're in the aircraft business,' said Sandyman. 'Your chappie Lugg, the Beadle at Brewers' Hall, he told me you were in "hairy nautical h'engineering" as I recall.'

'He would,' sniffed Amanda scornfully.

'Oh, yes, he insisted you were the brains of the family as well as the . . . looks, I think he put it.'

'I always said he was very astute,' warmed Amanda.

'We were lucky that this morning's test flight just happened to be in the direction of Gapton.' Mr Campion smiled inanely, which seemed to perturb Bernard Sandyman even more than having, at very short notice, a helicopter land in his back garden.

'How convenient,' he said with a hint of suspicion, then the tone of his voice changed to nervous. 'I suppose Torquil, or rather Victoria, is expecting you? Since Torquil's mother died I've kept myself to myself and let Victoria run the house.'

'Victoria did invite us to visit,' Amanda said carefully, 'though I doubt she expected us to take up her kind offer so soon. Of course, we don't want to put her out as she must have a lot on her plate, so we've booked a room at The Butt and Oyster.'

Bernard Sandyman, who had been a widower for several years and clearly trod carefully around his daughter-in-law when it came to household matters, tried but failed to hide his relief. 'Good, good, you'll be comfortable there,' he murmured softly, and then added cheerfully, 'and it's all good for the family business. Still, come into the house and I'll find Victoria for you. I'm afraid Torquil is at the brewery trying to get us back on track. Things have been pretty much up in the air lately.'

'I can imagine,' soothed Amanda.

'And you must be worried about Rupert and Perdita after last

night and the state they were in when they finally made it back,'
Sandyman said conversationally.

'State?' Amanda quizzed him sharply. 'What sort of state were
they in?'

'Dazed and confused, not serious – as we used to say in the
army, but I do wish you'd make Perdita see the local sawbones.'

Amanda turned on her husband like a hawk spotting prey.
'Albert . . .?'

Mr Campion's face quivered briefly with uncertainty then froze
hard and determined as he tightened his grip on the holdall he
was carrying and his pace moved up a gear to the quick march.

Perdita insisted that no one should make a fuss. In fact, if anyone
was entitled to make a fuss, then it should be her and, as she
was an actress, she *knew* how to make a fuss.

Victoria Sandyman, however, was under no such restraints and
was determined to make the maximum fuss of her unexpected
guests, which involved making a considerable effort on her part
– something she would point out in no uncertain terms to her
absent husband when he returned home that evening. It had been
she who had had to wash, dress and breakfast the children without
any help at all, single-handedly prepare a deceptively elaborate
rustic lunch of chicken and leek soup, baked potatoes, bread,
paté and cheese, and even wake Rupert and Perdita with cups of
tea and the news that a helicopter bearing important visitors was
on its way. It had left her with barely an hour to dress and make
herself presentable – no time at all when her guests included a
representative of the Suffolk aristocracy – before the roof tiles
began to rattle under the beat of rotor blades.

As a result of her efforts, noon saw the kitchen of The Maltings
transformed into a self-service restaurant with overtones of a
hospital accident and emergency ward and the Cabinet War Room
with Victoria, dressed for a fashionable cocktail party, presiding
as the perfect hostess with not a hair out of place and that air of
rarefied indifference which came as part of the curriculum of an
expensive finishing school.

Amanda, with an urgent need to inspect her son and daughter-
in-law, ignored Victoria's deferential fawning with a natural
politeness which no finishing school could teach, whatever the

fees. 'What on earth have you two been up to?' she demanded.
'Whatever it was, you'd better have a jolly good explanation, to
which I will listen carefully before I blame your father for
everything.'

At her side, Mr Campion blinked benignly and sighed. 'My
shoulders are broad.'

'You can't blame Dad,' protested Rupert. 'No one could have
seen this coming.'

'I most certainly can blame your father,' said Amanda with
mock severity. 'It's an obligation, nay, a duty, which comes with
decades of marriage. And I am usually proved correct. As Lugg
always says, your father has "previous" in these things.'

'Who is this Lugg?' Victoria Sandyman asked aloud without
quite meaning to.

'He's a retired recidivist with an overinflated sense of useful-
ness and an unfathomable loyalty to my husband,' said Amanda
disinterestedly, preferring to stroke Perdita's hair while examining
her face for signs of trauma.

Bernard Sandyman shuffled his feet and coughed uncomfortably as he always did when he found himself in a situation of
high emotion or in a crowd of more than one female.

'You don't mean Lugg – the chap who's our Beadle at Brewers'
Hall?' he asked uncertainly.

'Of course not,' said Mr Campion, smiling his most disarming
smile, the one usually reserved for disorientated clergymen or
vengeful maiden aunts. 'Different Lugg altogether, though they
may be related. Luggs are, in general, as loyal as bulldogs, which
indeed they resemble slightly. But enough of Luggs and their
slanderous and unsought opinions – answer your mother, Rupert.
What were you two up to last night and why did you leave your
darling Perdita alone and in danger?'

'How did you know that?' asked Rupert in puzzlement rather
than anger. 'Come to think of it, what are you doing here and
so quickly?'

'It was all thanks to my awesomely talented and well-connected
wife, your mother – who is capable of and quite likely to cuff
you around the head unless your explanation satisfies her – who
arranged a helicopter to transport us so we – the cavalry – could
ride to your rescue in style. I believe the American forces have

something called Air Cavalry and today, that's exactly what we are.'

'But how . . . how did you know we needed rescuing? I'm sorry; my head's a bit thick this morning, feels like it's been stuffed with cotton wool.'

'Ah, the old chloroform hangover. You must have had a massive dose but don't worry, a brisk walk in the fresh air along Gapton Spit will clear the furry brain.'

'How the devil do you know about the chloroform and Gapton Spit? I haven't told anyone except Perdita. In fact, I'm not too sure what happened myself, come to that; don't even know how I got back here.'

'You were delivered to the front door by an extremely large gentleman known as Mr Milton, the sort of chap who would feature in a bout of Catch-As-Catch-Can as we used to call it before the dear old London County Council banned it just before the war. I believe it's now called Professional Wrestling and is immensely popular on the television on Saturdays. Anyway, the only thing you really need to know about Mr Milton is that as well as the biceps of an elephant – if elephants do indeed have biceps – he is kind to orphan children and helps frail old gentlemen across the street. In other words, he's on our side and you were, quite literally, in safe hands.'

'But I have no recollection of this Milton chap – no recollection at all,' said Rupert plaintively.

'Don't worry, my dear boy, I'll fill you in on all the gory details when we go for our walk.' Mr Campion's eyes flicked behind his spectacle lenses in a not-in-front-of-the-Sandymans warning. 'Far more important for the moment is what the deuce happened to your lovely wife?'

Perdita did not need a prompt and took up her cue. 'She got tired of waiting for her foolish husband who had disappeared into the night, so she went looking for him. She found a fox instead, got scared half to death and pinned up against a fence by the local bogeyman, rescued by a dog called Dido and then escorted back here by two sisters called the Misses Mister to find errant husband slumped across the doorstep as if he'd been out on the tiles and had a skin-full.'

'My dear child,' soothed Amanda, cupping Perdita's face in

her hands, 'I didn't understand more than a quarter of that, but you've clearly had a shock.'

'She should see a doctor,' growled the elder Mr Sandyman. 'Said so as soon as I heard she was wounded.'

'Wounded?' Amanda instinctively felt Perdita's brow and bent forward to examine the pupils of her eyes.

'It's just a scratch,' said Perdita calmly, taking Amanda's hands in hers, 'on my shoulder, where I fell against that stupid fence out on the Spit. There must have been a piece of wire loose and I managed to stick myself on it. It's nothing, honestly.'

'I'll be the judge of that,' said Amanda, assuming command. 'You'll show it to me right now. Victoria, may we borrow a bathroom?'

'Of course, Lady Amanda, anything – anything at all,' gushed their hostess. 'You can use mine – please come upstairs. I'll show you the way. Should I bring the first aid box?'

Perdita raised her eyebrows and Amanda pursed her lips in return. The mental message which passed between the two women spoke volumes but it was not until they were ensconced in Victoria Sandyman's fragrant and incredibly pink bathroom that Perdita said: 'I really thought she was going to curtsey to you.'

'I'm sure she means well,' said Amanda sweetly. 'Now get that shirt off and let me take a look . . . Oh my goodness, that's not a *scratch*, my dear, unless you encountered a tiger last night.'

'Nothing bigger than a fox,' said the younger woman wincing under the gentle pressure of Amanda's fingertips, 'and he or she was more scared of me than I was of it.'

'Have you looked at this in a mirror?' Amanda stifled a gasp as she saw the black and blue circle with a flaming red core covering most of Perdita's right shoulder blade.

'No.'

'Good, well don't.'

'Rupert went rather pale when he saw it this morning.'

'He was always a squeamish boy, but that's not always a bad thing in a man and you shouldn't try and be so stubbornly brave. I'm afraid it looks as if you've been stabbed with a stiletto or, being less dramatic, a knitting needle. A strand of wire clawed you, you think?'

'From the fence and it didn't claw at me; I sort of impaled myself.'

Perdita twisted her neck to peer over her shoulder.

'Eyes front, my girl,' Amanda ordered. 'It looks quite grue-some, positively X-certificate, and I think Mr Sandyman is quite right about getting a doctor to take a look at it. At the very least you should probably get a tetanus booster and, in the meantime, don't think about wearing any strapless ball gowns.'

'Oh, I wouldn't dream of trying to compete with Victoria in that department,' said Perdita with a sly smile.

'Now, now, Perdita, you don't have to prove that fences are the only things with claws in Gapton. Pull your shirt back on and we'll see if Victoria has some aspirin, or those new tablets, ibuprofen. That's going to hurt before it gets better so you, my girl, are going to take it easy. Put your feet up in front of the fire for the rest of the day and let Victoria mollycoddle you.'

'I doubt she'll do that,' said Perdita, carefully easing the sleeve of her shirt over her shoulder.

'She will if I ask her.'

Without turning around, Perdita knew that Amanda was smiling broadly; and she knew it would be a smile of confidence, not a grin of malice.

Mr Campion had pecked at some bread and cheese more out of politeness than hunger but had insisted that Rupert devour a bowl of soup and a baked potato in order to regain his strength.

'Why do I need my strength?' Rupert asked suspiciously.

'Because, dear boy, you are not only my guide to the nooks and crannies of Gapton, but also my means of propulsion,' said Mr Campion.

'Propulsion?'

'Why yes, you don't expect me at my great age to man the oars and haul away under some bosun's cruel lash, do you? After all, it's getting on for fifty years since I tried out for a Blue at Cambridge, albeit as cox and even then I failed the audition. It seems my feet were too big to fit in the boat and took up the space normally allocated to two of the crew, or so they said. I think it was because I got sea sick. The Cam can be jolly rough when the wind comes off the Fens, you know.'

'Father, please.' Rupert held up the palms of his hands in surrender. 'I'll do whatever you want; just tell me what you're planning to do.'

Mr Campion cut another cube of cheese and speared it on the point of his knife. 'I thought we'd try a spot of smuggling this afternoon, with perhaps just a touch of trespassing.'

'Smuggling? Trespass? In broad daylight? Won't we be seen?'

'I certainly hope so,' said Mr Campion innocently.

Amanda declared her intention to remain at The Maltings to look after Perdita until a doctor could be summoned and offered to help Victoria with the household chores – and weren't there some children somewhere who needed amusing? Victoria naturally protested, though not too much, that Lady Amanda was a guest and scullery work was out of the question. When Lady Amanda politely but very firmly insisted, Victoria did admit that the children had always enjoyed an afternoon walk with Vibeke and that Perdita, during her brief stay, had revived their expectations in that department.

While this female summit was arriving at a peaceful conclusion, Bernard Sandyman remembered that he had books in need of urgent return to the public library in Diss and wondered whether the Campions *pére et fils* fancied a drive through the countryside in 'the old jalopy'. Mr Campion declined the offer, tempting though it was, as he had seen, from the air, Bernard's 'old jalopy' parked in the driveway at the front of the house and, unless he was very much mistaken, it bore a strong resemblance to a 1953 Lagonda drophead coupé, the one with the three-litre engine. Mr Sandyman squirmed with pleasure at Campion's tone of clear approval and muttered, 'Well, any time, dear fellow, any time,' indicating that Mr Campion had risen in his estimation to at least the status of Decent Chap.

Having dismissed a helicopter and spurned a Lagonda, Mr Campion urged his son to join him in a more traditional mode of transport by getting his 'walking boots' on, as he wished to get the lie of the local land from ground level while the light held and deliver his and Amanda's overnight bags to The Butt and Oyster.

'I'm sorry, Dad, I'm still a bit thick-headed. I thought you said we were going rowing?'

'No,' said Mr Campion, 'I think I said *you* would be doing the rowing, but to find our ship we must first go down to the sea.'

'You have a boat here?'

'Of course not. We're going to steal one – well, borrow one. I think we should probably aim to return it in one piece if we can.'

Rupert shook his head in a last grasp at clarity. 'You're seriously proposing theft?'

'I think, technically, it's piracy as we'll be stealing a boat belonging to Her Majesty's government, but it's all in a jolly good cause.'

It was only as the pair were strolling down the Lowestoft Road towards Gapton proper that Mr Campion seriously shared his thoughts with his son.

'Since you rang me with your last situation report, I've been rather busy,' said Mr Campion.

'I haven't exactly been taking it easy, you know,' Rupert said defensively.

'You've been in the wars, and so has your beautiful wife,' said Mr Campion, resting a hand on Rupert's shoulder, 'and it's not your fight, not your fight at all.'

'Whose fight is it then?'

'Do you know, I'm not really sure; well, not yet anyway, but I am putting two-and-two together slowly. At the moment I'm up to about two-and-three-quarters, but your stirrings of the silty waters around Gapton Spit have been very helpful.'

'They have?' said Rupert, stumbling slightly in surprise but taking comfort from the way his father's grip on his shoulder tightened reassuringly.

'Oh, yes, dear chip-off-the-very-old-block. Your telephone call yesterday unearthed a fox for me, so to speak, although not literally. It sounds as if that's Perdita's department. My fox happens to be the late Mr Francis Tate.'

'But he's dead,' protested Rupert. 'I saw his body in the morgue.'

'I know; that's why I said the *late* Mr Tate, but it doesn't mean he's not worth running to earth. Goodness, I didn't mean that to come out like doggerel: late and Tate, worth and earth . . . That sounded dreadfully flippant.'

'That's OK, Pops; I know it's just your way.'

'"Pops?" A man in Soho called me that and we had a bit of a disagreement. I'm not sure I approve of "Pops" at all. It may be a perfectly good sobriquet for an ageing New Orleans cornet player, but someone hoping to be mentioned in a will one day – far, far in the future, I may add – should perhaps use it sparingly.'

'Point taken, *Pater*,' Rupert grinned. 'You were saying – about Tate?'

'Ah, yes, back to my metaphorical fox hunt and the mysterious Mr Tate. Your phone call helped to put me on his scent.'

'It did?'

'It was invaluable, my boy, especially your spectacular feat of memory about his passport number. That put an idle thought in the ball of wool which passes for my brain because I recalled that Ambassador Westergaard had said something about Tate perhaps not being English. As I still have one or two low friends in high places, I telephoned a couple of them and called in some old favours. It appears that Francis Tate was actually born Franciszek Ksawery Tata, and I hope I've pronounced that correctly, as it's quite a few years since I had to pretend to speak Polish.'

'So his passport's a fake?'

'Not at all, absolutely the genuine article, allowing the bearer to pass without let or hindrance – all that sort of stuff. Polish parents, father in the RAF during the war, married and settled here in jolly old Blighty and became naturalized citizens. None of that, of course, is suspicious in itself.'

'But something is?'

'Oh, yes. You see, while you and I – primarily you – were tracking Frank Tate in and out of his earth in Soho on behalf of a concerned father, someone was tracking us. I have to admit I didn't notice at the time as they were rather good at it, professional, you might say. When I did a little bit of investigating on my own, though, I was rather glad someone was stalking us as it turned out to be a very muscular guardian angel called Mr Milton, the very same angel who rescued you last night.'

'How do you know that? I don't even know that!' protested Rupert.

'You were out for the count, my lad, and for once had a perfect excuse for not knowing what was going on. Your rescuer reported to his boss – a man called Elsie for reasons too foolish to go into – and dear old Elsie disrupted my beauty sleep by ringing me around midnight to fill me in on your little adventure. Naturally, your mother insisted on flying to your rescue with as much theatricality as possible, hence the helicopter.'

'Would you mind telling me exactly what my "little adventure" was? It's awfully fuzzy in here.' Rupert slapped the sides of his head with both palms. 'Are you saying I was abducted by foreign agents – *spies*?'

'Dear boy, you were lucky; you were abducted by *our* spies, who are generally reckoned to be far less efficient than foreign ones: top of the class for enthusiasm but regular detentions for incompetence. It was our two birdwatchers on board the *Dulcibella* and they work for Elsie, or perhaps they don't any more. As soon as you told me one was called Carruthers, I picked up their particular scent . . . and talking of scent, would those delicious perfumes wafting towards us indicate that we are near the famous Sandyman brewery?'

'It's right there, just across the road.'

'So it is, and there seems to be some sort of industrial dispute going on,' observed Mr Campion.

'Don't worry,' said Rupert, 'the sisters Mister are there. It won't last long.'

Automatically the two men began to cross the road to the brewery gates, which seemed to be completely blocked by a pair of vehicles locked in a titanic death struggle while totally stationary. On the road side of the gates with its nose pointed into the brewery yard was a small blue car, a Hillman Imp, with the driver's door hanging open and a stream of rhythmic music coming from it. Facing it, inside the gates and pointing out, were the far more impressive (and steaming) noses of two large horses in full harness to a dray loaded to creaking point with casks of beer. Although neither vehicle moved so much as an inch, there was little doubt that a neutral observer with an open telephone line to a reasonable bookmaker could get favourable odds on the horses being able to trample the Hillman into tinfoil if push came to shove.

In the small space between chrome bumper and polished horse brasses were three figures – two dressed in traditional drayman's garb and a young, tousle-haired man wearing a sharply cut Italian suit in a shade of light blue which complemented the paintwork of his car.

As the Campions neared the gates the music from the car got louder, masking the sound of what was clearly a heated argument between the young man and, as Mr Campion realized, the two bowler-hatted dray-*women*.

'Are those . . .?' he began.

'Oh, yes,' sighed Rupert, bravely stepping into the fray to perform the introductions which propriety demanded, even on the battlefield of industrial relations.

'Miss Hyacinth, Miss Marigold, I do hope we're not intruding . . .'

'Of course not, Mr Campion,' simpered Hyacinth. 'We were just about to commence our delivery round. Things have got a bit behind this week, I fear.'

'And this fool Truscott is delaying us even further!' shrilled Marigold, clearly in no mood for peace talks.

The young man in the sharp suit identified himself both as the fool Truscott and the driver of the Hillman.

'I was turning in the gates, slowly and carefully as usual, when these two . . . ladies . . . charged their horses at me. If anyone should be done for dangerous driving, it's them.'

'Then you'll be pleased to know that I have absolutely no intention of arresting anyone,' Mr Campion announced, so making himself the focus of attention, to which he responded by blinking furiously behind his tortoiseshell frames.

'And who are you, squire?' asked the fool Truscott over the throb of music still coming from his car.

'That's Mr Albert Campion,' boomed a new voice as Torquil Sandyman strode across the yard into the fray. 'He and his son are valued and honoured guests of this firm, my house and this town.'

'So now we have two Mr Campions,' said Hyacinth airily. 'Does that mean two Lady Amandas?'

'There can be only one Amanda,' said Mr Campion with a polite bow.

'Ignore my sister,' said Marigold, offering a firm, almost violent, handshake. 'It's for the best.'

'Rupert didn't tell me you were coming,' said Torquil, joining the handshaking queue.

'Rupert didn't know,' said Rupert limply.

'No, you were well out of it last night. Hope you've slept it off. Sorry I wasn't around to meet your rather spectacular arrival, Mr Campion, but we're making up for lost time here at the brewery. Do we really have to talk over that racket, Brian?'

'But it's the Rolling Stones,' pleaded the young man despairingly.

Torquil curbed his temper and remembered his manners. 'I'm sorry, Mr Campion. This uncouth youth is Brian Truscott, who can be a perfect pain in the you-know-what but somehow manages to be the firm's best Free Trade sales representative, so we put up with a lot, but we don't have to put up with his music.'

The fool Truscott, realizing he was now not only outnumbered but outranked, shuffled back to the Hillman with the downcast hang-dog expression which boys naturally perfect as young teenagers and girls adopt a few years later when bored.

As he leaned into the Imp and reached for the dashboard, Mr Campion said: 'That's one of those new eight-track stereo cartridge players, isn't it?'

Brian Truscott's head swivelled around and his expression could not have shown more surprise if Miss Hyacinth had asked him to dance. 'Yeah, it is. How did you know that?'

'My wife described one to me. She saw one last year in America, in a Lear jet of all things, and though I have dropped hints, she has yet to get me one for my car.'

'I wish I'd never let Brian put one in the company's car, it's caused nothing but trouble with some people,' said Torquil, staring pointedly at the sisters Mister, who remained defiant in their aprons and brown bowlers.

'He had the blasted thing turned up so loud we could hear him coming down the street!' Marigold protested. 'We've told him time and time again and he still insists on having that damn racket blaring out.'

'We've told him, it frightens the animals,' added Hyacinth,

though the giant Suffolk Punches behind her continued to look supremely unperturbed.

'So you thought you'd teach him a lesson by blocking the gate?' Torquil shook his head. 'Well, you've made your point, though goodness knows what our guests think of us. Now, let's all get back to work. Brian, back the car up and let the dray get on with its deliveries, then come to the office and we'll plan your calls for next week.' He turned to the sisters. 'Ladies, I believe you have deliveries to make.'

As the Hillman reversed quietly back out on to the Lowestoft Road, Marigold climbed up on to the driver's bench of the dray, but Hyacinth hesitated, then stepped towards Mr Campion as if to impart a confidentiality.

'I'm so sorry you had to see us like this, Mr Campion,' she said softly. 'We don't have anything against young Brian – he's very good at his job; it's his music we can't stand. I mean, those awful Rolling Stones. They're so raucous, aren't they?'

'Oh, I wouldn't be so quick to judge them,' said Mr Campion to Rupert's jaw-dropping amazement. 'When we were his age I'm sure we listened to raucous music; in fact, the more raucous the better if it annoyed our parents. I wouldn't worry about those Rolling Stones. It won't be long before they have to give it up and get proper jobs.'

'But it's played so *loud* it could drive a person to distraction. Just like that horrid, noisy helicopter that flew over earlier. Thoughtless, I call it, downright thoughtless. People who play loud music and fly helicopters shouldn't be allowed.'

FIFTEEN
Barter Economy

As they continued to walk into Gapton, the Campions were overtaken by the Sandyman dray proceeding at a steady pace, the clip-clopping of the horses' hooves giving plenty of advance warning so the pair were ready to flourish the required enthusiastic waving of hands and arms which such noble beasts of burden require and expect.

'They're quite a force of nature, those two,' said Rupert as the dray clattered down the road.

'The horses or the sisters?' quipped Mr Campion.

'Both,' said Rupert, 'and both are throwbacks to a previous age.'

'In that case, so am I,' said Mr Campion, 'and rather proud of it. The sight of a horse-drawn dray resplendent with a cargo of fine Suffolk ale makes me wish dearly that I was wearing a hat so I could raise it. If that makes me a throwback, so be it.'

Rupert glanced at his father suspecting – rightly – that his rather ethereal musings concealed a more serious train of thought.

'You see, it takes a throwback to spot a throwback, and there's a strand to the mystery of Francis Tate which is a definite throwback to a bygone age.'

'But Tate is dead,' argued Rupert, 'and surely we should be concentrating on finding Vibeke Westergaard?'

'You are quite right, dear boy, but I have feeling in these ancient bones of mine that the late Frank Tate holds the key. If we follow his trail, I think it will eventually lead us to Vibeke; I certainly hope it will.'

'And where does the "throwback" come in?'

'Perhaps it's just a minor thing; in fact, I'm sure it was for Mr Tate, but it may have been his downfall. You see, Francis Tate was, among other things, a smuggler; a petty one, but a smuggler nonetheless. Did I ever tell you Lugg's wonderful rule of thumb for discovering whether he was in a smugglers' pub?'

'No, but I'm sure Lugg researched the subject thoroughly.'

Mr Campion smiled in agreement. 'Rest assured; he did. His basic theory is that when visiting a public house anywhere near the flung spray or blown spume of the ocean—'

'Hang on a minute,' Rupert protested, 'that's Masefield, not Lugg.'

'Quite right, but I'm sure Lugg would have appropriated the quotation if he had been caught unawares in a poetic moment. Anyway, the point is that when in a pub on or near the coast, his acid test is always to ask the landlord for either Rum and Shrub or a Brandy and Lovage.'

'You've lost me, Father.'

'Good. One should never outlive one's children, nor ever be outwitted by them. Shrub and Lovage are mildly alcoholic cordials which go back quite a way. In fact, I believe they were the Babycham of the sixteen hundreds. Later on they became invaluable when pernicious taxes made the smuggling of rum and brandy worthwhile and many a Cornish or Devonian fisherman would earn a decent living floating wooden barrels ashore when the tide was high and the moon dark. The thing was those old wooden barrels tended to leakage and the good stuff inside got contaminated with salt water, which wasn't good for sales across the bar down the local Smugglers' Arms until, that is, somebody discovered that saltwater rum tasted better mixed with Shrub and contaminated brandy was quite palatable with Lovage. The taste stuck and the drinks had a life way beyond the smuggling era. In fact, I think all the Shrub and Lovage cordials are made down in the West Country, where they know a smuggler when they see one.'

'And what, pray, does all that have to do with Frank Tate?'

'Very little, probably nothing, because Tate was a very modern smuggler who didn't deal in rum or brandy, or tobacco for parsons and clerks for that matter. He smuggled Polish vodka, or perhaps I should say traded for it with all that ladies' hosiery you saw him buying at Marks and Spencer's Marble Arch emporium. It's perfectly logical.'

'It is?'

'It is if you know that Poland – an unfortunate country in other ways – is very good at producing vodka, and in fact has a surplus of it. On the other hand, it lacks many of the boons of western capitalism which we take for granted, such as fashionable female hosiery. Denim jeans, I believe, are also much valued on what we used to call the Black Market during the war. I'm told that nylon stockings and jeans are the best forms of currency in good old Gdansk these days, and almost certainly worth more than the poor old pound sterling.'

'So you're saying Tate was trading ladies' tights for vodka?'

'Strong, *duty-free* vodka,' Mr Campion observed, 'which made it very attractive to some of the less – shall we say – well-regulated drinking establishments of Soho; establishments of which you and I were totally unaware naturally, but which Lugg could no doubt name in his sleep.'

'It didn't seem to have paid well, as a trade, I mean,' Rupert argued. 'I didn't get the impression that Tate was rolling in cash. It could only have been a side-line for him. He did have a regular job, after all, in that photographic place.'

Mr Campion pursed his lips. 'Have you considered that Tate's day job might also have been a side-line?' he asked enigmatically, but before Rupert could formulate an answer they had turned on to the Hard by Grundy's shop and the weather-beaten façade of The Butt and Oyster and Mr Campion, seeing the water of the lagoon before him, changed tack.

'Where would Tate have acquired his supplies of *wódka*?'

'Off a boat?' Rupert answered. 'That's the smugglers' traditional method, isn't it?'

'Correct, but specifically from a *Polish* freighter. Hence his frequent visits to Gapton.'

Rupert pointed accusingly towards the lagoon. 'But no boats of any size dock here anymore, Dad. Look at it; it's a marina, not a harbour. It's good only for small sailing craft and I doubt many of them could make it across to the Baltic.'

'Well observed, Young Sherlock, but as usual I have the advantage over you in that I am very old and very wise, and I have contacts in a most useful publication called *Lloyds List* which is almost as invaluable as the *Racing Post* when it comes to inside knowledge on a subject. From them I learn that Polish merchant

ships regularly ply their trade in the sea-lanes just out there' –
Mr Campion gestured airily with a swirl of his wrist – 'beyond
that rather large sand bar, out on the ocean blue. My chums at
Lloyds tell me they appear almost like London buses on a regular
schedule, carrying mostly timber, apparently, to ports further
south such as Harwich or Colchester. Those Polish boats may
not dock in Gapton, but they regularly pass by it close enough
to offload some alcoholic cargo into a small boat whenever there's
a Smugglers' Moon.'

'That is useful information.' Rupert nodded seriously. 'Do you
have similar contacts at the *Racing Post*?'

'Alas . . .'

Mr Campion looked crestfallen then briefly shrugged his shoulders before reapplying his regular expression of benign
bewilderment.

'Come on,' he said, striding towards the pub. 'Let's dump
these bags with the landlord before he closes up for the afternoon.
What time does he open in the evening?'

'I'm not sure,' Rupert answered, hitching the strap of his
mother's bag higher on to his shoulder and wondering, not for
the first time, what she could be carrying to weigh that much.
'Six, I think. The landlord's called Stanley; seems a decent enough
cove.'

'Yes, he sounded very nice on the telephone and obligingly
gave us the bedroom with the best view of the Spit.'

'There's not much to look at.'

'Oh, I think there will be. Later, when it gets dark.'

They were made welcome at The Butt and Oyster despite the
approach of what most Englishmen, and a certain M. Lugg,
Esquire in particular, regarded as 'the dead hours' when public
houses closed their doors for the afternoon, a temporary measure
brought in by Lloyd George to increase efficiency in munitions'
factories for the duration of the war against the Kaiser and main-
tained ever since, though no one could remember quite why.

The licensee, Stanley, could hardly have been more welcoming
and offered to carry any luggage upstairs, an obviously unique
offer judging by the loud intakes of breath from the two ancient
'regulars' sitting at a corner table meditating over half pints of

Mild, which they seemed happier to see slowly evaporate rather than drink.

Mr Campion accepted the offer of portage and, when he informed Stanley that his wife would be along later, he was forced to admit, 'Yes, that would be the Lady Amanda,' at which Stanley visibly puffed out his chest with pride, only for deflation to take place when Mr Campion said it was unlikely they would be eating there that evening and would probably retire early. Further disappointment struck the publican when his distinguished guest (or at least the husband of a distinguished guest) refused the offer of several drinks after closing time, as was his right as a resident – an offer greeted with distinct murmurs from the pair of Buddhist Mild drinkers.

'Thank you, mine host,' said Mr Campion loudly, 'but my son and I have some exploring to do over on Gapton Spit. Which is the best way to get to the moorings without getting our feet wet?'

'Out of the bar, turn left and left again, towards Gapton Thorpe. After the first cottage you'll see a wicker gate and the path that'll take you round the edge of the lagoon to where they berth the boats.'

The Campions thanked the publican and followed his directions, finding the wicker gate with ease thanks to the poker-burnt wooden sign attached to it saying: *To Moorings*.

It was only then that Rupert said, 'After that little exchange in the pub, everyone will know who we are and what we're up to.'

Mr Campion nodded in agreement. 'Sole purpose of exercise,' he said with a smile.

The *Dulcibella* was easy to find; in fact, it was difficult to miss, occupying the first berth in the moorings, a string of small sailing boats stretched out beyond it along the length of the lagoon. The state of its paintwork suggested the houseboat had seen better days and many of them, judging by the unkempt flowerboxes along the roof of the cabin, in sedentary, domestic use on a quiet inland waterway somewhere, for it was well known that while bargees on a canal might have the time and inclination to dabble in horticulture, no true salt-water sailor was ever any good at gardening.

To Rupert the boat, the mooring and the short plank connecting the boat to the path rang no bells in his still fuzzy memory of the previous night's events. Only the sight of the wooden dinghy bobbing on the end of a six-foot-long painter secured to a cleat on the prow struck a faint, unpleasant chime.

Mr Campion paused before he stepped on to the gangplank and looked carefully into his son's eyes. 'Are you up to this, my boy?'

'I think so,' said Rupert, nodding his head. 'Though I have no idea what we're doing here.'

'We're playing pirates, so stand by to board!' whispered Mr Campion. 'Don't worry, there won't be any trouble.'

After taking the single pace needed to put himself on to the deck of *Dulcibella*, he stamped both feet in rapid succession and said loudly: 'Ahoy there! Anyone home?'

At the stern of the long, narrow boat, a hatch squeaked open and a pair of heads peeped out followed by a slightly undignified pair of bodies scrabbling to confront the intruders.

'Who the hell are you?' asked the first. He was slightly the taller of the two, but both shared the fresh faces and unruly hair of young men not long out of a minor public school. They both wore jeans, sea-boots and pea jackets over turtleneck sweaters, the taller one standing with a distinct starboard list due to his right hand being thrust deep into the pocket of his jacket.

'We are the Campions, senior and junior,' said Mr Campion charmingly, 'and I believe you met my son last night, though it was not an occasion for formal introductions. I am assuming that you are Carruthers and Smith, though I do not know – or care – which is which.'

'Look, we're sorry about last night—' began the smaller of the two, only to be cut short by a snarl from his companion.

'Shut up, you fool!'

'Gentlemen, please,' said Mr Campion, holding up his hands as peacemaker, 'there will be no recriminations about last night at least on our part. As to any disciplinary measures pursued by your superiors, I cannot speak.'

'What do you want?' asked the one Mr Campion decided, on a whim, to call Carruthers.

'Mercifully for you, we are not seeking advice on birdwatching.

That is your cover story, isn't it?' Campion turned to his son, ignoring the two men. 'Did you know that the Royal Society for the Protection of Birds started as a campaigning body which opposed the barbarous trade in plumes for Victorian ladies demanding the latest fashion in hats? Egrets were apparently seriously at risk from the trade but, oddly enough, ostriches were thought to be fair game and excluded from the campaign. I doubt these two chaps could tell their egrets from their ostriches if their lives depended on it.'

'Are you barmy or just trying to be clever?' growled Carruthers, stepping closer.

'I have been accused of being both,' beamed Mr Campion, 'but also have medical certificates to prove I am neither. However, I have no intention of producing them for your inspection. For my credentials, should you require evidence of them, I am told you have a radio telephone secreted somewhere on board set to a military rather than marine frequency. Please feel free to make a phone call to Mr Deighton or Mr Milton.'

'You're not supposed to know—'

'There are many things I am not *supposed* to know, but somehow I do. For instance, I know – thanks to the excellent advice of the stupendous Miss Mae West – that you cannot possibly be pleased to see me and therefore you are indeed clutching a pistol of some sort in your right pocket. Quite honestly, my dear Carruthers, you're spoiling the cut of your jacket that way. It's a nice jacket; looks warm and snug, and I think I'd like to borrow it as well.'

'As well as what?'

'Your dinghy. Oh, don't worry, we'll return it in one piece. We're just off for a quick pleasure trip around the bay.'

'We should have pinched their sea-boots as well,' said Rupert as he trudged up the sandy slope of Gapton Spit.

'Borrowed, my boy, borrowed. One should always aim to return government property whenever one can,' Mr Campion replied, gratefully accepting Rupert's proffered hand to aid his ascent.

'I can't believe those two characters are actually spies,' said Rupert as he crested the ridge.

'Trainee spies, if one is being charitable, and they can't all be James Bond, you know. Spies come in all shapes and sizes.'

'I'm sure they do, I just can't believe those two are on *our side*.'

'I know what you mean. Sometimes it seems as if we insist on playing the Great Game by always putting out the Colts XI.'

Father and son stood side by side atop the dune ridge, the highest point on Gapton Spit, the wind off the sea in their faces, and the profile of Gapton, already milky grey in the dimming afternoon light, across the lagoon at their backs.

'The Ministry of Defence fence-line is over there,' said Rupert, pointing to his left, 'and the ship was offshore just about there.' He corrected the arc of his arm. 'There's obviously a landing place of some sort and the remains of some buildings left over from the war when the place was a Hush-Hush station or whatever they were called.'

'Huff-Duff,' Mr Campion corrected automatically. 'This place was a Y Station during the war, a listening post – the ears of our war effort. Jolly useful place to have back then, vital in fact, and could be important nowadays too if the Cold War warms up again. Now, show me where you were last night when somebody took a pot-shot at you.'

With Rupert leading, they slid gently down the slope of the ridge, each step producing a wave of fine sand which swirled over and into their shoes. The nearer they got to the shoreline, where six-inch grey and white waves drummed a steady rhythm, the more distinctly Mr Campion began to make out the shapes of concrete foundations and the stunted skeletons of brick build-ings beneath drifts of blown sand which had concealed them more effectively than any army camouflage unit could have done.

Rupert reached a right-angled structure – the corner of what had once been a low, single-storey building – and stood with his back pressed against it.

'I think I was here,' he said, jerking his head dramatically to mime peeping round the corner towards the sea, 'and the boat was parked just out there, offshore.'

'I think the technical term is "at anchor" rather than parked, but I get the picture. You're sure it was somebody on the boat that was shooting at you?'

'I saw the flash out to sea and there was nobody else on the Spit, not then, anyway. Those two schoolboy spies turned up later – and from the landward side.'

'Your nautical terminology seems to be improving,' smiled Mr Campion, 'but I want you to be sure about this. To me, at night, pistol shooting at that range would seem a hit-and-miss affair, not that I'm not delighted it was a miss rather than a hit in your case.'

'I think he must have been aiming at my torch, which I disposed of rapidly, and then I hid behind the wall here. To be honest, I don't think an actual bullet came anywhere near to me.'

'You took exactly the right course of action,' said Mr Campion. 'They say discretion is the better part of valour. I've always preferred showing a clean pair of heels myself.'

'That doesn't exactly tie in with some of the stories Lugg tells,' Rupert laughed.

Mr Campion bent his thin body back dramatically in mock recoil. 'And just whose word do you take on such matters?'

'Mother's, of course.'

'That, my boy, is always the correct answer. Now answer me this: could somebody have landed from that boat last night and you just didn't see them?'

'I suppose that's possible, but I wasn't aware of anyone on the Spit with me and the boat was never out of my sight for very long.'

'Could someone have come ashore in a dinghy?'

'There wasn't a dinghy, at least not one tied up to the boat like the one we just liberated from the *Dulcibella*, but there was a long plank from the bow down into the water. When the boat pulled away I distinctly heard the thing splash into the sea.'

'So somebody might have been ready to come ashore, but you disturbed them – is that possible?'

'Yes; they could have spotted the light from my torch long before I got here.'

Mr Campion walked slowly towards the shoreline. 'You were right – we should have borrowed some sea-boots. It's far too cold to take our shoes and socks off and go for a paddle, but I think if we did, we'd find the water quite shallow and perhaps even a concrete ramp just about here. You see, there would have been some sort of artificial dock built here during the war to get the equipment in to build the Y Station.'

'One of the sisters Mister told me the army uses helicopters these days.'

Mr Campion could not resist a smile. 'Doesn't everyone, dear boy?'

'Only to make an overdramatic entrance,' retorted Rupert. 'Anyway, the army was taking stuff away not bringing it in.'

'Don't be too sure of that,' said Mr Campion mysteriously. 'Let's snoop around in the dunes while we have the light.'

'Be careful, there are these rusty iron rods sticking up everywhere to skewer the unwary.'

'Those would be the reinforcing bars – as in reinforced concrete. Made you feel very safe, during the war, if you were in a pill box made of the stuff, but a bit of a blot on the landscape since.' Mr Campion talked as he walked into the dunes, his pace quickening. 'And here we are.'

'Here we are where?' Rupert, at his father's side, could see nothing of outstanding interest other than sand in front of them.

'If you went to the trouble of building a landing stage, then you had to defend it. So you built a pill box and put a Bren gun and two or three cold and bored soldiers in there, where they would pass the winter nights cursing their sergeant-major in order to keep warm.'

Rupert blinked and shook his head as if clearing his vision. That he had forgotten seeing the pill box the night before in the dark and the excitement of being shot at did not surprise him, but he had walked within ten feet of the structure not five minutes before without noticing it. Yet once his father had flattened a patch of marram grass with his foot and revealed the menacing, tell-tale letterbox slit, it became clear that it was a pill box, though its sharp-angled contours were blurred by the amount of sand which had drifted against it. If someone had told Rupert that a giant crane had at one time dropped several tons of sand from a great height in order to bury the pill box as effectively as a tomb in the Valley of the Kings, he would probably have believed them.

'If I remember my basic training,' said Mr Campion, 'the entrance is round here at the side and down a few steps – and so it is, and it appears we are the first visitors today. That's good, very good.'

'How do you know no one has been here and why would anyone?'

Mr Campion tapped his nose with a forefinger. 'My inherited Apache tracking skills, which sadly seem to have skipped a generation. Look at the sand. Have you seen any sign of your footprints from last night? The wind and the shifting sands have swept the place clean overnight and there are no fresh disturbances or footprints. Which means that our smuggler friend has not been to do a stock check today.'

'You mean this is a sort of pirate's cave?'

'I have a feeling it's more of a very well-stocked cocktail cabinet. Shall we take a look?'

Campion seemed to shrink magically into the sand as he stepped down into the sheltered well of the pill box entrance, where he was confronted by a very solid iron door secured with a padlock and hasp. With Rupert watching over his shoulder, his father produced a bunch of small keys on a ring the diameter of a half-crown piece from a trouser pocket. The third one he tried in the padlock resulted in a satisfying click and he smiled over his shoulder at his son.

'They were a present from Lugg. Please do not mention them to your mother.'

Campion removed the padlock and bent back the hasp, then pushed on the iron door with both hands.

'As I hoped,' he said, 'our smuggler has oiled the door regularly. Otherwise we might have needed dynamite to shift it.'

The door slid inwards into Stygian gloom.

'We should have brought a torch,' said Campion, bending his head and stepping inside.

'I've got a lighter somewhere,' Rupert offered, patting his clothing.

'Don't worry,' said his father, his voice echoing from inside the concrete tomb, 'the old gig-lamps are becoming acclimatized. Oh, I say, you wouldn't happen to have a honky-tonk piano and a line of chorus girls to hand, would you?'

'What?'

'If you had, we'd have the makings of a perfect speakeasy in here.'

SIXTEEN
Carry On Bodice Ripping

D r Milne breezed into The Maltings exuding the cheerfulness of someone enjoying the euphoric state that comes at the end of a refreshing holiday but before the realization of the daily grind has hit home.

'Ah, Doctor, welcome back,' Victoria greeted him. 'Sorry to call you out before you've even unpacked. Did you manage to get any skiing?'

'Yes, yes, quite exhilarating. Plenty of good food and you really can't beat the air in the French Alps, though one always takes pot luck on the snow this time of year.'

The doctor placed his leather bag on the kitchen table and flexed his arms as if ramming ski poles into deep virgin snow and to complete the image, he bent his knees and swivelled his hips from left to right. Amanda decided that the doctor's three-piece Harris Tweed suit and bow tie did not help his impersonation of a daring downhill racer.

'Bernard telephoned the surgery and said you had a patient for me, one of your house guests, so I jumped you to the top of my house calls, a favour which I hope will be remembered when the brewery's Christmas Party comes round . . .' Dr Milne beamed at Victoria then turned an expectant gaze towards Amanda.

'It's not me,' explained Amanda, 'it's my daughter-in-law. She managed to impale herself on some barbed wire or something. She's in her bedroom moaning about the fuss we're making, but I would very much appreciate it if you would examine her.'

'But of course. I'm here now so I might as well.'

'I'll take you up to her room. Her name's Perdita, Perdita Campion.'

'Charming, quite charming,' said the doctor. 'And you are Mrs Campion?'

'Lady Amanda Campion, née Fitton,' supplied Victoria, unasked.

Amanda and the doctor exchanged glances and Amanda noticed that underneath his raised eyebrows there was a distinct twinkle of amusement. Dr Milne, however, was not to be distracted from his calling.

'Well, let's not keep the patient waiting, shall we?'

The doctor proved to be that rare combination of politeness and efficiency, treating Perdita swiftly and gently while distracting her with a non-stop stream of anecdotes about the French (amiable but rather slack), the exhilaration of skiing (she really must try it), the different types and qualities of snow (many and varied) and the prices charged in the so-called 'duty-free' shop at Geneva airport (outrageous). So fluent was the doctor's chatty bedside manner that she only noticed the tetanus injection had taken place – and she with a childhood fear of needles – when she was urged to press a ball of cotton wool against the single drop of blood on her arm.

After cleaning her shoulder wound with antiseptic and applying a padded bandage with surgical tape, Dr Milne handed Perdita a small medicine bottle of pills.

'These will dull the pain and reduce the inflammation. There are only four tablets but that should see you through the night. I'll pop in tomorrow to check on you and leave you a prescription for some more, but after a couple of days I doubt you'll need them. While you're taking them, though, don't drive and don't drink alcohol. In fact, try not to have any fun at all.'

Perdita smiled up at him and fluttered her eyelashes. 'Does that mean I can't go skiing?'

With her husband determined to put in long hours to clear the backlog of work at the brewery, her underappreciated luncheon spread to be cleared away, dinner for who-knew-how-many to prepare and her children to amuse now that her understudy au pair girl was confined to bed on doctor's orders, Victoria Sandyman was not quite sure how she was going to cope. She added to her burden of woes that she also had a prominent member of the Suffolk aristocracy to entertain. However that particular problem (as she saw it) not only solved itself but answered another of her prayers.

'Victoria, my dear, I've had an idea,' Amanda announced as soon as Dr Milne had departed. 'You've got far too much on your plate and, though you are coping magnificently without staff, let me at least get out of your hair for a few hours and I'll take the children with me. Perdita tells me they went for a very pleasant walk yesterday and the fresh air will help tire them out. I'm told the baby – Beatrice, is it? – can be firmly restrained in her pushchair and the twins will make sure I don't get lost.'

'Oh, I couldn't possibly impose the twins on you – they can be quite unruly, I'm afraid.'

'They don't scare me. They could not possibly be as unruly, as cantankerous or as downright naughty as my two boys,' Amanda said firmly.

Victoria Sandyman, who felt she was well informed when it came to county gossip, looked surprised.

'I . . . I . . . didn't know you had . . . a . . . a . . . second son,' she stammered.

'I don't,' said Amanda firmly. 'I said "boys" not "sons", and I was including Albert.'

Unlike Perdita, Amanda had no trouble distinguishing between the Sandyman twins. As she prepared them for their afternoon exercise, she consulted the almost organic growth of coats and scarves on pegs in the hallway of The Maltings and, turning her back on the boys, she asked loudly, 'You'll both need scarves today. Whose is the pretty red one?'

'That's Jasper's,' said George, reacting as boys do to anything perceived as 'pretty'.

'Then the blue one must be George's, am I right?'

'Yes, m'lady,' the boys said together.

Amanda knelt down to tie each scarf round the appropriate boy and whispered: 'You don't have to call me that, whatever your mother said, though I do quite like it. I tell you what, when nobody's looking, you can call me Amanda. Now let's get Beatrice and you can show me the sights. I understand there's a very convenient sweet shop on our route.'

Jasper and George stepped to with enthusiasm and seemed perfectly happy to have Amanda as their commanding officer for the afternoon. And Amanda, now she had them colour-coded, was happy to let them lead the way.

The guided tour of the High Street was conducted at a brisk pace and with minimal touristic information – 'That's the brewery across the road where Miss Hyacinth and Miss Marigold make beer' – until they reached the Hard, where Red Scarf (Jasper) informed Amanda with the seriousness of an MP making his maiden speech that Beatrice liked to look at the boats in the lagoon from here while he and his brother visited Grundy's shop for supplies.

Amanda eyed him suspiciously, simply because she felt it was required of her, and said that they were allowed two minutes to make their purchases. The twins were gone in a blur, only the faint inkling of a shop doorbell indicating where they had gone, leaving Amanda to unstrap Beatrice, who seemed perfectly happy to be lifted and cuddled by a complete stranger, and for both of them to take in the view across the lagoon towards Gapton Spit.

'Look at those two funny men over there climbing up that sand bank,' Amanda instructed the baby in her arms, 'running around playing Cowboys and Indians, or perhaps it's Pirates today. I hope they haven't anchored that dinghy properly and it floats away when the tide comes in. That will serve them right. Take a good look, Beatrice, and learn a good lesson: whatever their age, boys will undoubtedly be boys.'

When the boys who were her immediate concern emerged with their booty, Amanda was delighted to see that the twins had thought to buy a chocolate biscuit for Beatrice. She would get in a terrible mess with it, Amanda knew, but it was by far the most sensible sweetmeat on offer, given the twins' joint decision to stock up on liquorice Catherine Wheels, Refreshers and Black Jacks.

'Now let us continue on our way,' said Amanda, loading Beatrice into the pushchair, 'and you can show me where Mrs Monk lives, just as you showed Perdita.'

'Do you speak Viking too, like Vibeke did?' asked George, unwrapping a chewy sweet as black as coal.

'Danish,' said Jasper, chewing vigorously, 'he means Danish.'

'No, I'm afraid I don't,' admitted Amanda, 'but I spoke to one

of Mrs Monk's Danish friends on the telephone yesterday and I
must call on her to pass on his best wishes.'

'She should be Viking,' George persisted. 'She's the only one
who goes to St Olave's church – and he was a Viking.'

'Well, I'm pretty sure Dorothy Monk isn't a Viking,' Amanda
said firmly, while thinking to herself, *But neither is she Dorothy
Monk.*

'How odd. You are the second Mrs Campion to have called on
me in two days.'

'We come cheaper by the bunch.'

Dorothy Monk was not exactly the woman Amanda had expected,
at least not from Perdita's description of her. She had prepared
herself for a severe, gaunt figure to appear before her in washed-out
monochrome. Instead she had been confronted by a relaxed, well-
groomed Technicolor woman wearing a cream cashmere sweater
setting off a necklace of polished amber beads and a blue-grey
knee-length Crimplene skirt in a half-moon print pattern. Her
make-up and lipstick were perhaps understated, but confidently so.

'You all seem to have charmed the Sandyman children.'

'I think the word bribed is more accurate than charmed,' said
Amanda, and Dorothy Monk smiled a really quite engaging smile,
which was another surprise. 'Some more effectively than others.'

Both women looked at Beatrice; a chocolate-stained Beatrice,
to be sure, but a Beatrice now angelically and completely asleep.

'I'm afraid I have nothing to offer the children today,' said
Mrs Monk.

'Please don't worry about that – they've been overindulged
with sweets, and in any case we have dropped on you out of the
blue. Surprise visitors shouldn't expect lavish hospitality.'

From the way the tall woman narrowed her eyes, Amanda felt
sure she unwittingly committed a faux pas, but the frown passed
from Mrs Monk's face as she quietly clapped the palms of her
hands together.

'Why don't you two boys go out into the garden and count
the boats in the lagoon? See if we have any new arrivals.'

The twins, realizing that tea and cake were off the menu,
needed no second bidding and were jostling for position at Mrs
Monk's heels as she unlocked the back door for them.

Returning to the living room, she insisted that she and Amanda should sit in the two armchairs, turning hers so that they could face each other. Mrs Monk linked her fingers, placed her hands in her lap and took a deep breath. 'I assume your visit means there is news of Vibeke,' she said, as though preparing herself for bad news.

'Indirectly,' answered Amanda after a pause. 'Vibeke has not been found yet, to my knowledge, which of course is a cause for concern, not the least for her poor father. I understand you know the Westergaards.'

'Vibeke used to visit me since she came to be au pair for the Sandymans. I found her very pleasant company; she was a charming girl.'

'I'm sure she still is.' Amanda prickled. 'But I said Westergaards plural. You know Vibeke's father, Greve Westergaard, don't you? And you've known him for quite a few years, I believe.'

Dorothy Monk's ice-blue eyes focused on a point somewhere over Amanda's right shoulder but she did not speak, and after a minute's silence Amanda was forced to prompt.

'I wondered why the ambassador suggested a place like Gapton for his daughter. Yes, I know he knows the Sandyman family, but he also knows Gapton because he'd hidden a Danish girl here before, hadn't he?' When there was no response, Amanda pressed on. 'Though you weren't exactly a girl, were you? You were a woman – a very well-known woman once – who wanted a place to hide.'

'How did you know?' Mrs Monk said finally.

'I was sure only when you opened the door to me, up until then I merely suspected, but I recognized you from twenty years ago. Although my daughter-in-law is an actress and my son aspires to be an actor, neither of them go to the cinema as much my generation did, particularly just after the war. They have too many distractions these days – pop music, cars, fashion, television – we had bombed-out dance halls and grotty flea-pits.

'The films we went to see were escapist bits of flummery, but even in black-and-white they lit up those grey days when it seemed the government would have rationed sunshine if it could, and none shone more brightly than those period pieces, those costume bodice-rippers, which always had a pretty young heroine at the mercy of a dastardly uncle. And no one could do a good bodice-ripping scene better than a young actress with long blonde hair and an intriguing foreign accent but a very English name: Jean Lerner-Scott.

'When it came to an eighteenth-century bustle, no other ingénue filled one better than Jean Lerner-Scott. She was of the next generation of stars who would surpass the likes of Jean Kent, Margaret Lockwood and Patricia Roc for popularity and talent and compete with the Americans and French in the glamour and sex appeal stakes. But it never quite happened, did it?'

Mrs Monk's mask of a face displayed only the slightest of ticks as she stared at Amanda. 'That was quite a speech, Mrs Campion,' she said through tight lips. 'Far longer than anything I was ever asked to memorise, and you did it in one take.'

'I make no claims to being an actress,' said Amanda, 'and certainly would not in the presence of one who has managed to carry off such a disappearing trick'

'Trick?'

'Oh, I would say so. One day your picture is on the cover of *ABC Film Review* and you have a fan club of devoted followers, then suddenly you disappear from the silver screen and years later – fifteen years maybe – here you are, unrecognized, playing the role of the reclusive spinster in a town the sea cut off and the railways never bothered with. I'd call that a neat trick, and good acting.'

'But I have not gone unrecognized, have I? In fact, you suspected who I was before you saw me.'

'Ah, well, there I have an advantage over the good citizens of Gapton. You see, I share my husband's suspicious nature and when I was told that the missing Vibeke had been friendly with probably the only other person in the county who spoke Danish, I assumed that the other person must be Danish too. And then I began to remember the newspaper stories . . .'

'Oh, yes, the newspapers,' scoffed Mrs Monk quietly.

'Stories about a waif-like Danish actress who had come to London at the end of the war an orphaned teenager, but who was set to be the next Ingrid Bergman.'

'She was much older, and Swedish,' snapped Mrs Monk.

The actress shows her claws, thought Amanda.

'But after five or six films—'

'Seven, actually.'

Definitely an actress.

'After seven solid British films and, I seem to remember, good reviews, Jean Scott-Lerner not only drops off our screens, but totally out of sight, only to be discovered living a hermit-like existence out here on the Suffolk coast.'

'It reminds me of home, but I suppose Greve Westergaard told you that as well.'

Amanda had the uneasy feeling that Mrs Monk was switching roles, from that of victim in the witness box to prosecuting counsel.

'He did not want to tell me anything, Mrs Monk, but I persuaded him to on the grounds that it might help us find Vibeke.'

'I have no idea what happened to Vibeke,' said the tall woman, seemingly growing taller even though seated as she bristled with indignation. 'I wish I had, partly because she is a charming girl and I pray no harm has come to her, but also because I might then be left in peace.'

'You have been hiding in peace for many years, Mrs Monk, or may I call you Jean?'

'As you seem to know all about me, you should know that I answer to both names but neither is strictly accurate. When I arrived in England from Denmark in 1944 my identity papers were in the name of Dortë Munk, but it was wartime and Denmark was an occupied country and that identity, of necessity, was false. However, it did translate conveniently into Dorothy Monk, which suited me fine but it was not classy enough for the film producers who spotted me. Hence, a screen name was invented for me and I became Jean Lerner-Scott. If you want the absolute truth, my given name is Bitta Krause, but no one has called me that for . . .' There was distinct hesitation, '. . . twenty-five years.'

Although she could not put her finger on where and how, Amanda felt that she was not being told the entire truth.

'The count – Ambassador Westergaard – helped you come to this country?'

'Of course; I owe him my life. He was not an ambassador then; he was a hero of the Danish Resistance.'

'You were in the Resistance?' Amanda could not keep the admiration out of her voice.

'I was a foolish sixteen-year-old girl who had been born on a farm in Sjaelland, which you would call Zealand, and never thought she would leave it. The war changed things and I was put in danger. Aage Westergaard had me smuggled to Sweden and from there to London. I learned English quickly and became a naturalized British subject. I was nineteen and working as a hat check girl in the cloakroom of a night club near Leicester Square when two customers said they were film producers and that they would make me a star. The girls I worked with said they were "shooting a line, not a film" and were drunks after only one thing, but they actually were in the film business. That was my biggest stroke of luck and my biggest mistake.'

'Mistake? You were an instant hit as far as I remember, all those costume melodramas – *The Duchess of Dartmoor*, *Assignation*, *An Ironside Heart* – you made an impact in all of them, you got noticed.'

'Playing the serving wench or the farmer's daughter, the one who always got ravaged by the local militia or the pirates, or whoever felt like it. It must have been my long blonde hair which made me irresistible.'

Amanda checked the face of the woman seated before her for a wisp of emotion, any emotion – cynicism, resignation, even perhaps pride – but the sharp face was as impassive as marble, and just as warm. She was either a genuine ice maiden or a much better actress than Amanda remembered. 'What happened?' she asked softly.

'To the hair?' Mrs Monk's right hand rose from her lap and had almost reached the back of her neck and shoulder before she controlled the instinct and the hand dropped back into place. 'That was the first thing to go after my career as one agent famously said. Once it was cut short and dyed, nobody recognized Jean Lerner-Scott and so Dorothy Monk was reborn. I called myself "Mrs Monk" and wore a cheap wedding band to keep inquisitive men at bay. That was not difficult.'

Mrs Monk's eyes flicked down to the fingers of her left hand; another involuntary reaction, thought Amanda.

'I meant what happened to your career as a film star?'

Now the icy façade did move, if not crack, as Mrs Monk shrugged her shoulders and curled her upper lip.

'Mine was not a unique experience. It became clear that my talent was limited. I was offered a part in a so-called comedy film set in a Lancashire wool mill. The title was *Three Ganders and a Goose*, would you believe? It was a truly awful script, which I did not understand one bit. I could also not do the correct accent and the whole thing was a disaster.'

'I must have missed that one.'

'So did most cinema-goers, but the critics did not. One said it had truly cooked the goose of Jean Lerner-Scott's career, and they were correct.'

'Don't be ridiculous,' said Amanda firmly, 'all theatricals have flops and everyone knows that reviewers are not to be trusted.'

'I proved the critics right. For a year there were no more film offers. I had no confidence for a role in the theatre and television, in those days, was a passing fancy which no one took seriously. I was young, alone in a foreign country and all the money seemed to melt away as quickly as I earned it. I was desperate and when a man came calling with a suitcase full of money and the offer of a film role, I agreed even though I knew it would be a film which today we would call "X-rated".'

'It was a blue movie?' asked Amanda, sympathetic rather than shocked.

'Very blue. They were called "skin flicks" in those days. And it wasn't just one film. They took the scenes I did and cut them into three unfinished films then added some stock footage. I doubt that the end result made any sense at all, but those particular audiences are not looking for a story or acting ability. I did not see them, of course, but others in the film industry did and it was made clear to me that I would never work again.'

'How did you survive?'

'I cut off my hair, sold off all my good clothes and exchanged a flat in Chelsea for a bed-sitting room in Bethnal Green. I started going to church again and took jobs as a cleaning lady in offices in the City. No one recognized that plain woman mopping the floor as a film starlet and that, I think, was my penance.'

'Why did you come to Gapton?'

'You seem determined to know all my personal affairs,' said

Mrs Monk severely. 'Very well, then. Greve Westergaard found
me and offered to intercede on my behalf in Denmark. My
parents' farm had been destroyed during the war and there was
a question of compensation. The count acted for me and had the
money transferred to England. I draw it as a sort of pension. It
is not much, but it allows me to live here near the sea in small
comfort and peace. Until now, that is.'

Amanda recognized the barb and could not, in all fairness,
deny the woman at least one.

'Was Gapton recommended by the ambassador?'

'Yes. He knew Mr Sandyman – the senior one, Bernard –
during the war and, of course, because he knew the Sandymans,
it was a logical choice for Vibeke to come here too.'

'Did Vibeke know your . . . history?'

'No, not at all, and I certainly did not offer to tell her. Vibeke
was just delighted to find somebody she could speak to in her
native language.'

'And you really have no idea what could have happened to
Vibeke?'

'I have told Mr Torquil Sandyman and the police that I have
not. I *heard* them, or rather I heard her boyfriend's motorbike
– it makes a very loud noise – on the night she disappeared, but
I did not see her. I wish I could help. I owe Greve Westergaard
and the Sandymans a considerable debt.'

And then, once again, the hostile witness became the pros-
ecutor. 'Now, may I ask what your interest in this affair is, Mrs
Campion?'

'It began as a social favour, if I can put it that way. Ambassador
Westergaard asked for the help of my husband and it was freely
given. But my husband, being my husband, also involved my
son and, last night, out there on Gapton Spit, someone took a
shot at my son from a boat. If it wasn't for Vibeke, my son would
not have been put in the firing line. That is my interest.'

'I am sorry, but I know nothing of such events.'

Amanda stood up and tugged her jacket tight around her
shoulders. 'Are you sure, Mrs Monk? From what I can gather,
Samphire Cottage offers a perfect view across the lagoon to
Gapton Spit.'

'That is one of its charms, but I have not been sleeping well lately, and last night I took a pill and was in bed asleep by nine o'clock. Now, if this interrogation is over, I am sure you would like to get the children home before dark. Shall we get the boys in from the garden?'

Amanda realized her mistake in standing up. The initiative had passed to Mrs Monk. At the back door of the cottage, she summoned the twins: 'Jasper, George, time to get Beatrice home.'

'Awwww,' chorused the boys. 'Can we come here again?'

'I really couldn't say,' replied Amanda.

Dorothy Monk, formerly Jean Lerner-Scott, previously Dortë Munk and originally Bitta Krause, stood in the doorway of Samphire Cottage and watched her unexpected, and for the most part unwanted, guests depart.

When Amanda, the twins and the pushchair containing the still-sleeping Beatrice had cleared the white gate at the end of the path, she began to close the front door with its brass fox-head knocker.

'They've gone,' she called up the cottage staircase, though not in English.

SEVENTEEN
Fermentation

I t really was too much, fumed Victoria Sandyman. House guests were one thing, but when they commandeered the house and treated their hostess as no better than a waitress, it was close to the last straw.

Lady Amanda, of course, had to be allowed considerable leeway, but the other Campion woman, who was supposed to be there to help her, was now treating The Maltings as a private hospital. And as for the Campion men, they were becoming intolerable, bursting into her kitchen with inane grins on their faces and sand pouring out of their shoes and trouser turn-ups – goodness knew who they thought was going to sweep that up! – and then persuading Torquil (without a word of consultation, mind) that dinner should be 'whatever cold cuts were left over from lunch' and everyone should sit around the kitchen table for an intelligence debrief, whatever that was when it was at home. Torquil even offered to be 'potboy' and fetch bottles of beer from the cellar for everyone, as if smelling and talking about the stuff all day wasn't enough.

Fortunately, the gracious Amanda offered to take charge of whatever victuals were required by the 'kitchen cabinet' – a phenomenon she said she was sadly familiar with – while Victoria saw to the children and their feeding, bathing and preparation for bed. It was an offer Victoria found impossible to refuse.

Mr Campion, jacket off and sleeves rolled, began slicing bread with enthusiasm, if not accuracy, while Rupert laid out plates and Torquil began to open bottles of Sandyman's finest pale ale. Amanda, doing everything else that was required, also suggested that Bernard Sandyman be summoned from the television room (where it seemed he always hid in the hour or so before dinner) to join them.

When Sandymans (including a silently disapproving Victoria)

and Campions (including a slightly groggy Perdita) were randomly seated around the long oak kitchen table and helping themselves to whatever was in reach, Mr Campion called for order.

'Ladies and gentlemen, thank you for attending this ad hoc meeting of the Gapton Home Guard which has been reconvened after a brief hiatus of a quarter of a century to deal with the recent local difficulties.'

'Oh for goodness' sake, Albert, do get on with it!'

'Certainly, my dear. I propose that we pool our knowledge by reporting what we have discovered today, and I suggest that Rupert and I make one report and you make the other, and then we ask our hosts to add in their local knowledge. When we have a full situation report, we allow our ideas to ferment a little and then decide on a plan of action.'

'Makes sound military sense,' said Bernard Sandyman, his moustache bristling with pride, but then Mr Campion spoiled the moment with flippancy.

'Rupert and I will report as Pirate Patrol and Amanda will be Viking Patrol—'

'Albert . . .'

Mr Campion took the hint. 'I am convinced that the finding of Vibeke Westergaard,' he began seriously, 'is linked to the murder of Francis Tate, who is of Polish extraction and was born Franciszek Tata. Not that there is anything wrong with that and the poor chap was a naturalized British citizen. He did, however, have a lucrative side-line in smuggled goods, exchanging decadent Western capitalist consumer goods for honest Communist vodka via the regular procession of Polish merchant ships which ply their trade along the East Anglian coast, conveniently close to Gapton. So far, small fry.

'But then things become complicated. Francis not only falls in love with Vibeke, but also comes under scrutiny from British Intelligence, which may or may not be an oxymoron, not only in London but also here in Gapton.'

'I don't believe it!' exclaimed Bernard Sandyman.

'I'm afraid it's true,' said Mr Campion wistfully. 'Gapton Spit is, after all, still Ministry of Defence land, and so it was thought prudent to have – shall we say an outpost – in the form of a pair of amateur ornithologists on a houseboat in the lagoon.'

'I knew it!' said Mr Bernard with some conviction. 'Never trusted those snot-nosed birdwatchers.'

'One can never fully trust a grown man with a hobby,' said Mr Campion casually, avoiding his wife's withering stare, 'especially when they are pretty awful at it. Unfortunately they seem fairly useless at intelligence work also, as they showed last night when they abducted Rupert here.'

'They seemed pretty efficient to me,' Rupert scoffed.

'Except they got entirely the wrong man. You were just in the wrong place at the wrong time.'

'Poor Rupert,' Torquil Sandyman sympathized with his old school chum. 'Just how the devil many people were they expecting to be on Gapton Spit at that time of night?'

'At least one,' said Mr Campion vaguely.

'Our smuggler friend?' Rupert offered.

'Smugglers? Spies? Birdwatchers? I don't know which is worse,' blustered the senior Sandyman. 'What in the name of God is going on out there?'

'Let me try to clarify,' said Mr Campion, giving Bernard his full attention. 'The birdwatchers, who go by the names Carruthers and Smith, are spies and not really interested in the small but healthy local smuggling trade, other than that it involved the late Francis.'

'So Tate was the smuggler?'

'One of them, but more importantly, he was also a spy.'

Bernard Sandyman paused raising a glass of beer to his lips. 'And a birdwatcher,' he murmured.

'I think the only bird he was interested in was Vibeke,' said Torquil sheepishly while patting his father's arm rather condescendingly.

'But he always had a camera round his neck. He was forever snapping away taking pictures of the Spit and there's nothing there except birds.'

'Bernard is absolutely right,' said Mr Campion.

'I am?'

'Yes, you are, my dear chap. Tate was a photographer and he would have been keen to photograph Gapton Spit but not for ornithological reasons. After all, it was, and is, a Ministry of Defence site.'

'But he would have been about twenty-five years too late for the Huff-Duff station,' Rupert protested.

'Of course he would, but that was the last war. Perhaps the ministry is doing something towards – heaven forbid – the next one. It was you, dear boy, who pointed out that the army has been using helicopters at Gapton, as well as' – Mr Campion beamed at his audience and flicked an imaginary lock of hair from his forehead – 'certain debonair adventurers who are blessed with well-connected wives, and if you'd kept your eyes peeled while on Pirate Patrol you would have noticed, among the ruined buildings, the pill boxes and the vast amount of illicit vodka stored there – several discreetly placed surveyor's stakes, where somebody has been taking measurements or soundings, or whatever it is surveyors do when they survey.'

'What on earth for?' snapped Bernard Sandyman, remembering his civic duty. 'I keep an ear to the ground on these matters and nobody's asked for planning permission for anything to do with the Spit.'

'I don't think the ministry needs anyone's permission and I really have no idea what they're up to, but let's put that to one side.'

Mr Campion took off his spectacles, produced a white hand-kerchief big enough to serve as a flag of truce, and began to polish the large round lenses with circular motions of finger and thumb. Amanda knew the signs well; her husband did indeed have an idea fermenting behind that rather vacant expression.

'Tate's smuggling activities, I think, were useful to him as a source of petty cash, but far more important as both cover and conduit for his spying. If he was nabbed in Gapton photo-graphing Defence property he could, if he had to, resort to claiming that he was birdwatching and if that was too thin, then reluctantly come clean and admit it was a cover for his smuggling activity; smuggling being a far lesser charge than spying.

'The exchange of Marks and Spencer's bespoke goods for overproof spirits here off Gapton Spit gave him a conduit not just for smuggling, but his espionage. Not only ladies' tights went out to those Polish boats, but almost certainly films and pictures Tate had taken in the course of his intelligence gathering duties. Tate was not only bringing things *in* but sending things *out* and that, I think, included people as well as smuggled goods.'

Although he had been mesmerized by Campion's spectacle-polishing act, Bernard Sandyman's jaw dropped open wide. 'You don't mean this chappie Tate put Westergaard's daughter on a Communist boat headed for the Iron Curtain like some damn white slaver?'

Mr Campion replaced his glasses very slowly, settling them on the bridge of his nose with the precision of a jeweller weighing out a troy ounce grain by grain. His wife suppressed a smile, as she well knew this was Campion's own mechanism for suppressing a fit of giggles.

'No, I wasn't suggesting that,' he said when bifocal perfection was restored. 'There wasn't a ship scheduled for the night Tate was murdered and, from what Rupert tells me, the police are certain he was killed on the civilian side of the Ministry of Defence fence, if I may put it like that. Not that a fit young man like Tate couldn't have scaled the fence if he'd a mind to; after all, Rupert managed it.'

Torquil jumped to his friend's defence. 'Steady on, Mr C., Rupert's still in pretty good condition and he was a jolly useful fly-half on the rugby field.'

'I hated school rugby,' Rupert swore quietly.

'Are you sure, old boy? You seemed like a natural.'

'My point,' Campion resumed, 'was that our birdwatching friends, and their superiors in London at the Royal Spy School for the Preservation of Birds, were convinced that Tate's smuggling route was going to be used last night to land someone on Gapton Spit. You see, they've had their eye on young Tate for some time, but he's small fry. The real target was the big fish who controlled Tate – gave him his orders, received his reports.

'Now our chaps, the ones in the white hats, know that this big fish, who probably wears a black hat, is called Dieter in the spy business, but that's about all they do know as they've never laid a finger on him. Their sources – sources to which I am not privy nor have any desire to be – tell them that Dieter may well be tempted to put in an appearance to find out what has happened to his trusted agent. If he does show his head above the parapet, he could arrive in any number of ways: on a charter flight into

Luton airport, by hovercraft across the Channel, by parachute dressed as a nun or stuffed inside a diplomatic bag. We just don't know, but there's a chance he will use a route, or a conduit, he knows has served Tate in the past – the Polish boats – and as far as Dieter is aware, it's a route which hasn't been rumbled. Yet.'

'So I was jumped by those two idiots because they thought I was this Dieter?'

'I'm afraid you were, my boy, and by the way I probably should have read the Riot Act to everyone or the Official Secrets Act before I started this debating society.' Mr Campion did not appear unduly worried by his omission. 'So I would politely suggest that we do not speak of these things beyond this room. We should invoke a sort of Kitchen Cabinet Confidentiality, if I may call it that.'

'Only if you really must, Albert,' said Amanda sweetly. 'Now would you like to hear what I've discovered this afternoon?'

'But of course, my dear. We are all anxious to hear the report of Viking Patrol.'

Amanda, who was used to getting her thoughts across to recalcitrant board members and to ignoring the frivolous moods of her husband, wasted no time in taking the chair. 'Using Victoria's dear children as camouflage, I paid a social call on Mrs Dorothy Monk, having been intrigued by Perdita's description of her and the fact that to have two native Danish speakers in a place like Gapton was a rather large coincidence. I took advice on the matter from Ambassador Westergaard, who was, understandably, anxious to help.

'As I suspected, Mrs Dorothy Monk of Gapton turns out to be the new identity of Jean Lerner-Scott, a young actress who featured in some forgettable British films in the bodice-ripping genre in the late forties and early fifties.' Amanda turned to Perdita. 'Do not blame yourself for not recognizing her; she was before your time.'

'No wonder she clammed up when I said I was an actress,' said her daughter-in-law.

'I think she still is,' Amanda said thoughtfully, 'because she was putting on a very controlled performance for me. Oh, and while I think of it, Perdita, did you notice if she was wearing a wedding ring?'

Perdita frowned. 'I think she was, but I couldn't say for sure.'

'I'm sure she does,' Victoria contributed, 'though I don't think she ever married. I think Vibeke once told me she wore it to keep men and village gossips at bay. She adopted "Mrs" as a sort of honorary title, though it seems her name wasn't Dorothy Monk at all.'

'It almost was.'

Six pairs of eyes swivelled to target Bernard Sandyman.

'Dortë Munk was the name she used when Aage Westergaard got her out of Denmark during the war, but that was a fake identity to fool the Gestapo and the SS. He was in the Resistance over there, she was a teenage girl on the run, and he got her out. I told you he was a brave man. He risked a lot for that scrawny slip of a girl. Her real name was Bitta something or other. Sounded a bit German to me.'

'Bitta Krause,' said Amanda, 'and she told me no one had called her that for twenty-five years, though—'

'Yes, my dear?' Campion prompted gently.

'She sort of hesitated when she said it, but then she was an actress.'

'You'd never guess she was a film star,' Victoria suggested. 'With the best will in the world her dress sense is so dowdy I thought it was a religious thing. She is religious though, isn't she? I mean, you'd have to be, to volunteer to look after draughty old St Olave's, wouldn't you?'

'Well, I never suspected,' Perdita agreed. 'If she was playing the role of a put-upon Plain Jane, then she did it well.'

'That was how you described her on the phone, darling, but when I called round today, I found a woman who hardly answered to that description. Smart, self-assured and definitely . . . sparkling . . . yes, behind the years, you could see the film star.'

'Film star, you say?' asked Bernard loudly. 'Would I have seen her in anything?'

'I hope not,' breathed Amanda.

'Not that I ever went to the pictures,' Bernard continued, 'not then, not now. To be honest, I'd forgotten about her until Westergaard got in touch asking if there was a cottage or a house available up here and I put him on to the sisters as they seem to own just about everything worth owning. As far I know she's been the perfect tenant. Never complained, always paid her rent on time, kept herself to herself, but always happy to support local charities and such as St Olave's. Film star, eh? Who'd've thought it?'

Amanda cleared her throat politely. 'My initial thought was that the mysterious Mrs Monk, alias Jean Lerner-Scott, alias Dortë Munk alias Bitta Krause, simply *must* know something of the whereabouts of the ambassador's daughter, but she convinced me that she did not. I'm sure she was hiding something from me, though perhaps she was too good an actress and wanted me to think that. I'm sorry, all, but I don't think Viking Patrol has contributed much to this Brains Trust.'

Now who's showing her acting skills? thought Mr Campion.

'Nonsense, my dear, that was most insightful,' he said. 'Perhaps it might be useful – although I cannot think why – if we knew why the original Bitta Krause had to be spirited out of occupied Denmark. She could only have been a slip of a gal, hardly a kingpin in the fight against Hitler.'

'You'll have to ask Westergaard if you want the details,' said Bernard Sandyman stiffly. 'All I know is that the girl was put in danger and needed his help. He's an honourable man and his word was good enough for me.'

'It's probably not important,' said Campion, looking at his watch. 'Can I bribe someone into making some coffee? My wife and I really should be repairing to The Butt and Oyster, where I insisted we were given the bridal suite.'

'Didn't know they had one,' said Bernard. Then: 'But hang on a second, Campion. If half of what you've been saying – about smugglers and spies and suchlike – is true, shouldn't we be telling the police?'

Mr Campion smiled. 'I would have thought it was obvious that they were already in the know.'

As they walked down the High Street, Mr Campion looped his arm around his wife's slim waist and drew her into him, the warmth of their bodies combining against the damp chill of the night as it came off the sea.

'What were you asking Victoria just before we left?'

'Just whether she'd ever seen Dorothy Monk smoking,'

Amanda said, her heart-shaped face pressed gently into her husband's shoulder. 'It's probably nothing, but there were cigarette butts in the garden just outside the back door.'

'Perhaps the Monk woman, whatever she's really called, prefers to smoke outdoors,' mused Campion. 'That woman has got to you, hasn't she?' he said gently.

'Yes, but I can't put my finger on exactly why. One thing she said might be important, though.'

'Do tell, my dear. I am, as always, all ears.'

'Well, she went out of her way to tell me that last night she was in bed by nine o'clock, yet I hadn't mentioned nine o'clock at all. About what time was Rupert having his little adventure out on the Spit?'

'That would be about nine o'clock,' agreed Mr Campion. 'Oh, look, straight ahead, the warm glow of a welcoming inn, its lights beckoning the weary travellers to a soft bed and a good night's sleep.'

The couple crossed the Hard towards The Butt and Oyster, the muffled hum of saloon bar conversation competing with the *slap-slap* of the water of the lagoon and, somewhere, over the water and out of the night, the cry of a fox.

Amanda disentangled herself from her husband. 'But we're not going to enjoy a soft bed and a good night's sleep, are we?'

'Not for a little while,' said Mr Campion gently, but on that matter Mr Campion was to be proved inaccurate and Amanda almost exactly right.

EIGHTEEN
Low Treason

'Can I say it before you do?'

'Say what, my dear?'

'*I see no ships*. Come on, Albert, you know you want to.'

In the darkness, Mr Campion smiled broadly, but he did not turn away from the lowered sash window through which he was looking with the aid of an enormous pair of binoculars.

'Actually, I think I did see one. Well, it was a dark shape and it could have been a ship, I suppose. Do you know if whales visit this bit of Suffolk?'

'Only in the mating season,' said his wife with a sigh. 'It's jolly cold with that window open.'

'Then why don't you climb into bed?'

'I am in bed! My Lord, for someone with a pair of binoculars big enough to spot the moon landing, you are remarkably unobservant. I got under the covers half an hour ago and, despite being fully clothed, plus the addition of one of Perdita's sweaters, I'm still cold.'

'I thought Victoria offered to lend you a jumper,' Mr Campion said airily, still concentrating on the night over Gapton Spit.

'She did,' said Amanda and then she too smiled in the darkness, 'but I wanted to show her I could fit into one of Perdita's.'

'I think that's what Shakespeare would have said was a hit, a palpable hit.'

'Well, if we're quoting Hamlet to pass the time, then I still say there's something rotten in the state of Denmark, by which I mean the Monk woman, alias Jean Lerner-Scott.'

'Marcellus,' said Campion automatically.

'I beg your pardon?'

'It's Marcellus who says that there's something rotten, not Hamlet, but I grant it is in *Hamlet*.'

'When I want tips on my English Lit. O-level, I'll ask for them. What I was trying to say is that I'm sure the woman is hiding something.'

'Clearly she is – her identity.'

'Which one?'

'Good point,' said Campion, then exclaimed: 'Ah-ha! And the light shineth in the darkness.'

'A ship?' Amanda's voice suggested support and interest, though she had no intention of removing the eiderdown from where it was pulled up to her chin.

'No. I thought I saw the outline of one earlier, but this time it's a light, a torch, on the Spit itself. Just about where Rupert and I found the smuggler's horde this afternoon I think, though I could do with fewer clouds and a bit more romantic moonlight.'

'I think the word "romantic" became redundant as soon as we entered this bedroom.'

Mr Campion closed the window and drew the curtains. 'I am sincerely sorry, my love, if I have – as usual – dashed your hopes, but if we are to bring this business to a close tonight we must press on as time and tide and all that, especially in this case the tide, waits for no man. Could you find the light switch, please?'

Amanda clicked on the bedside light to reveal her husband standing at the foot of the bed attempting to pull something from his overnight bag while the ludicrously large binoculars swung from leather straps around his neck and seemed quite likely to overbalance his slender frame.

'Where did you get those things, Albert?'

'These?' Mr Campion touched the binoculars as if noticing their presence for the first time. 'These were a gift from a Distinguished Naval Person – no, not that one – who took them from a U-boat commander somewhere off Ceylon in 1945.'

'Ceylon? U-boats in the Indian Ocean?'

'I know,' said Mr Campion with boyish enthusiasm, 'who would have thought it? Apparently the U-boat was en route to Japan with a highly secret cargo when the Royal Navy intercepted it and politely told the *Herr Kapitan* that, for him, the war was over.'

'And that thing?' Amanda's brown eyes grew wider as she saw her husband pull an equally bulky item shaped like a large brick from his bag.

'This is a walkie-talkie; American, but reliable none the less. I'm sorry I had to put the binoculars in your bag but I didn't want anything to bash the valves. Now, if I can just remember how to turn one of these on and press the right button when I wish to speak, we can get things moving, assuming I don't poke an eye out with this whip aerial.'

Amanda sat up in bed, but kept the eiderdown pulled up to her chin. 'I thought, love of my life, that now you are supposed to be retired you would have put away your toys, even if they qualify as antiques.'

Mr Campion, with binoculars in one hand and a walkie-talkie in the other, did his best to appear aggrieved, shocked and cut to the quick, while knowing that he could not conjure a single faked expression which would fool his wife, even though his ability to control his facial emotions had served him well in the past and arguably saved his life on more than one occasion.

'These are not toys, Amanda,' he said with mock severity, 'and neither are they antiques. Yes, they are old, but they are still useful. I believe the official term is that they are "valued collectibles". Just like me, in fact.'

Amanda could not quite believe how the large military policeman had actually fitted into the driver's seat of the enormous Land Rover station wagon; perhaps he had been squeezed into place. Seated behind him, it was only by straining her elegant neck that she could see, over mountainous shoulders, the beam of the vehicle's headlights on the road ahead. Despite the sergeant's stripes on his blouson, Campion had introduced the giant as 'Mr Milton' and the other passenger – a tall, slim fellow with a permanent smile – as 'the new Elsie' although Mr Milton, who clearly had more respect for authority and rank, addressed him as Major Deighton.

Mr Campion had spoken briefly into the walkie-talkie and received a crackling reply, then he had pulled on the duffle coat he had borrowed from Bernard Sandyman and said to Amanda, 'I'm just popping out . . .' but got no further before his wife had thrown back the bed covers, swung her legs out of bed and was pulling on her boots. Campion knew better than to argue.

As it was less than an hour to closing time, the landlord of The Butt and Oyster, Stanley, had cheerfully provided Campion with a key to the door for their return. The Campions, he assured them, would be welcome to a drink after hours as legitimate residents, but as far as the locals were concerned he had to enforce licensing hours so as not to get in trouble with the police. Amanda noticed that her husband had grinned broadly at that.

The rectangle of light spilling out from the pub on to the Hard illuminated the waiting Land Rover and the tall thin man Campion referred to as Elsie standing like a chauffeur holding the rear door open for them. He nodded curtly to Campion and then, more graciously, to Amanda.

Their journey in the Land Rover was cramped, uncomfortable and mercifully short. As they turned left off the Hard and bounced down the deserted street to Gapton Thorpe, L.C. Deighton turned his head to address his passengers in the back seat.

'Did you see the one-man show out on the Spit?'

'Enough of it to know that someone was doing something furtive, but probably not clearly enough to stand up in a court of law. I suspect Mr Milton's magic night-sight gave him a better view,' Campion replied.

'It did, but I doubt any of this will ever get to court.'

Amanda paid only scant attention to this exchange as her eye had caught the coal black outline of St Olave's church on their right and she realized they must be passing Samphire Cottage on their left. For a split second she thought she saw a light flicker in the redundant church, but her brain told her it could only be a reflection of the Land Rover's headlamps.

'It's just up ahead,' Mr Milton growled. 'Shall I park off the road, Major?'

'No, take us right to the door. No need to be shy.'

The Campions and Major Deighton clambered out while Mr Milton eased himself out slowly, the Land Rover relieved to be rid of him, and they stood outside the rendered façade of a utilitarian British police house, complete with, although unlit, the traditional blue lamp above the front door.

'Hardly New Scotland Yard, is it?' said Deighton.

'It sort of reminds me of home,' said Mr Campion dreamily, 'and I suppose it is as imposing as it needs to be in a place the size of Gapton-cum-Gapton Thorpe. Should we knock or find a phone box and ring 999?'

'Oh, he won't be back at his mooring yet,' offered Mr Milton, 'and we'll hear his engine before we see him.'

'So the cop shop, as an old friend would call it, is empty?'

'Possibly, but perhaps not. We'll find out when we talk to the temporary resident,' said Deighton.

'Temporary?'

'I doubt he'll be the village policeman by daybreak. Are you armed, Campion?'

'He'd better not be!' snapped Amanda.

'Only with my most disarming smile,' said Mr Campion, 'but he's hardly likely to put up a fight, is he?'

'*He* isn't, but he may have company.'

'Albert, what exactly is going on?' demanded Lady Amanda.

'I'm not one hundred per cent sure myself, darling. Perhaps we should ask a policeman.'

A thin path of crazy paving ran alongside the police house down to the narrow entrance to the lagoon, almost opposite the very fingertip of Gapton Spit. It would not be long – a mere blink in the unstoppable progress of sand and tide – before that fingernail clawed its way towards shore and hooked on, turning Gapton Lagoon into Gapton Lake, sealing the town off from all but the smell of the sea.

But tonight there was still enough room between shore and spit to allow the passage of a small motor vessel, the low throb of its putt-putt engine bouncing a deep bass note off the dark water.

Four pairs of eyes watched as the boat negotiated the narrow channel and nosed towards the moorings, the last few feet in silence as the skipper cut the engine. With a slurping, sucking sound and a slap of water, the boat slid into the last berth as if joining the end of a queue of yachts and dinghies lined up waiting for service at The Butt and Oyster in the distance.

Mr Campion's eyes were now accustomed to the night and he was close enough to be able to read the name-board *Betsan* on the prow of the cutter, but he could distinguish no significant details of the dark figure wearing oilskins and sea-boots which jumped from the deck on to the path, trailing a length of mooring rope which he – for surely the figure was male – secured through a large metal hoop set in a concrete block. The figure then re-boarded the boat and clumped to the stern, where he grabbed another mooring rope and again stepped off the boat and on to the path. As he was threading the stern line through another metal hoop, Mr Milton lit up the scene with a very high-powered torch.

'I'm afraid you're in trouble, Sergeant Davies,' said Deighton, 'and I would advise that you come quietly.'

The man from the boat had frozen bent over his mooring rope; his white, shocked face and staring eyes and his shiny black oilskins all adding to the impression that he was posing as a wraith for a Brueghel painting of nightmare folklore.

'You're not police,' said the wraith defiantly with a jutting jaw.

Mr Campion could not resist an intervention: 'No we're not. We are much, much worse.'

Gapton Thorpe Police House, to give it its official designation, had been built – as had all post-war police houses – with functionality in mind rather than luxury or architectural merit. Disappointingly, as far as Mr Campion was concerned, it possessed neither cells nor stocks, nor even a ducking-stool, and seemed to have been designed more with domestic rather than policing concerns in mind.

Sergeant Enoch Davies, being no longer married, had seen no need to add any personal touches which might have softened the décor. The rather bare kitchen, with its unsympathetic Formica-topped table and strip lighting, however, did make the perfect setting for an interrogation.

Davies, at first, attempted to plead innocence and ignorance in equal proportions, and did it in the hope that a broad Suffolk accent would aid his case. The opening statement for the defence lasted only until Mr Milton had taken up a position behind Davies, towering over him like a glowering Alpine peak, and had inter-laced his fingers and then cracked his knuckles with a sound, Campion thought, loud enough to have created an avalanche on a real Alp.

'All right, no need to get violent. I've been doing a bit of import/export on the side, but it wasn't like it was drugs or dirty magazines or anything, just a bit of booze to earn a few quid to go towards me pension. When the wife left me, she cleaned out the savings account and when the Force puts me out to grass, I'll have to find somewhere to live. So what if a few clubs and boozers up in London got some duty-free vodka? It's not a hanging offence.'

'But treason still is,' said Major Deighton.

'Oi don't know nuffing about such things!'

'We know you do. You've been in partnership with Francis Tate for some time and the late Francis Tate was a spy – a fairly low-level one – working for one, possibly more than one, Iron Curtain country. You were helping him.'

'Oi never did! Frank supplied the goods – women's tights, jeans, denim jackets, stuff like that which the Poles couldn't get back home – and we swapped 'em for vodka. Frank sold it in London and we split the proceeds. That's all it was.'

Deighton, sitting across the table from the agitated policeman, calmly folded his arms and leaned back in his chair. 'You really are a sorry excuse for a law officer, Davies. Tate was a photo-grapher and he photographed a lot of things he shouldn't have. He was sending his films back to his spymasters in among those fashionable clothes you were trading for vodka – and you were helping him.'

Davies's complexion took on a deathly pallor and his jaw slid open to reveal tobacco-stained teeth.

Mr Campion broke the silence. 'Mr Davies – I will call you that because I doubt you will be a police sergeant much longer – my name is Campion. You do not know me but you have met my son, Rupert, who is currently a guest of the Sandyman family.'

Davies, his mouth still yawning, stared at Campion with blank incomprehension.

'Last night you took your boat out for a rendezvous with a Polish freighter, as was your habit. I am presuming that the late Mr Tate delivered a consignment of Marks and Spencer's finest merchandise when he arrived in Gapton last Friday. You were just waiting for tide and Polish freighter to coincide, but things didn't go to plan, did they?

'For one thing, poor Mr Tate had got himself murdered in the meantime, which meant lots of police activity – activity by proper policemen, not the likes of you – and the good citizens of Gapton combing the countryside looking for Tate's missing girlfriend. And there were strangers poking their noses in, such as my son and his wife. Yet in the midst of all this – a murder enquiry – you still risked taking the *Betsan* out to earn a few illegal quid, as you so elegantly put it. You were, of course, observed. It was a foolish thing to do; you should have kept your head down. Are you a fool or just greedy, Davies? Or were you scared?'

Davies closed his mouth, then his tongue flicked out to moisten his lips. Campion felt Deighton sit to attention next to him.

'I didn't have any choice. I had this phone call, you see. Frank said he might ring if anything ever happened to him. Told me I had to make the run as usual and I had to bring the films from Frank's camera bag.'

'Which you took from his room in The Butt and Oyster,' said Campion firmly, 'almost as soon as Tate's body had been found on the Spit.'

Major Deighton's eyes flicked towards Campion, but his expression did not change.

'But it wasn't a usual run, was it?' Campion continued.

Davies shook his head. 'He was on the freighter, waiting for me. Took the films, then told me I had to bring him ashore, land him in Gapton. Otherwise—'

'Otherwise, details of your activity would be sent to someone like me,' said Major Deighton, 'and I would have come down on you like a ton of bricks.'

Behind Davies, the ton of bricks called Mr Milton cracked his knuckles again and Davies winced, then nodded meekly.

'Did your unexpected passenger identify himself?' Deighton pressed.

'I knew him as Dieter; that was all.'

'And why did he want you to land him in Gapton?'

'I don't know; he wasn't giving much away.'

'But he wanted to come to Gapton even though you'd already handed over Tate's films?'

'He insisted on it and he was not a feller to be denied.'

'But you didn't head straight into Gapton, did you?' Mr Campion accused him. 'You stopped just off the Spit.'

'Well, I 'ad all my merchandise to land, didn't I? I couldn't very well land it here, could I? Not in a police house.'

'You have a strange sense of moral propriety, Mr Davies, but that doesn't concern me. You didn't land your smuggled goods because you were seen by somebody on the Spit – my son, to be precise. You even took a shot at him.'

'Not me! That was that crazy Kraut Dieter. He pulled a gun and blasted away before I could stop him. I thought he was shooting at shadows, or the Gapton fox maybe, but it was best to get out of there, though, just in case. That's why I had to make another trip tonight, to unload.'

'And what did this Dieter do last night?' asked Deighton with the air of a man enquiring casually about the weather.

'He had a good look around this house, checking all the doors and windows at least twice,' Davies said rapidly, now anxious to help. 'Then he got me to draw him a map of Gapton on a bit o' paper, just rough, like, showing the streets and the church and the pub. It didn't take long, there's not that much to the place. And then he settled down in an armchair in my front room, where the phone is and said I was to go to bed. I told him I was on a six till two shift today and he said that wouldn't be a problem. It wasn't. When I got up to make a pot of tea about five-ish, he'd upped and gone. There were just a few cigarette butts in the fireplace to show he'd even been here – I'm a pipe man meself – and honest to God, I've not seen him since.'

Davies slumped forward dramatically, his forearms cushioning his head before it hit the table top. Mr Milton unceremoniously helped himself to a handful of the penitent's hair and jerked it upwards.

'Did he have any luggage, any bags, with him?' Deighton asked, ignoring the whimpers now leaking from the policeman's contorted face.

'No, no bags. All he was carrying was that bloody gun, but I reckon he was wearing a substantial body belt. Fair spoiled the cut of his jacket, it did.'

Mr Campion raised a finger, asking permission to intervene

again. When Deighton nodded, he said: 'Are you sure this Dieter fellow was German?'

'Oh, yes.' Davies tried to nod his head but Mr Milton remained in control. 'I don't speak the lingo but I recognize a few words right enough. When we saw the lights of Gapton he stood on the deck of the *Betsan* and started talking to himself, almost like he was saying a prayer. I didn't get the gist of it, but he kept saying "*Bitte, Bitte*" and that's German, isn't it?'

NINETEEN
Scouting for Peace

On L.C. Deighton's command, the soon-to-be-former-police-sergeant Enoch Davies was escorted by Mr Milton along the Moorings pathway to the *Dulcibella* where he was to spend the night guarded by 'the idiot bird-watchers'. Mr Campion had beamed his approval at the plan, gleefully commenting that at last there would be a Carruthers and a Davies on board the *Dulcibella*, which was as it should be.

Once Mr Milton had left with his slouched and dispirited charge, the Campions reclaimed their seats around the kitchen table and Mr Campion, with a flourish, waved Major Deighton to a chair.

'Two kitchen cabinets in one day,' he said, shaking his head, 'this really is unprecedented. I call upon the Honourable Member for Spy Town North to take the floor.'

'I was warned by my predecessor,' Deighton began, adjusting his smile back into place, 'that I should expect to understand only about a fifth of whatever you were talking about at any given time.'

'Elsie, or perhaps I should say the original Elsie, was far too kind. I count it a failure if more than ten per cent of my whiffle gets through.'

'That's enough, Albert,' said Amanda firmly, 'you two can swap playground pleasantries some other time. Now, Major Deighton, sit down and tell me the real reason this Dieter character is here in Gapton.'

'Lady Amanda, I really don't think you should worry—'

'Worry what? My pretty little head? Look here, Deighton – if that really is your name – in my work I've signed the Official Secrets Act more times than you've had hot dinners and I am worried about a man who shoots at my son and is clearly looking for Dorothy Monk.'

'I'm sorry, Lady Amanda, I'm not following your logic.'

Deighton's smile was firmly in place but he took a chair and sat down like a good little boy.

'Yes, you are, or you are remarkably good at being stupid!'

Mr Campion rolled his eyes, but said nothing.

'He wasn't saying "*Bitte*" as in the German for please, he was saying "Bitta" as in Bitta Krause, the real name of Dorothy Monk, otherwise known as Dortë Monk, otherwise known as Jean Lerner-Scott. Now what, Major, is the connection?'

'I am not sure I can—'

'Oh, yes you can, or do I have to telephone Count Westergaard at the embassy? This all has to do with Denmark after all, doesn't it?'

Major Deighton looked to Mr Campion for help or at least moral support, but found none forthcoming.

'You are, my dear Elsie, on your own when it comes to a cross-examination by my good lady wife,' said Campion benignly. 'If I were you I would answer her questions quickly and truthfully then throw yourself on her mercy. That has worked for me in the past – sometimes.'

The major took a deep breath. 'Very well, Lady Amanda, you are quite correct, this business goes back to Denmark during the war. Bitta Krause was a stupid but very pretty farmer's daughter who had the misfortune to fall in love with a young German soldier.'

'Falling in love, if hearts are true, should never be classed as misfortune,' said Amanda, 'though I can see the difficulties in that particular scenario.'

'As we in England were never occupied we can have no real idea of the difficulties,' said Deighton softly. 'The situation was made worse by the fact that it was October 1943 and the Nazis had decided that the Jews of Denmark – some seven thousand and five hundred innocent souls – had been living on borrowed time and were to be rounded up and deported.'

'But the Danish Resistance had other ideas,' Campion added sombrely, 'quite brilliant ones, in fact.'

Deighton nodded. 'The Danes managed to smuggle more than ninety per cent of the Jewish population out to Sweden, but some were rounded up and sent to the camps. Some, along with the resistance groups trying to help them were betrayed and shot on the spot. I'm afraid Bitta Krause was suspected of betraying an escaping Jewish family to her German boyfriend.'

'Suspected or proved?' asked Amanda.

'The Danes were pretty sure. The boyfriend in question was an SS Mann, the lowest rank, not even a combat soldier, but SS nonetheless, and the local Resistance cell had him down as a target. He got away, but they nabbed Bitta Krause and she was marked down for execution as a collaborator. Aage Westergaard was given the job of carrying out the execution but he couldn't bring himself to do it.'

'Good man,' breathed Campion.

'Instead he smuggled her out of Denmark on false papers in the name of Dortë Monk and she has lived in England ever since.'

'And the boyfriend? The German she fell for when she was – what – sixteen? Come on, Major, finish your story. What happened to the other half of the star-crossed lovers?'

'His name was Burckhardt Schönherr, Lady Amanda, and after the war he surfaced back in his home town of Leipzig in Germany – East Germany.'

'Don't tell me,' said Mr Campion. 'Let me guess. Burckhardt Schönherr, which I believe translates as "pretty boy", forged a new career in the East German Security Service, the Stasi – the "shield and sword of the party". The Communist Party, of course.'

'A suspiciously good guess, Campion – you clearly still have your sources. To be accurate, Schönherr became a high flyer in the Stasi's Department HVA, the Hauptverwaltung Aufklürung, which has responsibility for anti-NATO espionage. His operational name is Dieter.'

Mr Campion slapped the Formica table with the flat of his hand. 'Scouting for Peace!'

'Albert!' chided his wife. 'Explain that or stop being ridiculous.'

'It's what they call themselves, darling. The Stasi's Department HVA call themselves Scouts for Peace, though I doubt Baden-Powell ever came across such a belligerent bunch of recruits for Bob-a-Job Week. No doubt Major Deighton's department has a similar pet name, but it's probably top, top secret.'

'That wasn't quite as inane as I feared,' said Amanda. 'I will, however, ignore it. Do you think Dieter is still here in Gapton, Major?'

'I don't see how he could have left. There have been no reports of a car being stolen anywhere nearby and we've been watching the railway station at Darsham Halt. He certainly hasn't taken a boat anywhere and, if he wanted to get into London, he would have been better staying on the Polish freighter and waiting until it docked at Harwich or Southend.'

'So he deliberately chose to come ashore at Gapton. Can either of you gentlemen think why he might do that?'

'To rekindle his dalliance with Bitta Krause, of course,' said Campion. 'I say, she's not in danger, is she?'

The question was addressed to Major Deighton, but it was Amanda who answered.

'Based on female instinct alone, I would say that Mrs Monk or Miss Krause, or whatever she wants to be called, is not in physical danger at all. Emotionally I cannot judge, but I am willing to give odds that her dalliance with Dieter has already been rekindled. What concerns me is his interest in Vibeke Westergaard.'

'The missing girl?' said Deighton startled, clearly thrown off his stride.

'Amanda is convinced that Mrs Monk and Vibeke Westergaard are linked, and by more than just the Danish language,' said Campion, 'and you have just provided another piece of that chain. Vibeke is the daughter of the Danish Ambassador and Denmark is part of NATO. Surely that alone would be of interest to a spymaster of the Warsaw Pact.'

'And if the girl is frightened out of her wits,' Amanda hurried on, 'then she's going to turn to the one person she has befriended in Gapton.'

Deighton took in a deep breath. 'As soon as Milton returns we'll pay a call on Mrs Monk. I think it might be safer if we dropped you two back at the pub first, though.'

'That is very considerate, Major,' said Amanda politely, 'and normally I am the one who points out that my husband is no longer a young man and should not be exposed to undue amounts of excitement, shenanigans or danger. However, as I have no intention of being left behind, I suppose he'd better tag along as well. Whatever else she may be, Dorothy Monk is a damn good actress and quite capable of fooling a pair of men. You'll need me there.'

'Don't worry about us, Elsie,' said Mr Campion, 'if things turn ugly, Amanda and I will shelter behind that nice Mr Milton.'

Samphire Cottage was in darkness, but its white garden gate hung open like a missing tooth. In the rear seats of Mr Milton's juggernaut of a Land Rover, Amanda consulted the luminous dial of her Breitling Chronomat – an unfeminine but supremely efficient watch – to discover it was still not yet eleven o'clock, and though The Butt and Oyster still had a few minutes of legal drinking to enjoy, the rest of Gapton seemed to have called time on the evening.

'And not a creature was stirring, not even a mouse,' Mr Campion chanted quietly.

'Albert,' said his wife, 'this is not the night before Christmas.'

'I'm sorry, my dear. I was trying to think of something from Hans Christian Andersen, but the old brain cells failed me. Stupidly, I had not allowed for there being nobody home.'

'Of course she's at home, I just know she is. Where else could she go? Where else *would* she go?'

'Female intuition?' Mr Campion held up both hands in supplication. 'I do not use the term disparagingly. Far from it, I regard it as a unique skill which no one else in this vehicle possesses.'

'Call it what you like, my love, as long as you are thankful for it. I saw her eyes when she mentioned that no one had called her Bitta for twenty-five years. Her eyes said "until now" and that was a look no woman could conceal from another woman, however good an actress. Dieter has come back to her and if he hasn't left Gapton, neither has she.'

'I bow to your feminine logic, and if Miss Krause is still in love after all this time, I have to admit to a twinge of jealousy where this Dieter is concerned.'

Amanda's hand cupped her husband's face and drew it near to hers. 'You have absolutely no need to be jealous of anyone on that score, darling, and any twinges are probably down to arthritis.'

In the front seat, Major Deighton coughed discreetly. 'We have to make sure she's in there.'

'Of course we should,' said Amanda smartly. 'You and Mr Milton cover the back door. We will coordinate a frontal assault.'

'When you say "we", my dear,' Mr Campion said with resignation, 'you actually mean that I look on while you charge in where angels fear to tread.'

Amanda smiled. 'You know me so well.'

As it transpired, the taking of Samphire Cottage was a subdued, not to say anti-climactic event despite the military precision with which it was carried out.

Amanda gave Major Deighton and Mr Milton three minutes by her precise wristwatch to get into position and then she marched up to the front door and rapped out an opening salvo on the brass fox-head door knocker before she brought her main artillery to bear.

'Mrs Monk, it's Amanda Campion. I know you're in there and I know who you're hiding. It would be best if you let me in before things get out of hand.'

Surrender was as immediate as it was sudden and signalled by the twin metallic clicks of a key being turned in a lock and a bolt snapped back.

Dorothy Monk, or Bitta Krause as she must now think of her, stood in the doorway, her right arm extended and out of sight behind the wall. Amanda's first thought was that she was concealing a weapon and that her own self-confidence had been misplaced. Was it weak of her to be grateful that she could feel the presence of her husband right behind her, radiating calmness and strength? And was her relief too obvious when Bitta Krause's hidden hand did nothing more than flick a light switch, lighting up the room behind her like a theatrical set?

'You are a persistent visitor, Mrs Campion, and your friends are already blundering around in the back garden.'

'I'm glad we haven't got you out of bed, Mrs Monk,' said Amanda, taking in the figure wearing a belted blue raincoat in front of her. 'And perhaps it would be best to open the back door and let the gentlemen in.'

'They are police?'

'No, but they do have extremely big feet,' chirped Campion over Amanda's shoulder.

'This is my husband, Mrs Monk. He is an acquaintance of Ambassador Westergaard and our presence here in Gapton is simply to locate his daughter, Vibeke. The two gentlemen at the back door have other matters to discuss but I want to make it clear that if you help us, we will help you with them in any way we can.'

Dorothy Monk turned on her heels and headed for the kitchen, throwing her words over her shoulder.

'I cannot help you, Mrs Campion, though I sincerely wish I could. As for you helping me, I'm afraid you are twenty-five years too late.'

Amanda and Mr Campion exchanged bemused looks and hand in hand stepped across the threshold.

The place, as Mr Milton announced in a voice Lugg might have used to describe the state of his beer glass, was 'as empty as a drum'. Major Deighton, the Campions and Mrs Monk had waited uneasily in the sitting room, their faces turned upwards to the ceiling as Mr Milton's considerable weight creaked across the floorboards, examining the upstairs rooms. His descent of the staircase had been, in contrast, an exercise in stealth, and then suddenly his massive frame was filling the room.

'Where is he, Mrs Monk?' Deighton said, his tone a semi-quaver of severity down from a threat.

'I have no idea who you are talking about.'

'Dieter.'

'I know no one of that name.'

The Deighton smile quivered but did not crack. 'I'm sorry; I should have said Burckhardt Schönherr. You do know someone of that name, and please do not deny he has been here.'

Mrs Monk stared proudly and unblinkingly at the major. 'I learned long ago that people like you would not believe me whatever I said, and therefore I shall say nothing. I am alone here. You have searched and you are welcome to search again, for I cannot stop you. Do your worst, but you will find no one.'

Amanda's soft brown eyes flashed at Mr Campion as though in anger, but in fact to draw his attention as she silently mouthed the words 'Distract her'. Amanda then silently edged herself out of the taller woman's eyeline as Campion slid effortlessly into his role as buffoon-for-hire, clapping a consoling arm around the bemused Major Deighton's shoulder.

'I fear, my dear Major,' he declaimed, 'that one gets nowhere with a Viking when they have set their face against you. The monks of Lindisfarne and poor old Earl Byrhtnoth at the battle of Maldon found that out the hard way. If history teaches us anything – though admittedly it taught me little – it is that the Vikings were a particularly stubborn race. Though I think "race" is not the correct term as to go 'a-Viking-ing' so to speak, was to go raiding in those awfully impressive long ships with their dragons' heads . . .'

Deighton stared at Mr Campion, convinced he had taken leave of his senses. Fortunately, Mrs Monk was equally bemused and did not notice the other woman in the room take up a position squarely behind her.

To the amazement of all present, Amanda made a grab for Mrs Monk's neck and shoulders and pulled her raincoat sharply downwards, the material pinning her arms to her sides, and before the assaulted woman could squeal in protest, Amanda had thrust her own hands into the waist pockets of the coat. Too late, Dorothy Monk kicked backwards in reaction, the heel of her shoe catching Amanda viciously on the shin but she was not to be denied and withdrawing her hands from Mrs Monk's coat – now effectively a straitjacket – she was able to triumphantly hold aloft a trophy: a large, rusted iron key.

'What the . . .?' said Deighton.

'I say, Amanda, well done!' complimented Mr Campion.

'Gordon Bennett!' exclaimed Mr Milton.

'She's hidden him in the church,' said Amanda, only now wincing at the pain in her shin. 'St Olave's. It's just across the road.'

'How on earth did you know, darling?' asked Mr Campion, full of admiration.

'The garden gate was open and she was hiding behind the front door still with her coat on when we arrived, which meant she'd only just got back from somewhere. Don't you men ever notice anything?'

'But why the church, dearest?'

'The only place she goes in Gapton is St Olave's – acts as a sort of volunteer caretaker – everyone knows that. Don't you men ever listen? Now, can we go there?'

'With all speed, my love, but first you must tell me where you learned that trick with the overcoat.'

'I saw Humphrey Bogart do it,' Amanda said, staring into Dorothy Monk's furious eyes, 'in a movie.'

Later, whenever Mr Campion thought about the events of that night, he could never decide whether Bitta Krause (as he would thence call her), in locking the door of St Olave's Church, was doing it to keep her lover safe from the authorities or to prevent him from leaving her. Wittingly or unwittingly and whether driven by the heart or the head, she had imprisoned Burckhardt Schönherr in flint and stone.

'This could be a church worth visiting in daylight,' said Mr Campion as they stood on the short path leading to the dark maw of the porch. 'It's bound to have spectacular flushwork of carefully knapped flints – chequering or diapering, I think it's called – which is very Suffolk. A hammerbeam roof, perhaps? Possibly some impressive stained glass and a wall painting if we're lucky. Who knows, there may even be a seven sacrament font, another Suffolk speciality. By no means uninteresting as far as prisons go.'

'It's not a prison,' said Major Deighton coldly, 'it's a fortress.'

'But not a defendable one, or no more than, say, the Alamo or the cathedral of St Cyril and St Methodius in Prague where those Czech guerrillas fought to the tragic end after the Heydrich assassination. I do hope you are not considering a frontal assault, Major. If Dieter wants to make a last stand it could get very nasty and we know he's armed.'

'He's got to be winkled out somehow.' Deighton's voice was grim, his actions grimmer as he worked the slide action on the large automatic pistol which had appeared suddenly in his hand. There was an instantaneous echo of metallic ratcheting as Mr Milton did exactly the same, although the pistol in his hands appeared little more than a toy.

'Do we really need a firing squad, gentlemen?' Campion asked. 'He can't go anywhere. All we have to do is wait for the dawn, by which time you could have the church ringed with fresh-faced policemen and possibly an archdeacon or two just to be on the safe side. Why go blundering in there in the dark with all guns blazing? Somebody, as my mother used to say, is bound to get hurt as sure as eggs are unborn chickens.'

'And what if he's got Vibeke Westergaard in there with him as a hostage?'

'My wife,' said Mr Campion 'is right, as usual. We cannot risk the ambassador's daughter.'

'Vibeke is not in there,' said Mrs Monk, the first sound to come out of her mouth since she had been restrained by Amanda in Samphire Cottage. 'I have told you several times that I cannot help you find Vibeke, but like these men, you only hear what you wish to hear.'

Mr Campion took a step closer to her and leaned forward to speak softly into her ear. 'If Burckhardt is alone and has no hostages, I can see no reason to restrain these gentlemen. My wife may very well side with them as she suspects him of shooting at our son last night. I think I can understand why you wish to protect Burckhardt, but for Dieter this old church cannot provide sanctuary.'

'Can you?'

Mr Campion shook his head and shivered in the damp night air. 'No, I cannot. Once, perhaps, I might have had the necessary influence to sway events but I am now out to grass in the meadow of retirement and enjoying a life of modest leisure. I can offer no securities, merely the wisdom of bitter experience.'

Dorothy Monk leaned forward and returned the whisper. 'Can you promise me these men will not hurt him?'

'That I think I can do, if he comes quietly as we say. I may no longer be able to ride to the rescue as a knight in shining armour, but they know I would make a very troublesome witness for the prosecution if they were to overstep themselves.'

'I think I trust you,' said Mrs Monk, then she swung on Amanda, 'but not her. She is too clever. Now, will you trust me?'

Campion stepped back and motioned for Amanda to hand over the key she had lifted from Mrs Monk's coat pocket. He then courteously waved her forward and Deighton and Milton, pistols in hand, allowed her to pass.

Dorothy Monk inserted the key into the oaken heart of St Olave's door and, straining slightly, turned the lock with a loud *clunk*. As she pushed the door open it creaked loudly on its ancient hinges – as all deserted church doors are supposed to do – and she shouted into the dark, cavernous interior in a language that Mr Campion recognized as Danish, though apart from the anguished cry of 'Burckhardt' the phrase *Jeg elsker dig* was the only phrase he could translate. It was, however, a phrase which brought a smile of relief to his face; something noticed only by his wife.

'Is she doing the right thing?' Amanda hissed, gripping her husband's arm.

Mr Campion patted the hand which secured but also comforted him. 'I think she is, but will Dieter?'

Without warning, the lights of St Olave's came on, filling the church with an orange glow which transfixed the five people standing in the doorway. Deighton and Milton tensed, their pistol arms outstretched. Mr Campion blinked ferociously and Amanda's grip tightened.

And then, with a clatter, first an automatic pistol and then its magazine of bullets landed on the flagstone floor of the church, and both objects skidded to a halt at the feet of Mrs Monk.

'And there we have our answer,' breathed Mr Campion.

TWENTY
Cobras in the Mist

S tewart Granger perhaps, thought Amanda, or possibly Peter Lawford, though it was hardly surprising that a Jean Lerner-Scott would fall for someone with movie star good looks and almost inevitable that a teenage Bitta Krause would be smitten by the younger version. What was surprising was that in all her incarnations – as Bitta Krause, Dortë Munk, Jean Lerner-Scott and then Dorothy Monk – she had kept a torch burning for Burckhardt for a quarter of a century. That was either the mark of a woman truly in love or a lost and lonely soul. Was it possible for a woman to be both? Amanda looked at her husband's thin frame, his straw-coloured hair and his expression now totally serious and concerned, and she thought not.

'Herr Schönherr,' said Mr Campion, 'these gentlemen – the two pointing guns at you – are from our security services. In a short while they will take you away for questioning which, I am sure, will be conducted in a civilized manner and to standards and rules which, from what I hear, are unknown in your own organization. May I ask if you understand what I am saying?'

As they had entered the church, Burckhardt Schönherr, known as Dieter, had walked backwards down the nave and sat down in the first pew. Deighton and Milton had taken up positions in front and to his side with Mr Campion between them and Amanda, firmly holding Mrs Monk's arm, a pace behind. Apart from a brief, anguished glance towards Mrs Monk, his face had remained expressionless and he had remained silent. Surrounded as he was, he sat calmly, his hands clasped in his lap, as though concealing dirty fingernails. His need for a shave spoiled his matinee-idol good looks and, when he responded to Campion's question and turned his face up towards his captors, there was a weariness behind those cerulean eyes.

'I understand you perfectly well, Mr Campion.'

Amanda saw her husband's shoulders stiffen while simultaneously noting that this Dieter, who should represent everything she despised, damn him, had a deep and really rather sexy voice to complete the film star image.

'You know who I am?' Campion asked in the tone of a High Court judge who had never read *Photoplay*.

The prisoner smiled upwards and yes, thought Amanda, 'pretty boy' really was an apt translation of his name, though his answer was chilling.

'Of course, we have a file on you. It was quite a thick file at one time, or so I believe, but entries of late have been sparse.'

'I am well and truly retired from your world, Dieter,' said Campion, 'and I have no official standing – or interest for that matter – in what these gentlemen want to discuss with you, nor with what ultimately happens to you. However, due to my great age and a small amount of acquired wisdom, my opinion may be deferred to if you can help me. In doing so, I can confidently say you will be helping yourself and, more importantly perhaps, helping Mrs Monk here, who is almost certainly in trouble with the authorities.'

'How can I help you, Mr Campion?' Dieter enquired calmly, with the same emotion he would use asking the time of day.

'You can tell me where Vibeke Westergaard is,' Campion said coldly.

'I have honestly no idea. I know who she is, I have seen photographs of her and I know she was the lover of Francis Tate. But she is of no – shall we say professional – interest to me, I have never seen the girl in the flesh, and I have no knowledge of where she is now. If I knew – and if I could trade that information for immunity for Bitta – I would tell you in a heartbeat.'

'Do you know, I think I almost believe you,' said Mr Campion, breaking the silence, 'but if your presence here has nothing to do with Vibeke Westergaard, why did you risk so much by coming?'

Burckhardt – for this was Burckhardt the lover and not Dieter the enemy agent – gazed beyond Campion at Bitta Krause.

'I had to see Bitta, my Bitta, one last time. May she sit with me?'

Campion nodded to the men with guns that he had no objection. Amanda, to her surprise, realized that she had released her hold on Mrs Monk, who glided between the gun barrels and into the pew. As she sat down – as Bitta Krause once more, no longer Dorothy Monk – she allowed Burckhardt to take her hands in his.

'I had to come once I knew my Bitta was here,' Burckhardt said, then flashed an angry glare at Deighton. 'He knew that; knew that very well.'

Mr Campion removed his spectacles and pulled his handkerchief from his pocket. He concentrated on polishing the lenses for twenty seconds then replaced both items and sniffed loudly.

'There's a faint fruity smell of incense which never leaves a church no matter how long it has been out of action, isn't there? And being in a church what better place for a confession or two? I was rather thinking you should begin, Major.'

'I don't know what you mean, Campion,' said Deighton, far too smoothly for Mr Campion's liking, and Burckhardt was quick to pick up on Campion's disapproval.

'He has not told you, has he, Campion? Told you how *he* made it impossible for me *not* to come to Gapton.'

Deighton attempted to cut Burckhardt short. 'This has nothing to do with Vibeke Westergaard, Campion; you have my word on that.'

'That is true,' conceded Burckhardt. 'It has to do with the cobras in the mist.'

Now it was Deighton's turn to bristle and Amanda was sure she could detect static electricity in the echoing cold of the church.

'If you really do have a file on me, Herr Schönherr, you will know that I am easily bamboozled,' said Mr Campion, 'so I would appreciate it if you would elucidate, preferably using small and simple words, unlike "elucidate".'

Burckhardt smiled. 'The file does have an entry on the famous Campion sense of self-deprecation – is that correct English? It also advises that anyone who comes into contact with him should not be fooled.'

'And clearly recommends the use of flattery which, I assure you in my case, will get you anywhere. But please, why are there cobras in the mists over Gapton?'

'You will know that Gapton was a Y Station during the war against the Fascists?'

'Of course; it was a listening station and very important to the war effort. We used to call them Huff-Duffs and I believe the locals here still do, but the station is long gone. I tripped over some of its remains only this afternoon.'

'Did you see any signs of recent activity out there?'

'You mean apart from a pirate's cave of smuggled alcohol, courtesy of this parish's corrupt policeman? Well, yes, a few tell-tale signs that somebody, surveyors perhaps, had been out there of late.'

Burckhardt smiled again. 'Those were the first signs of a planned Cobra Mist system, or at least that was what I was supposed to think.'

'We're back to those pesky hooded snakes again,' said Campion flippantly. 'Aren't they the ones that spit venom rather than bite?'

'I am referring to the Cobra Mist system, an invention of your American allies. It is the modern equivalent of what you called the Huff-Duff chain of listening stations. It is a state-of-the-art radar device which operates "over-the-horizon", as the phrase goes, in order to spy on Eastern Bloc countries and detect hostile missile activity.'

'That's a rather trite way of putting it,' said Campion, 'but do go on; I'm intrigued.'

'Two years ago the Americans wanted to build a Cobra Mist station in Turkey, but the Turks refused their permission. Now the British government has offered the Americans a site on the Suffolk coast, here at Gapton. It would be ideally placed to spy on Plesetsk, the Soviet missile testing centre near Archangel.'

'Fascinating stuff, Herr Schönherr,' said Mr Campion politely, 'and I am sure we are breaking the Official Secrets Act by simply listening to you, although Major Deighton here does not seem especially perturbed.'

Deighton shuffled his feet but said nothing.

'He would be if it was true,' said Burckhardt, 'but the story is what we call a baited hook.'

'To catch a big fish, I suppose? A big fish such as yourself?'

Burckhardt gave him a short nod of condescension. 'I set one of our lower grade agents to work collecting intelligence.'

'Francis Tate.'

'That was his British identity, yes, and I encouraged his smuggling activities with your greedy policeman – a man who is a disgrace to his uniform, if I may say.'

'You may and you would not be alone in that opinion,' Campion agreed, 'though I can see where Sergeant Davies and his boat would come in useful. Yet if you knew that these particular cobras in the mist were as spurious as . . . well, as mist . . . why risk coming here?'

'On one of the films Tate sent back there were pictures of two women looking out over the Gapton Spit on a day when your army helicopters were landing there. The women were only an excuse, a safeguard, if Tate had been discovered photographing a military operation.'

'I think,' said Mr Campion, 'that we are rather more relaxed than you are about such things.'

'Or careless,' countered Burckhardt, 'but the women he had caught in his camera were Vibeke Westergaard and . . .' he turned to smile at Mrs Monk '. . . my Bitta. I recognized her immediately. Even though her films had not been shown in the DDR, as a Stasi officer I had certain privileges and so I had followed her career until she dropped out of sight. To find her again was more than I could have hoped for.'

Burckhardt released one hand from holding his beloved and pointed a finger at Deighton's chest.

'He knew that and perhaps even arranged that Bitta and Vibeke would become friends. He knew I could not be bought in any other way.'

'So you were being tempted into defecting?'

'By the only thing that would tempt me,' said the German, gazing deep into the moist eyes of Bitta Krause.

'You met during the war, didn't you?' asked Amanda, breaking the spell.

'Yes, we did,' said Burckhardt, still entranced by the face of his lost-but-now-found love, 'and I wore a different uniform then, that of an enemy. Fortunately, love does not recognize uniforms.'

'It got Dortë – Bitta – into trouble, though, didn't it?' Amanda pressed.

'I got myself into trouble,' Bitta Krause answered for herself.

'I betrayed the Resistance because I thought it would help Burckhardt. It was foolish and selfish and innocent people suffered, even died, but it was wartime and we took what happiness we could, when we could. I have prayed to God for forgiveness every day since and finally I think He has forgiven me because He has brought my Burckhardt back to me.'

'Bitta was saved by Aage Westergaard.' Schönherr turned his head back to look at Campion, his expression stoic and unafraid. 'I always knew that and it is something I am grateful for. It is the reason why I would never hurt him, or his daughter.'

'But you were happy for your spy Tate to seduce her,' Amanda said crisply.

Schönherr shrugged his shoulders. 'Who am I to say they were not genuinely in love? I do admit that their relationship gave Tate a perfect cover for his visits here.'

'Just as Tate's death gave you the perfect excuse to come here,' said Campion. 'I suspect that even for a Stasi officer permission to travel outside the DDR is limited – unless one has a wife and family to be left behind as surety.'

'You are shrewd, Mr Campion. I would not have liked to have crossed swords with you professionally.'

'Perhaps you did and just never knew it; but enough of this flummery. Your fate is decided, perhaps not by you and certainly not by me, but it is decided. The fate of Vibeke Westergaard is still undecided and her whereabouts unknown for several days now. Will you not help us find her?'

Burckhardt got to his feet and Bitta, holding his hand, followed at his side. Standing straight, almost to attention, in front of Campion – who half expected to hear heels being clicked – he looked the older man in the eye. 'I do not know what happened to Vibeke Westergaard. It is possible she killed Francis Tate, though I find that unlikely. If she did, and if I could, I would help her to evade the police. I would protect her in the same way her father protected my Bitta in the war. But I honestly do not know where she is. If I did, I would tell you, Mr Campion, though not necessarily these gentlemen, because I believe you still have some honour, which is a rare commodity in our profession.'

'My husband is no longer of your profession,' said Amanda firmly.

'And jolly glad he is not,' said Mr Campion.

The Campions, arm in arm, made their way slowly back to The Butt and Oyster, the damp, salty night air warmer than the ice-house cold of St Olave's.

'So Dieter has Bitta,' said Amanda, 'but Deighton has Dieter.'

'Indeed,' said a thoughtful Campion. 'I think that may have been the sole purpose of this exercise all along. I was stupid and wrong to link Dieter with the Westergaard girl.'

'I was wrong too,' said his wife. 'I was sure Dorothy Monk was hiding her. We have both failed Count Westergaard. What can we possibly tell him?'

'Nothing tonight, my dear – let us sleep on things. I really am quite tired; it must be all this sea air. Things always look brighter in the morning.'

Campion's frame seemed to shrink and his pace slowed as if defeat had become a physical burden. Amanda rested her head briefly on Mr Campion's shoulder, glad that he could not see the worry on her face.

She was unused to seeing defeat in her husband's eyes. To see despair was a new and frightening experience.

TWENTY-ONE
Smokescreen

D r Milne, or perhaps more accurately Dr Milne's bowtie, was the only flash of jollity piercing the gloomy atmosphere hanging over breakfast at The Maltings the following morning.

Mr Campion and Amanda, much to the dismay of mine host at The Butt and Oyster, had politely declined the 'full Suffolk' breakfast on offer and had chosen instead to stroll up the High Street through the thin damp mist coming off the sea to the Sandyman home. Apart from the occasional set of headlamps and several unlit bicycles, they saw little sign of human activity until they were opposite the open gates of the brewery. That at least seemed to be one hive of activity with the hum, rattle and clang of rolling metal casks being assembled in the yard for the day's deliveries. The other was domestic rather than commercial: the kitchen of The Maltings, where Bernard Sandyman was struggling to create that most important meal of the day for his three grandchildren and two house guests and doing so with the concentration of a field marshal deciding a battle plan.

'Ah, more Campions!' he greeted the latest arrivals cheerfully enough. 'Come in, come in. Take a pew if you can find one. Torquil's trotted off to work down at the brewery and Victoria's got one of her "heads" so she's having a bit of a lie-in, so I'm in charge of the mess tent, and to be honest you might find it a bit of a mess! Young Perdita will be down in a minute. She's on sick parade as Doc Milne is about his rounds bright and early. The kettle is, I am fairly convinced, on.'

As the Campions made their way into the kitchen, carefully stepping over children, their toys and an assortment of clothing which had either just been discarded or had yet to go on, Rupert helped his father out of his coat.

'You look shattered,' he said quietly.

'I didn't sleep well,' Mr Campion admitted, 'and I'm afraid I bear no glad tidings, at least not about our missing girl.'

'What of our smuggler friend?' Rupert kept his mouth close to his father's ear.

'Well, at least he's out of business, but that trail didn't lead to Vibeke. I was on the wrong scent entirely there.'

'Sit yourself down, Campion, and make yourself useful buttering toast and suchlike,' commanded Bernard, busying himself at the Aga in the way a novice engineer would struggle with the controls of a runaway train. 'And can I prevail upon you, Lady Amanda, to keep an eye on the twins? They're boys, you know, and they're always up to mischief unless they're busy eating.'

Amanda smiled at Rupert and said, 'That would be no trouble at all, Bernard. I've found Jasper and George to be absolutely charming and well-behaved, totally unlike my previous experience of young boys.'

They were settling themselves around the large kitchen table, dealing cutlery and passing plates and cups (Amanda trying to ignore the wisps of smoke coming from an ancient toaster) when Perdita entered, flexing her shoulder and smiling bravely, followed by Dr Milne wearing a flamboyant red-with-white-spots bowtie which gave the impression that he was being attacked by a vampiric butterfly.

'Well, well, a full house of Campions and Sandymans!' exclaimed the doctor jovially.

'How's the patient, Doctor?' Amanda asked.

'This one?' He pointed a finger – and his bowtie (which Amanda found slightly mesmeric) – at Perdita. 'She's healing very nicely thanks to all the advantages of youth, with no sign of infection and a bruise which will fade eventually. I looked in on Victoria, but she seems to be sleeping comfortably so I left her undisturbed.'

'Wise man,' said Bernard to himself, though not quietly enough.

'We've sort of invited ourselves for breakfast,' said Mr Campion, 'won't you join us?'

The doctor sniffed the air as if trying to detect a kidney being devilled. 'Perhaps a cup of coffee,' he said after a pause. 'My first house call this morning was at Mussett's Farm and Mercy Lee does a really good fry-up, which is certainly bad for the arteries but jolly difficult to refuse.'

'You started rounds early this morning, Doc,' observed Bernard, leaning back from a frying pan spitting fat at him.

'I think my patients have been saving up their illnesses until I got back from holiday, but it's nice to be in demand.'

'Mercy Lee's not expecting again, is she?'

'Couldn't tell you if I wanted to, my dear chap, patient confidentiality and all that, but I wasn't called out to see Tinker or his missus; it was Uncle Eppy I was interested in.'

'Eppy? That mad-eyed old bugger who roams Gapton Spit scaring people?'

'Rupert!'

Amanda's sharp reprimand brought her son up short and produced a look of astonishment on Mr Campion's face.

'But he *is* scary,' Perdita defended her husband. 'It was because of him I impaled myself on that stupid fence.'

'Eppy? Ephraim Mussett? Are you sure, my dear? I mean it was dark . . .'

Bernard Sandyman was giving Perdita his full attention and barely acknowledged Amanda taking charge of the frying pan he was brandishing like a deadly weapon.

'I've no idea who Eppy Mussett is,' Perdita said vehemently, 'but I know I was frightened. It was Hyacinth Mister who told me his name, she seemed to know him.'

'I can certainly vouch for his scariness,' added Rupert. 'I ran into him out on the dunes when I was with Hyacinth. She said he was four-fifths barmy after something that happened in the war, but that doesn't excuse him wandering around with a dirty great axe like he's just absconded from a loony-bin.'

'Now steady on, young Campion.' Dr Milne stretched his neck, making his bowtie flutter its wings. 'Eppy Mussett was damaged in the service of king and country and so we in Gapton make allowances if his behaviour is a bit odd sometimes. For the most part, he keeps himself to himself and doesn't bother anyone, and in fact we've all been very grateful for the smoked fish and meat he produces. I'm one of his best customers and proud to be so.'

Mr Campion used a teaspoon on a plate as a gavel. 'Excuse

me, but not for the first time I am totally lost. Exactly who are
we talking about?'

'The Mussetts,' said Bernard.

'Still wandering aimlessly, I'm afraid,' said Mr Campion
apologetically.

'Neighbours of ours, I suppose. They own the farm between
our paddock and the sea. Pelagius runs it and because that's a
damn silly name everybody calls him Tinker, probably because
he always got on with the gypsies who turned up at harvest time.
Even married one, a proper beauty called Mercy Lee, and they
get on with most in the town. Eppy though, he's Tinker's uncle,
is an odd cove to say the least, but he usually keeps himself to
himself and that stinking smokehouse of his.'

'And he's completely harmless, Bernard,' Dr Milne argued.

'My son and my daughter-in-law would seem to disagree,
Doctor.'

'Well, I'm sorry, Campion, but Eppy has been my patient for
more than five years now and given his condition, he's doing
remarkably well.'

'Without bending your professional ethics too far, Doctor,
could you give us a hint as to what his condition might be?'
Campion asked, keeping his voice level.

'Hyacinth Mister said it was something to do with his war
service out East,' offered Rupert.

'That much is common knowledge,' the doctor admitted. 'Eppy
was taken prisoner at Singapore and held by the Japanese for
over four years, Lord knows in what conditions but clearly he
suffered a complete mental and physical breakdown out there.
Physically, he's now reasonably fit for a man of his age, but
he suffers from a very acute form of tinnitus.'

'That's "ringing in the ears", is it not?'

'Yes, only it's worse for poor Eppy. Sounds seem to get magni-
fied to a vast degree – inside his head that is – and then he can
be difficult to control.' Dr Milne saw the shock on the faces of
his audience. 'But most of the time he's a quiet, withdrawn sort
of chap and it's usually an unfamiliar noise which triggers him
off.'

'Such as?'

'Such as that helicopter landing in your paddock yesterday,

Bernard. It must have come in right over Mussett's Farm and Eppy's smokehouse. No wonder he was acting up. He was out most of the night, walking the dunes and so worried poor Mercy Lee that she called me in to give him a sedative.'

'Would the sound of a motorbike engine trigger the same effect on him?' asked Rupert.

'It's possible,' said Dr Milne, 'if it was loud and close and unexpected.'

Mr Campion's face lit up and a weight seemed to have slipped from his shoulders as he stared at his son.

'Rupert, get your coat.'

They marched across the Sandymans' paddock, arguing as they went. Rupert led the way because he could identify their suspect, Dr Milne hanging on his shoulder to protect (or treat) his patient, Mr Campion because – well, because he was Mr Campion – and then Amanda, because she knew her husband too well and because she refused to be left behind.

Perdita had been left at The Maltings, and she had accepted her fate with good grace. For one thing, her shoulder hurt more than she had let on to either doctor or family and, for another, someone had to make sure that Bernard did not burn the kitchen down around his grandchildren, for the smoke and screaming would probably disturb Victoria's lie-in.

'I assure you, Campion, Eppy Mussett is quite harmless in my medical opinion.'

'Is your medical opinion ever sought by the police?' Mr Campion asked innocently.

'Often,' said Dr Milne proudly. 'I am the local police surgeon.'

'But not on Sunday, when Francis Tate was fished out of the lagoon,' said Rupert.

'Well, no, because I was on holiday, but Superintendent Appleyard has sent me a copy of the autopsy report out of courtesy. Not that I've actually had time to read it.'

'So you don't really know what went on here in Gapton last Saturday night?'

'I suspect I'm as well-informed as the next man,' said the doctor. 'Layman, that is.'

'I somehow doubt that,' said Mr Campion. 'My wife and I

have only nibbled at the edges of the goings-on in Gapton, but our son has been in the thick of things. Rupert, would you brief the good doctor?'

Rupert jumped at the chance. 'Francis Tate and Vibeke Westergaard were last seen on Saturday evening. On Sunday morning Tate's body was spotted in the lagoon and later so was his motorbike. There was no sign of Vibeke. I had the unfortunate privilege of identifying the body and examining at very close range the way somebody had smashed the back of his head in.'

Amanda gave a sharp gasp of maternal concern and reached out a hand to touch Rupert lightly on the arm.

'From what the police can piece together' – Rupert felt that quoting the police, however spuriously, rather than the sisters Mister, gave more authority to his story – 'the two of them went somewhere on Tate's bike that evening, maybe just for a burn up and down the local lanes, and later on ended up on the path round the lagoon. Tate was killed on or near that path through the dunes at some point between Eppy Mussett's smokehouse and the ministry fence that Perdita was impaled upon.'

'And you think Eppy may have seen something? Well, it's true, he does prowl the dunes at night, as your poor wife discovered. But surely the police have talked to him?'

'I'm not sure,' said Rupert, 'but I think Mr and Mrs Mussett were paid a visit.'

'Well, if you think Eppy knows something germane to the enquiry, young man,' the doctor began pompously, 'then before we set out as vigilantes, we should have telephoned the police house, shouldn't we?'

'I'm afraid there's nobody home there,' said Mr Campion lightly. 'I believe they've discovered an infestation and Gapton police house is closed for fumigation.'

There were, however, lots of people at home at Mussett's Farm and all of them Mussetts of various sizes and ages. Dr Milne identified a muscular, curly-haired man of perhaps thirty-five weather-beaten years as Pelagius Mussett ('but Tinker to his friends') and a small, perfectly proportioned woman with porcelain skin and long flowing raven-black hair as Mercy Lee Mussett, the mother of the children of the house who seemed to number half-platoon strength, but it was difficult to do introductions or even an accurate head count as they were constantly on the move.

Amanda's expert eye identified six individual children, two girls and a boy clearly dressed for school and two younger boys and a girl no more than a toddler still in pyjamas. Amanda also noted with a wry smile that in a kitchen half the size of that of The Maltings and totally devoid of labour-saving gadgets, and with twice the number of children, this was not a scene of chaos but a well-drilled execution of the family breakfast manoeuvre, with every child allocated a household chore. Mercy Lee, Amanda decided, was not only a strikingly beautiful woman but a darned efficient mother.

'Oi can't stop to chat, Doctor,' said Tinker, pulling on a donkey jacket which had seen better days, 'Oi've got to get the older 'uns to school in Gapton Thorpe. Oi won't be long if you needs me, otherwise Mercy here will look after you – might even cook you a second breakfast if'n you smile at her!'

Dr Milne beamed at the lady of the house and patted his stomach, an action which made his bow tie flap its wings.

'Oh, I couldn't possibly manage *another* and we did rather want a quick word with you, Tinker. Dear me, where are my manners? These are the Campions, Albert and Rupert and Lady Amanda.'

'Pleased to meet you, Oi'm sure,' nodded Tinker Mussett, 'but I just got to get these kids to school on time or Headmaster'll skin me alive. Oi shan't be long and Mercy can at least make you a cuppa tea. C'mon you lot.'

The three elder children kissed their younger siblings and marched out in their father's wake without a single howl of protest and Amanda noticed that Mercy Lee was smiling with pride. Then the small woman's smile turned on her.

'Lady Amanda?'

For a moment Amanda thought she was going to do something excruciatingly embarrassing such as curtsey, but Mercy Lee went on confidently: 'Would you be a Fitton, and from Pontisbright?'

'Why yes, I was – am.'

'My grandmother knew your folk when she was travelling. Said they were kindly and generous and blessed with twenty other people's share of charm. She reckoned they could start a family fight in a confessional box but charm the priest so that he'd not only forgive 'em but pay for the damage.'

Mr Campion let forth a controlled explosion of laughter. 'Your grandmother clearly knew the family well!'

'Clearly,' agreed Amanda, 'and I think Mercy Lee is more than capable of answering our questions.'

'Oh, you'll get more out of me than you would my 'usband Tinker,' Mercy Lee said with a broad and beguiling smile. 'I don't hardly get a chance to gossip these days.'

'We've actually come to see Ephraim Mussett,' said Amanda, taking responsibility for what must have appeared to be a boarding party.

The lady of the house did not seem at all concerned by the invasion of strangers into her kitchen.

'Uncle Eppy? Oh, he's gone.'

'But he was here an hour ago,' protested Dr Milne.

'Well, 'e ain't now. Spends all his days and most of the night over at that stink-hole of a smokehouse of 'is; even takes his meals there. Took a big breakfast of eggs and fried bread with him this morning soon 'as you'd gone, Doc – and a pint o' milk which will leave me short, I shouldn't wonder.'

'Does he take all his meals at this smokehouse of his?' Amanda asked casually.

'Never used to, but to tell the honest truth it's good to have him out from under my feet at dinner times. He don't say much, old Eppy, and though he's not quite right in the 'ead, he's rarely any trouble until 'e 'as one of his turns, like when that whirlybird went over yesterday.'

'We're very sorry about that,' said Mr Campion, 'we really had no idea. It was most thoughtless of us.'

'You weren't to know, sir.' Mercy Lee smiled and melted Mr Campion's large and malleable heart. 'It don't happen that often, just when he hears a loud and sudden noise he wasn't expecting. Then he shuts himself away in that smokehouse and no matter how many times I put them through the wash' – Mercy Lee was now confiding, woman to woman, in Amanda – 'I can't get the smell of kippers out of his clothes. They reckon the Gapton fox has her den under that smokehouse, as the smell keeps men and dogs away from her cubs, fair stinks it does, close up.'

'Mrs Mussett—' Rupert began.

'It's Mercy as long as you're in my kitchen.' She beamed and fluttered her eyelashes in a way that seemed natural and un-theatrical, making Amanda fear momentarily for the heart rate of her son.

'Mercy,' Rupert returned her innocent smile rather self-consciously, 'how long has Uncle Eppy been taking his dinners out to the smokehouse? I'm sorry to pry but this could be important.'

'I hardly call that prying. I said I fancied a good gossip. Didn't think it would be about Eppy, though. Come to think of it, he never used to disappear so much. Now he piles up 'is plate with a double helping of everything and shoots off without a word. If I'm lucky I gets the plate back the next day. But no, he hasn't been doin' it for long.'

'Would you say,' Rupert pressed gently, 'that he has been behaving like this for weeks or months?'

'Oh, no, only the last week or so, I reckon.'

'Since Saturday or Sunday perhaps?'

'Yes, that'd be about right.'

'Clever boy,' said Mr Campion quietly.

'Go out the back door and across the yard and never mind the chickens,' said Mercy Lee. 'It's quicker that way, across the dunes.'

No one had said anything; no one had shouted orders or demanded answers but Mercy Lee had sensed that the situation – whatever it was – was both important and urgent. All she had done was to look at Amanda, who solemnly and silently nodded her head, before taking up the smallest child into her arms and directing her visitors to the porch door at the back of the kitchen.

'Thank you, Mercy,' said Amanda, who paused to stroke the chubby cheek of the toddler she held as the men pushed by them.

Once outside in a yard made of cracked and uneven concrete slabs where a dozen brown hens scuffed and pecked at imaginary insects, it was Dr Milne who spoke first.

'I'm not sure what is occurring, Campion, but if we're going to see Eppy, shouldn't we wait for Tinker? After all, he's Tinker's uncle and the only family he's got.'

'I'm not waiting,' said Rupert, pushing open the thigh-high gate which linked the farmyard with the sand dunes leading to Gapton Spit.

'I suggest we follow my son's lead,' said Mr Campion, 'because if he's right, there isn't a moment to lose. Goodness knows, I've wasted enough time already.'

'I'm sorry, Campion, I'm not with you. If your son is right about what?'

'His theory.'

'But he hasn't said anything!' said the doctor, exasperated.

'I know what he's thinking,' said Mr Campion, 'and I think he could be right.'

They followed first their noses and then their eyes. The morning mist had thinned but not gone, its briny scent soon giving way to the perfume of wood smoke and then the more pungent notes of smoked fish and flesh. And then a gust of sea breeze waved away the thin cotton mist and they could see dark grey smoke rising from the square, brown-stained timbers of the smokehouse. It was then that their ears came into play.

'Listen!' Rupert held up an arm to halt their Indian file column. 'That's him!'

The sound coming across the grassy sand was regular rather than rhythmic and was a combination of metallic click and then dull crack.

'He's chopping wood,' whispered Rupert.

'Of course he is,' said Dr Milne, kicking out his feet to dislodge fine sand from his shoes, 'that's what he does. It's fuel for his smokehouse. He's always chopping up driftwood.'

'You haven't read the autopsy report of Francis Tate, have you, Doctor?'

'Not yet.'

'Well, I went one better and saw the corpse,' said Rupert grimly, 'the corpse with its head smashed in. The police surgeons said it was as if he'd taken a blow from a medieval weapon.'

'You mean, like a battle axe?' Dr Milne spluttered, his bow tie seeming to take on a life of its own, fuelled by his indignation.

'Well, an axe of some sort, like the one Eppy carries around with him to chop wood.'

'But Eppy doesn't use an axe to split his logs. He does it the old-fashioned way, with a hammer and a wood bomb.'

'Of course!' Rupert slapped his forehead – a gesture he had perfected in a short tour in repertory playing a constantly amazed country vicar. 'When I saw him he was holding a hammer, not an axe! What the Dickens is a wood bomb?'

'It's a particularly vicious blob of sharpened steel,' said Mr Campion, 'shaped like a huge fat drawing pin. You hammer it into the end of a cut log and it splits the wood evenly along the grain. The sort of thing that a medieval knight would have loved to have in his armoury in order to dish out a blow like a mace or one of those spiked balls on chains. I think we should hurry.'

TWENTY-TWO
Run to Earth

They crested a dune with Rupert already ten yards in the van, Dr Milne shaking his feet after every step in the sand and Mr Campion and Amanda following hand in hand at a determined, if more sedate, pace.

They could see the smokehouse now, a building no more impressive than a large garden shed but seemingly made out of driftwood and the trunks of fallen trees, which gave it a spiky outline rather like an illustration from a Grimm fairy tale. Its smoking chimney, or what could be seen of it, was composed of sections of metal drainpipe forced together at random angles as if constructed following a design in a Heath Robinson cartoon. To one side of it, in a small sheltered amphitheatre of grass-tufted sand, a small, wiry figure stood over a section of tree trunk which he was using as a chopping block. To his right was a confused pile of logs and to his left a wicker basket, either a large trug or a baby's carry-cot, which he was filling with smaller, split pieces. He was doing so with a mechanical action, his right arm rising and falling to bring down the head of a lump hammer on to a fat, shiny metal 'bomb' chisel, each movement producing a metallic *click* followed by a wooden *crack*.

It was not until Rupert was within twenty yards of him that the man looked up and saw the advancing party. Even further back, Campion saw the man's eyes widen in surprise and then the small, brown-skinned figure turned and began running up and over the dunes.

'Rupert, don't!' shouted Amanda, but she was ignored as Rupert lowered his head and charged after him.

'Ephraim! It's Dr Milne! Don't be frightened, we just want to speak with you!'

Dr Milne made as if to join the pursuit, but Campion restrained him sharply.

'No, Doctor, we have to check inside the hut. You may be needed here.'

'You think . . .?' Amanda said, already moving towards the smokehouse.

'I hope,' said Mr Campion, taking long, loping strides across the sand.

'Hope *what*?'

'That she's still alive,' Mr Campion shouted without turning round.

The door to the smokehouse was a ramshackle affair cobbled together from a piece of flotsam – a hatch cover? – and two planks of planed timber nailed on the diagonal to give it strength. There was a closed padlock and hasp on one side serving as a lock and though the metal was rusted and the wood surrounding it rotten, it held fast as Campion clawed at it.

'Damn it!' he howled as he put his shoulder to the door, cursing both the solidity of the lock and his own lack of strength.

He had taken a pace back and was preparing another charge when Amanda reached him, grabbing at his arm.

'Stop it, darling. How many times have you said brute force was never your forte?'

Mr Campion, breathing heavily, looked into his wife's shining brown eyes. 'Yes, I really should stop and listen to myself one day.' He thrust his right hand into his jacket pocket and produced a pearl-handled penknife. 'I will put my faith in good Toledo steel – that's Toledo, Ohio by the way, not Spain. My trusty Maher and Grosh whittling knife is older than me, you know. Given to me by an American chap. Said he was a cowboy but I never quite believed that.'

As he spoke, Campion opened the main blade of the knife with urgent fingers and began to stab at the wood around the padlock hasp while Amanda breathed a sigh of relief. It upset and unnerved her when her husband cursed aloud in frustration, but when he prattled on inanely, it was a sure sign that his mind was running with smooth, clockwork precision.

She had no intention, however, of standing idly by and her eyes flashed to Eppy's chopping block and wood pile, searching for a lever or a weapon.

By now Dr Milne, his face the colour of his bowtie, was

shoulder to shoulder with Mr Campion, attempting to assist him, his fingers groping for an edge to the smokehouse door. Yet for all the doctor's straining and Mr Campion's chipping off splinters of wood, the door and the lock held.

'Stand aside!' Amanda commanded.

The two men automatically did as they were told and saw, with astonishment on one face and uxorious pride on the other, Lady Amanda attack the padlock with a berserker's swing of a three-pound lump hammer, smashing it from its mounting with a single blow.

The makeshift door fell inwards and hot, thick, pungent air billowed out to envelope Campion and Dr Milne as they burst into the fetid gloom. It was a hellish scene, but a hell where the fires had been damped for the night. Long strings threaded with split fish and eels, oily and damp, festooned the ceiling timbers like ghoulish trophies in a troll cave. In one corner an ancient iron pot stove flickered with glowing wood, giving off tiny flecks of black ash along with curling fingers of slow smoke.

As his eyes became acclimatized, Campion saw metal pails of water placed at strategic points around the floor, presumably doubling as humidifiers and emergency fire extinguishers, and incongruously although not surprisingly, a pair of motorcycle helmets. Then he saw movement in the furthest, darkest corner; a splayed, frantic kicking movement made by a pair of legs in stained and filthy leather trousers, and above them a wriggling torso and above that a wide-eyed face with matted hair masking half of it, screaming silently from behind a thick woollen gag.

'Ssshhh, you're safe now,' said Mr Campion gently as he stooped to cut the ropes tethering the petrified girl.

If her Romany heritage had taught Mercy Lee Mussett anything, it was that rich and well-educated people could be really stupid at times, especially when they were dealing with country folk. Although she was by no means clear why that nice elderly gentleman and his son and the doctor and the elegant Lady Amanda had all gone haring across the yard and into the dunes like mad things, she knew the hens would not lay that day. She was not concerned for Uncle Eppy, as the good Dr Milne was

with them and he'd always had a kind word or two for Eppy.
Trouble was, Eppy didn't have kind words for anyone much and
'specially not strangers and he had a bit of a temper on him, as
all Mussetts had unless they had a woman's firm hand to restrain
them.

Not one of those townies though had suggested telephoning
for the police, so it couldn't be *that* serious; not that Mercy Lee
would have dreamed of asking their local lazy copper the time
of day. They probably didn't think simple folk like the Mussetts
possessed a telephone, but they did and Mercy Lee decided that
someone other than herself should know that there was trouble
brewing on Gapton Spit, so she telephoned The Maltings where
she spoke to old Mr Bernard, who had always had a smile and
a kind word for her.

Bernard Sandyman, delighted to be doing something other
than kitchen duties, immediately rang the brewery and informed
Torquil of developments which seemed to be coming to a head
out on the dunes near Eppy Mussett's smokehouse.

Torquil Sandyman had immediately asked Hyacinth Mister to
take over his management duties at the brewery as he believed
his friend Rupert might be in trouble out on the Spit. He was
not halfway across the brewery yard before Hyacinth had dele-
gated responsibility to Marigold who, within a few seconds, had
passed that responsibility on to Mr Rose the Head Brewer, so
that both of them could join Torquil in aiding that nice young
Campion, whatever he was up to.

Thus the three of them were ideally placed on the path which
led from the High Street around the bowl of Gapton lagoon to
see, on the skyline provided by the high grassy dunes, a small
brown figure with the rangy, gangling gait of a monkey being
run down by a taller, younger man.

When hunted and hunter seemed almost inseparable, the
pursuing figure launched himself in a perfect flying tackle, his
shoulder and arms taking his prey around the legs, the two of
them rolling together down the dune. It was the hunter who stood
up first, triumphantly, after they came to a halt in a storm of
flying sand.

'Look at that!' said Torquil with approval. 'You can't tell me
that's a chap who doesn't like rugby!'

The sisters Mister looked at each other and shook their heads agreeing, without words, that they would never understand men and then, as they had done during the war years, they ran on to Gapton Spit to do their duty.

Neither they nor Torquil noticed that atop an adjacent dune, peering through a clump of marram grass, was a large vixen watching this particular human circus with bemused detachment.

The menu at the Brewers' Hall – potted shrimps with brown bread, jugged hare with creamed potatoes and red cabbage followed by a ripe Stilton – was pretty basic fare by the hall's banqueting standards, but Bernard Sandyman hoped that his guests would understand that this was a private party and the catering had been left, at very short notice, to the Beadle.

The luncheon party was, in fact, being thrown by Aage Westergaard as a private thank you to those who had rescued his daughter, but being a private function he had thought it diplomatic not to hold it at the embassy. His old friend Bernard Sandyman had without hesitation offered the use of Brewers' Hall, where the Beadle had taken great pains to ensure that the table linen was bright and crisp, the silver table pieces polished, the wines carefully chosen, opened and decanted and the welcoming tankards of ale (Sandyman's, naturally) perfectly poured from a freshly tapped and spiled wooden cask.

The ambassador's guests, apart from Bernard, included Mr Campion and Lady Amanda, Rupert and Perdita, Torquil and Victoria Sandyman and the sisters Mister, and as they stood in the reception room nursing their tankards Greve Westergaard welcomed them with the news bulletin they were all anxious to hear.

'My friends, if I may call you that even though I have never met some of you,' he began graciously, 'I will be forever in your debt for returning my daughter to me. Let me tell you immediately that she has been discharged from hospital and is physically well although still recovering from the shock of what we all know was a terrible ordeal. She apologises for not being here today to thank you personally, but in truth I forbade it for she has only been home for two weeks and still needs to rest and build up her strength.'

A growling murmur of 'quite right' and 'very sensible' went around the room.

'The man Mussett did not physically harm Vibeke, although he clearly terrified her, and details will, of course, come out at his trial. The result of that trial is not in doubt and the poor man will be committed to a secure mental hospital as he is clearly ill.'

'Jolly decent of you to say that, Westergaard,' said Bernard. 'There's many a father would take a service revolver to him and be done with it.'

The ambassador offered his old friend a sad smile. 'We above all others here, Bernard, except perhaps Mr Campion, should recognize that Mussett was a casualty of war. Not our war perhaps, old friend, but a terrible war as a prisoner in inhuman conditions which made him not responsible for his actions.

'It seems that Mussett had been wandering the dunes of Gapton the night that Francis Tate's motorbike, with Vibeke as his passenger, roared out of the dark.

'Vibeke tells me they were looking for a quiet place where they could do their courting, as I believe the expression is, near the sea or the lagoon there. By pure chance they disturbed Mussett's night-time rambling and they did so *loudly*, in fact, the revving of Tate's engine must have been unbearable to a man with his condition. Vibeke has told the police that they had taken off their crash helmets and dismounted but Tate was still twisting the throttle, as young men like to. The noise was their undoing in more ways than one, as they never heard Mussett coming out of the sand dunes.

'He reacted by lashing out – as startled animals often do – and attacked Tate from behind. Thankfully Vibeke never saw the terrible blow he delivered with some sort of chisel used for chopping wood, for she did the best thing she could have done in the circumstances: she fainted.

'Perhaps Mussett was overcome with guilt or compassion; who is to know? He disposed of Tate's body, and his motorbike, in the lagoon. For some reason he kept their crash helmets, perhaps as souvenirs. Vibeke he did not know what to do with. We have to thank God he did not kill her as she lay at his feet. Instead he carried her to his smokehouse where he tied her up and hid her until she was rescued by Mr Campion.'

'I assure you, Ambassador, it was entirely a family affair,' said Mr Campion.

Westergaard bowed in deference. 'I am grateful to everyone in this room, for you all played a part even when the local police seemed to have given up hope.'

'Poor Vibeke had a terrible ordeal,' Hyacinth said gently, 'and to think she was right there under our noses all the time – the one place even Dido couldn't sniff her out.'

'That dog's a stupid mongrel,' snapped Marigold, 'not a trained bloodhound.'

The ambassador coughed deliberately in a diplomatic call for order.

'The point is Vibeke was rescued and is safe, and while I am sorry for Francis Tate, I can only feel happiness at this moment. I hope you will share my joy and join me for lunch which, I am told, is always served promptly at one o'clock here in this most distinguished guildhall.'

On cue, the sliding doors to the dining room slid open like the parting of the Red Sea to reveal a sight almost as awe-inspiring: the Beadle in full ceremonial robes, one hand resting lightly on a silver-topped tipstaff as though auditioning for the part of Malvolio in a furrier's warehouse.

'Mr Ambassador, my lords, ladies and gentlemen,' declaimed the Beadle stentoriously, 'luncheon is *served*!'

'My God,' breathed Lady Amanda, 'it's a bear pretending to be Lugg.'

The bear watched the party troop into the dining room and take their places at a long table of polished oak and when he was content that none of the guests had attempted to make off with the silver, he adopted a position behind Aage Westergaard's chair at the head of the table.

Tapping twice on the floor with his ebony tipstaff and with his jaw jutted, he called for the guests to stand for the traditional grace.

While chairs were being scraped back, the Beadle performed the most un-bearlike act of reaching into his frock coat top pocket and producing a pair of metal-rimmed pince-nez. Once they were precariously straddled across his muzzle, he took a piece of paper from another pocket, unfolded it and read slowly and confidently from it.

'*Me signante emittite canos infernos.*'

The company, too polite or too frightened to criticize the Beadle's kitchen Latin, watched open-mouthed as he carefully refolded and replaced the paper, removed his pince-nez, sniffed loudly and then signalled for the waitresses poised on their starting line to begin to serve.

'Lugg looks well in retirement,' Amanda confided to Mr Campion, next to her. 'It seems to suit him.'

'I think he's had fun getting old,' replied her husband. 'I know I have.'

'I wish, my love, that I could trust your use of the past tense or believe for a single minute that you actually know the meaning of the world "retirement".'

Mr Campion busied himself with a knife and potted shrimps as a furry arm – human rather than ursine – came over his shoulder and dispensed chilled Pouilly-Fumé into a crystal goblet.

When the arm and bottle had moved down the table, Mr Campion smiled at his wife. 'Even in retirement the old recidivist is still looking after me.'

'Somebody has to, Albert, you simply have to accept that your days of adventuring are behind you.'

'And would you still love and desire me insanely if I did?'

'I suppose not,' sighed Amanda, 'though insanity would definitely have to be a factor. But you do give me cause for worry, my dear, at your age, charging off hunting spies and killers.'

Mr Campion put down his knife and patted Amanda's hand. 'Now look here, my girl, you know at heart I am a devout coward and would never put myself in danger because the very thought of your stern disapproval would have me in a bright blue funk, as we used to say. In any case – well on this case, if we can call it a case – I have had guardian angels at my shoulder all the time. Lugg was there when he was needed, Mr Milton was a strong right arm and even Major Deighton . . . I know, one may not approve of his methods, but we should be glad he's on *our* side. And when it came to hunting our own Gapton fox – well,

Rupert and Perdita did all the hard work there. In fact, Rupert really did run the fox to earth, literally.'

'But you can't always rely on other people being around, looking over your shoulder.'

'You are almost certainly right, darling, so I will make you a promise. The next time there is any question of a fox hunt – so to speak – I will refuse a mount, remain steadfastly impassive when the "view halloo" goes up and limit myself to handing round the stirrup cup. How's that?'

Before Amanda could reply, a lugubrious voice over Mr Campion's shoulder growled: 'Somebody mention a stirrup cup? I'll see what we've got in the kitchen.'

9